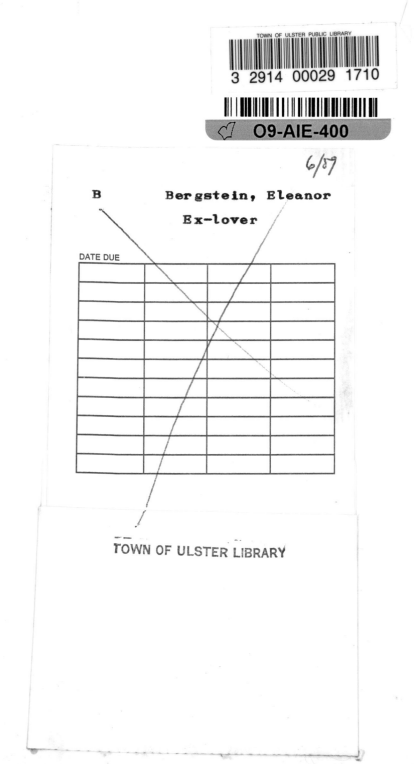

6/89

B   Bergstein, Eleanor

Ex-lover

DATE DUE

Also by Eleanor Bergstein

ADVANCING PAUL NEWMAN

EX - LOVER

EX-LOVER

a novel

ELEANOR BERGSTEIN

Random House New York

Grateful acknowledgment is made to the following for permission to reprint previously published material:

DOUBLEDAY: "Wish for a Young Wife" from *The Collected Poems of Theodore Roethke* by Theodore Roethke. Copyright © 1963 by Beatrice Roethke as Administratrix of the Estate of Theodore Roethke. Reprinted by permission of Doubleday, a division of Bantam, Doubleday, Dell Publishing Group, Inc.

W.W. NORTON & COMPANY, INC.: lines from the "First Elegy" from *Duino Elegies* by Rainer Maria Rilke, translated by David Young. Copyright © 1978 by W.W. Norton & Company, Inc. By permission of W.W. Norton & Company, Inc.

WARNER/CHAPPELL MUSIC, INC.: Excerpt from the lyrics to "Have You Met Miss Jones?" by Richard Rodgers and Lorenz Hart. Copyright 1937 Chappell & Co. (renewed). All rights reserved. Used by permission.

Library of Congress Cataloging-in-Publication Data
Bergstein, Eleanor.
    Ex-lover.
    I. Title.
PS3552.E7194E9   1989   813'.54   88-43211
ISBN 0-394-55306-3

Manufactured in the United States of America
2 4 6 8 9 7 5 3
First Edition

The author wishes to express her appreciation to the CAPS fellowship program for its support.

This novel is a work of fiction. Names, characters, places, and incidents either are the products of the author's imagination or are used fictitiously, and any resemblance to actual persons, living or dead, events, or locales is entirely coincidental.

FOR MICHAEL

If I cried out
who would hear me up there
among the angelic orders?

And suppose one suddenly
took me to his heart
I would shrivel

I couldn't survive
next to his
greater existence.

Beauty is only
the first touch of terror
we can still bear

and it awes us so much
because it so coolly
disdains to destroy us

—Rainer Maria Rilke
Duino Elegies

Man cannot prophesy. Love is no oracle. Fear sometimes imagines
a vain thing.

—Charlotte Brontë
Villette

EX-LOVER

I think of him at night. He comes to me in the middle of the night, or yet sometimes in the day in the crackles between the steam heat. Sometimes I greet him with fear and sometimes relief. It astounds me that I'm here and he's not. At times like this I cannot imagine my stomach without his pressing against it. My skin is smooth to his touch and then I feel him touching me. My face grows warm to his look and I smile back, think I know what's he's thinking watching me, and my lips curve in response. I think I know what he's thinking and then I know he's not, at all.

SECTION ONE

MIDDLE OF MARCH

I'm there at dawn—excited. If ever was a swell idea, this is it.

The big trailers are there, crew in puffy parkas, mouths making steaming spirals of vapor in the air as they bark commands, clipboards, Styrofoam cups with fuchsia lipstick stains or jagged tops, cigarette stubs in them, sawhorse tables with steel coffee urns, lights and towering cables that loom and sway, shouts and cries—a jumble to me now, but soon I'll understand.

The set of *Daughters and Sisters* has the power to cordon off a whole block of Third Avenue between Fifty-ninth and Sixtieth Streets, and me entitled to cross inside with a casual flair—NYC DEPT OF POLICE DO NOT CROSS—crossing inside with my usual flair, sure of my lines da da no one is there.

But my timing is on, so early in my career, and everyone is there.

Morris Jewel, the director (called Barney), is there, Sylvie, the star, is there, though in her huge trailer, the crew is there, and Barney is listening calmly to a tall, bearded young man in a khaki-colored down vest who turns away with an angry flourish.

". . . lose the light," snaps the young man, and swerves off furiously, his dark blond hair whipping around behind his neck.

Barney, left alone, smiles at me. "He's young," he says.

And suddenly all at once, so am I.

I am Jessie Gerard, thirty-three—optimistic and blazing—and as the crew rushes around, pushing platforms and dollies and shouting roughly in the cold air, I am inside the barricades watching a movie being made—me, who loves the movies, *truly* loves them, who grew up in the movie dark, learning of courtship, love, renunciation tied to higher motives, sex tied to choirs and song lyrics and most, oh most of all, to the unswervable possibility of utter joy achieved by two lovers running from either side of the wide shimmering screen toward each other . . .

And as they yell, "Action, roll, print that one," I am Jessie Gerard, described once by an interviewer as long long legs and thick thick

---

4

glasses. It is this blurred image of me, courtesy of *The East Village Other*, that I insert in the shot, blurring across the screen, loping, running, arousing every kind of atavistic implication of bliss on display as the music swells—no emotion here that passeth show but shows and shows and shows. And though this morning my husband, Sam, had to scrape me off the inlaid linoleum to get me to leave the house, now I am Jessie Gerard, playwright, who had a bad year full of crap and sadness, so took an assignment—the first journalistic assignment of my life—to write an article on the shooting of *Daughters and Sisters* for a rag of a magazine, the worst magazine I always read from cover to cover.

"This is how you write a movie script," a studio executive told me the time I pitched an idea for a film script at the Four Seasons. "What do you see, what do you see, what do you see?" I said my idea for a film script was about people moving in and out of growth, awareness of their responsibilities to the world and to each other. I threw in *growth* as the kind of trendy word on the back of an envelope I thought got intellectuals the big bucks for doing nothing. "What do you see?" he said, as he paid the check for my risotto with truffles and never got in touch with me again.

I see the same green car drive north on Third Avenue, circle the block, and drive north again, past Cinema I, Cinema II, the Baronet, the Coronet, come around again, and they yell, "Cut," "Do this," "Try that," and the crew rushes around like rowdy toddlers one sees tied together by their teacher in the park, bumping into each other, straining—but connected at the core, part of the same enterprise.

Round and round the green car goes. "Lower, higher, move the light, get this," they shout, and my heart stirs—how wonderful to feel your heart stir—and I suddenly have a handle on the material.

I bite the Styrofoam cup, letting carcinogens spin in the air, blow them from my lip. I will show how these people, so automatically mocked by the intelligentsia, who sit in the dark and watch their work, are presiding with the urgency of their hearts' energy over flickering images that can mean everything or nothing. I'll show them as wild and brave, these high rollers of nothing—with ambitions and stakes as grand as revelation itself.

I think of the desultory way friends talk of poetry, novels, and plays, and how when the conversation turns to movies the ground is suddenly shared and the conversation turns personal, cruel, alive.

I put down the crumbling Styrofoam, exchange it for a cruller. The white sugar coating collapses into empty space—the memory of it so sweet its absence is bitter against my teeth—sugar, flour, additives, wonderful forbidden joy.

I may come out of this well paid, understanding movies, writing the best piece ever written about movies and the best piece in the rag of a magazine I read from cover to cover . . . and then I'll get my own movie going and write the first piece about how original and brave Hollywood people are—and so reward Hollywood for getting me back in life again, by describing them with such fresh and generous precision in print.

The sheer good humor of the whole proposition makes the air smell like a coffee flower, sharp, fresh, slightly burnt.

And, at the very least, my movie stubs will be tax deductible for years to come.

I look around in delight, open my notebook, still full of pleasure at the whole notion of an assignment. Which means there's a daily reason for me to rise from my bed and leave my house with a purposeful stride.

For someone who works at a desk only steps from her bed, going outside means not working. Even euphemisms like taking a break, letting things jell, surface, come together—the crème caramel approach to writing—only underline being in the street as aimless self-indulgence, slippery in the mouth, no real substance to linger into tomorrow. Worst of all, your lagging step and wandering eye give it away that everyone around you has a more purposeful contact with the air, the sky. Once, in Madrid, I burst out sobbing in the street because everybody had someplace to go. And even though I was going back to a luxury hotel with the idea of dinner at nine or not at all and they were going back to steamy one-rooms from jobs they hated, they were connected and I was not. Being random leaches the soul. Or, on the lowest level of cosmetic necessity, it takes the lift from your step, the grace from the way you drop your token, the energy from your style.

But here I am, being paid to walk past barricades set up to keep others out, with a professional reason to meet a famous movie star about whom my teenage boyfriends fantasized in the Culver Theater even as they slipped their arms expediently about my sweater-setted shoulders.

Starring Sylvie Marlborough, Sylvie, as she's known, who moved from a musical-comedy stage debut to a prime-time comedy series— a Nancy Drew with telekinetic powers—then on to movies, where she first played the ugly duckling/beauty who won the boy from the pretty starlet, and then on to play the acknowledged star who got everything.

I plan to start at the center. Morris Jewel, the director, was known for serious Playhouse 90–type Technicolor films before he was blacklisted. After his trouble he went to London, where he's been making low-budget black-and-white films on small searing subjects.

He has a round bald head with a white fringe, pure blue eyes,

7

pink velvety skin. There seem no whites in his eyes; he is all pink and blue. A sky-blue shirt hangs out trimly over his pants. It is made to be worn that way.

Note: *Daughters and Sisters* is Marie Francesca Lowe's highly praised novel of a survivor daughter of a concentration camp victim, now an adulterous West Side housewife. She is sleeping around, watching her daughter grow, her marriage come apart; tales her mother never told her begin to inhabit her, as if she absorbed them in the womb. The book uses the technique of dimly intuited memories of the mother intercut with West Side housewife detail. An interesting choice for a movie.

I tell Morris Jewel (Barney) I met him at an antiwar symposium run by *The Nation* and ask about the material of *Daughters and Sisters*, what attracted him to it.

Barney says the thing he loves about moviemaking is that it brings everyone together—the electricians, the prop people, the gaffers. Not quite an answer, but I write it down.

Barney introduces me to Phil, the writer, a smudgily aging Li'l Abner.

"The book's a piece of shit," he says pleasantly, "but we're doing some interesting things with it."

A young girl is ducking in and out of the green car at the curb. She does it again and again and again. She is wearing a garnet crushed-velvet floor-length skirt with a flounce at the bottom, worn so that her rear shines, and a navy blue body shirt with runs—they look like vertical navy nipples. Because the camera is trained on her, she must have some importance, but she isn't really there. It goes on and on, ducking in and ducking out, and I get a little concerned, begin to lose my focus. My own mind and body are less there, too.

"Catch those clothes?" asks Writer Phil. "Being a stand-in's a crazy business. She's got to get attention some way." Just the kind of note I was about to jot.

Marie Francesca Lowe, the author of *Daughters and Sisters*, stands eagerly on the side. I recognize her from the book jacket. She looks terrific. I do not.

I bought these clothes I'm wearing because yesterday, on my way down to the set, it struck me that in my thick, shapeless sweater and wide-legged corduroy work pants, I was playing in the grain. That is to say, my brief experience of movie people is that they are into librarian-turns-into-bombshell-when-someone-removes-her-glasses-behind-the-stacks—"I could cry salty tears, where have I been all these years"—you've got it. And the bulkier the sweater, the thicker the glasses, the more inevitable it is that someone of them will paw my backbone with his index finger and say, "You know, under those big glasses you could be a lovely woman," or "Why are you ashamed of your body?"

Because it's only mid-March, and I'll be on the set at least through late spring when it grows warmer and I wear a ribbed turtleneck or a tank top, I want no one here taking secret smug credit.

So it makes a bizarre kind of sense to start out with tight oyster silk jeans and a fringed banana suede vest—writer-up-front-with-her-sexuality-knows-she's-first-of-all-a-woman. I'd rather bring my own clichés than slip into someone else's.

Or so it seemed yesterday. Today I'm feeling overdressed and overdetermined.

"You're a soft woman," men tell me when they start to love me. Today I'm animal skin edges and fragmented to the touch.

Enough of me. I take out my notebook.

Marie Francesca is wearing a long-sleeved cotton blouse with an eyelet collar, a loose man's tweed jacket, lime cotton-ribbed cardigan slurping out of jacket to keep her warm . . . cardigan stretched out of shape, blouse showing big hanging boobs, round nipples, messy knit skirt, uneven hem above knees. Her ginger curls have gray in them, her cheeks are fresh with a cinnamon blush, the one person García Márquez asks to meet when he's in town, is the darling of *The New York Review of Books*, she'll wipe me out with everyone as the real intellectual here, the goods, not a blocked Playwrights Horizons playwright trying to get her ink flowing. Even the outfit works. How did she think to combine the peasant eyelet the drooping skirt the bluestocking cardigan?

"There's Marie Francesca, the author, over there," says Phil, the screenwriter, "too Ralph Lauren, if you know what I mean." How can I not be irritated when it's exactly the level of mean, inaccurate insight that's me at my worst?

Spectators are starting to gather, women holding Bloomingdale's bags but not the real mainstream McCoy, only women out to shop at Bloomingdale's men's department or wanting to catch an uptown cab, so they're watching against their will, on their way somewhere where they have obligations to keep.

Mad Jane with the runny blue nipples crumples on the pavement and is scooped up by a powerfully shouldered silver-haired man in a blue topcoat, shoved brusquely into the back seat of the car. She comes out, crumples on the pavement, he scoops her up, shoves her in again. They do it at least sixteen times. Boring!

I try sorting out the poles and cables and ropes and sliding tracks and workmen standing around into some kind of coherent system. Finally I locate it—like the private parts of the enterprise—the camera. Froglike, it sits high on a sliding platform, beneath which two bearded, virile young men crawl on their sides, adjusting the wheels. On the leather swivel seat a grizzled man in a fisherman's sweater peers into the lens. The tall, impatient electrician with the dark blond hair stands alongside. Barney walks toward it and lays his hand lightly on the top. Its glass eyes bulge and gleam. It is covered with knobs and wheels and buttons, dull black and implacable. I stare as it bulges and tilts and gleams and selects—it's the real thing.

The camera swerves—and the center emerges and it all snaps to attention. Sylvie steps out.

A gasp springs up from the spectators. I walk outside the barricades just to walk back in and show my entitlement.

She really is all beige—high smooth hair, a chiffon scarf over the high smooth bones—but it makes beige an idea of glamour, a reflection of the spirit, rather than a neutral shade—all angles and cheekbones, though the features are there in their singular juxtaposition, long gray-fringed eyes, one slightly higher than the other, she is an idea of loveliness and glamour, more idea than flesh.

A young boy comes up to her, breaks through the barricades in his bright blue parka, holds out a pen and notebook. She starts to write.

And she is fragrance and air and fire and I am trapped, too substantial yet signifying nothing in my vest of animal skin and my shoes, earthbound, chained and dull to the pavement, while she is fire and grace and air.

"Next time you ask someone for an autograph, kid, make sure your pen works."

So she's real and she goes to work. They are wiping the pavement in front of the green car with paper towels and the broad-shouldered silver-haired man in an expensive topcoat scoops her up from the pavement and shoves her into the car. And then they do it again.

I slink over to her makeup box, which stands like a portable easel next to her makeup man, who stands, sponge in hand, ready to dab cream on her face.

The bearded electrician talks briefly to the makeup man, who is large, with a gray crew cut, cauliflower nose, like an old prize fighter, now there to dab contouring cream on Sylvie's cheekbones. Is it possible the cheekbones are made of plaster and paint and that anyone can have them? Closer to the box I see magenta, more shades of ocher and beige than Van Gogh ever saw on his palate, powders, creams . . .

With her silken poreless skin over irregular features, she seems cut out of a different cloth—perhaps it is a cloth for sale.

People have occasionally told me that I look a little like Sylvie— not constantly, and no one who really knows either of us. But with a wild surge of optimistic vanity I'm right next to the box, gingerly fingering the slate-green creams, when there's a thrill in the air and she's behind me. Barney quickly hurries up and introduces me.

"Jessie Gerard, doing a piece for mumble magazine, terrific playwright, won an Obie, *Jessie Gerard* . . ." Quick message: a spy in the house of love. Perhaps a serious person, so beware.

"You don't wear makeup, huh, Jessie?" Sylvie says. She has caught me staring into her box. Could it possibly be humiliation tracing a line across her delicate features?

Her voice that said, "Jessie," that public voice heard privately, trills in my wrists, but then she's gone.

Again, Sylvie crumples on the pavement, looks up pleadingly at the topcoated man, who shoves her brusquely into the car. Then they do it again, he brusquer, she more pleading, she less pleading, he less brusque, he less brusque, she more pleading. The hair person swoops forward and rearranges a tendril of hair and sprays it. There is a whiff in the air—the beginnings of spring? special star hair spray? I suddenly wish I'd worn my whory work jeans, wanting to assert my real body like a rasp of heavy metal, stamp on the pavement, have it answer my body with a wisp of city smoke steaming from the cracks in the pavement. Then he is brusque and she is less pleading and he is tender and she is pleading and then twice the same and he is brusque and it is over, and then it's time for lunch.

They've set up long tables around the corner, on the sidewalk and inside what seems to be a deserted storefront on Sixtieth Street.

A man in a beige nylon windbreaker asks who I'm writing for. He explains he's Men's Wardrobe, in case I've been wondering why he's wearing beige nylon with a zipper while all around him the crew is in Japanese coral plastic ponchos with snaps. He has mean, expectant wrinkles around his eyes. My first friend.

"There's Ms. Writer," he says, pointing toward Marie Francesca. "Book's a piece of shit," he says conversationally. I snap my notebook closed and walk away so as not to reveal some mean pleasure, realizing at that second I have snubbed him. Too late.

Sylvie slips off with Barney to finer tables—a restaurant, I'm told, where they seem to consult privately, so I line up at the big buffet tables, take mashed potatoes, chipped beef. Free food delights me under almost all auspices.

I take my heaped plate over to the long tables and see that the seating is democratic. The silver-haired powerful costar who shoved Sylvie into the car sits affably beside members of the crew, who introduce themselves as the propman, the gaffer, the makeup man. I slide in, ever so casually, next to the silver-haired man. He's eating, doesn't notice, so I eat too. We can drop into conversation after a few mouthfuls.

My appetite is high. I can come out of this understanding movies, writing the best piece ever written about movies, and I'll write about how brave and good Hollywood grips and electricians are and get my movie tickets tax deductible . . . and also learn to come out very gorgeous.

Next time you ask for a photograph, kid, make sure your pen works.

I see the silver-haired man and I are the only ones eating the real food. Some people are eating yogurt or an apple, others cheese and bread. The bearded electrician passes the food altogether, naps against one of the trailers in a spot of sun, his head flung back, his dark skin open to the sun, eyes closed.

"We two are the only ones hungry," I say to the costar. "I can warm it up for dinner," the silver-haired man says, and I see he's shoveling stew into a Baggie.

He asks me the time. He has an audition at three for a TV commercial, a Power Breakfast where executives insist on Blue Country Girl margarine.

He shoves the Baggie of stew into his attaché case, says he can warm it up on his hot plate.

His speciality is looking like a CEO, he tells me, and it is this speciality that won him the right to shove Sylvie into her car several times, as long as he doesn't say a word.

He'd hoped there might be some curses, a word or two, which would have gotten him a Day Player's contract instead of an Extra's one. Sometimes, he tells me, it can happen; happened to a friend. But no, the shoving was silent.

He checks my watch again.

Beats smell gigs, he says. Now he's talking about power margarine commercials as opposed to deodorants—the CEO knows the one thing you don't do at a meeting is show them you're sweating. He doesn't have a watch because they're always giving him a gold Rolex to wear and then snatching it away the minute he's off camera, but it's a nuisance to always remember to unbuckle his old Timex, even for auditions.

"God, she's skinny," he says of Sylvie. "Did you ever see bones like that?" and across the table the makeup man with the cauliflower ears stiffens, says he thought there was too much brown on the cheekbones, but the cameraman did two damn weeks of makeup tests. . . . Even I feel compelled to explain Jimmy meant her ribs under his fingers, and Gus, the makeup man, says, "They tell them to be skinny, that's the way they want them," and someone else at the table says, "Ever see her eat? A real pig," and Jimmy hurries off to audition for his power breakfast with his Baggie of stew in his attaché case.

From the back, he looks a little like my father did, brave, solid, family man, important in the world, at home needs support, protection, from his women.

I turn to my left to admire the furry angora sweater of Willa, the set designer.

She keeps it in her refrigerator, she says when I admire her fluff.

"Doesn't it get sticky?" I ask, and she looks confused.

"From the food," I amplify.

"If I have a party, I take it out," she says patiently.

We establish that what's in her refrigerator is coffee, champagne, and closed tins of pâté. Of course nothing's opened; she doesn't even need a plastic bag for the sweater. Is she rich? No, just working and on the move.

"I'd like my wife to wear a sweater like that," says Joe, identified as the focus puller. "She's an actress, could be as good as Sylvie. All I did was say yes, yes to getting married, yes to the kids, I enjoy them more than she does, all I did was say yes." And the wardrobe man says, "I know you girls won't believe it, but the thing that gives my wife the most pleasure is to have her elbows up into soapy dishwashing water—that makes her happy. My girlfriend says sometimes when she comes to visit my family, she never saw a happier or a closer family . . ."

But what am I to do with all this unless I'm going to, as the new journalists say, weave it into a tapestry? But I'm not one of those *Village Voice* writers who describe the vitality of the street littered with used gum wrappers, torn condoms, somebody's discarded belt buckle, and talk about energy in the air. "Energy in the air" is a crap phrase, I've never seen a used condom in the street, and tapestries never work for me without unicorns, so I look incompetent and miserable.

Everyone gets up from the table to set up the next shot. Everybody has a job to do but me. They say, "Excuse me," and push me out of the way or, worse, edge by me, until I see how hard it was to squeeze between me and the equipment. There are crowds behind the barricades by now—serious Bloomingdale's, Alexander's shoppers, senior citizens for the movie theaters, executives from office buildings. Long-haired girls with clipboards courteously move them back. And if someone refuses to leave, a man, a woman, anyone—

Rich, the Assistant Director, takes care of it. A short man, built like a fullback, he races over and bellows, "Out of here, away!" He yells in the way you thought once you were grown-up, no one would ever yell at you again.

I'm getting scared. They move me forward, back. I explain to everyone I'm here with a press pass, that I'll be here for the duration, and when Rich comes toward me, I'm shaking. If he shouts at me, I'll have to leave and never come back. Not because I can't explain myself, but because I'll cry totally, humiliatingly, like a child in kindergarten whose mommy's left. Everyone will be embarrassed and I won't be able to come back, will be the grown woman who stood drenched in puddles of tears.

It is easy to see that Rich is in control and will be the one who will throw me out, turn this into failure. He comes directly toward me, standing very close. It takes me a second to sort out that he's introducing himself, offering to explain the next shot.

He tells me my assignment was his idea; he used to work with the magazine editor who commissioned me. He says he worked with her in subsidiary rights at Dell "till I left the printed word went into the visual."

"By way of Papp village," he says. He set up props, cheese trays for Mike Nichols and Andrei Serban. He thought they were both assholes and tells me why, based on the kind of cheese they wanted. Does he have time, right now, for this kind of commentary?

He starts explaining the shot to me. "You have to suspend your allegiance to the verbal, Jessie, and move on to the visual." Is he being ironic? I can't tell. His diction varies radically with whomever he's talking to.

He has red eyes and is standing too close. "It's goodbye to the printed page and on to the visual," he says to me, and I can smell his alcohol breath. I back away and step in shit.

"Ooo," says the male wardrobe man. "Can't take you anywhere . . . ohh, ugh." I put my shoe up on my knee to wipe it off and— smash—on the ivory silk jeans. "Yuch. You're the kind who makes wardrobe men go gray." Phil, writer, looks away as tactfully as if it were my shit.

So much for feeling too perfect—shit on my silk jeans, newspaper smudge on my banana suede breasts. I am good in severe adversity. I will rise from this wreckage with radiant inner vitality.

I try to concentrate. Rich is behind me again. "It's hard to bridge the gap to the visual. Book's a piece of shit," he says, "but this is an interesting shot." A young girl lies strapped to a high table on wheels. She is not the tall one who was ducking in and out of the car. This one has a lashless face like an albino and extraordinarily muscular legs. A crew member releases the strap from a catch under the table, and she does a neatly executed jackknife into the lobby of Cinema I—mattresses there?—and then walks out, harnesses dan-gling, to confer with Barney and the guys around the camera. She has blank yellow eyes.

Rich is earnestly trying to help me bridge the gap to the visual. "These cords start a relay, and this button releases the tie to that cable so, at the moment this lever is pressed, that springs for-ward . . ."

Barney is talking to the stunt girl, and I'm trying to hear what he's saying. I think maybe here is the radiant generous texture I've been wanting to overhear. Together these unlikely people are creating a dream—Yip Harburgsville—"follow the fellow follow the fellow fol-low the fellow who follows . . ." Maybe it's old leftists, formerly persecuted Barney, talking earnestly to a hugely muscled, equally earnest eyelashless professional child. I sway toward them, trying to get their words.

"If you check that rolling track, the trolley track kind of thing," says Rich in my ear, "and think of the table running along the track like the trolley car, well under the table there's a release button, and when we push it, it flips her off and she goes into the somersault. I know it's confusing, but you have to suspend verbal assumptions and, to understand, you have to, you might say . . ."

"Bridge the gap to the visual," I supply absently.

Oh dear.

"I'm sorry," Rich says stiffly. "I've been overexplaining, I'm sincerely sorry."

Oh damn. I try to make it up. The stunt girl has placed a large astronaut helmet on her head, gray steel with horns and cords and cables protruding all around it.

"Won't that show in the camera?" I say, all perplexed serious interest. "How will you shoot around it?"

"Around what?" He's stiff, but still polite.

"That."

"What?"

Is he getting his pound of flesh? No, he really can't follow my question.

I explain again, humble and naïve. "That thing on her head, won't it show in the camera?"

The bearded electrician, woken up, back on the job, opens his eyes at my question, lounges against the camera, looking from me to Rich.

I ask again. No one has the right to be so mocking at my question. I want the answer. Won't it show? Why won't it show in the camera?

Old boy networks always get my dander up. Just maybe I'm pointing out a valuable mistake, a forest for the trees kind of emperor's new clothes that I can see, that this weird helmet will show in the camera, and I get shrill and insistent with Rich. "Won't it show, haven't you thought it will show?"

"But you didn't understand anything!" he shouts. How furious he is as he glares at me. "The helmet *is* the camera." It will catch her going over, matched together with other shots without the helmet.

Do I only imagine a chuckle behind me?

I slink off to sort out what it was I had in mind for this article of mine. A shoeshine boy adopted as mascot? Camera and crew praising each other in devotional fervor: "I was a pretty savvy guy, I mean a job's a job, but this project got to me . . ."? Love on the set?

No, I did have some intuition, if I can track it down. Something about the power of the flickering screen, some idea that working in a workmanlike way on magic creates a moment of moral magic in the act of creation. And because I am here, on the spot, I would see before my eyes a piece of such transforming magic, hear with my own ears some transforming exchange . . .

I do forget from time to time what a flair I have for bullshit.

At the curb now, the stunt girl, helmet/camera on her head, lies strapped on a high white table on wheels. The table has white rungs down either side. She is wearing a short white canvas smock, tied in the back. Protruding from under the sleeves and hem of her smock are plastic pipes in pastel colors. The pipes lead to a cluster of glass bottles of various sizes on a tin table, also on wheels, next to the high table on which she lies.

Though each item has been placed according to some predetermined plan, I cannot seem to grasp it.

The whole crew is spurred into activity. They buzz around carrying things importantly in front of them—flashlights, megaphones, large tin cannisters.

Under the Cinema I marquee leading to the lobby, the entrance is lined with laid tracks and two rows of high, powerful swaying klieg lights. Behind them are two tall ladders, men hanging off the rungs in attitudes of split-second readiness.

And as I try to sort it out—would listing them in my notebook help?—the whole hodgepodge of people at the curb begins to hurtle forward into the lobby. Clattering, rattling, tables swaying, bottles clanking, they run the gauntlet between the burning klieg lights and the ladders. Young men in sneakers are running alongside, calling hoarsely into megaphones, and then suddenly they're gone.

I'm left with the other sidewalk spectators at the end of the marquee, staring blankly into space, flanked by burning lights and the empty row of tracks where the table rolled past us. The real action is taking place inside the lobby doors blocked by the burly backs of the crew—keeping me out.

I feel the embarrassment of being inside the ropes and as puzzled as those outside. I scribble in my notebook as if my job is to record what happens outside. I write in my notebook: shit, shit, shit.

After a few minutes they all come straggling back, dragging the tables, the equipment, the stunt girl they call Georgeann, conferring, taking notes. It is hard to tell from their faces what manner of event has just taken place.

Then back at the curb they're setting up again. Georgeann, the stunt girl, is talking to Barney, the camera crew, adjusting the straps herself. They all listen to her attentively. I stare at it trying to make some kind of sense and something begins to whir as if a motor has just gone on inside me connecting my feelings and the air outside. This trolley moves that thread on this cable on this light.

They're moving people away again. Moving people back. "Jessie, you're too close," says Rich, amiably enough, can't read his mood.

But I'm lost about where this is in the novel *Daughters and Sisters*, which I read before I came. I don't remember anyone going to Cinema I or being strapped up on a table, or colored Rube Goldberg tubing going in and out and in and out and in and out.

"What's the point?" I say to the young electrician, who's closest to me. "What are all the bottles, what is supposed to be happening?"

"Suicide," he says curtly.

I jump, and he glances over at me.

I feel a chill I can't control. My body is shaking. My best friend Marilyn with the clown face who did it to herself last year, when I was too busy grieving about other things to notice. Who didn't let me know in time for me to change it, who died when she didn't have to, didn't *have* to.

And I see, of course, the high table is a hospital bed, the white smock is a hospital gown, those are tubes coming out of her sleeves. Oh Lord, a catheter—do they understand it's a catheter? They're draining a wound—pale pink plastic pipe? Behind the bed a bright blue pipe loops up and over a high chromium post, then down again through a hanging glass bottle. Is that an intravenous hookup? Don't they know that urine is yellow, plasma is clear, oxygen comes in opaque tanks—don't they have a fucking medical adviser? Draining the wound is a pipe dripping dark red clots into a globular glass jar—don't they know one drains a wound in bing-cherry-red circular discs strapped to the patient's bedpost like golden-hit million-disc blood records? What is this dripping globule jazz?

Could that man running alongside with a hurricane flashlight be making the globules of blood glisten? *Make them bigger, Sandy, harder as they come along, smoother, bigger,* says the megaphone. Behind the bed, also out of camera range, running alongside the hurricane flashlight man, is another young man, squeezing a rubber bladder connected to a tube leading under the patient's gown in back, protruding out and down the other side in front. He squeezes the bladder with both hands, sending blood shooting through the tube under the patient's gown, then out again the front side, pulsing down into the glass tub on the table. Out of the camera range, he squirts the bladder, the flashlight blinks on/off/on—testing? A clot oozes out, plops into the glass tub. Oh God, is it real blood? Is this the menstrual blood of script girls who want to be equal-opportunity assistant directors?

They lunge past me and are gone into the lobby.

"See, the thing is," says the set designer proudly, "it's all ours. She's coming out of a suicide attempt and she has this fantasy—you know, a head trip—that the doctor is wheeling her into a movie theater, and when she gets inside, she sits up on the bed, tubes hanging out all over, and somersaults down the aisle up onto the screen. Got a great stunt girl, always works with Sylvie . . ."

"And on the screen?"

"A newsreel—there she is Miss Ameeeerica, da da da being crowned by Bert Parks, only her gown close up is sort of striped like a concentration-camp uniform and the tubes are still sticking out of her arms."

And then he's got to run. It wasn't in the book, but now that I have it straight, my heart is pounding wildly and I want to turn and walk away and never turn back, shut my eyes squeeze them closed see only the patterns against the lids and yet I feel myself press closer and closer to see what's happening, walk along, stand on tiptoe, and the logic of what everyone is doing is so obvious it could be the Rockettes' Easter pageant.

There are three young men, all in a row, all out of camera range, walking rapidly sideways alongside the rolling table of bottles attached to the tubes leading under the stunt girl's hospital gown. The first man is holding a long curved steering rod with which he steers the table holding the bottles. The second young man is holding a bladder in both hands with which he pumps out the clotted blood through his tube to the connected stunt girl's tube and then down to the glass jar on the table. The third young man, holding a fluorescent hurricane flashlight, shines it on and off the blood for some manner of lighting effect. Three young men in khaki pants with little belts over their rumps, high tight little rumps scurrying along sideways, twitching horizontally over and over again—twitching along, to be sure, with some urgency. The globules get bigger. *Light, blood, light,* croons the megaphone, *faster, good, Sandy, smooth . . .*

They reach the lobby door and the stunt girl sits up, bends forward, presumably starts her somersault. I cannot see further.

But this time it all goes much more quickly. They're back at the curb readying to start all over again. Helmet/camera on her head, straps adjusted to relax when she somersaults, everyone in place, including the three young men.

It starts again, moving past me.

Not too close, stand back.

Clack: SUICIDE

My blood jumps.

Three young men, all in a row, twitching behinds, globules getting bigger, darker, redder *make them bigger bigger lights on okay.* Rumps are moving sideways, scurrying, twitching. *Good good faster slower light on right on keep on lovely lovely . . .*

And as they're passing me, oh for shit's sake, just as they're passing me, suddenly the high table falls off its tracks, tilts sharply to one side. A huge coiled lamp above sways, teeters. The sheet falls away, and with a frantic scissor kick of insanely muscular legs, the stunt girl tips sideways. She hangs in midair, strapped to the bed at the waist, her legs doing spasmodic scissor kicks, flailing in muscular terror.

The gown falls away. Reddish pubic hair curls around pink panties, no top, nipples flat brown leather buttons of terror, cunt open, screaming, spreading yellow-pink. Did someone lean forward, run a finger there? Yes/no. Blood pink—no, urine on pink panties. Her screaming antennaed head flails on its side in the air, eyes in shock of panic. Men are running.

Someone holds her, holds her head, rights the table, unstraps the leather strap. Her lashless eyes are rolling around her lashless face.

There is the smell of smoke from the swaying lamp—and suddenly, slam on my hand, scrape, notebook hurled to the ground, and Barney director stands before me, eyes wild, face glistening, pink shiny veins throbbing under forehead, mouth throwing spittle.

"You fucking asshole puking new journalists, saw you, murder people, fucking morons, asshole peaceniks, crazy fucking morons kill people, break their lives, turned it over—saw you push the cable off the track, reach out your foot, was looking straight at you . . ."

I did that?

First, let me see if I can reconstruct what happened then. Arms pulled Barney away and a man led me down a side street, pushed me, shoved me into a limousine. A little balding man who looked like someone's Uncle Moe got in after me and said, "Look, there's no reason you should listen to me, except that I'm saying to you, this is a decent man. You do as you please, miss, but this is a decent man."

It was dark and hooded in the limousine. He shook his finger in my face and said I had been playing with blocks, with dollies—what could I know of what they had made this man suffer? He said it was before I was born, maybe I read it in a schoolbook, the House Un-American Activities Committee. He said I had been a baby. "Barney has a little girl," he said, "looks like you, only now she's older, was a pretty kid." He said Barney's daughter came to Washington with her father when he went to testify, wanted to be with her daddy, and the reporters ran after her, called horrible things. He said she went wild for a while growing up, came back to Santa Monica to live, had a child. "One leg splays out like this, can't hold her neck up, wears a brace, all the drugs, the junk she took into her body when she was a girl." I cringed back in my seat, but there was nowhere to hide. "He sees his grandchild, it rips his heart out by the roots."

The Uncle Moe man pressed forward in my face. "She was a pretty kid," he said, "looked something like you. While you were having sodas with your boyfriends . . ."

The driver knocked on the door and handed in my bent and dirty notebook. But it wasn't until I saw Uncle Moe working to unbend it, watched his white hairy knuckles trembling, brushing the dust off, anxiously smoothing it down to make it nice for me, that I realized it wasn't about me after all. None of this was about me.

Uncle Moe was talking about how much tension there was, how Barney hadn't been wanted on the picture in the first place, how Sy and Bernie were just looking for an excuse. In my own relief, I couldn't seem to focus on the right words to reassure him. The only phrases that came to mind were too flip or too explicit. "Look, I won't send it out over the AP," or "I promise I won't tell a soul." I knew there was a tactful oblique phrase, but I couldn't seem to find it.

I asked about the stunt girl. She was in shock. As soon as he started talking about her, I realized I could have said, "It's okay, I understand," and we'd be finished. But *understand* had been so unlikely a word, under the circumstances, that it had been blocked in my head.

The stunt girl was in shock. Georgeann Cararra. The ambulance had taken her to New York Hospital. She was really too young to be a stunt girl. "They take gymnasts," said Uncle Moe, knowing he had me, but not sure how to consolidate his gain. "They're not used to this kind of pressure, they're only in exhibitions, meets."

"But aren't meets more pressure?" I asked, then bit my tongue. I hadn't meant to be contentious, just trying to be friendly.

"Yes," he said instantly, "much harder, a sports meet, much more pressure." I always forget, movie people never feel obliged to stand by what they've said minutes before.

We didn't have much more to say, so I touched his old hands. It was time to fit it in.

"Look, it's okay, I understand," I said with finality, and out it came.

"I don't mind telling you," he said, so he told me.

The deals he'd tried to put together over the years for Barney. Thinks he has one set up, and he gets home, sees his wife in the driveway, and she says, "They're on the phone," and it starts all over again. "I don't need this," he said. His boys have moved into TV now, he can pick up a phone and make more on one pilot deal in ten minutes. . . . I listened.

The studio car took me home, and that night I received a dozen red roses from Barney, with a note saying, "Thank you for understanding." Some tact is involved, because the picture is budgeted at enough to fill our arms with heather. I wouldn't, in fact, have minded an apartment overflowing with splashy flower arrangements; I like the big time. But these are from Barney and his agent. Probably his own money. I'm sorry.

The studio car picked me up the next morning to take me to the set and I wondered how Barney would face me, how I could make it easier on him. But no, I realized as soon as I saw him across the set, of course he's had other, worse humiliations before.

I recognized those bones in his face; they emerged as suddenly as those I saw in the Yom Kippur crowd outside Temple Emanu-El. To be explicit, I recognized them for the first time on Fifth Avenue and Sixty-sixth Street in the late afternoon, in the faces of the crowd coming out of Temple Emanu-El after services on the day of the Yom Kippur War. All at once, their minks and Cardin suits ceased to encapsulate them but hung from their unprotected shoulders like striped concentration camp hemp. Those bones don't nestle for long inside long-haired fur and pink velvet skin. At first glance, the second-marriage crowd at Temple Emanu-El seems to have the manner, the makeup, the style, even the jowls. But underneath are the bones, waiting.

I think of a scene one rainy Sunday night, waiting for a bus outside the Madison Avenue Delicatessen. Cold rain is flowing down. Eighty-sixth Street is moving closer to Harlem. The prices for a boiled beef supper are extraordinary, inflation comes and times are bad. Your money counts for less, as does the money you will leave your grown children and their children. Layers of protection are gone, and it is pouring and near to Harlem. The couples hesitated under the marquee. The husbands fetched the cars or hailed taxis, the wives hurried through the puddles and climbed inside. Oh, the beak noses, the eyes—the hint of adversity and out they come. I recognize them that morning in Barney. In his eyes and in his bones. Did thirties leftists plan to make the world safe for Jews?

Note: look into this

Barney is pleasant to me, kind to the actors. Someone tells me the stunt girl has a ruptured spleen; the shooting schedule has been rearranged. Pat, the PR girl, rushes up to deliver a large Gucci notebook to me, with my initials in gold. Knowing how much a tiny pocket address book costs at the Via Condotti store, I cannot conceive of the price of this. So the flowers were just a stopgap while the initials were being stamped. Delivered by the PR girl, the company paid. It is devoid of any personality. It has never happened.

Now you want to know if it had to do with me. And then you want to know why I thought it had to do with me.

For the first, no. I think not.

For the second, I will tell you things about a period of my life. It is freestanding; it has to do with nothing else. I tell you because I do not want you feeling you are in the hands of an ambiguous, perhaps deceitful narrator (one who invokes bones of survivors to get you off the track). Otherwise what I am about to tell you has no value. It has to do with nothing else.

A year and a half ago, I had a loss, a series of losses, in a short period of time. They were brutal, quick, and various. I speak not of symbolic loss, death of the heart, decay of the spirit. Those come along, often in the wake of real death, and I have known them, too. I speak only of irreversible loss. People without whom I could not imagine life suddenly ceased to breathe. And I have learned how ugly the world becomes in an instant.

I remember, with the first death, kneeling in the mud by an open grave, rain falling in wailing streaks. I remember, through the wail, a picture flashed in my mind of a huddled, weeping, crouching figure on a muddy gravesite in a bunchy raincoat. Me. It was so unlike the way I saw myself that I might say the world changed for me at that moment. It would not be, strictly speaking, true. I was too busy assigning people to limousines, supporting those with no resilience, setting the tone to take in the antechambers of the stunned. I was, in short, carrying on with grace. People marveled.

I, who had wondered what part of me, good or bad, would remain behind after this loss, marveled too. What was left behind was brisk, cheerful, full of soul and heart, and capable, most of all, of social amelioration in the face of tactless horror.

I was, nevertheless, startled to find the streets changed. I had been, in the past, propelled down city streets on bursts of affectionate favors from strangers. It is true. Hard hats called out, "Have a really nice day," a lady waiting for a traffic light suddenly patted my arm and said, "Bless you, my dear, you're a good person," a well-dressed man at Fifty-sixth and Lexington once thrust a bunch of spring flowers in my arms and disappeared. They had been a source of pleasure, bemusement, wonder.

I took to the streets soon after my losses, assuming, I suppose, that what had flattered and bemused would nurture and console. But the streets were gray and flat and granular and neutral. Nothing. It had vanished.

One might say I took to the streets to make sure I was still there, and found I was not.

I went back to work. One of my plays had a workshop production scheduled and friends said it was good that I was going back to work, so robbing my work of its professionalism and relegating it to useful therapy.

One day, I was obliged to leave a meeting to pack up a dead young woman's wardrobe for the thrift shop to pick up. My closest friend, Marilyn. It was elaborately arranged with my collaborators—no lunch and a blood oath to be back by one-twenty. I rushed off through the snow to the silent blank apartment and laid the clothes on piles of tissue on the empty carpet. The young black teenage delivery boy was warm-eyed and unexpectedly gentle. It was clear that he understood, as he handled the shaggy capes, the clear bright silks with lovely shells and beads, that he knew he was handling a life. Watching him, something began to relax inside me.

After he had left, I called work to explain I'd be ten minutes late. "Oh sure," they said, "why not take the whole day, don't rush."

I hung up the phone so sadly. I was sorry we had not talked, the

Irvington Thrift Shop boy and I, that together we had not held up each shining dress, each lustrous shawl, and told its tender story. But more than that was my chagrin that what I had seen as my collaborators' ratty show biz professionalism—"on top of that your ma and pa have parted, you're broken-hearted, but you go on da da"—collapsed in a second before my real-life woe.

But there was no reason to push beyond their platitudes, since the only action truly appropriate to my present state was to lie in a high burnt meadow and howl through the seasons.

What I mean to say is that I was surrounded by neither idiots nor villains and I continued doing what I was doing. I was accepting the unacceptable fact that my life, for the present, was simply filling time.

The losses continued.

We had loved them all immoderately—recklessly.

My mother died, my best friend, my husband's father, my cousin, my father, my unborn child.

My nightmares were so horrendous that I took to dropping off to sleep on the sofa, hoping to outwit them. See, it's not time yet, I'm just dozing.

Often I dreamed I was in a hospital elevator, rushing from floor to floor, pressing buttons frantically while around me nurses and interns joked and made coffee dates. They can't all die, I'd reason wildly, careening from one intensive-care unit to another. But however varied and vicious their imagery, the dreams kept one consistent design: they always remained one behind in the count. So when I awoke trying to bring in the real world to calm my shaking heart, I would go over the dream, saying, "It can't be that bad," and . . . oops, it was worse.

One rainy night in February, we were both in bed with the flu. Insistent calls were coming in from a distant relative asking that I arrange the funeral of her husband, as I'd had so much experience. A cable arrived from Europe telling us of the fatal auto crash of a young and loyal friend. Finally, Sam staggered out to bring us a hot meal from the only open pizza place I could find in the yellow pages, where, when I telephoned, the counter man made obscene sucking noises in Spanish. Toward midnight, we received a telephone call telling us that the one beloved person left, the one who had stepped forward to help and understand us both, had just been admitted to the hospital and was not expected to come out.

We sat on the bed, stared at each other, and started to laugh. Up until now we'd always hurriedly assigned the blows—worse for him, worse for me, one to grieve, one to watch, one to kneel in the mud, one to stand by if needed. This was the last death we could take. We turned out the light, sat together on the bed with our arms around each other, and rocked back and forth against the white wall behind the pillows. Sounds came out that neither of us had ever heard the other make. At first, I thought we were laughing, then sobbing. Then it moved into a dialogue, sometimes him, sometimes me, sounds as precisely rendered and particular in meaning as any hard-edged language I have ever studied or used.

Years before, on our honeymoon in Greece, mosquitoes had swarmed our white stone bedroom, and Sam, then my new husband, stark naked, had thrashed around for several hours in a furious rampage of attacks and ambushes till he got them all. In the morning, we saw the white stone walls of our hut were streaked with red where the bugs, glutted with our blood, had been smashed and died.

We rocked and exchanged sounds all through the night, Sam and

I. As the dawn light came, I remember an instant of surprise, for I had turned toward the white walls behind our pillows, expecting that they too would be smeared with our blood.

Life moved on. Let's make this fast.

After a time, I began to have lunch with friends. I sat for hours on leather banquettes and traded their lives off briskly—a friend in a job squeeze, a friend with cystitis, a friend in divorce court, and so on. Now *there's* a trouble you don't have, was my subliminal message, one to the other. I compared, contrasted, and prefaced my response, too often, with, "Well, when there are irreversible problems in the world . . ."

I passed endlessly severe, uncalled-for judgments on tragic pretensions in books, plays, movies, and death of household pets, and I delivered myself often of such insufficiently researched insights as that ghetto youngsters had a more instinctive understanding of the soul's chaos then the middle-class college freshmen to whom I gave a class on playwriting.

From time to time, over a lunch table, some conscientious or caring friend asked me "really" how it was. The grief spilled over; it was not imperceptible moisture glinting from the corner of stoic eyes. It drenched the crepes and went on silently until I could stop. We would both be surprised, she and I.

I had many minor ailments. I wrote charming essays for specialists on Everything I Can Remember About My Throat. I put on paper hospital gowns and drank substances whipped up in Waring blenders and radioactive ones cooled in mini refrigerators. I waited in windowless cubicles, reading copies of *Time* and *Newsweek* about contemporaries of mine whose books and plays and movies were sprouting incessantly in the cold sunshine. Then I was called inside and clamped between huge gleaming machines while technicians scampered out of the room and called through steel doors, "Breathe in, no in in in, then out."

In late spring a young mother in the back of a taxi with me said that her tiny daughter had asked, "Mommy, are you going to die?" She repeated to me the little platitudes she'd given Lisa Kim about Mommy's death and asked for my opinion. At first I did not understand. I have no child, and I have written neither for children nor about them. As soon as I understood why I was being so humbly consulted on how to put it to Lisa Kim, I was furious. I wanted out. I was ready to resign my professional status.

We spent the summer in the company of strangers. Without our credentials of suffering, we were just folks.

By fall, the show was over.

Okay. Now where are we, and what remains?

1. I have had wide and deep experience of death. I honor it neither personally nor professionally.

2. I think some things are not useful as material. Early suicides of gifted friends, death of aging parents in nursing home. When I see them invoked to validate the profundity of beginners, I grow furious.

3. I dislike suicide. I have known too many people who wanted to live and were not able to. I do not care for the bottles and tubes keeping alive people who chose not to live.

4. I know about chapel costs, grave plots, cremation procedures, and that tin coffins are a shill to torment the inexperienced mourner.

5. I know that the first few weeks are the easiest, and I can spot a problem griever instantly, by the little ways in which she calls attention to her matter-of-factness.

6. I can spot an insincere, faintly pleased, slightly grudging, or smug condolence note, and have learned to purge all such elements from between the lines of those I write myself.

7. I know how to acknowledge someone else's grief in a way that honors it and when not to refer to it at all, because it shames them.

8. I know how ugly the world turns in an instant. But I have already said this.

What else remains?

In discussing work projects with directors, I discover, as we talk concept or story, that I cannot see the world as wistful, some artful combination of sad and good. I did not plan to be disqualified from bittersweet, but it has happened.

It eliminates many projects for me, especially movie ones, which often start from a very funny situation and turn tragic, or the other way around: "There's this guy, dying, right?" or "There's this orphan, wants to be a clown."

But I posture. And perhaps I insist too much on this being free-standing. Because it occurs to me I have one story left to tell. A few months ago, riding on a crowded bus, I stood next to a young girl who was trying to make the acquaintance of the young boy sitting beneath me. She gave him her packages to hold. "What street is this?" she asked, leaning across me, over him, to look out the window. "It's my last day," she said.

He looked up.

"Oh, it's not my last day, I'm not dying, I'm visiting from Vancouver staying with my cousins, ugh ooo what did you think, I was one of those people with tumors, hah?"

An ordinary little girl, standing, on her last day in New York, trying to make a little connection with a nice young man, sitting. I got a seat in another part of the bus soon and forgot her.

Sometime later, at my stop, I rose from my seat and saw the little girl in front of me at the exit door. She glanced back at me, crashed out the door, and started to run. At the dark corner she stopped, looked back at me, and ran again. I have no idea what she saw. I wore an expensive tweed coat and thought my face expressionless. I tried to feel it with my fingers, but the mouth seemed passive. I tried to hold my face in the same lines till I got upstairs to consult the mirror, but the doorman stopped me with some junk mail and a comment. My husband was not helpful. That sweet face? And I found there was no percentage in taking it all too seriously.

But I owed you this tale.

All right, I was wrong. It is not freestanding.

But I do insist grief gives one nothing good. Socially, sexually, artistically, aesthetically, pretty-clothes wise, hollowed-cheekbones, deep-eyes wise—nothing. It comes to nothing.

Only one day, when it seems to be gone and you are saying, "I used to feel"—suddenly it's off again.

My father, sitting in the Oyster Bar, begins to cry into the chef's salad. "Your mother made me into the man I always wanted to be," he says. It is the most intimate thing my father has ever said to me. He looks up, our eyes meet, and the tears fly down. At some point, typing this, I cry again. Trying to make my words as hard as stone, I cry again, seeing the lettuce, the ham, our tears, the get-your-shoes-fixed-while-u-wait shops on Lexington Avenue where my father and I walked hand in hand, tears streaming down our faces, arranging to have the soles of each other's shoes fixed. "Do you need new soles for your shoes, of course you do, come I'll take care of it."

I am describing my father (now dead), buying me soles for my shoes, so he could be my mother for me, then me, so I could be my mother for him. We were father and daughter, but it was my mother we were after. We went to the opera and he held on to my hand, my mother's flesh.

Because loving flesh is all, you see, and grief is being deprived of that most particular loving flesh. It is what I miss the most—the hand smoothing my hair, cupping my chin, a touch of my unsucked breast swollen with milk for the child never fully formed—these have been ripped away from me, and even now there is a rising wail of outrage when, inattentive, I allow it through my body.

But we have already spent too much time on this. Because the truth is, one day it ends. Out in a red day-sailer, coming about, making-the-best-of-it in spades, life jumps in your wrists. "Shut up about your losses," said Aristotle Onassis, and suddenly, you do. Excitement ruffles your hair, sends it streaming back against your cheeks. Sexual promise sizzles in the air and welcomes you back as if you had never been away. It slaps you in the face that all this has been going on all this time, and you race along to join it—you must join it. For the first time, it crosses your mind that everything is not wonderful and something is wonderful. The formulation seems magically to close the torn space between the person who was and the person who is. You say it again, out loud—everything is not wonderful and something is wonderful—and once again you are a gleaming whole, the person for whom something is wonderful, whose plays are played, whose soufflés rise, whose husband sings in the shower after love, whose sails, most days, are filled with freshening breeze. The person, in short, you used to be.

And from that time on, it is easy, open—home free, as we yelled, triumphant, on Brooklyn nights. You go along and feel your joys, insist on your triumphs, recognize others' pain—just as important to recognize others' pain as to insist on your pleasure, you've always known that—and insist that the people around you insist on their triumphs too.

But why, you say, did you think even for a moment that any of this stunt-girl accident had to do with you?

Because now and again, without warning, anger slams through my soul.

And then it is gone, and I'm back again. The world is full of blazing promise and power, spinning, speeding, laughing.

And you, urged on by me, perhaps you too insist on your joy. And then, laughing, dipping, billowing out, you skim around a bend of endless possibility, out of my sight, as if none of this had ever been at all.

And I, I am left with my expertise.

SECTION THREE

I clutch my swank aubergine Gucci notebook. I approach the new location—a mall of walking, talking people. A quirky feeling of luxury bubbles along my woolen arms, evaporating in the cool, fetid air. Maybe it comes from starting my day's work in public transportation—the exhilaration of going OUT OUT, no matter where. Even the Hudson seems to waft a freshening breeze.

The new location is a supermarket plaza behind Sixty-sixth Street and Columbus. I'd never even noticed it before, since you have to crane your neck from the bus. I thought it canny of them to have discovered a suburban mall tucked in midtown—so saving the cost of transporting their equipment down the Jersey Turnpike—and discovered they were, in fact, immensely pleased because they thought they'd chosen the archetypal urban West Side neighborhood store.

The company will be here for many days, and they've established their turf—blocks and blocks of trucks, trailers, equipment you can't miss from the bus, from the street, from the air.

Passersby and shoppers stop, spectators pass, the extras dressed as shoppers mill around, the only discernible difference between them being the extras' free access to the long tables of bagels, cream cheese, waxy apples, and Oreos.

I am watching people watching people watching people. Something inside it all stirs.

This is why I'm here, to locate that something. So far, nothing. I am not yet sure just where on the set I will track down my material. I tell myself, when it comes, I will know.

Most of the time is spent setting up the shot. Occasionally in the course of a day, a shot is ready, and this counts as a peak moment. Then I am watching people watching people watching people work.

It starts like the days before. There's a fight between Barney and young, dark blond Harry, grim and angry, about the first shot.

Harry says, "We'll lose the light," and Barney says, "We have all day."

Harry says, "Not if you won't commit to the first shot."

Barney walks away, and Harry says, "You can't reason with directors in the morning. They're like very young men."

What?

"They think the day is endless."

Young men? He looks no more than late twenties himself.

And in the afternoon?

"They see that the light is coming to an end," he says patiently.

Yesterday I discovered that Harry, whom I thought the electrician, is the Director of Photography. The older grizzled man with his eye to the camera is the camera operator—lower on the totem pole. Harry looks in, sets the shot; the other man actually touches the levers and moves the camera. Union rules.

Harry is the Director of Photography—D.P., they call him, as in the camps. I call him the P.D. and they correct me. Doesn't anyone but me find D.P. an odd phrase for a dark-skinned young man, his hair long on his neck, sun-streaked, like a little boy at the saltwater pond?

He's tense, full of preoccupied energy, like boys with toys, on the barely courteous edge of impatience. He keeps his head slightly to the side when one talks to him, framing the shot, I suppose, hoping whoever it is will go away.

But it turns out the reason people are not starting yet is that Sylvie is being made up in her trailer.

I check the mood among the milling people. It's mixed. It's not as much fun as people imagined. People who want to shop in the supermarket have to go in the side doors. The clerks will be used as extras and are excited. Women who want to watch are pleased, but they have to do their shopping. Rich, the assistant director, and his crew are busily herding people out of the way.

Sylvie comes out of her camper at Rich's begging, to meet the store manager. She's grumpy to Rich but sweet to the man. When she goes back inside, he shows everyone the autograph: For Allison. "That's my daughter," he says.

In the book, she is always shopping. Her memories of lovers past and present and fantasies of her mother's memories are intercut with supermarket shopping, so they'll be doing a lot of connectives. There'll be close shots of her coming out and wide shots of her as a little dot coming out of the wide plaza doors.

No medium shots. They bore Harry, I heard Rich say.

"Background," shouts Rich through his megaphone. The women extras, the ones entitled to free bagels and Oreos, march out, arms loaded with celery. Have they all bought celery? I wonder. No, it's probably somebody who decided celery was visual.

"Background," Rich shouts, and the extras move.

The real women, who look like the extras but a little more vivid, complain. They have bought frozen things; they must leave. Their schedules are not all that flexible. Rich's lieutenants are herding them behind barricades anyway. When will it start again? When will Sylvie be there?

"Will you still be here on Thursday at three?" one woman asks the Amazon lieutenants. "My niece Nina could come if I knew, I don't want her to come if you're not going to be here."

"Move on, move on, no time for questions," Rich shouts. "Background!" and the imitation shoppers walk by.

"Background," bellows Rich, and a stand-in goes in and out the door so they can set up the camera and the lights for the next shot, and this will be as good a time as any to discuss Rich, the assistant director, the man who knew my magazine editor, Rich, whose diction varies with his audience and who is my access, my friend.

He has red eyes. They hired him because no one else was free. When he is not around, people speculate he was fired from all his other jobs.

He calls Barney boss, and Barney says of him, "At least he's loyal to me." The fact is, he isn't. Hired as a kind of Sancho Panza to the director, he makes fun of Barney behind his back.

Once he trashed all the files. Went into the office drunk and threw them all around. The next morning he was not around, and dull-eyed men (and one woman) from the crew warned us how he would be feeling. "Don't be harsh," they said, "he'll be very ashamed." He arrived on the set late morning, subdued for a day, and I noticed how many of the dull-eyed prophets always drank Diet Coke and Perrier after wrap. A crew of AA?

But the day after that, he shouted again.

His A.D. crew smokes nonstop around the camera crew, who are nonsmokers and claim it's bad for their equipment.

He's in charge of directing the extras and treats them badly, even the older ones, when they complain about the greasy cold gruel they're given to eat or want to go to the bathroom.

He goes to the makeup camper, yells into his megaphone at the door, "Let's get moving!" so that the spittle on the mouthpiece dribbles to the ground. Then he walks a few feet back to where Barney and the cameras are and yells into the megaphone, "Waiting on makeup!"

Everyone, I find, is always waiting on hair and makeup or on wardrobe. Hair and makeup claim they're waiting for wardrobe and wardrobe claims they're all ready but have no time to get their people ready because hair and makeup take so long. None of them say that Rich's shouting at them makes them slow up, but that's obviously the case. They grit their teeth and say, "It'll take as long as it takes."

By the time the actors arrive late on the set, they are an aggrieved monolith with their hair, makeup, and wardrobe people, on whom they rely for their on-screen appearance. The actors claim that if they come when called, they sit on set and wilt until the cameras are ready for them and need to be retouched anyway, and Barney must spend some time getting everyone in a better mood.

Not, as they say, a well-run set.

I hear the mumbles that it doesn't have to be this way, that this is a particularly poorly run set, but my role with Rich is as the one person outside the system who sees he's only doing what has to be done. Like Himmler's doxy?

"If I don't do it," he's telling me, "I'll be a nice guy, but the movie won't get done." I meet his eyes. I agree it's a tough job but he has to do it, that the crew are babies, that all around us the extras are a bunch of sissies who want to lie down on the job and go to the bathroom, that the actors diddle over spit curls while the days roll by. He wants the producers and the studio to admire him. He wants his sister, the art-book publisher, to admire him. So I'm his Eva

Braun, no, his Boswell, and he doesn't give me a hard time. I've made worse bargains. It's not a bargain with the devil, only an alcoholic ex-theater propman trying to keep a job. He'll make the dollies run on time.

Sylvie emerges. She'll be coming out the revolving door on the supermarket plaza, a tiny dot in the long landscape.

She finds her mark and confides in me, "I've been putting on four shades of eyeliner for the daylight to match with the inside fluorescent shot done yesterday."

She says, "So it's a long shot and so nobody'll know, but I'll know, you know?"

She's applying to me to endorse higher standards because I write plays that make no money or because I wear thick glasses.

But they're losing the light and it *is* a long shot. I know Renoir says everyone has his own good reasons, but I like to point the finger of blame.

So I nod noncommittally, and as I see her going in and out of the swinging door—a speck in red, to be sure—I think maybe I've blown my chances for a higher rapport with the juiciest subject around. Pointless.

As she's waiting to walk out again, I sidle up to her and I say, "Well, I see what you mean about the makeup even if nobody sees . . ." and she looks right through me. I say it louder, and then again louder—I can't just walk off and be ignored, it's too weird, and she snaps, "Don't talk to me when I'm acting."

Acting? Walking in and out of a revolving door in a long shot?

"Don't *you* concentrate when you work?" asks Harry, the sun glinting on his streaked hair.

I guess I said it out loud.

Oh yes I do concentrate, but she's being made up for a long shot and losing the light, so why is he saying this? I thought he was the one frantic about the light. I'm losing my handle on it and have to move fast to get it right.

"So who's right?" I ask. He shrugs. "It depends on how selfish you are." Who?

I watch the other day's stand-in, Stephanie, the tall girl who kept being pushed in and out of the car. Only today she's changed out of the long cut velvet skirt and is crouching alertly with a clipboard. She does everything, a DGA trainee. Directors Guild. She'll have a series of jobs. Today she wears pink cord culottes and a sleeveless paisley flowered blouse and a heavy lavender crocheted shawl. Short curly hair, long legs emerging from the wide-bottom culottes, strong arms, she is frail on a tall scale. She rises from the ground like a high unfolding bridge chair. From the back, her shawl is lacy over hockey shoulders. Mixed styles.

I often fall into conversation with her. I like to look at another woman at eye level. It's easier and more natural somehow, and something I rarely get to do.

I watch Ms. Writer of the novel, Marie Francesca, who has a faint accent. Middle European, even though she mainly grew up here. When asked what she thinks of the drastic changes they're making in the novel, she says, "They're serious people and they won't disgrace me." She smiles shyly. I wonder what her young daughter, who watches with her, thinks of us all.

When they've taken shot after shot of Sylvie going out the door—to be matched with the close shot of yesterday and a back shot—there's a hiatus while they set up the next shot.

I overhear Rich herding people into a back room to audition an actor, and I ask if I can watch. Perhaps now I've presumed too much, but he says, "Sure."

If not for Rich, who would let me in? Now no one questions it. Though the publicity department of the film promised the magazine I would have the run of the set, without Rich's agreement it would be like a pass through war-torn Berlin given by a clerk who's long ago disappeared. I remind myself the next time Rich's spittle hits someone, we have a pact—access for approval.

They're conducting the auditions in a storage room of the supermarket, filled with cartons of Hunt's tomato paste and Bounty paper towels.

One of the actors playing a lover of Sylvie's dropped out—his TV series was picked up—so they're making a last-minute replacement.

The casting woman is an ugly, mildly harelipped woman named Babs, grim and competent, like a children's librarian who doesn't like children.

Perching on a stack of cartons is Maureen, a young actress with hair like fuzzy chocolate milk, and lounging against the wall, the guys—Barney, Phil, the writer from yesterday, and a balding man named Albert, who, it turns out, is the writer of the screenplay before Phil did the rewrite. He explains he was not available for the rewrite but has come back for the polish.

Maureen with the fuzzy hair and a Woolworth pink-lipsticked mouth is playing a seduction scene with a series of young actors. Her passion wanes and flares matter-of-factly. She is reading Sylvie's part.

The auditioning actor's objective, as Uta Hagen would say, is to woo her from the sofa to the bed, from the Windex cartons to the cartons of Hunt's tomato paste. The actors hold the script sheets, which they glance at to refresh their memory. One young man makes vague ineffable motions in the air, flapping the script, another toys with the pearl buttons of Maureen's baby blue sweater, a third one whispers so everyone has to lean forward to hear him.

When each leaves, Babs turns to the actress, Maureen. "Sexy?" she asks.

"Nah, nothing," says Maureen, or, "Hey, you know the hairs stand out on my arm." "He was trying too hard. So, no." Or, "You really should let my husband audition, he's had two small bits on *Miami Vice.*"

Once Babs says, "What did you think?" to me, and, startled, I say, "Um," as she says, "Nothing, right?" and scrawls NOT A TURN-ON in bright red ink on the card of the dark-haired actor who toyed with Maureen's sweater buttons.

She waves the card nonchalantly to dry the ink, and the red letters gleam down over the three of us, Babs the grim, Maureen the fuzzy, and me, three women like a hanging jury, under the red-lettered flag of our assessments. This, for my taste, is too much like a man's fantasy of women's bonding in the steam room—muscled, naked women sitting on slick stone benches, steam rising from their killer lips as they mock, dismiss . . . break into cruel laughter. The three witches from *Macbeth* at the Health and Racquet Club, cackling about penis sizes, judging the entering young men in turn for their facility in raising the short hairs on our arms.

The men in the room are momentarily silent.

After each reading, Albert takes the script and strikes out some lines.

"Less is more," he says enthusiastically. A few lines remain.

HE: I look at you and I want you.

SHE: But last night you were with her.

HE: It's easy—that twenty-year-old skin.

(beat)

Look, last night I was with another woman and I wanted it to be you and I didn't like that.

(beat)

I always leave a little piece of my gut in you.

(beat)

I'm happy with you.

And then there's a dialogue about killer ants moving in a swarm, and then they're in bed.

The "twenty-year-old skin" goes, the "piece of gut" goes, "I look at you and I want you" goes, and Albert says enthusiastically to Maureen, "Now *you* try the ones left, honey."

"Last night I was with another woman and I wanted it to be you?" she asks worriedly.

"Oh right," says Albert, "okay, we'll drop that too, less is more."

No one questions why they don't drop the killer ants.

The last actor to audition, a comedian named Trance Farber, plays it for comedy, inverting the emphasis weirdly so all the lines seem funny.

"Sexy?" says Babs after he leaves. He has rubber, affectless lips and some reputation as a cool urban comic. Not for me. But I only shrug.

He's down to the killer ants line and "I'm happy with you."

"You know you really should let my husband audition," Maureen says with mournful bravado.

Then Rich comes in with the news that there's a hitch with the union about Sylvie's hairdresser. He's English, can't get his union permit after all, and Sylvie refuses to let anyone else touch her hair, so in the forced break it is decided they'll go over to the soundstage

49

and videotape the scene with the two finalists—the whisperer and the comedian.

We go over to get in the cars. Sylvie is coming to read with the two finalists. The food table is set up, but clearly no one is stopping for food, so I grab two chicken legs to eat in the car. I pass Sylvie on the way from the table to the limo.

"I'm very generous," she confides to me. "I only wish when I was in their position, people had been as generous with me." Presumably she means to read with actors.

The driver tells me it's nice to meet a real person. Presumably he means the chicken legs. Sylvie agrees enthusiastically. It seems I'm forgiven for interrupting her.

The soundstage is huge and cavernous, but there is a dusty sofa and a dusty bed. The whisperer and the comedian both do the killer ants scene with Sylvie. Then the dialogue, almost down to no lines— "I look at you and I want you"—as each actor tries to move Sylvie to the bed from the sofa. She's kittenish, surprising, responsive, turns to stone, plays along, doesn't. You never know where it will come out, you lean forward, you wonder . . . I'm impressed.

Clouds of dust rise from the bed.

Albert, the writer, is scribbling away, making black squiggles over his lines. Less is more. Sylvie comes and confers with them. She prefers Trance, the comedian.

"How important is it to you that they hit the sack at all, Albert?" says Barney.

Albert's eyes sparkle.

I suddenly find I can't breathe. The comedian is talking, talking to me . . . and now I remember how actors take up all the oxygen in the room, even on this vast soundstage.

"It makes no sense if they don't make it," Trance says to me urgently, staring beyond my pupils, down into what feels like the base of my throat.

"Wouldn't she want it?" he says. "It makes no sense if she doesn't want it. I'm a very sexy guy, I can be very intense on the screen, I could show you a blowup of a take on my last movie they cut it out, I could blow it up on your wall. . . ."

My mouth is open and I take shallow breaths, trying to get some, enough, air in.

They use up the oxygen in the room, actors do. They're direct, like animals. They want what you have—your total admiration and love and attention, and then any specific they can use.

Note: We lived in a house for a while whose previous occupants had left Katinka, their Siamese cat, with the neighbors. Every morning she would come across the street and, though I have never liked cats, would rub against my legs with such delicate and fervent devotion that I could not but feel beholden—till I realized she had figured out I had the key to the house she wanted to get into.

She wanted to get in the door, which was why she rubbed up against me. I was immeasurably offended. "I never liked her," I said.

My husband, Sam, said I was too hard. "Come on," he said, "She just doesn't know how to dissemble. She can't say, Let's have tea, what an interesting play you wrote, oh, is *that* your house? She uses what she has."

She'd rubbed up against me, she'd implied she loved me, she'd curled up against my toes to keep me from walking away from her . . . and so do the actors rub up against you.

"Wouldn't you want it?" Trance says rudely. "When's the last time your husband told you you were still a beautiful woman?"

He's trying to convince me he should keep his nude sex scene with Sylvie.

I'm afraid they'll hear my shallow breaths and I'll be asked to leave, and I feel a pair of hands massaging my neck. I jerk around, long fingers, hair glinting on suntanned wrists, the pressure firm and experienced. I'm breathing again, and Harry, the D.P. moves on—calls of a similar nature?—and Trance keeps talking. I listen with a cold interest.

"Wouldn't you want it, Jessie?" he says. "Of course you'd want it."

He's making two basic mistakes about me. One, because he's a New York actor, he assumes the woman in the room is the writer and has some power. (In the way a Hollywood actor assumes the unknown woman in the room is the script girl.)

"Wouldn't you want it?" he says. "I'm a sexy guy."

Second, I'm back in my baggy work clothes and, as I said before, I'm back to men thinking I'm their secret discovery—i.e., they'll get me to put my hair down and deal with my passionate gratitude.

But now I'm a means to an end to get to move onto the sofa with Sylvie, and fuck you, mister. That is to say, I'm more annoyed than it warrants.

Sylvie says, "That line—'I'm happy with you'—I want it back in, Albert, only I think it would be better if I said it, don't you?"

Albert says, "Less is more, less is more," and rolls his eyes toward me. As Trance assumes my support on the issue of wanting more sex, so Albert thinks I'll be there on the crucial issue of his polish. But I'm not a serious writer on this job, just journalist for a day, and like the last holdout on a hung jury, I dig in my heels and won't meet anyone's eyes.

Sylvie says, "I'm so generous . . . Jessie, remember that line, 'I'm happy with you,' he says it, where did it go?"

Albert says, "Darling, it's a finer thing to have somebody say it to you—you know, you make him happy."

Trance says to me, "Look, Jessie, if a guy says he loves you, you want it, right? I could show you a blowup on my wall. I'm very intense on the screen. Right now I'm fucking a very famous star. She's a married gal, like you."

He is going crazy. What he's just won—the part—is turning to ashes if he can't move Sylvie off the sofa.

Sylvie says, "Jessie, that line 'I'm happy with you.' I think it would be better if I say it, don't you?"

Albert is saying, "Always remember, Jessie, less is more, less is more."

We're called back to the set. The others stock up with peanut butter cracker sandwiches from the vending machine to eat in the car. Outside I see the second finalist, the whisperer, gathering up his things sadly. I want to say, "Look, maybe Trance won't fuck her either," console him for his loss of a flickering fuck, for his approach, after all, was a reasonable one—but our limo is waiting, doors open.

Sylvie says to me, "You wouldn't sleep with every guy around, right, Jessie?" Like she does? Or like the fan magazines claim she does, with younger and younger guys?

I'm starting to understand the terms. A real person doesn't use makeup or have a lot of sex or sleep around, and eats real food instead of shredding off the cellophane with her teeth to gobble crackers in the car as the others do, peanut butter scent in the upholstery, nuts caught between their teeth, crumbs on their Ultra-suede safari jackets.

The conversation in the car on the way back has shifted to which is worse, losing a lover or a mother.

"Oh," says Sylvie, "a lover, because maybe you've done something wrong."

"Oh, a mother," says Barney. He sounds too shocked to even open it to discussion. It is the most definite I have seen him.

"Oh, my mother," says Trance the comedian. "I call her every day, she wouldn't ask me to, but I do. She couldn't live without me."

Albert says, "My mother is a saint, lives for me. My father, she puts up with him, but when my mother hears my voice . . ."

"Oh sure," says Sylvie, "a mother's great, nobody like her, but a lover? That's something different."

The men sigh. The teamster driving the car touches the rosary on his windshield. His position is clear.

"My mother hates to touch me," says Trance suddenly in my ear. "So does my grandmother. They like to touch my daughter and my daughter likes to touch them, my mother and my grandmother, but they don't like to touch me, they never have."

I wonder, if the teamster's arm was jostled, if he swerved into the tractor trailer coming from the other direction, whose name would head the obits? Oh, Sylvie's for sure, but Barney in *The Nation* or *The New Republic*, *The New Statesman* even, me in the *Times* and the *Dramatists Guild Newsletter*, Bernie in *Variety*, Trance—sure in *Variety* too, but everyone everyone would be also in the car with Sylvie, we'd not get space of our own, anywhere. "Also riding" in the car in which Sylvie Marlborough was killed.

Back on the set, the hairdresser crisis has been negotiated. A member of the hairdressers' local will sit on the set and do nothing (actually, she knits), be paid scale while Florian, the English hairdresser, does the job.

The light is going. I can feel it like another person in the room, the way I first experienced wind in a sailboat.

They're falling behind on the shot list and Barney is tense, pushing at Harry.

"How long do you expect this setup to take? You said twenty minutes or I would have given up the reverse. We've got to move to the next master. What's taking so long? Don't any of you take responsibility for schedule?"

Harry says, "We're going as fast as we can."

The light, as the man predicted, is coming to an end. The crew rushes around on their hands and knees setting up little sticks on the grass that make a track like a caterpillar trail, a dolly track for the camera to roll on as the light fades and grows dimmer around them. They need another matching shot with the day's light.

Sylvie goes in and out the supermarket door. Her newly coiffed hair by Florian is shining, flips over a shoulder.

Harry and his guys huddle by the camera. They agree on something and an arc light is adjusted. Their moves are quiet, full of purpose. I want in.

"Oh, I see," I say to Harry and the other guys if they're listening, "why it was worth losing all those hours. Hair does make a difference, if it didn't gleam in that way . . ."

"It's movie star shit," he says.

Sylvie's hair flips back and forth and back and forth. The union hairdresser assigned to sit in a folding chair drops a stitch, picks it up. For the moment, I'm watching people watching people watching people work.

They are shooting inside the supermarket itself today, and Sylvie waits her turn on the cashier's line. She starts to unpack her groceries, someone yells "Cut!" and they do the whole thing again. Each time she lifts the box of Cheer, someone yells "Cut," there's some dead air, and then they do it again. Patricia, the script girl, checks what each of the extras was handling when they stopped. "No, you were picking up the toilet paper," she says to the checkout girl. "No, you were holding the chips," to the packer. "You had the milk in your hand."

I came on the streets today with the sense that something was about to stir. After all those miles of dead streets, my footsteps had their own rhythm—I felt them hurrying toward something urgent, alive, to do with me.

For the first hour, there is one counter open for real shoppers, and they rubberneck as they empty their carts. The real employees are excited. The young actor hired to play a counter boy in a later scene is learning how to ring up the register from a fat, dimple-armed woman. He does it over and over, determined to get it right, and the other clerks hang around calling advice. He needs to look like it's bored second nature and they're showing him movements charged with the excitement of the occasion—but it's getting better.

In *Daughters and Sisters*, the heroine goes to the supermarket constantly, when she's going to a lover, when she's remembering a lover, when she's imagining her mother in the camps. I have no way of knowing which is the one they're shooting now, when she holds up the box of Cheer. They'll probably decide in the editing room. I wonder if Cheer has any significance, but don't ask or I'll reveal myself, as Rich would say, "trapped in the printed word, unable to make the leap to the visual."

They'll be matching this shot with one where she takes Cheer off the shelves, so those shelves, even in the first hour, are cordoned off and shoppers who planned to buy detergents are out of luck.

Phil, the writer, explains the scene they're shooting here is when her mother's memories are haunting her and she's just run out on a lover she doesn't want.

"Do I cry here?" Sylvie asks Barney. He says no.

Patricia is also called the continuity girl, which I prefer, because I've always associated script girl with miniskirts and long hair, not Patricia with her shirtwaist dresses, her pageboy bob, and her neatly curving shelf front of a fourth grade teacher, seemingly unseparated by hills and valleys.

She and Willa, the angora-clad set decorator, are busily working out what is in which wagon and which were in the last shot. It's a little like the boredom of grocery shopping squared to a manic degree, emptying the cart, checking your list, filling it again, emptying it again, checking your list, and then oh, yes, all over again from scratch.

I know it can't be this boring. There's got to be a pulse or I've made a mistake. I feel myself starting to exist less, it all starting to go. In bad times, times of grief, I look stretched, as if someone took to the roots of my scalp and the soles of my feet and tugged.

Willa is wearing peach angora today instead of the lemon color of the other day—little soft points of fur, harmless balls, and round little eyes. She seems to be working her way down the fruit salad spectrum in little furry balls. She says she had to fight her way into the union—they made her do worse things than any of the carpenters. She flexes her earned muscles under the angora sleeves and sateen Oshkosh overalls. "I used to come home at night and cry from pain, but they never saw it."

I like little girls like this and I like them to like me. And I forgive her her caviar and pâté in the refrigerator while she cried from pain.

And then Stephanie, the tall Directors Guild stand-in from the car and later the clipboard, asks me if she can ask me a personal question and asks how I became a playwright. Then Willa asks me if she can ask me a personal question and asks where I met my husband.

I answer fully because maybe this is where it's all leading to, Women on the Set.

Women always ask other women about process. When a woman says, "Do you mind if I ask you a personal question?" it's always process, maybe because going from nothing to something is still such a risky convulsive uncharted leap. That early trying to be somebody or meet somebody is everything, and the secret seems to lie in process. What did you do? Call? Ring the doorbell? Use wing-tipped pencils, Wordstar, a turban, rinse?

I use "be somebody" and "meet somebody" interchangeably and do not compare and contrast the personal questions of Stephanie's and Willa's because, in my case, the organizing lines of judgment and irony would be blurred, because I wrote my first play as a college assignment and continued to write because of my ardent crush on a visiting older director.

Note: though I am now older than he was then, I cannot say he was a young director and be true to the way it was for me. Then there was a real mark between a boy and a grown man. Gray threading the short hair, a body slightly heavier, more heavily muscled around the midriff, army khakis to show he'd been a man in a man's world.

I see men dressed as boys now, their bald heads above their open shirts and jeans—they haven't understood that young girls will not be swayed by aging versions of their contemporaries. (And I know now that the game for the most celebrated lyric poet, painter, uxorious or esoteric though he be, is of course the admiration of young girls.)

But I am avoiding the embarrassing memory of me glued to my dormitory desk, writing, discarding lines of dialogue, trying, trying, knowing if I got it right, if he laughed out loud, his eyes might roam over me appreciatively.

And when I got one right, I jumped from my desk to try out new outfits for seminar—teal-blue mohair to pick up the fleck in the tweed skirt. We thought, in those days, men responded to fabric and color when they looked at a woman.

He did not seduce me. He did not want me. I sat in the plush seats of the college movie theater-turned-playhouse and lusted for his corduroy jacket on the seat, his midriff, of which I have already spoken, his belt. I had a more extravagant sexual response staring at his empty pigskin glove on a chair than I had previously experienced in response to the erratically probing fingers and imagery of undergraduate courtship.

He told me the two most important things in a woman were posture and nerve. He had a red-haired wife who was pigeon-toed. I never heard her speak, but I imagined her nerve to be like a sharpened carving blade, hidden from casual view for its blinding, lacerating slash. I kept out of her way.

Once I checked his schedule and took the bus to New York on a week I knew his wife had taken the children to visit her parents in Georgia. He was directing an off-Broadway production of *Orpheus Descending*. I thought he would have his needs and I would be there. So little did I want for me. I would have, I believe, contentedly replaced his wife in the dark like some Mariana, so much did I see it as an experience to attend—in the first row, so you could see best.

The young blond actress in the play had waist-length silky hair and narrow lips. A man talked about her thin transparent skin. Her bare feet squeaked caressingly on the stage boards and she said, "The act of lovemaking is almost unbearably painful, and yet, of course, Ah *do* bear it . . ."

I was sure she was available for his needs, and I was without hope. I took the next bus out of Port Authority.

My skin is, in fact, more leathery than not and needs some prodding, but I began saying it was thin. It took my sexual vocabulary years to recover from that matinee. I was forever drawing around me the mantle of that irresistible trio—posture, nerve, and thin skin.

I was too ambitious for transforming delights to be stopped: I sneaked in the back way. I wrote six more one-act plays as assignments that semester—the art and sullen craft of schoolgirl seduction—and finally, indifferently, he took me. I was so full of throbbing expectation and careful notation that I scarcely noticed how indifferent it was. It was still more excitement than I could come by without him.

The next semester I wrote four one-acters, and at the end of the school year he put two of them and one from the first semester together and made a New York production that launched a new star, gave freedom to a fabulous set designer (which I now think was the whole point), and put together a production that transformed it all. It's still being anthologized and performed by companies around the world.

The production was extraordinary. I took no secret credit for it at the time, nor do I now.

He said I was an extraordinary talent. I took it as PR hype, even when he said the same things to me privately as he said in his interviews. I thought it was to maintain his consistency. I knew my play would not exist without him. I doubted I would have had the incentive to go on working without him or to know what to do with the work unless he was there. I didn't believe he could really think that well of my work, because he was so smart, but I hung on anyway.

I have never been more humble or more ruthless.

He was a briefly clever fool. I do, in fact, have something that is mine. That I am now trying to isolate it and control it is another story. What I needed from him then, I want to be able to do now, myself.

He did not do so well. He went off to Hollywood for a while. A director does not exist without his material. How could I not have understood this?

He came back years later. He needed me for his career, and that made him much more fervent in my bed. When it was for career advantage, he really put his balls into it. There must be some message about a man's sexual connection to his work, because I could swear his organ got bigger, and after all, I had stretched during the years. Anyway, failure made him a better fucker, which should be some consolation to someone.

He wanted me to refuse an assignment I was being offered unless he was named as the director, and he put his whole self into the effort. It was as if he couldn't screw me wholly when his career was upward—but when screwing me was a totally compromised act for me, it became a whole one for him.

He didn't remember his pronouncement about nerve and posture. He was delighted with himself for having said it and made me repeat it twice so he could keep it in his mind.

What does this say about what I wanted before? Didn't I want sex to do with my mind, my heart? Why, when it had to do with my talent, was it irrevocably compromised?

Anyway, it was too late. We were not partners, and I want to do it for myself now.

I look around the supermarket—women playing women in a supermarket. Something here?

Marie Francesca, the writer, comes over shyly to stand next to me, her soft Middle European accent shades her words. As a survivor child whose mother was in Dachau, what does a supermarket mean to her?

I should make clear that her novel, *Daughters and Sisters*, is often affecting, plausible, not a piece of shit.

Her hair is tightly curled today, and her firm fresh-skinned arms emerge from what might be called an Orlon house dress. She asks me softly to call her Marie instead of Marie Francesca, it was stupid of her to have let them use the Francesca on the book jacket.

Sylvie breaks ranks briefly with her makeup people and rushes over, this being her chance to assure Marie she sees this as her first serious role and that they're all working for scale.

"I have a scale at home," says Marie and giggles, but Sylvie is already gone.

Marie tells me she wants to write like Dorothy Parker. She's happy comedians are making this, she was distressed that reviewers took her book so seriously. If she had to do it again she'd take out all the survivor child stuff—any child has a problem with her mother and sisters, she says. She has an idea for a TV special for Sylvie.

Trance, being fitted for wardrobe, comes to meet Marie, tells her how he admires the material. She says she admires his standup work, was so happy he was chosen. He says he can show her a blowup on his wall of a still where he's sexy—"She knows it, too," he says, pointing at me. "She knows how intense I can be."

Sylvie whispers to me, "Nobody could take him seriously in bed, right? You wouldn't go to bed with him." And I understand he's been cast so probably they won't get to bed at all, and even if they do, she won't seem promiscuous because he won't seem like going to bed with a real person.

I watch them milling around the supermarket, Marie telling Sylvie she's glad it's a comedy, Sylvie swearing it will be serious and real, Trance assuring everybody he's both real and sexy, Sylvie assuring me she'll never sleep with him because it won't feel real on screen. They're like figures on a gift shop Grecian urn, linked forever by the constant use of the word real.

Trance says his agent would kill him if it got out, but he wants her to know, for her material, he's working for scale.

"I have a scale," Marie tries. I smile for her sake, but in fact working for scale is unimpressive to me, especially since Hollywood scale would keep off-Broadway theaters in Dom Perignon for breakfast.

Stephanie comes by and suggests we duck out to a luncheonette for coffee. Our lips suck at the thick crockery, veined with black cracks, which seems luxurious after nothing but Styrofoam. She picks up the check because she is serious, she wants to know about me and my life. She seems very admiring for one so tall and strong and young. When I stand next to her, we are automatically friends by being the same height—over the table it is more of a commitment.

She got her pink culottes at a discount when she was Miss Clearwater College college representative at the college shop in Perkins' Department store in West Virginia the summer after her freshman year at Sophie Newcomb, when she was obsessed with her first abortion, being arranged by her cousin, the mean bastard who'd knocked her up, whom she'd been in love with for thirteen years, started when she was ten, who told her to go riding bareback three hours every day before sunrise, so she got up in the dark and rode on the beach till dawn, when she raced to answer Perkins' coeds' questions on Psi Gam rush tea outfits.

She presents it all to me with an energetic, cheerful optimism—life goes on, doesn't it?—and my questions, ever so slightly skeptical, elicit an even more effortlessly rolling narrative.

Or once she stood at a traffic intersection watching a blinking yellow light for seven hours. Seven hours? ask I. Yes, her parents did come looking for her, but only after it was clear she was late from her Beaux and Belles meeting, and then Daddy came only because her best friend, an old lady, had been found hacked to death with a butcher knife in her rocker the month before and it had been Stephanie who'd found her.

Once she was crazy for a month and she had a therapist with a beaded curtain in her office who treated her with metaphors about being a wild bird being shot down by those who could not fly.

An energetic all-inclusive southwestern Gothic Americana, optimistic, energetic, cheerfully bizarre, always good-humored, with the details of memory, dress, humor, and desire so effortlessly and intricately flowing, offered in advance exchange for my story of Sam. I stall as long as I can.

Stephanie has a guy she sort of lives with while they're shooting, the young bearded director of photography, Harry. I watched her tell him we were going off for coffee, she standing, he sitting. He'd lightly circled her thigh with his hand, so high his knuckles almost grazed her cunt. Young love doesn't turn me on these days, it's too explicit, they've taken the yearning out.

Years after it happened, my high school boyfriend told me he could always remember that moment I walked down the stairs in a green skirt, and it's of that that love is made—it is cloaked in language and symbol, in green skirts attached to shy and trembling for-the-first time sensation. My dear young first boyfriend, Terry, whom I met again at a political dinner, told me that every year, on the first day of spring, he races from his executive office and runs around the street thinking he'll find me. "Oh, she's not on Fifth, she must be on Madison," he says, "oh I guess I'll go up to Fifty-third." After five minutes the craziness is over, and he goes to lunch. He has a pretty wife and family and we never even met for lunch, but such is the stuff of young love. Green skirts, trembling, verbal and romantic in origin. Young love now is too localized, genitally oriented.

Stephanie is asking me about Sam, and if it wasn't to be a quid pro quo I was obliged to cut her off earlier, so I try to explain him. One day, in the bad days, in the sleet, when people were unkind and the world full of hard graying ice, we arranged to meet downtown, and he came walking toward me on a city street. His smile was the only sweetness while everything else was gray. Oh, we can make it, I thought, and I clung to his lips. They were warm and I thought, oh, we can make it. And we did.

I describe him in cool phrases. He meets a payroll. He knows about irrigation.

But my mind wanders instantly to what I would never say out loud.

He can be harsh with his children, has a heavy touch, but his soul is whispering, gentle.

This is too intimate. I tremble to write it. We are connected by a narrow cord of shining steel, the wire from the center of him to the center of me. The voice no one else hears, the movement no one else sees. Sometimes we live on the wire, sometimes one of us wanders a little away, like a dog on a leash. Oh, but we always know the wire is there—and to turn too far away is to yank out one's own heart.

What is he like?

We bump clumsily against each other sometimes. He is bearlike and heavy. We do not explore each other delicately. We roll around until we find it.

I seem incapable, this Thursday noon, of cool description.

It is always a labor, describing Sam's work for laymen. "My husband is a civil engineer," I say, "involved in Water Resources."

"Oh, he makes dirty water pure," says Stephanie, making him sound like those purple beads through which you run your water faucet to protect your steam iron from rust.

But we've lingered too long, and we rush back to the set.

There is a general announcement. While they set up the next shot, several counters will be open for the store's regular customers. They suggest that anyone on the set, cast or crew who has shopping to do take the opportunity.

Marie and I are the first to head for carts. We are clearly the only ones who'd needed to shop at the end of the day one way or another. She asks the butcher for knuckles and feet for stock, gets giant family containers. My shopping seems, by comparison, both frivolous and gross, but we both know when it is the moment to splurge on asparagus. She pushes the best bunch toward me, through the gritty water. What is she guilty of? We both know about produce.

Stephanie is collecting whole grains and vegetables for Harry. Sylvie comes by and stuffs chocolate in her little son's mouth. I had forgotten she had a child, and he clings with the other hand to his freckled nanny. He seems a pleasant enough little boy, and Sylvie barely knows what to do with him. He says something to her in a small voice.

"He wants a snack pack," she announces loudly to the world. He doesn't even flinch, as children do when grown-ups repeat their words. He seems to expect nothing of Sylvie. He's chattering to his nanny about going to Meredith's house, and his mommy seems a little like an aunt he's got to placate. He and his freckled nanny wait till it's all over, then they chatter earnestly about the party and other things and hurry away.

The real stirring seems to be here in the real supermarket, not supermarket as set. The space between me and the actions around me seems to be closing, coming together. We skid around buying things where the real women have walked, where the actresses playing real women have walked. Who are we, these straddlers of both worlds? Is this the *handle*?

Real women playing pretend women walking where real women walk? Or pretend women playing real women walking where real women walk?

The neighborhood shoppers are complaining because the two

shelves of Cheer and other detergents are closed off. So get it to-morrow, the manager says.

Sylvie smiles at me happily. It's a real we-could-be-any-women-shopping smile. Stephanie holds up carrots, brown rice—and grins. Healthy dinner with Harry?

I turn away and let out a short laugh. "Jesus Christ," I say, and it comes out harsher than I intended. I begin to laugh to soften it. Sylvie looks at me inquiringly.

"Look," I say, "one roll of toilet paper." It is a transitional sentence that gets everyone's attention. "No housewife buys one roll of toilet paper. A Hollywood cart."

They're ready to start shooting again, and I'm pointing at the movie shopping carts, carefully checked to take their places in the line for continuity. Marie says anxiously, "But that's what's so wonderful. It's the movies, right? A real cart we can see any day."

Sylvie says, "What's a real cart?"

I go through the items quickly—colored napkins, not biodegradable, one roll of toilet paper, single-ply paper towels—not an Upper West Side sensibility. A small original bottle of Windex—you buy the big size and then a refill, makes no sense . . . suddenly I see Willa flushed and angry and Sylvie talking furiously with Barney.

A few minutes of intense conversation—every item will be changed. The shots will not match, and worse than that, they have to throw out the master.

"The brown lettuce is fine," I say anxiously. No one listens. A morning's work is trashed. Some people blame it on Sylvie, others on Willa's incompetence.

A lot of money is being lost. I try to explain to Willa it's not her fault. Someone who keeps sweaters in her refrigerator doesn't buy toilet paper in bulk.

"Everyone needs toilet paper," she says coldly.

"Yes, but this is a housewife," I say. "You run out of everything but toilet paper and if you run out of that you buy the economy pack. Look," I say, "you lead a different life. You couldn't keep your angora sweaters in a real refrigerator because it would be full of sticky things—half full, half empty, partly covered—ingredients, not food."

"Ingredients," says Sylvie behind us, "and make sure, you, when we get the refrigerators they're full of *ingredients!*" Sylvie is beaming and this whole thing is ridiculous. These carts are not for real. I pat the peach angora shoulder in apology, but it hardens like rock under my touch.

Harry comes over to ask Willa for a time estimate.

"It'll take as long as it takes," she snaps. I realize she's near to tears.

He says something with a slow smile that makes her laugh. His hand rests lightly on her furry back. "Now that's soft," he says, and she hurries off smiling.

He takes a book out of his pocket, lounges against the camera, and begins to read. I can't see the title, but the point is clear. Because of me, there's nothing to do now but wait.

I see Stephanie watching me.

Marie watches silently; she knows about assigning guilt and responsibility.

And it wasn't Willa I meant to undermine, in her satin overalls, who finally made it into the union against the guys.

The health food set me off.

Patricia, the continuity girl, has to change everything on her lists and her matching. Willa has given her her orders. "Paper towels okay?" she calls spitefully.

"Ask *her*," says Sylvie, pointing radiantly at me. She is sure Marie thanks me, too.

Sylvie tells me last summer she bought beach chairs, two hundred and fifty dollars a chair, for her deck in Malibu. And then she had a party. Six of the chairs were stolen. She called the police and was ashamed in front of them to admit that friends she'd invited to her home would do this.

"It's because I started in comedy," she says to me. "They'd never do it to someone who hadn't started in comedy. And TV? I'm surprised they didn't take my car."

"Tide okay? Or does it have to be Cheer?" Patricia calls to me. And I've had enough of a hair shirt because I'm sorry I caused trouble, but in fact I think I'm right. That is to say, I explain to Sylvie, when details, i.e., props or settings, are not precise, the screen goes dead. When a laid-off metal worker leans back in an original Eames chair to tell his wife his life has no meaning, no actor can carry the day, however skilled, because the screen goes dead and phony, though most of the audience could not say exactly why.

As I speak, Sylvie is nodding with a how-true, how-true gesture of the kind we wrote in the margins of our paperback novels. Her hair, shiny, done by Florian, flashes around her shoulders.

I explain with the precision I am demanding. As a little girl I saw *Letter to Three Wives.* Linda Darnell drank crème de menthe and turned out to be the one of the three wives whose husband left her. Only after I saw it again on television two years ago with Sam did I understand that for twenty years I have never drunk green liquid for fear of losing my man.

Call it superstition, suggestion, the fact that the mouths are so big, the words so few, whatever it is about movies, the moral lessons grip you by the throat and say, "If you do this, this will happen— if you do that, that will happen." Or perhaps it is that the screen is so bright, the audience so rapt and huddled in the dark. So there is a kind of obligation, if you have any pretense toward serious subject matter, say I, self-righteous and surprised by my fierce humorless commitment to it—you have to be honest with your audience with everything from story to language to set detail.

"How true, how true," cries Sylvie enthusiastically, turning with her shoulders to include anyone who can hear.

"And *Letter to Three Wives* is in black and white," I say as she dances off toward wardrobe, past Harry and the camera, twirls gaily under his arm, disappears into her trailer, leaving me with the prop and set people. A real-life cart goes by—a woman with gray-streaked hair wearing an army duffel pushing her cart of one roll of toilet paper, a small bottle of Windex, single-ply paper towels, colored dinner napkins, blue sneakers, Indian tote, unmistakably Upper West Side housewife. Everyone avoids my eyes. Hah.

I walk outside, where they're setting up the final outside shot. Okay, I'm out, I've declared myself—no turning back—I'll find my place with the tech crew, who are, after all, the heart of the enter- prise. I step across the caterpillar dolly tracks, the crisscross tracks made of individual sticks of wood, which were laid down so care- fully by the big, curly-haired dolly operator in the stubby grass of the plaza. The camera will move along this track to follow Sylvie coming out of the door, moving away from the door. It must be very smooth. I'm always very careful not to disarrange any of the pieces of wood, to pick my way through the sticks, step only on the grass. One of the gang. I turn around behind me to see the big dolly operator squatting down on his haunches, smoothing down the ground between the tracks, where my heels ruffled the dirt.

"Why didn't you stop me?" I ask. "I was trying to be so careful. That's why I didn't rearrange the track. . . . I didn't realize the grass in between had to be redone every time I went by."

He looks up at me indifferently, shaking the dirt off his fingers. "Anything can cause a bump, means it won't be smooth," he says. So I've been clomping across the canvas of his work since I first came on the set, and it never occurred to him to tell me, to stop me, to apply to me standards of courtesy, decency, much less professionalism. It never occurred to him to tell me not to. Everyone who was anyone would know better or, if told, would instantly modify his or her behavior and have the courtesy to walk the extra ten steps.

I understand with the bleary intensity of an uninvited child how outside the party I am—the birthday party that the whole fourth grade is attending—and standing there at that moment has triggered every memory or intuition of exclusion and rejection. But the grown-up in me forces me to know that when you lose you move forward, not back.

"He's crazy, you know that," says Barney to someone behind me, and bursts out laughing. "That guy's not afraid of anything."

"Harry wants a reverse," Rich mutters in my ear. "An extra shot." He disapproves.

"Why so many setups?" I ask Harry. His eyes are green, when they light on you, they darken. "Couldn't you tell the story with less?"

"No," he says politely. "Say we're having dinner. If it's about you talking to me, we need a shot on your face, a reaction shot on mine. If it's about me talking to you, we need a shot on me, a reaction on you. If the shadow of the salt shaker is pointing toward you it's menacing, if the shadow points away, it sets a different kind of mystery altogether . . ."

There's a shout—the checking is done, the shot's beginning, everyone starts to rumble like a sleepy avalanche of which I am no part, and I rush out of the way. It's something that isn't me that's happening, so why doesn't it feel that way?

Hands in pockets, jeans low on his hips, canvas shoes, thick hair, streaks of gold, mouth open and alive. He's pasted to the camera for a last second.

And menace or not, shadow or not, it's about you pointing at me and me pointing at you and they're saying I'm a real person, but who is the unreal person? The CEO executive off for his margarine audition? Willa in refrigerator angora? Sylvie the TV comedy queen longing for history and dignity, Marie full of history and dignity, longing for TV comedy . . . or me, dragged off the inlaid linoleum by husband Sam? Was told I was a real person because I wear glasses/ hold a notebook. Was told I was a real person by a comedian whose mother won't touch him, because I was stuffing myself with a chicken leg and cole slaw when everyone else ate crackers from the vending machine—first stuff your face and then talk right and wrong, says Brecht. So where is this real person, sifting, choosing, judging everybody's work with clever morality based on a green liquid I never drank—and what else have I forsaken? celery juice? limeade? Afraid tomorrow I will lie depleted on the linoleum again, not make it out the door? It's about you talking to me or me talking to you and oh, Jesus, there it is.

His quilted vest is flung over the chair. Look at ANYONE ELSE! There's a woman with black slacks rolled up, pale calves, she is motionless. Girl in light blue windbreaker hunched, moving back and forth, child picking up stones, further on, girl in striped jersey, white jeans. I am shaking and I want to bury my face in the tufts of his vest and I'm shaking. There's no mistaking it, I tell my earnest writing students, when you've found your material, there's no mistaking it, you know it.

Goddamn.

SECTION FIVE

Did you see it coming?

I did not.

It is not about Stephanie, women on the set, detail and theme for my assignment. It is about him. It was there, howling, all the time.

Time now seems a huge daylight-filled cavern of hours to get through before I see him again.

All things are organized in retrospect. I see my attention to people working, the camera, equipment, power, movements in the air, he was the only one. I see what most of my preoccupations have been about. You shall have to take that perspective into account.

Nevertheless: trust my descriptions.

SATURDAY, MARCH 27

I wake at dawn wanting to cancel boats, trains, taxi rides, trips to the kitchen. I want to lie here where I am. My emotions do not yet have words assigned to them, and I am afraid they will spill—puddle merging into puddle—if I move around too much. But today is the day we must drive down to Bucks County to see Sam's ex-wife, Bernice, and her husband, Leonard.

In the car I try to concentrate, because although some part of me needs to organize, isolate, identify, put heated lemon oil and hot towels on my hair, soon the press of events will take over, will become as immediate as now the hours till Monday seem numb. Today may be many things to many people, but it will not, repeat, will not, for anyone, be a day to walk through.

Harry.

As we drive, I remember driving down here in the early days of our marriage, when the tenderness we observed between my husband and his daughter, Petra, set us all off. We would see them sitting together, she with her wood nymphy charm, flowing hair floating past us into the air. An emotional hustler, I thought, with her flowing hair, murmuring through her flowing hair to Sam, only to Sam. As she grew, long-haired swains came calling, with silver flowers, leather-braided amulets. Into handiwork, were her lovers. Were their hands clever with her, too? Did Sam wonder?

We wondered, all of us, what she thought of us.

"Attaboy," called Leonard, her stepfather, to their neighbor on a power mower. A phrase Sam would never use. What did Petra think?

I used to imagine her conversation with her girlfriends about me, and I dressed to be described to preteeners—vests, workshirts, long, rough cotton skirts the color of pumpkin bread. No pleated skirts or well-cut gabardines to be noticed and mocked.

If she noticed at all.

But you wonder at the past tense. Although I am rarely noted for my smart remarks, I said one Thursday to Sam, "Our contemporaries no longer have mad wives in the attic, they have mad stepchildren in the basement."

And that was the Thursday before the Friday at dusk when we pulled into this very driveway that we're pulling into now and there was Petra, barefoot, in one of her endless granny dresses, staring into the garage door. When we tooted, she turned and drifted toward our headlights and her eyes were blank and wandering over the landscape.

But this was a year ago. We pull up now with the weight of history behind us, and no one is one up on anybody anymore. Game called on account of madness of the pivotal player. Or is she the scorekeeper who never bothered to keep score? And here we are, endlessly trying to find her scorecard among her confiscated belongings, the drawings, the poems, the caches of thread and dried flowers.

My remark? A disgrace only in my memory. Tragedy is never topical.

Bernice and Leonard come out to greet us. There is always a little awkwardness when we emerge from our car because we are so much taller than they are. She's the same height, exactly, as Leonard, who's a hard, lean little tanned man. They're such a hard little couple, not an ounce of soft jiggling flesh on either one of them.

Do not trust my description of Bernice (nicknamed Bun). Read it through my irritation and anger that she was Sam's first wife.

Leonard used to tell me how much he saw of Bernice in Petra— no doubt to minimize tactfully for me Sam's collaboration in the whole event. But I never saw it at all. Petra was boneless and floating. Her mother is taut and small. Her nickname, which, to be fair, she loathes, is wrong. A bun is squishy and oozing luscious scarlet jelly or honeyed cream. I used to think she named her child Petra to be the opposite of bun. But Petra turned out boneless—she could pass through rock and come out the other side.

We try so immensely hard, Bun and I, not to play so tacky a game as one-upmanship that I truly thought we didn't compete at all. We play with their two charming babies, who tumble over each other and chortle. The day last year I felt her no longer hating me—ah, that was a defeat where I had never known I'd triumphed.

I've always put it together with my miscarriage, but it was also the time of Petra. Not a time of triumph for any of us.

I see from the food on the Hot-tray that the news is not good. Dark meat and beans lie dormant in deep pots. Bun puts elaborate care into such details. Her cooking is not good enough—she selects and alters recipes with a heavy, uncertain touch—but the gestalt is impeccable. Today there is nothing to carve with a flair, nothing leafy, nothing spurting. Nothing to be eaten with the slightest festive ceremony.

And the news is bad. There are decisions and revisions that no moment will reverse.

Leonard and I sit silently and speak when spoken to. Leonard is spoken to first—a look from Bun.

"So I'm a surface guy, okay," he says, "but it seems to me that at least the Elavil made her look out the window. . . ."

Do not judge him harshly by his introductory clauses—"So I'm a surface guy . . . so I'm pretentious . . . so I have a Sunday supplement slant"—which seem to be introducing an ass. They introduce his straightest, best remarks.

And they are a healthy step away from the pretentious, terrified bridegroom I met years ago, who almost broke his pride trying to keep in temper his Bun, who would not, would not, sweet heaven, be married to a surface guy.

He is a middle-level media executive, and he has, to be sure, ridiculous traits. He uses "we" and "they" constantly and indiscriminately. One day "we" is the huge conglomerate for which he works, and the next day "they" is the other three middle-level media managers who disagree with him on prime-time rates. I have never heard him use the first person pronoun in talking about his work except when Bun tells us he's gotten a promotion.

But he is a work in progress, and I take a certain pride in him. I encourage him and I give him clues, which he picks up.

(For instance, one day, I mention an article I read on top executive types. I make clear that the best of them regret being away from their machines, their laboratories, their basic products. Two weeks later, I hear him say he misses the cutting room. Not true, he hated working on documentaries and loves scanning proposals, but he got the point.)

We are complicitous without being in the least attracted.

I guess we are both a little on edge because Sam and Bun have two unfinished children together.

My respectful attention and surface flirtation help him through his eggshell of a marriage.

I believe I can destroy his marriage by showing some sign, in front of Bun, that I am contemptuous of him. But I am not. He is a smart surface guy.

He met Bun when he came to interview Sam for a white paper on environmental geology.

I will give him a hint, and he will drop the introductory clauses. *That guy's not afraid of anything.*

Bun pushes the dishes away. The sexuality drains from her face and she is a concerned mother. There is suffering around the table, but it has nothing to do with me.

Except once.

Seven months ago, Petra, home from the hospital, sent for me to come up to her room. It was late hot September. She motioned me to close the door behind me. Then she ripped down the top of her dress and showed me her breasts—and gave me a ripe tomato with her bare breasts showing. She was like a baby, scarcely rippling nipples, and I covered them with my hands. They grazed my palms, they were erect—seductress stepmother? How could her boyfriends not be moved to tenderness? The foulest imagination would see in this seed of flowers poetic concepts bursting to ripeness. She said in her high light voice, "I brought a tomato for you, Jessie." It was the ripest reddest one I'd ever seen, and she'd never used my name before.

So I walked down the stairs holding the tomato. In the living room they told me about the vegetable garden at the loony farm, and no one asked me what Petra had said.

I worried and winced for days about whom to tell and whether it was useful and how to put it and how much it had to do with me. I wondered whether I should tell the doctor it might be a literary reference, because the only play of mine Petra had ever seen—bad idea, I'd thought at the time—was the off-Broadway one that showed young girls sunning on a rooftop in Manhattan, taking off their bikini tops before being raped by a stranger playing WBAI on his transistor. But by the time I'd almost gotten ready, they'd discovered Petra's blood chemistry changed drastically just before her worst sieges, and were giving her no analysis at all. Since then she has been on various drugs at a place where the psychoanalytic faction is not even allowed in the door. So there would have been no one professional to tell. But if the other faction ever comes back into favor, I shall step forward.

Sam's son, Daniel, is away at prep school, and I am relieved. The last time we saw him, he'd had his hair cut, at Sam's insistence. His neck was long and bare, an adolescent's bones, to be sure, but I felt—so foolish, how do I say? Daniel had looked better in the long, matted pageboy fluff he'd tried to keep. It showed his face more angular and boyish than now.

Don't borrow trouble, or lend it.

But Leonard and I sensed it, and share the fear we may be sitting on another keg.

I think: I could be away from all this pain. No, to be accurate, I do not think this. The image of Harry, sweater, beard, jeans, zigzags through my body, trailing slowly dying delight in its path.

On the end table, under the blue glass lamp, is a picture of Len's son by his previous marriage. I first met him when he was fifteen, in from La Jolla for a visit—a husky, large-toothed, fifteen-year-old beachboy—and wondered how Len and his dark, rodent-faced first wife—viper image of Bun—had produced Andy Hardy.

"If I had that kid's opportunities, I'd be dead in a month," Len said often that week. But he was wrong. Gary didn't live inside his sexuality any more than the Ipana kid. Now he is a resident in psychiatry at UCLA, tracked down facilities for us, and found friends everywhere, one of whom supplied a room for me to lie down in at Petra's first sanatorium, when I was pregnant and all of us were sore and battered.

Enough. Bun, let us save for another time. Bun and Sam. She and Len were already a couple when Sam and I met. On paper, he stole her away from Sam. In the flesh, such ordering of the events is palpably preposterous, however chronologically precise. It rarely comes up, except through Bun's occasional insistence on being ostentatiously tactful with the past.

She asks me about being on the movie set.

Bun practices ballet. There is a barre in the house. She talks about dance with the edge of anger. It is a kind of fetishism I haven't figured out. When she speaks of ballet, her face turns tight, wary, slightly scornful. Her peak expressions of outrage are against others' crimes—a dance teacher, Gelsey Kirkland, a fellow pupil in Bucks County. Ah yes, people will always be treacherous, commit crimes, or have faulty turnout. I feel her world is made clean and unambiguous, livable, by seizing on a single standard of judgment. No, I'm unsure of what I think here.

Petra really dances. She waves like wind through leaves. Unlike her muscled mother, sweating, doing tours jetés in a turquoise leotard, Petra sways like the wind, ripples like leaves.

But now Petra cowers in a corner of a sanatorium room, defecating and smearing it through her hair, so they have to cut it off, masturbating and leering, so that the new place does not want to keep her, so that we moan, so that Sam and I are back in the car going home and his heart is so low I feel myself keeping him alive. I keep up a steady flow of pulsing on-with-life talk, just this side of gibberish, but carefully, oh so carefully selected. Nothing that can seem to matter too much or it will be dismissed, but nothing that can matter not at all. Just enough so that the heart will keep pumping blood to the brain, which will send impulses to the hands on the steering wheel and courteous replying sounds to me, the currents will keep going. *Thank God no one read my mind.* We will lie tonight, humming in each other's arms, and perhaps at one point he will cry out and his cheeks will be wet. He will fall heavily asleep and in the morning he will be implicated in *my* life.

I prefer to make these visits on Sunday, because Monday he has promises to keep—but tomorrow it will be my life. We are going to visit my brother, and Sam will keep me from getting angry, bothered, riled about my father's widow, who will be there, her bad grammar, his good money. I can think about her money all the time, all the time . . . and she is forever finding new ways of swearing he didn't die of intercourse.

SUNDAY, MARCH 28

It turns out we are not going. Dora cannot come, and careful questioning establishes that my brother has work to do, my sister-in-law has prepared food that can be easily frozen, my nieces have friends with plans. But I'd looked forward to seeing my brother, who is one of those rare, genuinely funny men who doesn't need his audience, and my sister-in-law, Edythe, with her serious brow, and my two nieces with their serious brows, all of whom I adore.

So, instead of a day on a stage of people, among whom we share sidelong glances, Sam and I are one to one all day. I heat lemon oil and sit with a soaked towel in the room where Sam does some work, then we take a nap, then we get up, go out and wander. We walk slowly. An unplanned day. I am his again and I am relieved. No sorting through was necessary. It has not happened. We come to sunset over the river, a red ripple flares through me—*slow smile, beard*—over and out, and I am over it. No more. The sky is a mellow blue, no undertones of pink; we drink sherry. I am a little sad but so relieved, so clean. We move slowly to dinner. We have a silent dinner. Ceremonious. We smile over creamy vinaigrette on the asparagus. We come home holding hands on the lighted bus. We sleep heavily through the eleven o'clock TV news, then stagger up to turn it off, and bump into each other. We go back to bed, slowly make love without a word. Our pillows seem drenched in sweet exhaustion.

I dream that my mother is crying. On the balcony of a Paris apartment. She will die in a few months, and dreads what they may be. Oh, she doesn't want to die. I stay inside the dream. How can I take comfort in knowing, when I wake up, she is already dead?

I wear a striped shirt and a fresh cord skirt. I am pleasant. I ask Harry modest questions, to show I am at a place in my work where his answers are useful. I praise others when possible and eat lunch with Marie to show I know a worthy when I see one. Several times I go to the wardrobe trailer and splash my face with cool water. I conceal my profligate, moist, and wriggling rue, for I have accepted my degrading temporary bind, and leave early, explaining I want to catch the bus before rush hour, the cab being too expensive. I am clean, thrifty, clever and calm.

Stephanie has a terrible sunburn. The skin is stretched over the knobs of her shoulders like moist summer squash. It glistens with pain.

It is an elite and extraordinary pain, I tell her, unbearable but finite, found its inception in pleasure and will disappear as if it had never been, no, leaving a rosy glow of loveliness. In the interest of moral economy, I say, think upon it, to understand the glory of being without pain, the pleasure of pain that will irrevocably stop. In fact, the weight of personal experience I imply is unearned. I speak neither of childbirth nor terminal cancer—only severe menstrual cramps. But I have, after all, had years more of them than she.

Stephanie and Harry listen respectfully. I say, "When I was your age," including them both, implying ease with my age, experience, weight of life's knowledge. I establish Stephanie as a dear child I wouldn't hurt for the world, and expose my tender fondness for young lassies . . . and lads.

I am clean, thrifty, clever, calm, *and* compassionate.

WEDNESDAY, MARCH 31

I think I can move things along. I am standing in the supermarket next to Harry when Sylvie fluffs her lines. The scene is one of the first I've seen with dialogue. She is coming from a night when hallucinatory memories of her mother's life intruded on her and her new lover in bed. Now, the next morning, she has rushed out as if for refuge to the supermarket, to the place she considers her normal life—and there has an irrational fight with the checkout clerk.

They keep fluffing their lines. First the boy who is playing the checkout clerk, the one who practiced learning to use the register, fluffs his. Then he fluffs again. "Hot enough for you?" he's supposed to say, and she says, "What's that supposed to mean?" and off they go, into double entendre, he assuming she's coming on to him, she assuming he's mocking her mother. It's skillful in the book, misunderstanding piled on misunderstanding. But Sylvie and the boy can't even get the dialogue started.

She is buying meat and the blood spills over into the lettuce. That will be a separate insert shot.

Barney calls a pause and speaks with the actors. They start again, but the counter boy fluffs again, then Sylvie. Then Sylvie fluffs again and then again.

Once, they get through it, but it doesn't work. It's arch, he's mean and arch and she's hysterical.

Then she blows the line again.

It is painful to watch and seems a good opportunity, so I step up to Harry to express my compassion. Especially for the young actor.

"It's worse for her," Harry says, and goes to speak to Barney. Looking over in the corner, I see Sylvie, elbows up, while the makeup people dab deodorant under her arms. I catch her eye, look away not quickly enough.

And then Harry is speaking to Barney and, oh yes, they clear the set, good idea. Me too?

Me?

And there I am, banished. Banished on the sidewalk, full of dismay and spite.

Into a Spanish delicatessen I go, but nothing has names, and I stare into the refrigerator case, which doesn't seem to be working.

Out they come. I see through the window. Harry pushes Stephanie ahead of him, poking her with a finger in the small of her back— no, doesn't hurt, the only non-boiled part, and they go down the street, she on the point of his finger.

I go home and get into bed. Sam is away this week. My ire and bile have closed my stomach. At eleven I get up, make myself a slice of bread with peanut butter, and eat it on the way back to bed.

The eleven o'clock news reminds me it is April Fool's Day. Hah! I'm thinking like a hack.

I am drained and still. Relief from hope. No need to keep on trying. I sprawl on the steps and Harry sprawls next to me. His long lean leg in jeans slants near to mine.

"What happened to you yesterday?"

"I went home and got into bed."

"That doesn't sound like you." And he's gone. And with him a slit, a whiff, a promise, no, a presentiment of intimacy.

I leap from the stairs through the slit and there's no stopping me. I am next to him, I talk, I get our lunch, I ask him questions, I take notes, I bring him coffee on the set—out in front groupie of the day.

Harry's aesthetic. What Harry hates most: overoperatic angles, search for effect, overdramatic wide angles, vulgar colored lights.

I take notes, oh, I write it down.

Mystery is important, beauty you understand in a few minutes is boring. Shadows excite and surprise with mystery.

Interested in close shots and long ones, bored with middle shots. But I'd heard that.

Plays with contrasts of light and dark, mixed light colors with a filter, sometimes they misfire, but you don't know till the dailies.

I write it down, I listen hard, but then I talk.

I cannot stop talking, it is useless for me to try.

Instead I drawl to control my hypervivacity, and I can tell it's working, slowing me down, but not slowing the drive. Through the fray of my words, I feel certain themes emerge. My line of attack is clear.

1. I talk to everyone in the line of work. This is nothing special, nothing to do with you personally. Today the director of photography, tomorrow the grip.

2. I am old, older, oldest. I have experience, the weight of a crowded past and present. "One evening years ago in Madrid," I say. "My stepson likes to say . . . my agent has been swearing for ten years . . ."

3. I mean no harm. I have neither edge nor spite, and tend to be passingly appreciative in a hearty way. "Is that your dog? Isn't that a sensational ring, a terrific child?"

4. I am busy, really busy. My eye is on a wide number of cross-referenced, intricately related, personal and professional sparrows. Should it, might it be, that you have caught my eye with your informed remarks about light and dark and filters, and that, should it, might it be, that we coincidentally hit a free moment together, near an unobserved bed, chances are, with my schedule, it will never be coordinated in a like way again.

In other words: Here is a shot at a chance encounter with an older, experienced, accomplished woman who, coincidentally, has a few minutes to spare.

Do you hear me, young man? I am clean wise experienced vastly impersonal and will scarcely note your curious and inquiring one-night excursion.

It will interfere not at all with your life, your work, your evening meal, your tomorrow, or Stephanie.

In other words, in precise words: why not?

How economical is unsatisfied lust. It is a simple aim I have. It is cold. He is the adversary. My words are totally focused toward having the brain instruct the blood to harden the penis. And then, in, deflate, and it will be over before Sam gets back from Atlanta.

I concentrate on the key. If I can push the right psychic buttons it will be up and over, unlock me from this obsessive concentration, and it will be gone. And the next day, notebook snapped closed, casual, charming—"I think I have all I need to know."

It is all so disembodied, it relaxes me. I feel I have never been so cool and dispassionate and compartmentalized in my life, and it seems a good sign for my future work schedules.

Note: and just in case, Harry, you fear to squander your creativity with random acts, don't you think the fact of hardly noticing it at all can be interesting in itself, even briefly insightful?

FRIDAY, APRIL 2

My hair is crinkly. I see the parallels. With my first lover, I mean. Why do I always try to get in the back door, explaining in advance I'm not to be taken as me? I'm either too young and inexperienced for it to matter or too old and experienced for it to matter. I am resentful and martyred. My hair is crinkling because it is damp, the linen pants are creased around my hips. In damp weather, my skin turns moist and dark; on islands people ask to buy my seashells. As summer comes, if I suntan and my hair grows red, strangers fill my drink at parties and ask what Jesse Jackson really wants or say that Leontyne Price is one of the conscious artists of the century.

I have arranged to pick up an article on day-for-night lighting in Harry's room, but it has all become wearying and absurd. Stephanie will be there. I wish to seem bloodless when I arrive so they will not guess at my past few days of overheated, unbecoming folly.

FRIDAY AFTERNOON, HOTEL WARWICK

I walk inside the door of his hotel room and we are drowning inside each other. Moving across the floor, I rear my head back to make sure it's him.

Our sex. We are mouth to cunt, inside out, talking, no, sighing—rolling, waving grace notes. We have slipped inside each other's skin like satin pillowcases; we are shiny and slippery and gleaming and bridal and pure. And, oh Lord, the quivering waves are sweet, sweet Harry, they have to do with him, with him, no. Not *sweet Harry*, stop that, do not call him sweet Harry.

But dear Lord, it is it is, it is him and me. I am awash with my odors and his, the sweetest is holding him limp—no triumph—done, done.

There is no ending or beginning. Lights and shadows and jokes and lengthening shadows.

There is a bone in his shoulder—he is in me, thrusting, his shoulder pushing on my neck. Its pulsing frightens me, for it is a wild heart beating . . . *his* heart, what else can it be? The rhythm is galloping, it is galloping away from me, wild and desperate. Not so fast, I think, though it goes on and on and on and on—it will not be rushing past me it will go on and on beyond me, it will go on and on.

Go on with him, I try to think, but I am terrified. I fear it will kill me. He is reckless and strange and I try to feel like the proud free woman who would love it, welcome it . . . but it is me and for me and with me. Thrills rush down my arms and legs, like those of a feverish child, curled in Mommy and Daddy's bed. The paths of my curling nerves grow wild and convoluted and clench around me and shout free and clench again . . . and slowly die away. But when we are quiet the air still crackles and trembles and there is terror in the room, and sweetness.

It is me, Jessie, but I'm not alone.

We can barely speak.

Survivors of a fire, a wreck, chaos. We stare at each other and his eyes blaze green, then blue. We face the world and cover each other.

I drop the sheet, the towel. We protect each other. I want to pray from the tenderness.

The tears are from him to me and back again.

There is no one else in the room.

In the world.

Where did this come from?

Oh Jesus, we understand each other.

1. We are together on a narrow bed, under a harsh hotel laundry sheet.

Our limbs seem flung around the narrow surface, interchangeably. It all has to do with the two of us. I cry. We are exchanging sweet tears.

Surprise at the end for both of us—it's *you!*

2. In public.

My body has no stiffening organizing spine. I yearn with whatever flesh is closest to his. Though I think I think public yearning tacky in the extreme, I change my shoulder bag as we walk coincidentally side by side, in the event that the back of his swinging wrist might brush my hip and—like to the marriage of true limbs—admit impediment. He does not touch me in public, and I become aware he will not.

As dusk comes each day, my body is assailed with blows. Memory of contact—tongue in mouth, penis against membrane, knee against thigh. They hit me from without, separate blows, surrounded by spidery dying chills. I try to lean against a wall. Seen in the round, I am afraid I will seem to be reeling slightly.

I would say it was flesh calling to flesh, but it is thought that does it to me. Memory in words in my mind, that starts it happening. So then, I could say, it is this joining of words and bodies that I want in drama. But this is a lot of crap. I am learning nothing.

Sometimes it is words themselves that start me. "You," he said. Specifically, as in, "Will you move a little to one side, please, we're setting up a tracking shot."

I fear that my body flutters under my denim skirt like beating wings.

I find myself ridiculous.

3. In private.

Harry's room is dark, jammed with equipment, mobiles, wires, spools, toolboxes.

"Do you like to make things work?"

"Yes."

"Do you mind when they don't?"

"Yes."

"People, too?"

"Yes."

This is false dialogue, too gnomic to be insightful. I repeat it to hint that our tangled limbs are spiritual rather than dirty.

In fact, it turned into a sexual game. Harry, murmuring to himself, curious, experimental. "Hmm, what makes this happen, is it this? Is it that? Is it when I press this, push that? Let's try this, no, not that, this, then." I, lying back, rocking slightly with pleasure, self-delighted, reared up slightly, to show myself tenderly more knowing of him than he of himself. I saw his smile. He was mocking the insightful inquirer curving and quivering in his bed.

He is very smart.

I said I would not invoke your griefs for mine. Can I invoke your pleasures? Descriptions of sex are humorless or harrowing. Birds in flight? Questionnaires on mustard-yellow recycled paper asking, "Does the base of his penis stimulate your clitoris sometimes ( ) often ( ) never ( ) ?" Either genre of description makes me lonely. I would not make you lonely.

Or another time. He looks at me, his eyes darken, and my body—muscle, bone, veins—wrenches through my layer of skin and faces him. It was just a flicker of his eye, maybe a trick of the light.

4. Let me tell you about Harry.

He is the best director of photography "in the business," says everyone. He came out of the union, made a film with a man he says was a saint, who taught him everything. Harry was only a camera assistant, but the word got out that the old man was dying on the set and that Harry did everything. The film won a lot of prizes, and everyone wanted Harry. He made a film with a new director and the director became famous. Like me, he has made someone else's name. People are after him to have him do it for them.

The director of photography is the pivotal person on the set. He is responsible for the look of the film, the pace of the production, the appearance of the actors. The actors flatter him and fear him. He holds their appearance in their hands. Harry's known to take care of women by sensing what makes them look good. He analyzes how light falls on their faces, creates with his lighting cheekbones that aren't there. Actresses have passed the word around, request him for their projects.

In public he seems so other, it's hard to remember him as intimate. With sloppy work he turns cold, scornful, closed.

He is often laughing with his crew.

He is strong, strongest, stronger than me. He started as a cameraman, lifts heavy equipment. I see him lift a camera once, his mouth tightens. I try it, it will not budge. Though my arms are sturdy, I cannot make it move at all.

I watch his movements in the middle of an action shot, quicksilver, angular, on the alert, every muscle tense, part of the equipment with his faded corduroys, graceful when relaxed, his leg up, the lines so long, I watch his lips, so sweet, hot green eyes.

Harry loves his equipment. I watch him touch it, curve his long, tanned fingers over it. He dismembers it at night and puts the various parts together into swinging mobiles that hang from the light fixtures on his ceiling. He does not secretly fancy them in a Madison Avenue gallery—when he needs something, he unscrews it. I secretly think they might be art.

He is a good salesman and he hates it. People buy. He was a traveling salesman once, in college, sold paintbrushes and drafting boards. Because he draws back at the moment of the deal, people press forward.

At Yale, the sons of famous fathers were his friends. The fathers wanted their sons to be more like Harry. They offered to fund them in setting up regional theaters or small magazines. Then, too, he drew back. He is everyone's ideal son. I, too, am often my friends' parents' favorite grown-up child. The child-grown-into-woman they wished to have had. What is there of the child grown-up-well about me—about both of us—as opposed to simply adult?

Stick to Harry.

I see I want to convince you he is the best. As in grade school, when erotic impulses could only be sanctioned if they were toward the smartest boy in school, the president of Arista, the best cameraman in the business, or the boy who got a full scholarship to places where they weren't taking Jews.

And why am I trapped in images of childhood at the first truly adult—adulterous?—act of my life? *Unfaithful* is so devastating because it implies, correctly, that there was adult faith, broken.

5. And so we properly get to Sam and what this has to do with him and if I have ever done this before. Sam is keeping his distance because he thinks I am working through something in my mind. And your answer is once, once before, and I never thought of it as such till now. It was in our bad period, when we were bone-dry, bleached in the aftermath of blazing loss, and I was always afraid a flare might consume us. I remember that I felt my secretions as tears. The substance of ulcers, they say, when analyzed under microscopes, is the substance of unshed tears. And so I felt about those vaginal secretions, body juices. The bitter juices might wash out of me with someone else and finally cleanse me.

Did I feel guilty about Sam at the time? I wanted only to eliminate all the fluids that would have scalded him, bathed him in bitter acid. I wanted them to flow away.

I picked someone I had known long ago. Oh, I had no heart for new romance and I felt it to be no betrayal, since it was someone I'd known before I met Sam. He was a grown man I had known before, a doctor, southern, courteous, and I had chosen not to marry him.

97

And until now, I never saw it as having been unfaithful to Sam. More as an attempt to prepare myself, purify myself for him. Bad show.

A crack, a space, appears. I can do without Harry yes/no. Thinking about Sam makes me think I can do without Harry. Yes/no/yes/no/no. Not yet.

Spaces appear and I rush into them, get flashes of what life could be without him.

I feel myself swarming, arms in his hair, laughing, joining, not tender about anything. I can barely handle it. I save my best observations about life on the set to tell him while tracing the curls on his chest. I wonder if it will seem cold-blooded to publish little movie-set anecdotes I am whispering first on his skin, hair.

Aha! Am I thinking of a time without him, when I can get along without him? No. Like a contraction of pain it closes again—no space at all.

His head is on my breast, a glossy shock of thick soft hair, I run my fingers through the bright streaks—seen in public, mine to touch, just mine. I cannot keep in mind the two states—wanting him and doing without him.

MONDAY, APRIL 12

We are shooting in a playground.

I have decided to work with blazing precision. If I can think clearly

I will have a fine piece, be back to my work, and impress Harry at the same time.

I have figured out the reason the PR people and Rich are allowing me so much access is that they think my assigning magazine a finer thing than I do. They feel it will validate them in some glossy coffee table way—a magazine whose ideal piece would be Elizabeth Taylor on Samuel Beckett's sex life, with a sidebar by Sam on Liz's art.

The trucks and towering equipment loom over the miniature playground, so shading it and stunting it that they are painting the jungle gyms and little swings in bright primary colors like Beaubourg, and the trade-off in keeping the neighborhood children out for a week is they'll leave the bright paint when they leave.

Instead of leaving teamsters to scrape it off? I wonder who in the city government made this deal.

In the story, the heroine takes her child to the playground every day as a place of sweet and graceful safety and boredom.

"Do I cry here?" asks Sylvie, thinking perhaps the ennui of the playground may get to her character.

The last scene they'll shoot before leaving the playground location will be when a park policeman walks by in uniform, the ordinary cries of the playing children suddenly meld with the screams she has heard in her dreams.

The playground is flooded with stage mothers, real mothers, real children.

The set is boring in a brand-new way. Something is in the air. Phil writer (the aging Li'l Abner, not Albert, the original writer and polisher), spells it out for me, what everyone is whispering.

It started with the sight of the neighborhood mothers standing around, mesmerized by watching Sylvie act out their lives—wipe her pretend child's nose, zip his parka, take out his jelly sandwich. And as Sylvie acts out their secret fantasies of being a star, she is acting out her own. That is, Sylvie's secret fantasy of being a housewife, mother, devoted watcher of progeny in the playground. Judging by the clumsiness with which she closes her pretend child's parka—catching his soft double chin in the high zipper—it's always been the freckled nanny's job with Sylvie's own child. The irony here has been passed around to the lowliest grip. Sylvie's life is shitty, she can't keep a man, her kid hates her, she's financed this movie just so she can play the role of these ordinary women who stand here in clusters behind the ropes, wishing with their exhausted hearts—it's snack time and their children moan and whine—that they could be her. It's the kind of real life/movie life irony that everyone connected with the set is capable of grasping instantly. A sort of perk, making them feel they work in a glamour industry.

But there is no ignoring that there really is a kind of sullen trapped vitality in the faces of the neighborhood mothers as they stand for hours watching the insistent boredom of the set.

Between shots it scares me. I rush into Sylvie's camper—to show I can go in whenever I want, as opposed to the other watchers?

She is having her shiny tan hair blow-dried while a little groupie sits at her feet, knitting an earth-toned mess.

Sylvie is talking about not letting people take advantage of the kind of person she is. She says one of the P.A.'s (production assistants) comes in late, has attitude, so she isn't going to put up with it, there was a time she would, but now she'll just tell him she's on to him.

"It's beautiful that you don't want to be loved," her little hanger-onner is saying as Rich comes to call her to the set.

Florian gathers up his combs and Sylvie goes "to pee." She doesn't close the door all the way, as if her imperial tinkle is music to our ears.

Back on the set, Barney motions me forward. "C'mon," says Rich, "it'll be dynamite for your article," arranging for me to be pushing a child on the swing in the path of Sylvie's entrance, smiling at Sylvie as she comes past wheeling a stroller. A bit part. It all goes very fast. I push the child in the swing. Sylvie comes along. I smile hello with a tinge of amusement, welcome. The subtext of my smile is endless. I'm glad to see her but find her a little false and have my own thoughts. And then she's walked by and it's over and I feel I could have done it better. "Good," says Barney approvingly, so I must have been more effective than I thought. I also think when the dailies come the realness of my real person's greeting may sweep Sylvie off the screen.

But then they give us slips of paper and send us all to makeup and wardrobe. This was just a run-through for blocking, the other extras explain to me. I'm forced to exchange my jeans and shirt for a horrid paisley blouse with puffed sleeves that hit me where my elbows jut out and an ill-cut wraparound skirt that an impatient young man fixes at the waist with a safety pin that jabs into my side, and then it's the makeup trailer.

The people in hair and makeup are hurried, and though I am seated in front of a mirror, their bodies block it. I am unused to combs in my hair without consultation either on style or on the clouds of scented spray that suddenly envelop me, and allowing a stranger's fingers to roam over my eyelids and face with liquids and powders makes me helpless and angry. My brief glance in the mirror is pleasing because I seem a gleaming version of myself—but it's nonadjustable, which is to say, my hair is sprayed too tight to rearrange with a breeze and if I touch my finger to my cheek, it draws a line through the heavy pancake. A beige line through the pinky beige powdery cheek.

"Hands *off*," says a pink-skinned makeup man, a bright smile of irritation on his face as he sponges the repair with a filthy pancake sponge.

Looking into the mirror without task or expression was odd for me. If I had to describe myself I would say I, Jessie, have a good head, long legs, tapered hands, and rarely see my face as others see it. Sometimes in our mirrored hallway I catch it, exploding with welcome—all eyes and teeth and creases. The worst poker player in the whole wild world. My face shows everything.

Even when I could swear nothing has changed, it happens under my cheekbones. And when I speak and people stare at me, ignoring my words, it is not my loveliness that strikes them—they are staring at what is really me, what I'm thinking in my heart.

It's a reactive face—I mimic others too easily, try to monitor it. It's hard to imagine one expression on my face when I have another. People who meet me for the first time when I'm angry don't recognize me when I meet them laughing.

And I look like Sylvie—people sometimes say that, except when they're with us both in person or know either of us well, as I've said before. In repose, passive, no one would make the connection. As soon as we animate, the affinity starts in motion. Our aspects, not our bodies. I'm bigger, high-waisted, turn-of-the-century round-hipped, she's delicate, no waist, flat ass. I have dark brown hair, springy to the touch, turns reddish in the sun, as her smooth, silky tawny hair grows pale; heavy skin that darkens, flushes under the surface, as hers is clear, translucent; but something there is that this peevish makeup man will never see, that makes people say we look alike.

Outside in the playground, they place me in front of the third swing. The little girl I am pushing on the swing has one tooth out, which makes her distinctive. I wonder if her hideous stage mommy knocked it out for this moment in the sun. I smile at her as I push her, and she turns around and grabs my wrist.

"Listen," she says, stroking it seductively, "you're supposed to be my mommy, right? Why don't we let me fall off and I'll scream and you look at my knee and then I throw my arms around your neck?"

I ask what time I can leave, inventing an appointment, and realize, too late, I'm in the master shot, which means I'm here all day doing this again and again.

My hair blows and my body lumbers behind me. I lose all sense of style. I start out worrying about nuance of behavior, but it soon deteriorates into preoccupation with my hair. If a breeze blows it wrong, I need to call to someone to adjust it—or it flows by itself, a horizontal Medusa tendril. It has been sprayed so stiff that when I try to pull my own comb through it, it grows wild and crazy, and I hear my voice as one of the near hysterical mewling ones, "Come over here, fix it, quick me meee . . ."

Once I think I have it all together and right. The hair in place and expression just right—then realize this was the setup on Sylvie's face and on the back of my head.

And when the sun is at its height they set up another shot. I turn to smile and my heart leaps in fright—for in place of Sylvie, it is lashless Georgeann, the ill-fated stunt girl from the first day, who strolls by wheeling Sylvie's child's stroller. It is so unexpected that my much-rehearsed casual greeting curdles—my mouth stays open and Georgeann is understandably startled by my response. She pauses but, pro that she is, though young, keeps on walking. I remember now that somebody mentioned she was coming back, would be given temporary work as Sylvie's stand-in, not a usual job for a stunt girl, but she was not recovered enough yet to do stunts.

Life has many turns as have stand-ins in the movie, but let me set it out in sequence. Sylvie's ordinary stand-in is pregnant, which is why tall Stephanie, the Directors Guild trainee, was standing in for Sylvie (or, one might say, for her pregnant stand-in) when I first arrived. And now, Georgeann Cararra, the androgynous stunt girl, will be Sylvie's stand-in till she heals enough for her to somersault off tables again, or until Sylvie's regular stand-in has her baby, whichever happens first. In the meantime, lashless, sexless George-ann, built like Sylvie except for the muscular legs and flat breasts, but the same height, can move like her from the back, wheels the stroller back and forth in the hot sun, used to me by now, smirking at all around—a pretend mama? a pretend stand-in? a pretend Sylvie? Who can tell?

Sylvie, of course, is resting in her trailer, cool cucumber on her brow, while we stand in the sun blocking the shot for the camera crew for the next setup.

I grow more sullen than the sullen watching housewives who have, at least, the option to head home or gossip. The child actress I am pushing grows querulous with missed opportunity and wanting apple juice, which has run out. I think if they were the delicate bones of my own child, I would let her fly, come back safe to my palms, fly higher—I would feel the delicate bones of her back in my palms and push just enough to let her fly and bring her back to my palms, cradled and safe, oh safe in my hands.

I stand, rearranging a smile, checking my hair, talking to this horrid child actress, pleading to have my hair fixed, keeping an unaggrieved expression on my face because at any moment Harry may be looking into the lens. I am thinking of Sylvie in her camper with cool cucumber on her brow—and why does she have Florian there just for her?—and the more I stand there the more aggrieved I get, so that the final shot, which I learn was a close-up on my face as the sun is about to be going in, is my worst, most irritated "Who in hell do you think you are, I'll be polite but I'm exhausted and I just want to go home."

But then some wild last-ditch vanity makes me think even this is so real, it will wipe Sylvie off the screen in dailies. Like Trance blowing up his scene SEXY . . . right?

After the last shot, I step into Sylvie's trailer and she's crying. Her silky, small face crumples, her mouth opens like a bird being fed, she's all open yowling creases, no features visible. I have never seen anyone cry so totally. The production assistant she was complaining about has been fired, is already paid off and gone.

"I didn't mean off with his head," she weeps.

Nobody liked him, we try to tell her.

"I was just complaining, you know, like everybody else," she says wildly. "Suddenly they say, Okay, he's gone." And then she's crying again.

I've never seen a transformation like her crying. No wonder she wants to cry in a scene. I mean to talk to Harry about it.

I appear at his hotel room. He says it is getting warm. He has his suit to go to the cleaners. "See," he says as evidence, "I have my suit to go to the cleaners," and he takes my breast, traces it till I think I will faint. I shake, tremble, I've waited so long, so hard, hard sticking through his trousers coming toward me, stirring odors and waiting tips. Where do you want me?

We don't talk of Sylvie's crying at all.

TUESDAY, APRIL 13

I think something is hidden here about the lights in daylight, lights more powerful than daylight. About women in daylight.

It occurs to me that all my plays have been about women in daylight.

At night, women have grace. They are wanted. They are the lights behind all the sparkling windows on the dark city streets that men prowl in states of urgent, impersonal longing. It is easy to have grace behind a lighted window.

When someone says spring, I always think of the first days that grow longer, when girls go out on dates with their evening makeup showing in the daylight. As soon as I see their unprotected powdery faces coming toward me on the street, I know it's spring and I feel a lurch of pity. For they haven't managed the transition yet, these girls, and the man beside them may be drawing away, dusky mystery being replaced by powdered dulled freshness. They are drawing away. I can tell. I know I will not see Harry tonight.

The new set seems a mine field of betrayals. I don't know where to stand or what is happening. I try to steady myself.

I remember the first time with Harry. He was so grateful, he wept, his beard soaked with tears. Could he be as grateful as I?

Stephanie has bought my plays, and tells me she wants to be a producer. I bring her home to dinner.

I feel I have supplanted her without a trace. Can this be true? And I need to keep her under surveillance, make her like me, never betray me, if ever she should find out. She seems eager to be my friend.

She and Sam make each other laugh. He and I only smile—a glint in the eye is enough to indicate comprehension, don't you think? But she laughs out loud, and with her so does he. She doesn't ask if he makes dirty water pure.

She is wearing a loose flowered smock, and her legs are like glistening orange matchsticks.

She turns out to know about precipitation runoff relations and stream flow routing in the Southwest. Her father was away at war while she grew up. She talks about the phenomenon of rural daughters.

I never thought girlish girls would carry the day. The exhaust fan over the stove goes, and Stephanie helps Sam fix it. She holds the fuses. She is obviously admiring of him.

She looks up, hair away. Yes, no—she waves like Petra, very like.

And, very like, she waves so gracefully into center stage, just when I least expect it and think it's all about Sam with *me*.

She wants to be a producer. She talks about percentage deals, deferred grosses. She's smart and can put together the financing of a movie for Harry.

(He wants to make a film out of an anthropological article about Indians and the first airplanes. I cannot help him. I cannot write things like that. I had thought of helping him, had fantasies of clipboards on naked laps—till I saw the material.)

Stephanie is lovely. Her eyes, her determination, her youth are lovely. Her family is large and weird. Her brother is a scientist, doing government-funded research tied to atomic matters. A fascist, she says. Her sister is conventional on a manic scale—lives in an imported Austrian castle in a little town in Idaho. Her other sister sells franchises and started a nationwide company for panty-hose vending machines. She, Stephanie, does all their taxes.

She is an appreciator. She went to Samuel French and bought all my plays. Are they lying around Harry's room?

After she leaves, Sam says she was smart, knows what she wants, no edges, sweet. Like me a bit, he says.

Good-looking?

"Yes, strange, not conventionally, but yes, certainly good-looking."

Like Petra?

No. He is wary. What is this?

Okay. He never goes back over things, bears a grudge.

Tonight Stephanie knew all about methods of land irrigation, tax percentages, bombs, and franchises. None of the wild bird crap.

Sam says that encourages him about Petra.

Does everything have to refer to Petra? I snap.

He (mildly), "I thought you were making the connection to give me some hope."

Keep your mouth shut, Jessie. His hair sticks up weirdly but I'm afraid to smooth it down. I'm afraid I've lost my touch.

I lie there silently. He'll always fit my behavior into nice motives unless I force him not to.

In the kitchen, Stephanie told me shyly she thought Sam was wonderful.

THURSDAY, APRIL 15

Now comes the part I do not understand. I do not understand how it got from then to now—what the line of events was. I will try to describe it, but I am uncertain about which details to select.

This morning I drank coffee with Barney and Marie, who seem to have become friends. I thought I understood why. They have both suffered in the same way: wars, politics, have entered the fabric of their lives. They are both cross-referenced to the real world eight times more than I am. They are both wise and both weary. They have earned living in this time and of this place.

On the way out to the cemetery, I praised Barney and Marie to Stephanie and Harry. I contrasted them swiftly with young radicals now, many of whom I find cruel and idiotic, theoretical terrorists playing at dying young, who have seen of death only their grandmothers aging slowly in private rest homes. As I talked, I became aware something was going wrong. I meant only to posture as I had with Stephanie's sunburn, but it was going wrong. They were listening to each other, not to me. There was a private language they were speaking that was excluding me, nay, mocking me.

I may have been talking about easy answers, smug judgments, rigid kids. Why I could not write a play about people too young to know about death. In any case, I just meant to posture, as with Stephanie's sunburn.

We were going to the cemetery to shoot the scene that Sylvie said she would give her right arm for. She said that when someone tried to cut it for economy's sake.

This was where Barney would tell her she could cry. I kept my distance. I was not going to let this do me in. Not a movie scene of a cemetery, I mean. They set up long shots of Sylvie, close shots of her, and then a long shot from behind her framing her huddled by the grave in the side of the frames, lots of empty space. Even the naked eye could see how lonely she looked. "Always put the camera where you least expect it," Harry says. Like Storaro does. The best director of photography in the world, Harry says.

I ate the lamb stew from the caterer's pots. The caterer said I was his best eater, offered to make me anything I wanted the next day. Rich told me the caterer did disgusting things to his assistant behind the pots, and with the food. The caterer came to get his special order from me. I said baby lamb chops, the only thing I could think of unredolent of substances.

So did my day go. I tried to ignore the teenage members of mourning families, who wandered from the graves, unable to believe their luck in seeing a movie star on what otherwise might be a wasted day burying Granny or whoever else.

I didn't know which star-struck cemetery official had allowed *Daughters and Sisters* to come with our trucks, but I didn't want him burying me.

And then in Sylvie's long-awaited close-up crying scene, she cried wrong. It was external, phony, overdramatic. Not, that is, the way I saw her cry the other day.

It seemed such a waste. The trucks, the lights, the caterers had transported spring lamb stew for eighty-five on the Long Island Expressway, and she was crying wrong. I probably shouldn't have come.

I came because I was allowed to ride with Harry in the camera truck, which rides in front of the car and shoots back inside it. We sat huddled, cramped against each other as at a hayride, on the floor with the microphones and the generators. They had found room for me on a box. By now the film crew accepts me as there. I take constant notes to show the reason. On the way back we used a little video tap, a black-and-white monitor, which showed Sylvie inside the car driving, weeping, and talking to herself. Barney was crouched out of sight in the back, giving her direction. I expected, though it was too blurry to tell, that she was crying wrong here, too.

Then we started shooting the skyline. I mentioned that Sylvie was crying wrong, and Stephanie told me the cemetery scene was left in only for the establishing shot of the skyline.

"That's wrong," I said instantly. "There shouldn't be a shot of the skyline here."

Stephanie said with all the LA interiors, it's one of the few chances to establish New York.

"I guess you don't know," I said rudely. "Coming back on the highway you don't see the skyline. I've come back from cemeteries more than you'll ever know, and I never even knew it was there."

She tried to interrupt me.

"You've left someone you love underground," I said, "that's what you're thinking about. You have tunnel vision, you're looking at the ribbon of highway, you're not looking at a *skyline*."

I can't stop. Because, for God's sake if it was true with my father, my friend, it was even true with awful Jeremy, my cousin, who tried to make me shuffle grave slots, bury him two graves closer to my mother than he belonged.

"It's like those awful awful kids today at the other funerals, thrilled to see a movie star . . ."

"They're just kids," Harry said. "Let them have a good time."

I hadn't known he was listening, he'd been looking through the camera. It made me even tenser.

"They're kids who don't understand that someday they'll be buried too, who don't understand . . ."

"Maybe *you* don't," said Stephanie.

I was startled, tried to make it less rude.

"Well maybe I don't understand . . ."

"I don't think you do," she said coldly.

"Well, I'm not a kid," I say, "maybe I'm too old."

"Maybe you are," she said.

Harry said nothing. He was looking at her and said nothing.

Oh I am old I am old I shall wear the bottoms of my trousers rolled.

Back on the set, I tried to make sense of it all. I had only meant to let off some steam and it had gotten out of hand. But there was a way in which they were allied against me. And my stinking history of death? Or was I being presumptuous about choosing a shot? This was his work? Or am I crazy, distorted on the subject of grief, did I have an edge to my voice that put me over the line—over the line of people who live with death.

After the wrap, down the street they danced. She reached out her long legs and hit his rear with her foot. And he did it to her—Jerome

Robbins heterosexual and young—the horseplay that has never come with us, and down the street they ran as I watched.

> May your limbs ever flash
> in the sun,
> in the sun,
> when I am undone
> when I am no one

Stop that.

The next day, nothing seems to have changed. Stephanie and Harry are both remote with me. I have frantic thoughts. I do not know how to reestablish myself in the world of the young, of the sexually alive, of the untainted by death. I talk about a play of mine that was taken up some years ago in which murdered rebel leaders return to life. It was full of smug assumptions—a mean party skit, in fact—but it raised a lot of money at rallies and college performances.

This is to say my treatment of death can be rakish, irreverent, oh so young, and used for raising money from fondling couples at campus events.

I try to work it into the conversation.

As the day goes on, I remember Stephanie said she got my plays from Samuel French, so she must have the antiwar one. But then I remember it was published by a trade house. Did French do it, too? I wonder if I can find a private phone booth next to the set and call my agent. But I am afraid to leave. They may all drift off any second and I want only to announce that I will be free for the weekend, that Sam is away, consulting in Washington.

I say something oblique to Harry.

"I hope the cherry blossoms are out."

"Yeah?" Polite interest.

As dusk comes I am frightened. We have not spoken, and I rush into the tiny cubicle they use as a bathroom. When I come out, he is gone.

I walk the streets in a shrunken T-shirt and hip-huggers, my navel showing. Men glare at me. I do not think to button my coat. I sit on the steps of deserted office buildings. I think I will wail. I am out of control.

Then spaces appear. Like labor contractions. It begins for a second not to matter—to matter—I cannot keep the pressure and the absence of pressure in my head at the same time.

I think I do not like his knees. Yes/no. I try to hug it to myself as a secret. I meant to bring it out later—not yet, but soon. Even now not yet . . . but soon.

I cannot get through to him. After several calls, the hotel operator recognizes my voice and says, "Funny, I could have sworn I saw him go up."

Is she smirking at the desk clerk with whom I rigorously avoid eye contact? Where is the switchboard located, anyway?

At night, I dream of an empty sorority house, girls in rages, frozen into frozen splatters of frozen blood, waiting by a bank of telephones for calls from men. I am trying to run to class, but I can't find the room. When, finally, out of breath, I find it—oh, with a dying fall, it's only a woman teacher.

Obligatory dream. Recycled feminism.

I smooth my anguish in the mirror, wish for Marilyn. She cut her fringe of bangs one day. She frosted them, spiked them, then tinted them blue, once tried pink. A serious composer of some growing fame, she pasted tiny iridescent stars all down her chest and arms. I watched her play the piano in her living room, amidst equipment, composer friends, tiny stars moving up and down, glittering on her fleshy arms. I thought it would be fun to try, would do it someday soon, when I was merry and she was free.

I need her here to talk to now, to plan with, cry—though would I tell her something Sam must never know?

I am trapped inside this lonely pain, for I cannot speak to Sam and who can know what he does not?

Tomorrow if the weather is good they will shoot a scene on the docks. It's a scene Harry hates, with a beached ship. "Like her emotions are beached," Sylvie says, and he finds it a hackneyed image, but though he fought with both Sylvie and Barney, he's lost this one, and if it's bright I'll see him on Sunday.

I am scanning the sky for weather more eagerly than any time I can remember since the May Fête in grade school.

It rains.

He has not called.

I am assailed with a physical longing so intense I sit down, abruptly.

I keep remembering the one time he wanted to go to bed and I could not. I went home to prepare dinner for guests, and that lost opportunity burns in me till I think I will go crazy. I think if I could have that time to do over, I wouldn't care if I never went to bed with him again—and then I snatch that back. No deal.

I remember words and grow sentimental. I remember bending over him, my hair brushing his naked stomach, he holding a piece of camera equipment in his hand. He was playing with the parts, showing me which parts were replaceable and which not. He caresses his camera, his spools, his cans.

I said, "Am I replaceable?"

"No."

And as I sat there bathed in self-delight, he came back and climbed over me, hairy thigh separating my knees, hairy knee separating my thighs.

He could have said, "No two people are ever truly replaceable."

Why would he bother? But I replay the "No, no, no" in my head.

We all have words, Reagan, Nixon, Stalin, to explain our actions, and I think Harry could say, "No two people are, in a certain sense, replaceable. Unless they're standard parts, they fill different needs, make different things work. It's personal. You're not replaceable and I just don't want you anymore."

And then I'm back to knee separating thighs, the moment just before his entering me, because I can't remember his entering me. I try with my finger but it's no use. I'm relieved Sam is not here because I don't know how I would behave. I remember my hair brushing his naked stomach, he beginning to grow hard, feeling it press against my breasts. And he's not here, it's only my stupid little finger.

MONDAY, APRIL 19

It all seems to have been for nothing. I am in his room, he wants me, and he tells me he was working all weekend, checking out suburban locations, Barney leaned on him. When he is inside me, he is trembling and I realize I forgot the trembling. He wants me. I recognize how much he wants me. Forever. I'm confused. Somehow I'd forgotten.

He goes into the bathroom. I swing my legs over the bed and there is a sneaker on the floor. My feet are square and wide. The sneaker is narrow, too narrow for my foot—oh Jesus—Stephanie with the long narrow feet.

I confront him, screaming. I am shuddering all over, the proof in my hands, shaking the Ked, screaming, "You lied to me, you lied."

He stares at me. "Yes, I lied. Why not?"

We are in bed. He is trembling. He cannot do without me and I am in terror. What? Back in bed, you say? I needed time to think. "Yes, I lied. Why not?" He is trembling inside me and he cannot do without me and he lies. Cannot do without me? I mean the way he fits himself against me—knee against knee, calf against calf, bone against bone—wrist, elbow, arm, knee. He shudders against me, each bone of his pressing against each bone of mine. The insistence is remote, implacable. As if he wants to be me. No. As if he *will* be me. This is not erotic folderol. The savagery is unmistakable. And he lies, why not.

I wanted the obsession to be mine so I could control it. Anarchy and obsession. This is what I have feared all my life.

I am back at home.

What is this all my life business?

My first memory of obsession. Joey Marcus, a little boy in my fourth-grade class, proposed marriage. He planned to be a lawyer when he grew up so he could buy Jess a mink coat. Everyone called me Jessie, he called me Jess. One day his mother gave a surprise birthday party for him. They walked in and everyone yelled, "Surprise!" and sang, "Happy birthday, dear Joey, happy birthday to you." He whirled around. By chance I was hidden by my mother's peplum. He leaped upon his mother, knees digging into her sides, shrieking, "Jess! You didn't invite her, you didn't invite her!" flailing her chest with his fists. Mrs. Marcus wore a fur jacket with a scarf of little animal heads flopping at the neck. They popped and flew around her as Joey beat her with his fists.

My last memory, a few weeks ago on Fifty-seventh Street. I sat at the Vim and Vigor Health Food bar, eating spinach noodles in slimy cheese, when the girl sitting next to me left and a man with a little Omar Sharif moustache jumped onto the vacated stool and told me I was his destiny. He heaved a large tooled-leather portfolio onto the counter and flipped over page after page of glossy prints of himself in varying poses, with and without the moustache. He said he had followed me in from the street after seeing in my face the reason he had been led from his little town in the boot of Italy to come to America, to this very city, to this very street, at this very hour. No one else would find me beautiful, he said. "That beautiful girl with the blond hair sitting in the corner, do you see, she is beautiful but she does not interest me." I was married? Only with my husband? Well then, he would follow us, he said; everywhere we went, he would go. He would become a friend to my husband and would never be more than a few steps away from us both, as long as we all lived. He would explain it until my husband understood that it must be this way. On the pretext of getting a carob bar from the opposite counter, I threw down five dollars and ran. Amazing.

Amazing refers to my hasty exit. This is not a new occurrence. Versions of the above have happened to me, as I expect they do to some regular portion of the female population, with waiters, lawyers, elevator operators, fathers of small children, assorted men on the street.

What does interest me about the Vim and Vigor is why *this time*, this day, this month, instead of pleasantly excusing myself, did I flee in terror? Why did I run as if my life was at stake, gasping in my throat, turning my ankle, a little twinge I feel still today.

TUESDAY, APRIL 20

Which brings me back to right now.

The air is queer. Nothing is going right. We can't get things back to normal—whatever that was.

After Monday night, I thought it was all right, but he is laughing with Stephanie, and I see, after all, it *was* about her. I've tarted up simple jealousy. I've talked about Joey Marcus and narrative devotionalism and homogeneity in the culture, but he's laughing with her and maybe it's because she's younger.

LATE AFTERNOON

What do you see? What do you see?

I see a man and a woman wearing kimonos. It is as if they are both going to undergo some regrettable surgery. There is a black photographer with flashbulbs waiting to record it.

I see a minimum of people. The young woman in the robe is gravely going over the list of her demands with the director. "I don't want you to show my crack," she says quietly. "I don't want cassettes made up. I want to speak to my lawyer and my agent." Her voice is rising. The director looks more and more tired.

They sit going over a list of names. "Does Rich have to be here?" No. Margaret? No. Laurie? It is a large bare room with a bed and camera equipment. The sound man, a jolly sort with four children and a gray beard, lies sprawled on his back, the microphone around his head. He will, it seems, do his work facing backward.

There is a burst of laughter from around the camera. Perhaps the sound man has murmured something into his microphone that the camera crew hears on their headphones. His lips are not moving now. Everyone is nervous.

"Look, I don't mind the world seeing," the woman says, "it's my doorman and my father."

Tinny Japanese music starts as background music.

"There's a window," the woman says, and meets my eyes.

"I'll keep my eyes on the window, Sylvie," I say. "I'll see nobody's there."

The young man and Sylvie shrug off their robes and whisper to each other. The lights shine. I see their flesh warm and glowing with pink amber light, but only around the elbows of the camera people. I want to see more. The cameraman and director confer.

Sylvie flips off the sheets. She has been pulling them up about her for all the whispered conferences. She looks full front at Harry.

"Now you see it, now you don't," she says, and flashes.

Then they're back in bed.

"Don't kiss, it hides the faces, we want the eyes at the moment of penetration," says Barney mildly.

She sits up again. "Oh come on," she says . . . and calls the director over. He sits on the bed, his body blocking her bare breasts. They begin another whispered list.

During the break, I wander outside the soundstage. Jean-Claude, the young man from the bed, French Canadian with a strong accent, asks me where he can get a soda. He is wearing a terry-cloth robe and clogs.

All the banished crew are sitting watching a Mets game on a closed circuit TV without the sound. They glance up at me, the messenger from the inside world. Rich's cheeks are pink with the pain of exclusion. It is unheard of not to have the A.D. inside.

"Believe me," I say, "it's the most boring thing in the world."

They concentrate on the silent screen. As far as I can tell, it's a boring moment in the middle of an uneventful game. When we're called back inside, I get up tactfully, so as not to emphasize my insider status.

As I walk in the door, Barney greets me. It seems the list has gotten longer. The makeup girl and the script girl and—oh shit— me too. Outside, angry.

Outside, the crew still sits before the silent monitor. When I come and sit with them, they are perfunctory.

"You too?" they say.

"Believe me, I'm relieved," I say. "It's the most unerotic thing you can imagine."

We can hear the tinkling music as the sound inside the soundstage plays out to us. Suddenly there are low but unmistakably female grunts and moans. They shock me. They are the moans of orgasm. Too unbecoming and hurled out, little short grunts, to be simulated or acted.

The crew stares at the screen. Either they are gentlemanly to an extraordinary degree or obsessed with the player at bat.

During the next break, I come up to Harry as the focus puller says, "I guess he rubbed it against her clit and she came." I want to kill them both.

I do something terrible. I find a window. The very one I was supposed to protect from the inside. There is no one left inside to monitor it. The leading man steps out of bed.

He has an erection. So do most of the crew, I'm sure. How can they not?

I see myself, cheeks flushed with exclusion, sitting with men around a TV campfire, men in parkas, whose delicacy shames me.

The sound does not recur.

We all take our meal break. Sylvie comes to take her food in a pink chenille robe. She has worn the same robe before to protect whatever was her day's costume, but now it seems to be covering her nakedness. No one will look at her at mealtime. She brings her plate uncertainly to a table. People keep eating, go back to get seconds or pie, and return to a different table.

I avoid her eyes, too. I think it is because she banished me. But I also feel her shame.

The next day at mealtime she apologizes to the crew and everyone in sight for having been such a brat.

Harry brings his tray and comes to sit with her. They talk comfortably, smiling. I hope they spill their trays. I hope she has chosen the salmon. I hope they choke on the little bones—either of them.

There is a burst of laughter inside. Inside where?

I turn shooting the sex scene into a story at home. The ultimate in being an outsider at a party. Sam is embarrassed.

For the first time since I have been on the set, I sleep at night hugging myself in spite and relief, assuring myself that I am not her: I am Jessie Gerard. I am not Sylvie.

Stephanie's body is younger. There is no doubt about it. She is wearing a kelly-green minidress with a hip belt, the kind of dress you mean to try over pants someday. In that out-of-style early sixties number, her breasts heavier than I thought and her legs smooth and boneless, she looks like a fresher-than-memory version of the girls I competed with when I was eighteen.

He can't see me tonight. He has an appointment.

WEDNESDAY, APRIL 21

The next morning, while I'm talking to Marie, the men's wardrobe man breaks his foot. A light pole falls on it while they're setting up a shot. I've tried unsuccessfully to avoid him since he saw me step in shit. By afternoon he is back on the set, dragging his cast behind him. He crouches under trouser hems, pins in his teeth, his already soiled cast splayed out to the side. I can almost see it throbbing.

Barney shows concern.

"Nah, it's nothing," the wardrobe man says. His face, around the clenched pins, is dripping. He needs the job. I don't want Harry to see me as steeped in impairment. I stay away from the wardrobe man and his cast.

They're doing a close shot, before they leave the playground, of all the children screaming. It's supposed to be a normal moment turned wild and scary, but there's neither passion nor power in the children's cries. They just shout. Barney gets the joy out, but then it's just blank shouting.

Marie shrugs when I complain, and I can see her bra straps through her blouse. Her waist is supple as she bends for a dropped toy. A supple waist in old lady underwear.

Barney says it would take all day to get the particular wild sound I mention was in the book.

"Can you put it in later?" I ask. "In the sound mix?"

"If anyone wants to bother," he says.

Of all the things he says, this is the one that makes me count him out. No wonder Harry more and more literally calls the shots.

Early afternoons, they pile in limos and cruise around looking for what the script describes as lonely streets. I hang around like an irritating puppy, claiming I know lots of lonely streets. I keep asking Harry to walk with me downtown, in Chinatown, by the South Street Seaport, Wall Street at dawn.

We're falling behind, going into overtime, golden time, they call it, platinum. (Golden time is double; platinum time is triple time, etc.) My daydreams are of moving through city geography—dawn, Chinatown at dusk. Anyplace with Harry, I realize, seems lonely, because I am imagining a future when I will walk there after he's left me.

Once, rushing home on the subway, I feel our lovemaking still sliding along inside me, hate to carry it into my shared home with

Sam. I think this means I'm beginning to realize where home is.

I fear that Harry has confided about us to Stephanie, who will tell Sam or somebody else or, worse still, secretly patronize or pity him. My feelings of self-loathing and protection of Sam relax me even with their violence, for they must mean I am ready to go home.

And then, sitting on the subway car, I think I am walking into Harry and his blooming new wife. She has short blond hair, cut to the nape of her neck with a razor cut sharp to the fingers, and her hazel eyes sparkle with humor and optimism. She tells me how much Harry admires me and I know she will tell him how much she admires me, too. How they share the same taste in interesting women of substance. Perhaps on their next trip to Greece she will suggest bringing home a thickly woven cloak for my old bones for the winter. But then it is my stop, and I can't shake my misery and I can hardly speak when I get in the door.

In Harry's room the next day I speak of how sorry I am about the wardrobe man.

"You told me you couldn't stand him," he says. "You hated him from the first day."

Oh, he does think me cruel! I rush in to urge my case. I, too, dragged a foot once, only a broken toe, but I remember the depression, the fear. I put in a few earnestly thought out feelings about fragile bones, decaying bodies. I am full of feelings. On the other hand I make jokes about it. I'll get him on both sides—full of feelings, light and gallant. He is remote. It is getting worse.

I praise Sylvie, who asked for ten takes before she was satisfied today. "Professional, sincere," I say.

"A killer," he says. He means the way she quizzed him on the lighting.

We make love, but it is as if through a gauzy curtain. "Bodies" may remind him of Stephanie, darting by today in a hot-pink muu-muu, covered to the ankles, tentlike, which after yesterday's tiny green makes everyone remember minutely what's underneath.

He has an appointment, we don't have much time. It is still through gauze. I thrust myself around, but that makes it worse. His penis stays erect, but the circumference seems to shrink away from me slightly. The tip remains deep where it was. He is almost irrit-able—once he pushes my hand away, rubs the spot where it was. So my touch is not instinctively magic to his flesh. Does he keep the lights so low so as not to see me? I imagine he will swell out, swollen with young lust for Stephanie. And then when he comes I am so sure it is for her that it is sour with my jealousy. Then I want to snatch my thoughts back—rerun the reel. It was me there, after all, and I missed it. But he is damp and small and has an appointment.

THURSDAY, APRIL 22

I am frightened. The film is finishing up in the playground today. Insert shots—empty swings, discarded push toys upturned on the ground. The playground before anyone arrives, after everyone's gone. On Saturday we are planning to visit my brother. I will not be able to see Harry, and I am afraid he will spend the day with Stephanie. I am beginning to imagine how I will suffer, smiling with Alex and Edythe and my nieces. What is it now? Spring? I picture myself seizing a crooked rake and dragging it savagely through the budding geraniums. I have never known such detailed sexual jealousy before.

As dusk comes, I see Harry look at his watch. Behind him, the housewife spectators are tiredly buttoning up their children, shoving plastic pails and shovels in their canvas tote bags. The brighter-than-day lights are still burning on the playground set, but on the fringes, the voltage is slipping away. There is no longer any excuse for them to stay.

I move to Harry and start to entertain him. Out of my "Ideas" folder, I act out people waiting for a free gift on a bank line, women at a Macy's white sale, manager at the Korvette's New Tire Center in Queens. I am a good mimic only when it is instinctive, unconscious, so what am I showing off? Am I saying I am a playwright? That I can use other people, while they can only use themselves?

My dialogue is precise. Quoting the Columbia student trying to court the big black man with the shoulder-strap battery phonograph, I suddenly recall that such precision without an ordering vision leaves out the sweetness. Too late I remember my early gift was to leave out the sweetness—and how I fought against it. I stop for air, my face hot.

"Do you remember every word people say to you?" Harry says politely.

I plunge quickly into an account of my first speech to a playwrighting course at a fancy girl's school. "No dialogue admitted about men being ridiculous in the act of love." Oh. The grossness of why I have spun into this is suddenly apparent.

Nothing plays.

We see the dailies of my scene. My smile is grotesque and forced, my features heavy and stiff. Sylvie walks through in her jeans smiling at me—the radiance of beauty shimmers, she is a glory. One wonders why she even greets this lumpen woman by the swing. There is a burst of laughter after the scene. I am sure someone made a bad remark. No one meets my eye when it is over, and I am exhausted with shame. Harry is talking into the phone to the lab in numbers: "No one told you forty-five," he says. "Between twenty-eight and thirty-five. They printed it up wrong." His voice rises in tension.

Sam at home says it can't be as bad as I think. I ignore him.

Thinking of my nice family, I am sad for the way I shall be sifting through their words tomorrow for anecdotes as bizarre as those of Stephanie's hillbilly kinfolk. I am sad because I shall be rearranging their cherished normality into zany patterns.

(Note: remember Harry once said of the parents of the girl he almost married, "I never saw people so mean to each other." So the keynote is crazy, but loving.)

I am in his room, trying to memorize the warm rumpled bed, the curve of pink lip smiling under his beard. We are smiling together, he has stopped and is talking seriously, but I keep smiling. I have not had a chance yet to tell him I will not be available tomorrow.

If he is about to tell me it is over, I will keep smiling as if nothing has happened.

"Okay, you feel this way now," I'll say, leaving the door open to sneak back in later. How useless it was for me to hoard the way he hugs his knee, holds his arm, winces when no one is looking, like a tic. I saved them up to break my bond—things I didn't like about him—now he's doing them and I don't care.

After a while, I reason, he will forget my image in the dailies and remember there was something in the flesh that attracted him once. Anything is possible, I tell myself.

He is telling me Stephanie is going to die.

What?

He tells me she has cancer of the bone marrow, has, at most, six months to live.

I am stunned. Gooseflesh springs up all over me. First reaction is: quiet, absorb this, Saturday doesn't matter. Second is quiet spreading sorrow. All the energies in the room flow into something larger than us.

To my surprise, he wants to make love again. He is thrusting and interested, much more this time, but I am cold and proud of it. I am still covered with gooseflesh. See, I am thinking of Stephanie. The gooseflesh turns to a rolling chill and I shudder from head to toe. Cold beads of sweat race down my legs, my thighs. My hair is damp in my ears, from tears I don't remember shedding. Orgasm? Death rattle?

SECTION ELEVEN

The first thing I do is tell Sam, who is more upset than I expected. I tell him as I am ladling carrot soup, and he cannot eat. It might be his identification with Petra, but no, he is genuinely unhappy about her/Stephanie. And, to give me some credit, so am I.

I clear away the bowls, thinking of all the carrots scraped, the washing out the coffee grinder to grind my own coriander and cumin seeds.

"She's a lovely woman," he says. I saw her as a strange girl. As young.

SATURDAY, APRIL 24

We go to my brother's house. There we laugh till we choke. I am a slow laugher but my brother Alex's bits send me into whimpers; ten minutes later I am still giggling to myself. Edythe smiles. His daughters are indulgent. Their sense of humor is slowly improving as they grow; they usually like his dumbest stories.

Edythe is clear-skinned, blue-gray eyes, fire in her cooking, plays the piano and the harp, is good at playing duets and taking out splinters. Her brows always suggest to me that she wears her hair in a braided coronet.

I think it likely that I infuriate her with my admiration because I expect so little of her. I think everyone should have a wife like her.

I tend to picture her where they met, she, the dance counselor at the camp where Alex covered the waterfront. "She's my squaw," said Alex, introducing her to me, giving me my first whiff of brother-as-man, so I always picture her at campfire, buckskin fringes hanging from her budding, deep-grooved young boobs, doing the Cherokee mating dance past lascivious Bud the tennis pro into clean Alex's arms.

She was a music major at Smith. At the wedding, her roommate told me of Edythe's racing out of the music cubicle in happy tears when Alex turned up unexpectedly.

She's half-Jewish. Did we find her less smart, my mother and I? A girl who didn't look half-Jewish, she's half-Dutch—almost exotic. Unlike Bernice, who won ballroom dance trophies in the Catskills, Edythe wore out her leotards at Smith and Camp Janice. Actually, I find both their preoccupations with dance a little stunted, weird and airless. Edythe, at least, looks a bit more like a dancer. Her stomach stays flat and her hips curve back. It is as if she spreads sideways, never forward or back. Bun is narrower, but has a little pot sometimes. They both ice skate well, have medals, but never flaunt it. I occasionally play them off against each other—dancing, mating, skating. The competition is in my head. Edythe and Bun meet briefly, only at funerals. They are not invited to the same celebrations.

I like to think of Edythe as a sturdy peasant, although she has a long aristocratic nose and her mother is a widow in Shaker Heights, active in the temple.

Edythe is terrific in the kitchen, where I have seen her slicing pockets inside pounded-thin veal scallops, boning ducks—today it's lamb. As she grows older, her nose flares out more sharply and she is less sturdy, more elegant.

My nieces want to know if I've met Sylvie. Edythe asks if it's tiring me. Alex asks how long it will take me to finish doing this journalist number and write another play. In the roast lamb filled kitchen I remember Stephanie quoting her father saying, "Once more, daughter, you have been a grave disappointment to me." I have always had approval bouncing around me, as now. Is approval protection? Against how much?

At the table Alex is hilarious. His routines are of that moment. I have seen him refuse any number of audiences; he will not be the lawyer at the party with a talent to amuse. He is now, however, being very very funny about Robbie, our middle brother, who lives in Ann Arbor and has married a girl who is such a ringer for my mother that it is embarrassing. Middle child syndrome? Alex is being maniacally funny about Abigail's hair style and the way Robbie has her dress. Then he swings into so savage an imitation of my father's widow that I can only think it reveals the depth of his grief about my mother's death. Because they were really friends, my mother and Alex.

But tonight there is some static in the air. Something is always happening in families—and Alex spills it. It seems one of my nieces said she wanted to be a tree surgeon when she grew up. Fine, why not? And not have children. Oh. It seems Edythe was very upset. Edythe's face gets red. Alex should not have repeated it. Can this be serious? No, it's over. It's last week's upset.

Then what does she think of me? That I should have tried again sooner? Be trying now to have a child? But I cannot bring a new life to this world in fluids drenched in death. Not till I am free and new with hope. Soon.

I follow her to the kitchen and she seems fond of me. Buxom over the leg of lamb she is boning, scooping, slitting. I really love her cooking.

Back at the table, my nieces sit in their granny glasses, blooming behind their ringlets. They open their bright eyes and gleam at me, then at Alex, then at Sam. I never see their eyes in the process of moving. Cleaning up, I tell Edythe about Stephanie. She is sad and knowing. At my father's funeral, Alex had a spasm and was carried out. I was amazed at the knowledge on Edythe's face as she walked alongside the stretcher. Or maybe she looked like a Shaker Heights widow.

Alex comes in, smooths my hair. He wants to know how it's really going. I don't know *him* well, I guess. It's all about me. I don't know how to sort out his law friends, golf friends, school friends. Adores football, won't watch hockey. Why? Is he funny in bed? Oh I'm sure he's lots of fun, but is he funny?

Edythe is murmuring to him about a young girl on the set of whom I've grown fond. He tugs my hair that he's just smoothed. He makes it stand up all over my head. The message is clear. Don't let it get to you, babe, you've paid your dues, we all have, our tiny remnant of a family.

We stand in the slanting kitchen with the cluttered dishes and pots, the warm heat of Alex, the perfume of Edythe, leftover lamb and gingered pears. They have to gently push me out.

Alex and Sam like each other. Back in the living room, they both stand up. They are both tall. When they stand together, as I brush my hair down, I feel protected and excited by these two tall men

I've brought together. Note: what does eroticism have to do with bringing a mate into family?

No, Pinter did that.

SUNDAY MORNING, FIRST LIGHT, APRIL 25

When I first saw Sam I said, "Oh, I'll be all right."

I still haven't sorted out whether everyone feels that way when they first see him. In those early days, there were moments when I felt a thrill of sympathetic horror for his estranged wife. I didn't know how someone could stand to have him and then lose him.

Looking at him asleep on the pillow, his cheek pink from the friction—black hair, pale skin, man's shoulder, man—I wonder again. Oh.

This morning is calm, very quiet and calm. I make myself an enormous cup of café au lait in a black cup with a gold rim, warm a roll with butter.

The story of Sam, for you.

The first "Oh" was on the sidewalk in summer dusk, in front of the Evelyn Wood Speed Reading Center on Forty-fifth Street.

I felt he was the reward for goodness. Not that I deserved him, but I begged God to let me have him in advance, if I swore to be good from then on.

He is good. His only sins are those of omission. He didn't care for his then wife, Bun, but he only gave up on her when he found he'd married an unfair woman, an unreasonable one. He has always confused the two.

My game was to be smart, reasonable, decent, the best. Better than me, in fact.

Because, in truth, I know she was neither unreasonable nor unfair.

I know how in despair one thought does not follow another. It billows out like an aching sail, a poignant spinnaker, when the first thought is, He doesn't want me. And that initial thought, whether he admits it or not, was true. Bun knew it.

I was taking the Friday evening six-week Evelyn Wood course. Six summer Friday evenings—a loser's schedule.

Sam was taking the course because—oh, it's so hard to separate what I know now from what I knew then of what was going on.

It was on the street that we met, both turning in to the same doorway. We chatted in the elevator and sat next to each other in class. So life can be like this, I thought. The following week, we had dinner after class in the awful creperie next door, with canned ratatouille, because it was too big a move to go out to dinner. I remember only my immediate feelings. A lifetime with someone else seemed so wearying. *Else* being the key word. Hours to get through when it rained or the weather was nice or it was just a collection of hours, making a day or a year.

The week after that (third), we walked down to the Algonquin and had sandwiches. It was almost empty.

He asked me to lunch at Tavern on the Green the next day, Saturday. It was leafy and still. All the food had heavy sauce, and most of the women wore little straw hats. It was beautiful. He said, "I have friends on a lake, do you have the afternoon free?"

"Oh yes," said I. We rented a car from Avis. I remember wondering what would have taken place by the time we stood again, turning in the car in the narrow Formica office.

We visited his friends. I remember little of them because, inter-
estingly, in all these years we've only seen them again once. It was
on Candlewood Lake. There was a young girl, learning to play the
guitar. She was starting Cornell in the fall.

I swam with rounded strokes. I am you and you are you and we
are one and we do well together. All rounded sounds.

I saw him cut the water away from me and his strokes were
ferocious.

Coming out of the water, through the plants that flapped up against
us, he brushed a leaf from my midriff, gave me a sexual look, and
squeezed my stomach.

Bless bikinis.

The host urged us to stay overnight. I was eager. We did, but in
separate rooms. I wished we'd driven back in the darkness of the car
to my silent apartment. I hadn't thought fast enough.

Early the next morning, he drove me back to the city and left me
downstairs. He returned the car himself. His daughter and son were
coming. I didn't know.

"See you in class," he said.

That wasn't till Friday.

He called that night.

"What are you doing?"

"Washing my hair." Thinking of you?

"May I come?"

The downstairs door was not open. He called from a drugstore
phone booth. Our new superintendent's security measure. I met him
downstairs, immediately turned back up the stairs. Halfway up, I
turned, he held me. We kissed, made our way to my apartment. I
was dizzy.

He cooled it.

"Washing your hair?"

STOP TALKING

"Lovely apartment."

"Your hair . . ."

"It's wet," I said.

He said, gently, "Would you like to make love?" and I said steadily, "Yes."

I did not bury cheeks in shoulder, swarm, duck, ring out, fling back wet hair.

We went into the bedroom and separately got into bed. Yes.

He said, laughing, "I feel like a young boy."

I had never realized how intimate an act love could be—a secret whispered between two children.

We might have been two angel children in a pageant pledging eternal love. No, we said nothing.

I felt a newborn's helpless trust in the arms that held me, trust that they meant me love, would not send me crashing to the ground. When all I had to go on was the blurry scent of a warm particular flesh, the circling strength of a particular arm, the hint of a caring love. The sigh that he trusted me to hear made me ache to comfort him.

I woke weighted with hope. It was his arm flung over my breasts.

The following Friday he came home with me after class. He stayed till Sunday. We went out, shopped for food, read the paper, did speed-reading homework, and ate radishes in sour cream three separate times.

I'd talked up not quitting the class, to give the method a fair chance (and give me a six-week shot with him). Now I talked up the lifetime membership in refresher classes. (That would mean I could endlessly bump into him.)

"No," he said, "that doesn't make sense. If it doesn't stick, you give it up as a bad job."

I worried it over after he left.

I found out later the divorce papers were just being served.

The following Friday he came to class with a small square suitcase. He was flying to the Cape, going sailing, should be nice.

"Yes, it should be," I said.

I went to have my hair trimmed. Flipping through the summer Vogue, I came upon a layout of lean young models twisting like tensile vines around the masts of a sailboat. They seemed to be twisting in my chest. All night long they writhed in my skin. By morning they moved inside my brain, and suddenly they went out, leaving me dull, tearless, and depleted. I stared at nothing all day long.

Sunday night, unexpectedly, he came back. He called from the airport and appeared, hot-skinned from the sun, ruddy, wearing a striped polo shirt and canvas jacket.

Life spun around.

I couldn't believe my luck. I almost ate him up, tried to control my mouth and hands. We were wild. He too seemed reckless. He said he had two weeks of vacation time. I asked if he was going away. "I won't go anywhere unless I take you with me." They were the first personal words he'd ever said to me.

I moved ahead calmly. My time was my own, I said. I, too, had planned to get away. I went for the Sunday travel section, out of the kitchen garbage. I stood in the kitchen in my nightgown, my hands steadying themselves against my cheeks.

(I know now it was the wife of a friend of his who'd invited Sam to the Cape and made a clear move toward him. He was shocked. He'd always liked her a lot.) Timing. If we hadn't been together before the trip to the Cape, if he'd been without a woman all that time, if in the salt air, after scotch, wine, she'd heard that sigh . . . he would have felt bound to consider her, having slept with her. Men are so careless, or so innocent. Sam is just so innocent. I know him. I got there just in time.

We talked about vacations. I know now he'd thought he might spend it on the Cape, at the woman's house. She'd offered to invite his kids, clear it with Bun, arrange everything. Now he saw the terms.

The excursion packages were junky and expensive in the small print. We looked at Mexico, Barbados, California, London. He had things to do in England. I should go to London, I said. It was a lie, but I wanted it to seem less like a commitment to take me along. Though I was anxious for frozen rum drinks, velvet sand, flowered ruffles curving under tanned shoulders—I do well that way—all the resort packages were discouraging and he was growing tired, saying "I" instead of "we." I felt if we went to sleep without making plans it would be over, so I pushed England and we made it firm. Co-incidentally, we were going to the same place on business. It was rather comical. I called my English agent, who didn't quite know what to do with me. He and his wife invited me out to dinner, which was exactly the wrong thing, because I couldn't invite Sam lest he discover I had no reason to be in England at all. Then we rented a car and drove through industrial towns in the north for a series of Sam's appointments. It was an itinerary so drear that we seemed at every turn like ruddy and loving birds of passage from a vigorous and ambitious country.

When we got home, I thought of the flower-scented airports, candy-striped jeeps, chiffon caftans and bongos—all the accoutrements of temporary Technicolor coupling—and counted my blessings. Those were weeks when I wanted all the special lighting I could get, and the drizzle of the Midlands, the soiled London Fog raincoat every day, no central heating, and even the lumpy puddings set us off just fine. If we were happy—and there was no mistaking it, we were—it came from our being together. If it was laughter, warmth, dazzle in the air, and a jungle beat we were after, we were the whole show.

On our way to the airport, we dashed into Harrods and bought each other presents. Sam bought me a red flannel nightgown. Have I made myself clear?

In the fall, he said he'd stop seeing me for a while. He said he had other commitments. He said he should tell me he might be going out of my life for good. I didn't know if I'd been too loving or too independent.

"It will be a great waste for both of us, if that's true," I said.

Bravado/compromise.

"That may be so," he said.

Bun was hinting she wanted him back. He owed it to Petra and Daniel.

I worked on my play.

I behaved as if any moment on the street he might see me.

I thought, if this is not true, nothing is.

I kept moving slowly, circling, no abrupt movement, my face slowly curving, inclusive.

On Thanksgiving morning he called me, and we spent the day together.

I had no rights. We were family, though. I cooked us scrambled eggs.

We drove to see the leaves in Connecticut. They were, of course, on the ground. He had bought a car without me.

During the weeks that followed, I tried to control my outrage. In the best graduate-of-Evelyn-Wood manner, I concentrated on a technique to close my lips and prevent the flow of spontaneous words. I took to mashing the knuckle of my index finger against my mouth, much like an absentminded child gnawing candy. My knuckle came back with a wriggle of blood but I kept in parentheses my sharp and raving peevish self.

Why outrage? Because by then I didn't want to have known he existed if he wasn't going to be for me.

We began to look for an apartment for him. The *Times* again. We circled the classified ads and checked them out on cold Saturdays. One Saturday, in the Copper Lantern Coffee Shop, with the paper between us, he said, "We want to live together, don't we?" and I said, "Yes," and he said, "I would like us to be married," and I said, "I would like that too." Conditional?

"Shall we?"

"Yes."

ME (out of turn): "When?"

HE: "Tomorrow."

Oh, I could never swing it in another language. Shall, would, might.

We burst out laughing. It was relief. It hadn't come apart.

We ran and got married and met each other's families and talked about our past. Our families were more relaxed and folksy with each other than we had been. My brother and his mother confided in each other about how worried they'd been and how much we needed each other and agreed they'd never really thought anyone else worthy of us before.

We began to laugh together after we were married.

Then there was sorrow that we shared.

Always happiness.

How have I betrayed this?

Can I tie it to the death of my mother? My baby? My cousin Jeremy? No, I did that with my southern doctor.

During our courtship, I moved slowly, holding my best self in my arms, slowly turning this way and that so you could see me rounded all over with a base embedded in goodness, goodness, good earth, public works, utilities, water works.

It was not surface I was showing you. You made me the person I wanted to be.

Am I composing the letter to ask forgiveness, win him back?

How could I have done this, you ask.

I don't know. I simply don't know.

REMORSE. CODA

I solidify us all day. Plans for next Thursday, two summers from now, ten years from today, this afternoon.

Bun is in the city, taking her babies to the ballet. I invite them to stop in on their way home. Tiny Lolly is wearing her first panties. They are flowered. As we talk around the sofa, there is a sudden rush of hailing drops on the hardwood and Lolly's brown eyes grow round and stricken. Bun lifts Lolly, and slides her teal-blue gabardine knee under the little girl's crotch to stop the humiliating sound. "We almost had an embarrassment," she says lightly, and keeps talking of other things till Lolly looks less stricken. I'm impressed. There was no hesitation.

I tell her in the kitchen as we wipe the knee—ruined?—that a girl on the set is going to die. At least Petra is reversible, I say. No one has ever told us that all of this with Petra cannot reverse, like a bad dream.

She is grateful, she kisses me at the door, and tells Sam what a lovely person I am. A coherent scenario, having to do with grief and death, may excuse me. I knew first, I didn't know, it upset me when I learned, though I'd sensed. I push the chronology this way and that, should the truth about Harry and me ever come out. Coherence? Reprieve?

Weekend is over.

"I guess tomorrow will be rough," says Sam, putting his arms around me. He knows his loyalties. Comfort Jessie, who will have to face Stephanie.

SECTION TWELVE

Today, I'm having lunch with Stephanie. It is more than two weeks after I heard the news.

Last week, I was with Harry once. Why? At first I kept my distance. But then I did not want to play the I'd-love-to-but-it-wouldn't-be-fair-to-roommate-Brenda dodge. I didn't want my scruples to leave him annoyed at Stephanie. Which is to say, no, it can't be on the heels of the news about Stephanie that I suddenly refuse him. Also, I wanted it so little I thought it would be my punishment.

But once having changed my position on this, it was hard to arrange to be with him. He had never been persistent, but this time I had to do some dogged pursuing to show him I wasn't refusing him. I had it in my head that it should be at the latest next Monday or Tuesday, before I started the cycle of my new life. And just when I began to see the comedy in the whole thing, our schedules meshed and we spent a late afternoon together.

Though I'd meant it to be penance, it was surprisingly nice. We talked about my work, about the dramatic ordering of events and dialogue. I have gotten away too long with random actions covered with funny remarks in most of my plays. Cleverness papered over holes in logic or want of revelation. Now I want to use events that, once having happened, change everything. In other words, I want events that make bodies move in a way they have not moved before.

He'd spent the afternoon shooting a dramatic scene with Sylvie in the dark. She had a pimple on her chin. "Once you know a face," said Harry, "you can shoot it in the dark."

He seemed to understand why nothing I'm working on now satisfies me. He spent Sunday at the Frick, staring at "Officer and Laughing Girl," because you can learn more about lighting from those paintings than anywhere else in the world.

I talked about the play I cannot finish—where the subtext of every line is "don't count me out"—and how I can't keep up the urgency, the sense that it matters. It dies on me.

Everything that acts is a cruelty, says Harry, quoting Artaud.

I mentioned Sam's new system at the Coliseum show, analogous to prelighting by computer?—no subjects are verboten now. And I offered again to show him lonely streets. He doesn't know New York and the location scout grew up on army bases. I even offered the laundry room of our apartment building, and he said thank you, very politely.

We had a nice time.

The only mention of Stephanie was when I talked about the time I found myself wanting to dive across a bus aisle, to nestle inside a black patent leather purse with a tortoiseshell clasp resting on the lap of a strange woman. It was only later, when the yearning had subsided, that I remembered a similar bag my mother had owned.

I don't remember how that came up with Harry. I can't remember what we said before it or after it. But there seems no doubt that it is over, already distanced in the most graceful way, all things considered.

And, in other words, it was nice. I think there is no emotion in common between what I felt for Harry and what I feel for Sam, and that is interesting about human sex. But Harry is smart, we are friendly, and with a slight rearrangement of chronology, I can, in the future, remember once, briefly, sexually comforting a gifted young director of photography on his way to being a director, at a time when he learned his lovely young girl was doomed.

When it was over and I was out the door, in the cab, I felt sad for all the things it will not be. We will never get around to checking out what we thought when we first saw each other. I still don't know. Nor will we ever explain what we first thought sliding in each other's skin. Nor why we still slither along inside each other's skin—never deep inside—still in the space between skin and bone. Because we were just passing through?

I feel a certain gratitude toward him, my blood, so drenched in sorrow, now bubbles through my veins with optimism, pounding with pleasure—and for the first time, instead of dwelling on the little daughter I lost, I think that someday maybe I will have a son, hair curling on his neck, who bends over machines and computer toys with Sam, both laughing at how Mommy can't understand how anything works.

I swayed inside the rattling cab, my optimistic blood pounding, planning duck pâté for Sam for next week, don't count me out— because I'm just starting.

The sound of city horns will propel us through, crash of happy cymbals, with a small discordant sour note—sympathy for Stephanie. Really tragic, that tall young girl. But nothing me dismays. Like Eddie Felson in *The Hustler*, I'm back!

This morning Sylvie is playing a fantasy sex scene with a young brat-pack superstar, who agreed to do these tiny scenes because they bookend the movie and, as he says to an interviewer on the set, because he had these "awesome fantasies" about Sylvie when he was a child in Texas.

The scene is a seduction in a health food store that ends up with coupling on spilling sacks of alfalfa sprouts. In the book it was very funny, involving the carrot juicing machine. Here they've moved it outside. They want as many New York exteriors as possible, they tell me. So it's in what is presumably the back lot of the health food store, a messy back lot with a view over some raised highway all the way over near the warehouses on Eleventh Avenue. It's a loony place to imagine a health food store but they've built a facade on the abandoned store, and the ever-present trailers, honey wagons (temporary toilets), etc., make it, again, as much its own environment as if it were on the Hollywood tour of the Universal Pictures movie lot.

It's so barren an area, even the presence of the brat-pack superstar with the "awesome" fantasies as the seducing clerk hasn't attracted much of a crowd.

Down by the temporary toilets, Sylvie tells me she can't stand the way he kisses.

She seems truly unhappy, asks my advice. Actually, I see him as pallid, self-delighted, nonsexual, but I take the PR view. I tell her every woman in America will think she's a stick if she doesn't respond to him, so she better watch it.

As Stephanie and I leave for lunch, Rich tells us Sylvie is now "on top" and managing better. He's clearly not the only one smirking about what he thinks this means.

Stephanie and I agree that probably this way his rather rubbery lips cannot descend on her and blot out her air supply. Then we chat about men's lips, what it would be like to kiss for money or fame.

"Or food for starving children," I bring in, just to make the conversation marginally less frivolous, a small bridge to what is coming, and because there is some discomfort in our having a conversation about good kissers.

Stephanie is wearing pale tight jeans and a worn black tank top. Her shoulders are bony and muscled. She looks rail thin—like a young pony?

I've chosen the restaurant with some care—a cozy Hungarian place a few blocks away from the crew—but at the entrance I abruptly change my mind and steer us across the street to a plastic and Formica Chinese restaurant. I must be edgier about this than I thought. I want something not smelling of candles or sex or family, but of order. So Formica Chinese isn't so bad.

As we order, separate dishes, I swiftly sketch in Sylvie as a girl who will never be happy. Finally, my grossness dawns on me. The unsaid clause in the sentence is, "Even if she lives to be a hundred."

But face to face with Stephanie, the blooming cheeks, the light in the eyes, I begin to finger the plastic packets of soy sauce that slide under my fingers. All my thoughts seem ones I cannot say out loud and I am afraid the agitation will spread to my fingers and the brown red liquid will begin to slurp all over my hands and crust and stain the white cloth like some hideous metaphor.

Stephanie is tentative.

"Did Harry . . . he said he'd talked to you." Don't lean away. Terminal patients feel alienated enough. Touch. So I lean across the table, put my hand on her arm and say straight out, "I'm so sorry."

It's true, I am. My throat is clogged and I feel very affectionate. I see why I veered away from motherly waitresses and homemade noodles. She is a lovely young woman and I don't want her to have to comfort me into brisk, acceptably kind behavior.

"Oh, don't worry about me. I don't matter."

What?

"Well, I can't presume to know you well but you do matter to me. You're a lovely young woman . . ."

"Don't worry about me. It's Harry I want to talk about."

Okay, got it. The reason for the lunch, the reason for her insistence on this lunch. To establish how much Harry loves her. So she knows about us.

"It's hard on everyone," I say.

"It's hardest on Harry." She is curt.

Okay, she's made her point. I'm not sure I buy it—sentimental and dubious in any case, about it being worse for survivors. But if I was invited to agree to how destroyed Harry is going to be and to tacitly swear never to couple with him when she is underground, that's fine. I am angry that Harry told her, yet must keep on her good side, she has a weapon over me, is she threatening disclosure? but it doesn't matter either way, whatever she wants, she's got it.

Though I'm willing, even eager, it seems hard to get it said. "Look, I can't help it," I try. "I'm more concerned about you." This seems to irritate her even more.

She keeps talking about a film script Harry has taken an option on that she wants to produce. She thinks she can get the financial backing, but it's a matter of how long the preproduction will take, and even with a negative pickup the distribution people insist on physicals, and what do I think? Me? Wait a minute. Is she giving him to me, to take care of and console?

What kind of junk is her head stuffed with? Is it her pop psychiatrist? Will he write her story, about the wild young bird being grounded? A cross between *Love Story* and *Jonathan Livingston Seagull*?

To get us off the topic of distractions for Harry, I begin my life-is-full-of-strange-turns monologue. Joe is given a death sentence, outlives Moe who has a coronary. Sue hit by a taxi killed instantly while Lou is in remission . . .

Stephanie looks disappointed, rumpled, tired, less pretty. But she's back, gamely, into options, contracts, negative pickups, post production schedules, round-the-clock work for the next six months.

Does she want this film as a monument to her?

SHE: Finally it's up to Harry.

ME: No, it's up to you.

What *is* this devotionalism?

SHE: It's his life.

ME: It's also yours.

SHE: I wouldn't have expected you to be this way.

ME: Look, this is getting nowhere.

Okay, she wants straight talk, she'll get it. It is dehumanizing to the terminal patient not to get irritated with him/her.

"You want to set up a film for him. Fine. And you're afraid the time will be too short, the backers need certain promises, in some cases there are physical exams needed. Well, the thing to do, then, is bring someone else in and coproduce."

Blankness.

"What good would *that* do?" followed by outrage. "That doesn't make any sense at all." And then suddenly Stephanie stopped, looked at me face front, cold, wary stare. "What exactly did Harry say to you?"

Oops, tread carefully, something has gone wrong.

"He told me you had a . . . serious health problem."

"Oh."

It was clear, and then I knew or had known all along.

"He's dying," I said.

"Yes."

All my juices slam in one direction, stop, then flow in the opposite one. Like certain sauces, they should not be mixed. They have their own laws. Had known all along? I don't know about any of this.

At home, Sam instantly has to know about lunch. I hadn't prepared myself for his questions. He is, first of all, joyful, relieved about Stephanie. And yes, astonished. But sweetly, continuously, smiling with pleasure. Stephanie was the show. Miracle, reprieve.

Care about Stephanie's boyfriend dying? No sir. A liar? A cruel, capricious liar to cause poor Jessie such unnecessary apprehension. No, not exactly, I am not being fair to Sam.

Poor bastard, poor kid, poor guy. He says one of the above. Just as I am afraid Sam will begin to puzzle out the intensity of the thread between me and a lie so extreme—the bond between the liar and the lied to—Sam says, "He must hate her because he has to leave her."

So it's all about Stephanie. The intensity is all about Stephanie. I'm just an innocent bystander.

Is this right?

NEW SET ON A STREET WHERE PEOPLE LIVE

I walk onto the new set and swing around. We are on the Lower East Side, on a long street where people live. It is a scene where Sylvie will come to track down old friends of her parents' from Europe, other camp survivors. She will find only their children, who have a survivor-child workshop she doesn't want to join.

A freckled production assistant stands with his clipboard and tries to keep people from walking on one side of the street, where they are running cables for a tracking shot.

"No, I will not walk on the other side of the street," says a red-haired young woman. Her hair glints and flames.

"I'm looking for my sister," says another woman, shouldering by him, big tits swaying through her Popeye T-shirt.

A fat Puerto Rican high school kid in a V-neck white Orlon sweater delivers his groceries. He elbows his way stolidly through the cordon, his cart clacking along the cable tracks. What can you do? Groceries have to be delivered.

There are afroed blacks on bicycles, old people who lean on each other taking a stroll, a blond woman with bleached bangs who yells through her barred window for Barney to come over and sign his autograph on her little fat lime-green pad. (He rushes to do so, knocking over his director's chair.)

The whole movie company seems backed against the wall. They've set up their lights and cables and California types in the middle of the street, spread out as if they've taken it over, but they seem pale, strained, backed up against the wall.

When a portion of the sidewalk is finally cleared and the professional extras come out to mill on command, the street looks denuded, skinned.

FRIDAY, MAY 14

With all the real-life people always alongside, it is Friday before I am privately face to face with Harry.

I say, "Stephanie tells me you're sick."

"Well," he says, "yeah."

That slow sweet smile again, the sweet lips curving under the beard. I never remember that.

Jeans low on his hips, thick sun-streaked hair over his eyes, he looks straight at me, and to my surprise I circle his hand, my fingers stroking the golden hairs on the back of his wrist.

"Look, you're not alone," I say. "The worst thing is feeling isolated—as if the rest of the world is exempt and lucky, as if it's only you. We're all in the same boat, only nobody knows exactly when, the difference is statistical . . . what I mean to say is that it's me as much as you."

Silence.

I want so much to help him, make him less alone, but it's not working. I keep talking, hoping the act of talking itself will reach him.

"In the week since I . . . talked to Stephanie, I've almost choked on a bone in my chicken sandwich, had my desk covered with daggers of glass, lost my heel on an escalator, almost pitched down to the bottom, and went to a movie where a sniper turned out to be hiding in the theater."

A flicker in his eyes.

"Yeah?" he says. "Well, keep trying, maybe you'll get there first."

Jolted, I turn, pull my hand away, but he catches my wrist. I jerk it away hard, harder—a lurch of panic, he can't hold on to me, does he think he can hold on to me? but he pulls so hard I feel the pain, and it happens so fast.

He's pulling me out of the path of the cherry picker—a crane with the hundred-pound camera swinging down to where my skull was headed.

He drops my hand and the aftershock is in the raw bruise on my wrist, the ferocity with which I tried to get free of him.

"Waddya *doin!*" yells the swinging camera operator, hoarse with outrage. I start to stammer thanks, excuses, but Harry's sharply gone.

I spin around to find him and almost collide with Georgeann Carrara, the stunt girl, now stand-in, standing in a lilac-print cotton dress, in the shadow of the artificial rain towers.

Since I was surprised by her in the playground, I've seen her all over the set, pink with pleasure, presumably mending even as she stands.

I have kept my distance from her before, but she's right near the camera and the only excuse I have for lingering till I can catch Harry's eye.

The company sent flowers to her in the hospital every day, signed "Sylvie," and I've overheard Georgeann describe them to everyone in sight—a series of breathy anecdotes told in the exhilarated way of shy girls who have never before told stories against themselves.

She seems puzzled about who I am, and I have to prompt her,

take out my notebook, but once started, she tells me that in the hospital she was sure she was dying, going over and over the last minutes of the stunt that should have worked, had been planned to work . . . "Should have worked," I write in my notebook.

"So I'm lying there thinking, get real, Georgie, you're buyin' the farm, and the nurse comes in and I go, 'What, more flowers?' So I go, 'Oh, they must be for the room next door.' So I go, 'Wait, hey, let me see the card,' and it says, 'I need you back, Sylvie,' so I say to the doctors, 'Get your charts out, docs, I may have messed up, but I'm not buying the farm yet . . .'"

Note: "Buying the farm" stuntman's expression for fatal stunt.

As she talks, I inch nearer to Harry. I am standing too close to the equipment, but I want to seize a moment to say, "Thank you, I'm sorry, I was trying to get away from you, I don't know why."

He is moving around the high tower rain machine. It's been sitting here for three weeks waiting and is being used today in the glaringly hazy sunshine because it's committed in the Northwest in four days. The only rain method Harry says he trusts, he's running it through its paces—on command it sprinkles slow, hard, gentle, angry showers of rain over the wedge of sidewalk going from brownstone doorway to the curb. I begin to find it mesmerizing.

Around the wedge of sidewalk, of course, is blinding sun, and it is here my central confusion resides. Rain has always been for me the one manifestation of the heavens where my mood and heaven's whim seem naturally to correspond. At all my funerals it has rained, nay, poured. The very air itself splashed darkly and wetly—properly, I might say—of misery and loss. If there was ever a time for me to munch apples in the spring rain with a young lover, it has long passed. Rain is sad for me, unequivocal. Seeing Harry make the rain harder, lighter, flatter, wilder, stop altogether, let in the sun and start again . . . confuses me.

Georgeann still talks, sprinkling her narrative with "I'm so crazy" or "I'm such a nut." The articulation of either phrase seems to cause a slight though perceptible erotic flush to creep up under her pale skin.

Seeing Harry change the filters, the flow, the direction of the sun, running through the rain into the sunlight—technique is raised to the level of revelation, joy and pleasure seem possible, and I think suddenly anything can be what it seems.

Georgeann tells me she did her first stunt on Sylvie's TV comedy show when she was just a kid. She was slapped for Sylvie, she says. She says everyone's desire is to find an actress you look like and become her regular. "But you don't look like Sylvie," I start to say, but then I guess she means from far away. She says her grandmother was slapped hard for Judith Anderson: ran into the room, grabbed the killer, and he slapped her. She says that once she went out on the wing of a plane with a rubber mask so exactly like the face of the actress that the pilot almost freaked out, thought it was the expensive actress on the wing. Instead of expendable Georgeann?

And that Hal Needham, King of the Stuntmen, has broken forty-five bones and his back twice.

They call her in and out to block the shot, and each time she comes back, she seems trying to place me again. I hold up my notebook as identification. Remember? I'm the one asking the questions? Her attention span is stunningly short.

She tells me she's an expert in falls, in ditches, lakes, pools, through trapdoors, from piano tops, over chairs and tables, down flights of stairs and laundry chutes. She's also good at being hit by cars, bouncing over the car, lying flat dead on the pavement.

They call Georgeann into the scene, she rushes from doorway to curb and gets drenched. Comes back dripping and shivering. Stares blankly at me again. Is it that she thinks I look like Sylvie? Doubtful.

"What will you do next, Georgeann?"

"Depends on her."

Will you go to California? Paris? Would you like to travel around the world?

"If she does," she says.

She runs back into the rain several times and then Rich bellows, "First team," and Sylvie emerges in the same lilac dress, little pearl buttons, but so different than on this muscled albino child, where the puffed sleeves droop and the little pearl buttons flash, that at first I think the same fabric is a trick of the light.

Sylvie runs from doorway to curb in a few seconds, is wrapped in thick terry robes and returned to her camper, where wardrobe and hair will work on her for another forty minutes to prepare her for the next run in the rain.

"Second team," shouts Rich, and Georgeann does two more drenched runs, stands next to me, and sneezes again. I'm not ready to abandon my place, so I try to deepen the level of discourse.

"Does it make you feel odd, being dead?" I ask.

What?

"I mean after the car accidents when they take twenty different angles of you dead on the street, or at the bottom of the stairs after one of your falls?"

"But I'm not dead," she says.

I have to smile. Fair enough. I'm a washout as an in-depth interviewer.

"Hey, Georgie," Sylvie yells from her trailer, "wait in here, you'll catch pneumonia."

Georgeann throws me a triumphant look. About what? The wardrobe trailer is three blocks away and she's shivering. It's the least Sylvie can do.

"I know I'm a nut to worry, but she's the kindest, most generous human being, she understands things before you say them," confides Georgeann. "I keep thinking it's like before, you know, when I would no more dream of marching up to her . . . *camper* than you would."

What?

"Really nice talking to you, ah, *Bessie*," she says, smiling graciously. The haughty who-are-you-anyway glance. It's not her teeny attention span, it's noblesse oblige, for God's sake. She's been humoring me. Sylvie's name was on the card saying, "I need you," and she's been humoring a peasant.

I don't recognize instant noblesse oblige when it's laid down before my eyes any more than I recognize instant mashed potatoes. That is, unless it's composed of the real ingredients—years of breeding, a body of first-rate work, Idaho potatoes boiled and skinned—I simply don't catch on. Not if it's whipped up from nitrate chips, sodium phosphate, and daily posies from the PR desk to be billed to cost accounting.

Sylvie runs in and out of the rain—one might use the word *bedraggled*, the way one would use it on oneself, but I've been down that garden path before. "She looks like a drowned rat," mutters one of the extras gleefully. But I know she'll be translucently damp, caught in the rain squared to glory.

Nine identical lilac-print dresses are being checked out by Ginny, the costume designer, who wears elegant loose woven black clothing—Bedouin boutique.

"They tell me my budget should be big enough," says Ginny,

"and I say, sure, except look who you're dealing with." She says she's never been on a nonperiod show where so many dresses had to be built instead of bought. Ginny says this was only partly because Sylvie got it into her head she wanted to wear the same dress in different scenes. She'd seen in a European film where a French actress wore the same skirt with another blouse in two scenes.

But why not buy nine copies instead of "building" them? If they're ordinary West Side housewife garb, why not get nine at Bloomingdale's?

"Because we had to build her body," snaps Ginny. She lights up a cigarillo. "Shoulders, waist, it's all inside the clothes. Not to mention the boobs we gave her."

So her body was made more extravagant. Hips narrower, shoulders wider. But her breasts were fine the way they were.

"Even so," I ask, "*nine* copies of the same dress?"

Her young male assistant, the one who stuck me with a safety pin and never saw any resemblance between me and Sylvie, sighs.

"Rain shots?" I say.

"She sweats," he says. "We use giant shields and then the armholes need cover. The lights are hot and lots of them sweat, but she's a real pig."

The rain comes down and down and down. And Sylvie rushes back and runs through the rain to the curb. And then she changes her clothes and gets her hair dry again, so we can see over and over, in close, in medium, in long shot, the moment dry Sylvie gets pulverized by rain. Then she's dry and swept up by hair and wardrobe, who hate her, and then she's out again. I wonder if she's sweating.

And then it's done. The rain is loaded on a truck to go to the

Northwest, fickle as woman's love, implying we had control of mood and season only for a while before it left on a truck to the Northwest.

Ginny and her crew, carrying away a sodden mass of lilac cotton, laugh and laugh.

Item: I should explain about the slivers of glass on my desk. It happened on Tuesday, in my den. I was sitting at my desk, Sam in the chair by the window, beginnings of a lilac and coral sunset tinting the white walls. We were working, drinking sherry. The phone rang in the kitchen. I got up to answer it; Sam followed me out to re-fill our glasses. As I answered the phone by the kitchen window, I saw a small black cloud whirl in front of the sunset and heard a crash. Back in the den, the chairs on which we had been sitting bristled eerily with glass daggers of every size and shape. The room was still deepening in shades of lilac and coral as we lifted them—machetes, cleavers, stilettos. There seemed thousands. I insisted irrationally that put together they would form more than a window.

The rational facts are:

1. We would have been horribly mutilated.

2. The storm windows should not be left down alone. They are not meant for high floors. The frame had slipped off its track, and after that it was a question of pressure. I had done it to frame the sunset without the paned partitions of the regular window. Sam blames himself; he knows better, he simply didn't notice.

3. The sudden wind gave no warning. If the phone had not rung, we could not have escaped. I call back the casual acquaintance to thank her. She is embarrassed, does not welcome this significant part in our destiny.

4. All week I find daggers behind books, in folders, in a partly

opened file drawer, in the leaves of a magazine lying on a bookshelf. I feel I shall find them all my life.

I dwell on just how mutilated we might be had the phone not rung.

Sam sees no reason to dwell on it.

But "almost" must count for something. Grace?

The chicken sandwich had a piece of bone in it; I choked. We were at a diner on Route 1, at a long table of people. Sam was on the other side. I was choking and I saw the people at tables around me look delicately away. I didn't want this to be my last sight—people looking out toward the parking lot, putting quarters in their jukeboxes, trying to pretend this wasn't happening, or discussing the Heimlich maneuver, which they'd never mastered. It was slow motion. My mouth made sounds I could hear less and less. Was this brain damage? I saw Sam racing around the table. People put their quarters in the jukebox. It cleared.

The escalator at Saks suddenly jammed. I pitched forward and saw preteen sleepwear coming toward me. I was hurtling down, but a big motherly woman was near the bottom—she turned and caught me in time.

We emptied the theater while the sniper was found and removed. He had a handgun. We were seeing a comedy. We all walked back inside and watched the movie. Going back into the theater, the audience talked about the movie. I couldn't believe it. I did too. But suppose the sniper had a friend, still uncaught, in the balcony? Sam didn't want some sniper to change his plans. No crazy is going to tell him how he spends his evening.

Today we're going to Marie's daughter's bas mitzvah. All of us. Doesn't she have friends from before? It's at a seedy temple on the East Side.

Several details. Sylvie, taking it all seriously, arrives on time. Barney is there, with a yarmulke on his head. He rocks back and forth, knowing all the words. Marie Francesca wears a blue silk print dress, with a pin holding it together at the top so it will show no cleavage. I watch Marie breathing. I am always aware of her, her packed flesh moving slowly up and down inside her clothing. She never wears good fabrics, but the pumping of her life mesmerizes me when I watch her. I don't know why. Now that I see her clothes as failed attempts at topical chic—and failed in the eager miss-the-point charming way that is so particularly Marie's—I find her perfect. The little girl, with her honey-colored Afro, looks sullen and defenseless. The synagogue is old; it reeks of survivors from somewhere else.

AFTER THE SYNAGOGUE

Harry and I go with a driver on a brief scout for lonely streets. I drag them down to a wharf, but there are deliveries and an embracing couple and kids are playing, and I drag them around to two more, Fifty-sixth and Eleventh, but there's a hooker; Wall Street—too far and too tendentious. And though I have the driver turn left here and right there—a cul-de-sac, a play street with no children—wherever we go, the looked-for lonely street is on the edge. It's full of less vitality than other streets, maybe, not really lonely. I thought I had so many options, but none of them work now.

We try Fifty-fourth Street—no good, and the West Side docks have a blazing sunset.

When we come back to the set, the driver leaves and we have a few minutes alone in the studio car. Harry is wearing his yarmulke, which I take off his head. He wears a cord suit, tie—the outfit he wears to the doctor? That he wore in college on dates?

He asks how my piece is going. Badly, I say, but even if I do a terrible job, I will get a kill fee. Only I stop before I say the phrase out loud.

"This is so bad," I say, "so bad."

"Yeah, it sucks," he says. "So where do I lodge my complaint? Tell me where to send the letter, Jessie, and I'll get it right out."

His eyes change, hot into my heart, and then it's gone.

I tell him I would like to help him consult another doctor. Another specialist. If he has none in mind, I will consult my network. On me, of course. Friends are family. I will have the fee from the article. It becomes true. Are we family now?

"Let your friends help. It's too lonely this way." Lonely is the key word. We embrace, almost in public. I grip his knee in the light fabric and he winces a little. I remember my mockery when he rubbed his joints, his habit of hugging his side. Still out of the sight line of other people, I touch his calf lightly, back of my hand, scarcely any pressure, nothing sexual, just friends. It is a lonely time. We are grieving together.

I have a disgusting thought. I think the wharf, the dock, the cul-de-sac with empty play street, all the streets I saw are less lonely than before because I will be able to walk down them in peace, knowing he is not in the world with someone else.

Can I be this appalling? Certainly not. The streets just seemed less lonely. Clearly, they will not do. I apologize for the waste of everybody's time. "They're sort of lonely, aren't they?" I say. Not enough, I guess, but sort of?

Later that night he calls me. Sam and I are in bed already, two wineglasses on the night table and the bottle of Grands Echezaux '73 brought from France, the only wine I feel in my knees for weeks later. We are smiling at each other before the phone rings, relaxing into the forms of the man and woman who married in happiness and blossoming hope.

"Can you talk?" Harry says after a few minutes.

"Yes," I say.

That was the perversity, not what Sam did next.

I couldn't hear too clearly what Harry was saying. I rolled on my side. I wondered later if he remembered the timbre of my voice when I'm lying on my side, because, of course, he knows it.

No, I am being evasive, reluctant to describe this. Sam, cradling me from behind, began to touch me. I responded, moved toward him. My duty. I trusted Sam to be saying, "You are so loving, to that poor boy, even on this night that is only ours." Something like that. Giving and loving and responding in two directions. Then abruptly, it was all gone. Harry hung up.

Sam turned over. Within an instant, the voice in my ear stopped and so did the finger and pressure of belly on back. Sam rolled over. I was afraid to speak.

What Harry was explaining was why the streets I chose would not be as lonely as I planned. The fact is, he was saying, film makes everything look beautiful.

In the next few days, by any standard criterion of what constitutes an event, a lot of events happen.

1. My oven blows up. The second I put my head in to check the leg of lamb, it explodes, and my hair catches on fire. Straightening up, I see the wall of flame out of the top of my eyes, and clap my hands on my head in despair—so, putting it out. It is all over instantly, but the slowly dying cry of terror, mingling with the smell of burning hair and pungent lamb, remains too rich to bear, drenching my body. The top of my hair has singed gray ends, which I finger obsessively, thinking of my eyelashes.

2. I introduce Petra as "my daughter" to Sylvie, words that have never before passed my lips.

(Petra is abruptly much better. Out of the hospital, she blooms in an instant.)

3. A dog, foaming at the mouth, races toward me in Paley Park.

4. Barney asks to use our apartment for a brief scene. It is partly because of Sam's room-size terrarium, partly because he thinks it's an intellectual's slum, and partly because they need more New York cover shots for when it rains. (Sam, surprisingly, enjoys the idea. He says we can use the money, which is irrefutable.)

5. Before my eyes, Sylvie eats four packages of Yankee Doodles

and one box of Mallomars, with no effect on creamy skin or boyish hips. She seems naturally gorgeous by divine right. That had not occurred to me previously.

6. Sam's demo jams at the Coliseum. An accident. He comes home with his man's shoulder taped.

7. I track down a specialist for Harry, one who is using laser beams. The nurse, over the phone, says, "He's the nicest man you'd ever want to meet. I had a problem with my own family, and he couldn't have been nicer, not like some of those others."

8. Sam and I decide to take a long weekend on an island where we hope to find a house to rent for the month of August.

9. A sudden thunderstorm erupts. Huddling behind a scaffold— I'm never sure what attracts lightning and what repels it—I give Harry a card with the tentative doctor's appointment for him to confirm, show him tips of my singed hair, tell him about the dog in Paley Park, and say I'm never sure what to do about lightning. He says maybe the odds are evening. "What?" say I. "Evening?" Some regional pronunciation of the end of daylight? "You mean thunder is different in the evening?"

"Statistics," he says.

10. The wrong chain steps arrive from Hammacher Schlemmer. They would only take us down to the eighth floor in case of fire. Coming out of the tub, my foot slips scarily; when I plug in my blow dryer, it spurts current from the socket; about to use an opened can of chicken broth, I suddenly sniff it, find it strange, and notice the bottom end distended; and on the number 5 bus, a woman urges on me sugar cookies from William Greenberg, Jr. "They used to be full of sugar," she says, "and now they put in something else, oh, it's not sugar, it's full of something else now, I can feel it."

But then, leaving the set early to go home and pack for our trip, I feel I'm willing things into events. Dusk seems to blow away the uncertain lists in my head; I think perhaps they are all in a long day's journey into New York of a working housewife. Is this the way you found them?

Walking down Eighth Street, I grow romantic about the young girl coming toward me. Her clear face peers over her large bag of groceries jammed with succulent vegetables, a spurting small planet extravaganza for her healthy lover. She wears a trench coat; her hair spills over the collar. We are walking toward each other when her face lights up, and she greets someone walking behind me. As they meet, almost alongside me, her face crumples into desperate tears and she begins sobbing wildly.

End of events list.

We are about to leave.

Statistics lie. But so does Harry. Odd phrase.

Years ago, when chill November, a broken romance, and a failed play entered my soul, I bought a ticket to go far away. On the eve of my departure, a cousin/therapist said, "What do you expect going away to solve?"

"Everything," I answered in surprise. And it did.

THURSDAY, MAY 20

We are going off to a secluded island for four days. It is an island largely peopled with the summer homes of doctors from five states. We are going to look for a house to rent for August, now that Petra and Daniel may be coming with us.

On Wednesday, a dog foaming at the mouth came toward me in Paley Park. He threw himself on my stomach, but as I staggered back, he raced away, didn't break the skin or tear my coat. I staggered onto the street. A man wearing a sandwich board was crooning, "God loves you God loves you." A well-dressed woman who I recognized as married to a publisher walked up to him. She put her face in front of his and screamed, "NO HE DOESN'T!"

I'm driving because of Sam's shoulder, but I'm a good driver, and we have a nice trip. I love the distance I am putting between us and New York, especially when we go across water. Except that we're first on the ferry and the boys waving us on, forward, perilously forward, are long-haired and college-boy chic. I preferred the square farm boy types of last summer, trusted them more.

FRIDAY, MAY 21

We are staying in the biggest hotel on the island, the only one open off season. We are almost the only guests and our mailbox is immediately crammed with telephone messages from rental agents.

I, who brag of throwing down my possessions anywhere with the sound of waves and a wide wooden porch, am made to seem most particular—even more so than usual this year—and I am. I do not choose to spend a summer shushing neighbors' children, but if we want to see the rolling waves on any decent budget, the houses are so close together. The agent assures me that this tree flowers in the summer, hides that window next door—but what if the tree should have blight? Then my bathroom will look into my neighbor's kitchen, or his bedroom into my hall, or his bathroom will be so close to my kitchen he can snipe me with his shaving cream while I fry my egg.

SATURDAY MORNING, MAY 22

The silliest agent, the one who fluctuates between promising us privacy and promising us prestigious neighbors (being uncertain as to wherein true elegance lies), shows us a house buried in the woods with direct access to a private beach where we can moor a sailboat. We sign the lease and rush to swim on the public beach while there is still a little sun.

Our heads bob, decapitated, in the grayish silver black-green water. On the float, Sam meets a man he used to know, a doctor. There are a few of them on the float. We all return to the water. Our heads bob around, introducing, smiling. Someone is stung on the eye—jellyfish? Doctors' brown faces float on the dark gray waves; I hear a clap of thunder . . .

On the beach I watch a mother flirting with her four-year-old son. "First you get undressed, then Mommy gets undressed. First you take off your top, then Mommy takes off hers."

I find I am shuddering.

SATURDAY NIGHT, MAY 22

We are invited to a party by Bernie from the float. Heidi, the hostess, is more casually polite than I would ever be able to swing. I would duck and weave and crease my eyes into a parody of earnest welcome, especially if the unknown guests are not really welcome at all. We really are not. This is a party that was planned the year before by friends on the island who would all come this third weekend in May to open their houses. It was last Labor Day that the sponge cake was bathed in ports and liqueurs and set away to marinate patiently for this very night.

It is an ostentatiously mixed crowd. Mixed professions, mixed marriages, mixed states of the union. Good legs on the women.

The host is very nice. I have the crème anglaise, don't eat the cake drenched in friendship, to which I am not entitled.

Heidi doesn't urge it on me. She plays Ping-Pong with all the men. The host tells me the kind of story I most enjoy. He played the trumpet in Catskill orchestras to work his way through college and medical school. He describes the other musicians on the bus and the Hatikvah pageants. I wonder how his mother felt when her doctor son brought home German Heidi. How can I ask? Suddenly it's not going well. It is turning off in both directions. I'm turning contradictory and cold and he's becoming a correct host, thinking of his other guests, wondering why he lingered so happily with me.

In the hallway mirror, I see I unaccountably put on lipstick and forgot to blot it, rubbed it into my cheeks like clumsy rouge. With my hair frizzy from the damp, I'm at my worst—beady, aging, artificial.

Back at the hotel I think about doctors I have known who tried to court me with some anecdote that would make a great play, or quoted *Streetcar* or *Happy Days*—when, in fact, they could have more effectively urged me toward their beds by talking to me of dialysis machines or cardiac valves or the urine test for diabetes, "See, little girl? It turns different colors." I love men who are good with their equipment. Good with their equipment and clumsy with me.

Like Sam, who loves his machines and is blind, fumbling and wondering each time. He is lovely with a jib, with a fishing line, with his machines, with every outside thing he touches. But with me, I feel the blind fumbling each time, the wonder, the hugs and embraces. He seems to remember nothing from one time to another. He is a big, magic, shy, ecstatic, trembling bear.

He minds having another man in his children's lives, even little Leonard. I will myself to remember this in the morning and be tender.

SUNDAY MORNING, MAY 23

Sam tumbles out of our warm bed in the dark and leaves to go deep sea fishing with our last night's host. He smells of oilcloth and, the outdoors already. I get out of bed after he leaves, put on a bathing suit under a sweatshirt and jeans, and drive to an ocean beach. My car is the only one in the parking lot. The sky is wide and overcast. It is easy to love empty sand, gray waves, sweeping breeze.

I poke around the deserted beach houses, back in the dunes. They are all gray, many-windowed, perched on stilts. Through the windows I can see cobweb-shrouded wooden tables on their sides, rolled-up Rya rugs in plums and corals, kitchens full of piled cast-iron pots and lids. The houses have not been opened yet. They are no-frills, meant for bare feet, sand. They have freestanding fireplaces and are $30,000 to rent for the season. I know, I've inquired.

Walking down the beach, I feel it will be too chilly to swim. A man is walking toward me down the deserted beach. He is wearing boxer-style blue trunks.

I imagine when we come face to face he will pull his penis from the elastic drawstring top and guide it toward me. I veer off before we are face to face and scramble up to the dune grass, lest when we pass I begin to giggle.

The dune grass is high and gives me a clear view of the whole beach. I watch the slow procession of a man on crutches in madras slacks and a woman wearing a chignon and exercise tights. When they approach below, I hear her say, "It's going to be a long haul coming up." Does this mean his injury is temporary? I look away tactfully as they struggle on below me in the soft sand. They interest me.

It is growing darker. I sit with my knees up in the wild dune grass, watching the increasingly violent expanse of swirling waves, in sight of the closed-up $30,000-a-season houses full of custom-size butcher block tables on their sides and Le Creuset seventy-dollar eight-quart casseroles.

And here she sits, ironic city rat, sitting on the beach pricing Le Creuset casseroles and butcher block tables, sitting steps away from the dune entrance because she felt drops of rain and a bit of thunder and is never quite sure what the word is on lightning and an open stretch of sand.

The sky clears and it smells fabulous and free.

From far away the horizon is deserted, except for the one figure of another man getting bigger and bigger. We will be entirely alone on this deserted beach. When he reaches me, he can murder me.

My friend Lorette is taking a judo class. She is taking it because her friend Audrey huddled in a closet in her studio apartment, where she was shoved when a man delivering art supplies turned out to be a sadistic thief. The point is, she had many opportunities to fight back, run out the open door while he rummaged in a drawer, race down the stairs. But she stayed where she was, untied, huddled in a closet. It was where he told her to stay. And when he finished rummaging through her drawers, he beat her up horribly.

A question of attitude.

The man coming toward me can use my sharp pencil point as a weapon, but if I break it he will not have it. However he can drag me into one of the empty beach houses, shatter a glass window, and have as many sharp-angled daggers as weapons as I have in my den at home.

I have never been this exposed in a city apartment, unprotected from all directions.

But, of course, he could carry me to the ocean from the wooden house on stilts, carry me out to the ocean, where he could drop me. Exhausted and stunned, I would sink to the bottom, drown cleanly without a mark on me.

I still see the ocean as sandy, pain-free, passionate blue-green. Though, yes, I have read Melville and, while reading him, am convinced of the ocean of sperm, broken sacs, miscarriages, and blood, blood—sometime later, the dutiful poetry-ridden girl inside me reasserts herself.

But I will die on a city street.

My lone man is approaching. He is an overweight jogger, anxious, double-chinned, apologetic. How my fantasy would please him. He schlogs by me like Mother Courage dragging her wagon. Soft sand, uphill, will do it to you. When he disappears from view, the empty water line draws me. I have never had the means of painless suicide before me before. I feel a slight pull into the ocean and hastily put on dark sunglasses, glad for the distance of the width of the sand.

Perhaps, for all my talk of turbulent landscapes, gray waves, wild wind, I want to watch it all with a motel staff behind me in the next room, tactfully arranging a turkey club with little toothpicks in each section.

A car has driven up in the deserted dune parking lot, next to mine. It is a carload of middle-aged people. They have short hair, graying crew cuts and chopped dutch bobs, heavy faces. They move past me on the smooth dune passageway. Under the gray sky, they walk to the beach in a cluster. They make a semicircle facing the water. Because I am seated on a rise in the dune grass, I can see in front of them, inside the semicircle. One of the group, I see now, a stocky young girl wearing jeans rolled up to show heavy hairy calves, gets on all fours and emits strange hoarse animal sounds. She grunts and wails and howls. Then she makes little playful cries and kicks out her heels in what seem to be cavorting ways. After a while she gets up. The others brush the sand from her knees with little slaps. Then they all walk past me back to their car and drive away.

Okay, here it is, folks, the moment we've all been waiting for, and no dice.

Because this was the moment I was going to say, "Sitting alone on the sand, the car door having slammed on the group of short-haired people, their car having screeched away, I realized the world is mad, and evil lurks in the hearts of men, and Harry my ex-lover is trying to kill me."

But no dice, because do you know, oh, I understand how far back this goes. It's true, all right. He's trying to murder me. But I've known it such a long time.

And the fact that I have come here to sit on a bare beach and have a tatty revelation about life and death and madness, triggered by some incident—man on crutches? crazy girl on all fours?—so that seeing this, I could say, "Oh ho, seeing this, I, for the first time understand that people can be crazy—and Harry is," or "Oh ho ho, the world is mad and so is Harry," or some other syntactical variation like, "Seeing this I believe in evil evil evil lurking in the hearts of men."

More particularly:

I think Harry is trying to kill me/Sam.

Both.

One of the above.

Notwithstanding Melville, I expected the truth to be bleached bone-white, windswept, cloud-tossed—clean and fresh and turbulent and moving.

But I shall die on a city street. Violent shreds of tissue like flesh will be flickering out all over me, unraveling my insides. My hair is thick with spray; it whips at my face like sharp salty snakes. Shredded pink inner tissue, telltale tissue flesh will be leaping out, licking at the retreating universe, while on the street around me people run on to parties, where they will be consoled by people like the person I used to be.

Last year Wendy arrived at a party, shaken by having just seen a man killed in traffic. Expert me! "Enjoy, enjoy," I said, "you'll have your day, you're making a big mistake if you let it spoil your party." I convinced her to have a good time anyway.

And so they will with me! I am frantic, changing my tune, *don't have a good time anyway, not when it's me!*

Calm down. This is self-indulgent if I've known it all along.

Windswept beaches are simply not my scene.

I go to the car, roll up the windows, and sit still to figure it out. Beach, wherever, number your thoughts. It's got to be done calmly.

SECTION SIXTEEN

Statistics lie—but so does Harry.

Odd thought.

1. I put the idea in Harry's head with my chatter about statistics. About how we were, all of us, in the same position.

2. Sitting in the car, I begin to tote up the accidents. Storm window shattering on my desk chair, oven blowing up around my head, escalator jamming with me at the top, blow dryer spurting current, and Sam's demonstration machine. Oh, in my Events lists I confused the issue by adding ringers—sniper on roof of Plaza theater, dog foaming at the mouth in a man-made park, woman with William Greenberg, Jr., sugar cookies, and weepy maidens on the street with groceries. It was not the human/animal crazies, it was the machinery malfunctions that were the real thing. And though I didn't hurtle forward, catch on fire, take in slivers of glass through my heart, electric current through my spine, I was left alone often enough with the slowly dying after-echo of human terror both in the scream I let out in the air and the inner hurtling scream in my soul—that I should have made *something* at least out of the accumulation of events.

Most of the accidents began after the night I spoke to Harry in Sam's arms.

It is beginning to rain.

I remember my bedridden Uncle Merv calling me from Arizona the day I'd buried his son Jeremy's body. "Did it rain, are you sure it rained, Jessila?" he kept asking, though in fact we are a factionalized family, and I'd been pulled into service to shuffle the gravesites because of some old 1920 feud between Merv and my father about who got the money for medical school. And because Jeremy, from his hospital bed, tried to make me do it. Jeremy, named for the same grandfather as me. The saying is if it rains at a funeral, the person didn't want to die. "He didn't want to die in the worst way, oh that boy, he didn't want to die in the worst way," wept my rotten Uncle Merv, who will live to be a hundred.

Suddenly I am furious with Sam, who is making me retaliate. Because only because of Sam's shoulder am I even considering retaliating, you understand, because Sam is, after all, blameless. Sam, who angered Harry by touching me, who often forgets to and has to be guided to it. Sam, that is.

Oh, lonely lonely Harry, who doesn't want to die in the worst way! I think of him raging, angry, trapped in a silent room under huge steel machinery. Because even oxygen tents are of human dimension. That is, you might claw your way through them, if your mind didn't remind you they were helping, not smothering. But with huge, stainless steel monsters being lowered from the ceiling toward you by buttons on a panel outside an iron door . . . oh, sweet Harry, who doesn't want to die in the worst way, who controlled the rain for many hours till it left on a truck for the Northwest.

I remember a fight with Stephanie and Harry in the early days. It was something about Stephanie's sunburn and elite pain and bodies underground in gravesites, and I was carrying forth with high moral tone.

Was this when Harry decided to be interested in me? Or was it later? And at what point did he decide he wanted me or wanted to get me? Did it have to do with my pursuing him? with my body? my eyes? my tendentious remarks? that caused a dying boy to go after me with vengeance to show me I knew nothing?

Or is it just out of loneliness—to show me I don't understand how lonely a person can be?

I'd moved into the future, leaving him behind. The day I'd thought we'd ended, I left his room ringing with life, happy. Sorry for Stephanie, of course, but ringing with life. Somewhere I probably knew better. My ringing turned harsh in the cab, was a tinkling sound heralding false freedom, disaster.

Harry had been with the crew who came to inspect our apartment as a possible location. The window was off its track. Harry worked one summer during college doing elevator repairs. Are they the same as escalators? Why didn't I mention it before? Because who thought it was important? I myself told him about the Coliseum. And did he push toward or away from the camera swinging at my head? The further back my mind races, the less I welcome it.

The odds are evening.

The rain has stopped. A car swerves up next to mine in the empty parking lot. A group of boys jump out and take their piled surfboards off the top. They glance over at me.

Gang bang?

Big deal.

No, they are looking for the perfect wave. They get back into their car and drive away.

I know now my vocabulary in picking a house—"sniper" with shaving cream, "exposed," etc.—meant I was worried even then.

I know I turned rude to Sam's friend last night lest he begin to find me more appealing than casual, frosty Heidi of the penwiper grip, and so push Sam off his deep sea fishing boat today, the better to win for himself my Semitic widow's grief on August's sand.

So much for my calm, weekend-in-the-country thoughts. A peripheral casualty.

It's Sam I'm bound to protect.

I drive back to the hotel. Sam and I have a good time. Ferry, lobster, peace. The next morning he drives north to a business conference and I fly home.

AIR NEW ENGLAND, MONDAY, MAY 24

A woman with a fine young strapping son of about twenty-five is sitting across from me on the small plane.

"Every human body of sixty should have at least an ounce of scotch a day, but you wouldn't touch it!" he shouts suddenly at his mother.

Then he jumps into the aisle and says

> I'm a kangaroo
> I'm a kangaroo
> I'm a kangaroo

His eyes roll wildly around his head, and his large pink tongue lolls on his chin.

When he returns to his seat, he croons, "I'm a kangaroo, I'm a kangaroo," and, "There's a tree in the meadow, where my thoughts often lie," for the remainder of the flight.

If I hadn't found my epiphany yet, this would have been it.

SECTION SEVENTEEN

BACK IN NEW YORK, TUESDAY, MAY 25

Clearly, I have to act almost immediately. At least before next week, when they move into our apartment to shoot our scene and Harry will be able to make his move.

Once I tell Sam, every balance will shift. The power of my family, my rightness, my sanity, my health, will come crashing down around Harry's body. I think of his body, through whose ribs and furrows and marrow the grittiness of death is slowly moving. I give that thin body in its cotton ribbed turtlenecks one day of reprieve.

Instead of going to the set, I go to Georgette Klinger for a facial. To purge my face of all impurities? Warrioress in battle? Miss Posy has been squeezing, patting, and poking my skin for years.

Today, Miss Posy is upset. Her hand trembles and the pot of boiling water, fetched to steam open my pores, passes over my up-turned face and a drop, just a drop, grazes my skin. It could have scalded my eyeballs. I recline, frozen.

Have I caused this fearful and dangerous agitation? No. The hus-band of Miss Posy (Pazmany), survivor with her of Budapest, Tre-blinka, Cape Town, and La Paz, was mugged on West End Avenue. His fifteen dollars freely offered, he was then kicked and stomped.

"Die, die, cocksucker," he was told in both Spanish and English, and left with a punctured lung and shattered ribs and ankle.

My words of response, the words necessary to keep civilization going, must straddle a tenuous line. But today, all I can think of is how close Miss Posy's boiling water came to scalding my eyeballs. I do not trust my balance. I murmur sympathetically as the almond paste is put on my face, allow it to harden into a mask of horror and commiseration.

When it is bathed off, I scoot.

Outside, it is raining, and with a thrill of alarm, I hail a cab and speed home, cursing the traffic. They ran out of cover shots—inside locations to use on days of rain—a few days ago, and sure enough, the trucks and trailers are outside and Rich is arguing with Julio, our super, who is refusing to let the movie company in.

Because it is raining and they ran through their cover, they're here a week early. Couldn't they have waited to use real rain instead of fake rain and needing to run inside when it does rain? I don't even ask.

I'm jubilant.

I calm Julio, flutter a little at the unpreparedness of my house, but truly it is to cover my crow of triumph. Sam will not be back in town until this evening. We have finessed the script.

I'm feeling so fine I remember to call Petra, whose amusement was one of the reasons Sam agreed to do this at all. Bun dispatches her on the Pennsylvania Railroad.

A few particulars: The set designer runs in with his prop boxes. I said before that it was tacky to put down movie people but what am I to do with the spectacle of the set designer who races in to make my place a West Side intellectual's apartment with a music stand, an empty French horn case, a copy of Christopher Isherwood's *Berlin Stories*, and an acrylic lace piano shawl he drapes over our Danish sofa?

The casting department and the propman haven't coordinated their efforts, because the actor who walks in would never be caught dead living here. The little shudder in his eyes shows that. Another problem: he's the chic-consumptive Chopin mold of musician, chest too thin to play the French horn. No one with that Sulka ascot would live here, nor could his slender wrists diddle around in Sam's huge-stalked hairy terrarium.

The scene in the script is an aborted seduction. The heroine arrives early, looks around, abruptly realizes she's not yet ready to accept life. The seducer arrives and she runs out.

(I do believe that up until he walked in, the actor secretly thought that if the apartment was cool and he played his cards right, he might persuade the Star-as-refugee-housewife to stay and be seduced, so expanding his part immeasurably. One look at our apartment and he knew it was no go. No way. He gave up and wandered around fingering things, looking tired and sour.)

Marie and I stand in a corner having a nice dirty time talking about the figure Marie had in mind in her book, a horny little balding West Side flutist, a real cocksman—"come see my scores"—who loves plants and women and sweet onions.

Marie is wearing a shapeless old lady shirtwaist with lace on the collar—a mix of Laura Ashley and Triangle fire. She smiles happily and I think of college productions, i.e., fresh-faced nineteen-year-olds in white woolly wigs, who make you think old age won't be so bad at all—the eyes so bright, the step so fine. Till you remember inside the white woolly dowager hump is a young and radiant girl, and so Marie, this day with her shapeless flower-sprigged dress, her pretty skin and eager smile, reminds me of nothing so much as a nineteen-year-old Lady Bracknell.

Barney is not satisfied with the way things look. He holds the French horn case. Something is wrong with the shape, he says. What? The propman is not dismayed. He brings in a cello, a trumpet, an oboe case, and a clarinet. Nothing has both itself and its case. He covers most of the terraced terrarium (the whole point of using our place) with a Lautrec poster, offending the plants, who peek through sullenly. They move the furniture, hide the *Sports Illustrated*, and banish Sam's football and his squash racquet. He's going to be a highly rarefied little seducer. No wonder she runs out.

Do I care? About the apartment being changed? Nah. It is only the same walls they're using, inside which our lives usually take place, suspended above the street. They have temporarily changed the space with acrylic shawls and peevish actors. We will hang there again when they leave.

And if Sam's plants are irritated, serves them right. They're much too vain and self-important anyway.

Marie and I are getting gigglier and dirtier, talking about oboes, flutes, and stubby fingers, when Petra arrives, and we stop.

(There is a way in which I haven't described my space. When Harry walked in, at first there was a hum, unpleasant and jarring. My arms and legs started to tingle and there was a high-pitched whine, as if two clashing vibrations were making an ugly sound, hissing steam pipe against sputtering electric current. Jarring, dangerous. Then it died down.)

The other thing I haven't mentioned is that Stephanie has gone back to California for a few weeks to help the postproduction coordinator. She left a message with Marie that Marie tries to pass along but may have garbled. She seems to be thanking me for letting her leave now. I don't question Marie too closely for all kinds of reasons, but anyway it doesn't matter, now. I'm on my own.

Georgeann is coming in my door again and again. She is wearing a parody of Sylvie's costume—a silky plum-colored sweater and tight black pants. Georgeann's version is Orlon, with Chinese cotton coolie pants.

They have found the fire door and opened it to consider another shot—reveal dark, oddly curved stairs I have never seen before, would never see except in disaster.

Barney asks Georgeann if she's recovered maybe enough to fall down stairs today, they could probably squeeze it in at the end of the day, and she says every stair fall is different, a stair fall in a house is different from one in a subway, the size of the stairs, the width and steepness matter, and instead of forward somersault you touch down gently, turn the head to one side, roll onto one shoulder. It needs planning, planning and preparation, doesn't he understand?

"So you mean you're not recovered enough yet?" asks Barney. Her regal affrontedness has passed him by.

My neighbors—some I like and some I don't—hang around my hallways waving to me. I try to stay out of eyeshot. It's not up to me to invite them in. Rich's staff urges them away.

"I have permission to stay," says a neighbor whose horrid children press all the elevator buttons so the elevator stops on each floor. Rich checks with me. Why has he picked this moment to be courteous? Why not scream at her, humiliate her as he does with everyone else? For my sake?

"Who gave you permission?" I ask her politely.

She flushes. "Stan, the doorman."

Out she goes. It's not up to me, I signal. My hands are tied.

I understand many of my preferred neighbors will be hanging around shyly in the lobby. The company has used other apartment house locations before and I've seen with my own eyes the inevitable arc of tenant response. Pleasure, excitement skid swiftly into inconvenience, irritation, mixed with shame at having been excited in the first place. Then we pack up and go, leaving a card tacked up in the lobby—"Thanks to 517 West End Avenue from the *Daughters and Sisters* Company"—and a monstrous tub of pistachio nuts, which everyone eyes with jeering contempt and eventually, sheepishly, eats to the bottom. It's a deflating cycle when you know in advance where it leads: shelled nuts on the lobby floor for the Julio in each building, who wanted the company least, to end up sweeping away.

Made more complicated for me here, in my own building, when I find I'm saying "we" instead of "they" about the interloping company. When did it start? Did you notice it? Sam did.

I do my duty when Petra arrives. Sylvie and she go into my bedroom while Sylvie changes her makeup. Is Sylvie going to paint up Petra's peach petal face? Sam will have a fit. No, I slink in the doorway while Sylvie is explaining how she puts on completely different shadow, lashes, and mascara for each shot, because the lighting changes. "So it takes forty minutes, and then, when they show the dailies, no one will know the difference, but I'll know, you know?"

And Petra, it seems, knows. She gives Sylvie an I-know-exactly-what-you-mean look.

But when the shot starts again—Sylvie running out the front

door—Petra blurts she's got to leave and slips out when the lights go off (the front door is in the shot). I walk her to the elevator. She seems excited.

"What do you think of our Star?" I say.

"She seems like a nice person." Slam.

You only met her because of me, honey bunch.

Sylvie begins running in and out of my front door crying, "You'll just have to forgive me, this was a mistake," slamming my door behind her. In between takes I get to go inside my home. The actor watching her leave is looking truly dashed.

A serious young stage actress named Ruth rushes in wearing a plastic rain poncho of the kind that folds up into an envelope. Her large eyes shine out from her crumpled hood. Her agent just tracked her down at her health club. Her one scene with Sylvie, supposed to be on a bench on upper Broadway, has been moved inside to be additional cover for today's schedule. Not especially pretty, a wonderful stage actress who was once in acting class with Sylvie, she was insisted on by Sylvie for a small part.

I've seen her do a wonderful Masha, but she's been Nurse Suellen Shea on a soap and we all pounce on her. Will Dr. Jerry marry her? Is she really mad? Is it his child or his brother Jake's? She says she's left the soap, can you imagine they want her back to haunt Jerry? Why not? we cry. She's so pleased I saw her as Masha, she doesn't want to talk about Dr. Jerry, who's gay and a real woman hater, and she tries to tell Marie and me that she's going for a Mamet audition on Thursday.

It's professional girl talk—and a pleasure for me. It may be my last day of play. I must stay alert. Where is Harry?

Where is Ruth's Broadway bench scene going to be shot today?

"Somebody's bed," she says cheerfully.

I race to Rich, to Barney. They are busy blocking out our bedroom. They clearly never expected unreason from me.

Harry solves it. In a square room, there's no room angle to hide the light. "A square room is the worst," he says, and the subject is closed.

They finally choose the daybed in my workroom and start setting it up so that it will seem like a corner of somebody else's apartment, not the rarefied seducer's. So my apartment will be two apartments.

But it, too, is awkward to light, the headroom unacceptable, and they finally move the daybed out into the dining room and make it a pretend corner of a pretend room. Harry wants to shoot from the side to give an impression of isolation in the placing of the two women, so they set up a pretend bed in a corner of the dining room, using Sam's plants after all.

Ruth and Georgeann sit on the bed while they set up the lights. I mind that such a serious actress, a real Masha, is used just setting up a shot, but she doesn't. She's the kind of person who brings out the best in people, and I hear her learn from Georgeann that her hair is so thin as a result of its having been stripped and dyed in seconds when it doesn't "read right" in the camera. That is to say, with seconds to spare, it's discovered that she needs to be more strawberry blond or fiery red, the better to match from a distance some dainty star who would never dream of falling overboard in a canoe or scrambling from a fiery plane. Hair stripped to match some dainty star's from a distance? Any bitterness here? No, it doesn't matter, because now she plans to get her hair as much like Sylvie's as possible and just keep it that way. There is no complaint.

And then Sylvie comes out and she and Ruth run through the scene once, and then, as in class long ago, they try an improvisation. Ruth makes the hair stand up on everyone's neck. She is using the original language of Marie's book. She apologizes, says she read it over last night, for groundwork.

There is a small conference around the camera. Barney agrees, everyone agrees, they will use the dialogue of the book. Marie is pleased but not overjoyed. She never thinks she knows better. And besides, she wrote the words a long time ago in a book. Now she's working on something else.

I'm impressed with everyone's judgment. Oh, the excitement when something good seems to be happening.

They do the scene again. Ruth is wild. Beauty doesn't matter. She is sensual, amazing, alive. It's a "No, now *you* listen to *me*" scene, turning the tables on assumptions. And when Ruth has finished her tale of her marriage, she cries terribly, her tears are huge and contagious. Even the focus puller has tears in his eyes.

Sylvie consults with Harry and Barney about the lighting. She wants to protect Ruth's performance. I have never seen her so protective of another actor. It is hard to remember Sylvie is in the scene, though she has half the lines.

They go through the scene again. The crew cries again, huge tears. Even when Ruth does her lines off camera for Sylvie's reaction shots, we are all shaken. I had forgotten we were here to do something of value, of art. Barney seems to have done nothing, but I am grateful he did not get in the way.

Ruth rubs her eyes and smiles briskly. She hugs Sylvie, who has been so generous. The crew gives her a round of applause. It will be her movie debut.

———

That something has taken place of this much emotion in my house shakes me. I want my house back.

In the bedroom, women are sprawled all over our bed, idling, chattering, playing with the tassles of our bedspread. Georgeann is saying Barney thinks you just wake up one morning, no planning, no concentration, and fall down the stairs like that. Sylvie's dresser says her son could be another Glen Campbell, only shorter. The groupie doing petit point embroidery says, "Wow." Georgeann, sitting cross-legged, holds up Sylvie's hairbrush, pulls out long silky strands of hair and lets them drift down slowly onto the bedspread. "Mmm, like a baby's," croons the needle-stabbing groupie, putting her canvas down in front of Sam's and my wedding photograph, and I want them *off!*

I grab Rich in the hall, explain that everyone must leave my bed. I must be dressed. I am going out. It is close to five. He understands. Oh surely. He does.

They all gather up their things and begin to trail out, Georgeann last. I feel a spasm of irritation in my hands, and the slight hostessly pressure on Georgeann's back turns ever so slightly toward a shove. Hurry up!

But they are out and, alone, I turn on the TV news. My point is only half made, because Barney and Sylvie come right back in and sit on the bed and talk in soft voices. Nothing applies to her. I wish I hadn't turned on the TV, so I could hear what they are saying. The noise is a wall.

I go into the adjoining inside bathroom, feeling spiteful. When I come out in a robe, Sylvie is there alone, pulling off her costume— the silky plum-colored turtleneck—over her head. "Going out to-night?" she says to me.

We both stand in front of the dresser mirror, looking more vaguely alike than ever. The crew calls goodbye—so Harry has left. No one is left but us. I refuse to undress under my robe, as in camp. I pull my sweater off, then my bra. They have all left; I am safe.

We are both naked to the waist, staring into the mirror that reflects the TV, two women naked to the waist in panty hose.

The news is bleating about the death of a famous union boss. The President praises him and talks of the grief of the labor force, the world, his own personal grief.

"He was a bad guy, a good guy, no?" Her celebrated breast, lovelier than when tampered with, wobbles uncertainly toward the screen. She is afraid of making a fool of herself.

No, I will not mock her. In a time when long-haired headbanded kids picket the Boston schools with placards reading "Nigger Go Home," when the President praises a former Mafia hit man on the six o'clock news, who am I to knock her confusion?

We seem in the shadowy room like a black-and-white movie with sepia tints.

Our breasts are the same. Not large, they just start high, lots of cleavage right away, not much in profile. In the mirror, smudges within shadowy circles.

They should have left her bustline in her clothes alone.

I take a black turtleneck out of my drawer, and she takes one out of her bag and we yank them over our heads. Then we stand in our panty hose before the mirror—two black-topped spiders in the shadows, rearranging our tousled hair.

I am sure we have both seen *Persona*.

"I'd hate my waist," she says, "if I had one."

She chose the one body part where I excel, and I know she means well.

She is not a bad sort. She longs for normality in an elite way.

She wants to be the acknowledged beauty on the block, and if she leaves the block to go marketing, she wants to be the star of the marketers in the supermarket—not the Star marketing but the star marketer—and so it goes. She wants to win the Miss Normal Life pageant. Miss Upper West Side Politically Aware Housewife, Miss Refugee with Bad Dreams, Miss Whitest Skin at Bloomingdale's White Sale.

Of ambitions, this is surely not the cheapest.

She reaches out and holds a lock of my hair for an instant. We pause.

"Do you ever act in your plays?" she asks.

No. I smile.

She pulls on gabardine pants and I a flowered skirt. We are ready to leave.

"You have a real kid?" she asks.

"I had a miscarriage," I say. "A girl."

I never say that.

Sam comes in the front door, early—we were supposed to meet later at the dinner—and disappointed that everyone's already left. His shoulders seem huge. Odysseus returning in his trench coat.

Sylvie is shy with him.

When I tell him Petra was here, he flashes me a big pleased smile that Sylvie sees. Women watch him—slow, quiet, gray eyes, dark brows, male.

Oh, look at him, I want to say. But she already has. How lucky I was.

Sylvie is hurried out.

Harry said only (in my den), "It looks like a good place to work."

Oh, it was such a dumb idea to think something would happen

here. A Roger Corman rip-off of a Hitchcock spin-off penciled in late at night in someone's hotel room when even the Kelly Girl steno has gone home.

I think of the shadowy moment with Sylvie.

Interesting moment.

SECTION EIGHTEEN

I tell Sam a few days later, before we leave for Bun's house. I try to keep calm, make sure I have eight hours' sleep the night before. I hedge my bets a little by introducing Harry as the boy who originally lied to me about Stephanie's being ill. Once I am talking, I relax. The big question to me was whether I was going to do it at all. Now that my voice is speaking, my words forming and changing the air, natural forces will take their course. I explain that dying—or at least the knowledge of dying—has altered Harry's brain. I say brain instead of mind because it sounds more clinical, less potentially erotic. I take a lot of blame. Why me? I am prepared to spend a lot of time on that. I explain it was because I chattered on to him about how all of us will die someday, it is statistical who dies first . . .

Sam cuts me off. "Yes, I know."

Know what? That all of us will die? Or is it that this statistical business is one of my routines that he's heard before?

I continue. It is a mechanical problem to be solved. Technical, one might say. I try to scant on the human dimension, to defuse the forces of enraged protection that will rage forward and envelop me in their inexorable path.

I talk a long time into silence. Then I stop.

"What do you suggest for the next step?" asks Sam. His voice is interested, even cordial.

I do not understand. I am confused.

I go over the incidents again.

"Yes, yes," he says. He is a quick study.

A whole new scene flashes through my head. No one will believe me—no-one-will-believe-her-till-it's-too-late. But no, it is over and out before I say another word. He believes me.

What next?

But I hadn't expected to be asked. I thought everything would envelop me at this moment—loving arms, protection, plans, devices. I didn't think beyond saying this, of suggesting a way to proceed. I expected the air to tremble, the sky to shake, everyone to close ranks about me, ranks Harry could never penetrate. I expected to be nodding meekly to a thundering set of instructions, and the head I saw myself shaking had a ribbon on it. So I guess I saw myself as a little girl having the grown-ups help me.

Sam is still waiting.

"I thought we should get some professional advice," I say. When you're grown-up yourself, you turn to professionals.

"You mean speak to Gary," says Sam. (Len's psychiatrist son from UCLA, in town for a conference.)

I guess that's what I'd had in mind, why I'd told Sam just before we left for Bun's. I always believe in family for doctors, lawyers. You can trust them with your life.

(My doctor father always took the fallen eyelashes from my eyes. When I woke in the night, I went whimpering into my parents' bedroom and he lifted me gently in his arms, carried me down two flights to his office. The year he died, I woke in panic in my marriage bed, wondering what other people did. Do they call a doctor for a house call in the middle of the night? I've got an eyelash in my eye? This is to say I've never been sure what a doctor and what a daddy does.) And driving in the car with Sam, my forehead feels hot and I long for my father's cool Dr./Daddy hands to tell me I should go to bed.

We are quiet in the car.

Gary, Len's big-toothed-wonder psychiatrist, is sprawled on Bun's sofa. Not my idea, really, of a doctor. Petra seems to have a little crush on him. Just how broad-minded *is* Len?

Petra is drifting around in corduroy jeans and a loose flowered smock of spilling goldenrod. Her young swain-in-residence is there, Jerome. They both seem unsurprised by either her having been away or her being back. Jerome is the weaver. He sent her a lariat and a shawl in "the place," which she called "awesome." Everyone is delighted to hear her use so silly and trendy a phrase. Drifting is an unfair word for them. They have been stuffing little cherry tomatoes with egg salad for a party.

Petra seems grave and free. She kisses her small half-brother and -sister before she leaves; she's tender with them. She probably wouldn't mind Daniel, her whole brother, turning out to be gay.

When she is gone, Gary tells us that Petra told him that Jerome Margolies is simply her favorite person in the world "of the same age." Leaving the rest of the field for both Daddy and the big-toothed wonder. (Stepfather Len is obviously not in the running.)

Gary is deferentially consulted on her condition.

"Oh, she'll always have to be watched," he says carefully. "Especially she'll have to be watched after the birth of her first child."

I find myself irritated beyond what is reasonable. Why assume she'll have a first child? Because all normal women do? Because her mother did?

Four-time mama Bun, her tight little hips flashing under her bulky sweatshirt, strides self-confidently into the kitchen. I follow her, just to get away. But Bun in the kitchen is rumpled and furious.

" 'Always be watched,' " she bursts out. "In other words she'll always be crazy." Yes, I guess he did mean that. Oh, the things one doesn't notice when it isn't one's own child.

"What do you do when your stepson tells you you're a hysteric?" she says, jerking the refrigerator open, slamming it shut. "That everything you do from babies to chopping parsley is to prove to yourself that you're a better woman than your mother or your daughter?"

And suddenly we're two stepmothers. It had never occurred to me before: that big-tooth Gary is the child of Len's first wife, that he sees Bun as the woman who broke up his parents' marriage. Not true, in fact. Did big-tooth's mother, Len's first wife, resent Bun? And Gary thinks Bun's at fault for Petra?

We both think at the same second—wouldn't it be terrific if Gary were to crack up, drop out? mess up, at least? The child neither she nor I nor Sam has responsibility for? It would take the pressure off everyone. We see it in each other's eyes.

Bun is laying out the stuff for the blender béarnaise. The shallots, the tarragon vinegar, the margarine in a saucepan. It's always more trouble than you remember.

"Oh . . . fuck it," she says, and we hurry back inside. Just another minute in that kitchen and we'd be showing each other flowering pear trees.

After dinner (plain broiled steak), I tell my story, dully. Someone has gotten it into his head to harm me and I don't know how to proceed.

Len responds instantly. What? Some Crazy Guy hurt this nice little girl eating at my table? And for the first time I think the unthinkable. I unbelievably wonder if Bun hasn't done better for herself. Here, at least, is someone who reacts as I rather expected the world would. And though little Len always makes me feel overly tall, I suddenly feel right size, the size to ask for and get protection of a sort.

Bun rushes around the table and puts her arms around me. I'm amazed. I smell her perfume. She has never touched me before.

"Well now, Jessie, are we talking about commitment here?" says Gary. "Are we talking sign a complaint and send him to Bellevue, where they'll pump him with drugs and the attendants will bugger him and he'll go crazy in any case?"

(And where they give you drawstring pajamas without the drawstring so you can't hang yourself, and you have to walk around with your pajama bottoms bunched in your hand. I've read about it. Who could make him spend the last few months of active life locked up?)

"Commitment is a tricky thing," says Gary.

"So is somebody out to get you," says Bun. The kitchen paid off.

"So," says Len to Gary—father to son, "how to best handle this?" He clearly loves my consulting Gary. Their family is in charge.

Sam asks Bun if she remembers Miyuki, his Japanese secretary when he worked at Lockair. Oh, she certainly does. (I have never heard of her before.)

It is a baroque tale of Miyuki, who fell in love with a non-Japanese young man. While she agonized over breaking the hearts of her traditional parents, he revealed he had a rare blood disease and only a year to live and urged her to marry him immediately. It was the Personnel Counseling service that discovered, inadvertently, that he was also secretly engaged to each of Miyuki's two Japanese room-mates, and further investigation revealed two wives and children in separate California valleys, unware of each other's existence. And he was not, incidentally, ill at all.

I stare, dumbfounded.

"You know, I was just thinking of that story," says Bun enthusi-astically, and goes back to sit in her seat. It is all shifting and she and Sam are a couple.

It is not her defection that matters—on that, I can't say I'm surprised.

"Were the other wives Japanese?" asks Len. He's in there trying to get back in, but he led with his chin.

He is rewarded with a blank outsider's stare from both of them. No, they murmur, don't know, don't remember.

Sam and Bun go on, invoking a past when there was no stepson to hint you have children to prove yourself a woman and drove your daughter crazy, and no wife with a colleague stalking her and stopping escalators and loosening window frames. My brief alliance with Bun over the blender béarnaise has gone by the boards, and who can blame her? I can blame her, for sure. But Sam? What is he doing?

I am cold with shock. Beyond anger. I go to the tiled bathroom, just to have a reason to move. When I come back I stand in the doorway of the kitchen watching him. He smiles up at me pleasantly. How can he do this?

From Bun I never expected better. This is too seductive. And she's had a bad week.

"Yes, and how do we know this guy's really sick?" says Len, finally tuning in, finally getting the nasty subtext of the story. Incipient bully that he is—all short men?—he joins in.

Anybody know but you, Jessie?

"His girlfriend," I say.

"Yes, but what kind of girl gets mixed up with a boy that sick, anyway?"

And then he asks if Harry has AIDS, if he's gay, is he with his girlfriend to prove he's not gay, and I say I sent him to a doctor— and Harry has to defend himself against everything, it's not fair . . . someone's left to die of cancer, remember?

"Look, maybe just keep out of his way for a while. Not many men could handle a woman as successful as you." Bun glances over at him. Len's not going to have an easy night either.

"Well, Dad, assuming for the moment he's really sick *and* really crazy, what is there to do?" asks Gary—unexpected reprieve.

"Good thinking," says Len.

Father-and-son team. Professionals. The alliances stink. And I have no one. At least he has someone.

Gary talks about fathers who commit sons who are stoned, and there's some joking about Len's finding him with pot. They too go back to a happier time, when Len was married to Gary's mother. Just as Bun and Sam move back, they all wish to be back there— and the only face missing from all those family albums is me. So we've moved from this to legalizing drugs and a homosexual's court-martial when Len was in Korea. The anecdotes move to and fro with verve, deftly avoiding anything to do with me, till Gary suggests I see a lawyer.

And that suits me just fine. Because I want to go back to my own family, to my blood relatives, to my brother the lawyer, to be exact. I can't get out of this house soon enough. And away from here.

Everyone here has a blood relative except me. And they've all gravitated to them. But Bernice and Sam are not the same blood. It just mingles in two other people.

When she puts my coat on, Bun holds my shoulders, but I'm too angry. She must be standing on tiptoe to reach, but I'll have none of it. You can't play it two ways.

I am frozen on the car ride home.

At home, in bed, we are frozen. But I can't be without anyone. It starts slowly—gets worse. "What were you doing? I stood in the doorway, I thought who is this person, this man I live with, share my life with? If there was one thing I thought I could count on, if there was anything I knew, it was that if I was in trouble I could count on . . . I thought, if there's anything I can count on, it's that when I tell Sam . . ."

"Why must I always be perfect with you?" says Sam. He raises his large arms above his head and throws a pillow past me with all his might. Splat. The violent action of a loving man. The eyelet corner grazes me.

And belatedly, sadly, I look at Sam, my husband, the man I share my life with and see what I have done to him this day. I have blown in an evening what we built up slowly, carefully. I have approached his ex-wife's family with a mess, a humiliation, brought it to them to handle. But it was Sam I wanted to protect.

It is time for me to move forward, to reconcile, heal with words. In the crunch it was his welfare—I would have taken chances on myself—because I love him like my family. Whatever it is, I must make him understand it is because I love him like my family that I did this . . . I physically move toward him in the bed. The effort is so labored I feel the sheets wrinkle under me. I smile before I speak, so as better to arrange my tone as loving, healing.

But instead I say, "We wouldn't have had to ask free advice from Gary if we'd had enough money to consult a professional, if we hadn't spent all that money on . . ."

your crazy daughter?

No, the unsaid words hang against the air. I would have said the treatments that didn't work, all the things we were happy to try, the clinic in New Haven, the place in France . . . God knows. I would never begrudge . . .

crazy daughter against crazy Harry.

In the year I was bereft, he loved his children still. He loved them more than I loved my future.

Ugly, ugly, ugly. I didn't know I felt this way.

He knows enough not to answer. We reach for each other and touch, but we are afraid to move.

SUNDAY, MAY 30

Now it's on to Alex, lawyer, brother. My sister right or wrong, family forever. I am calm on the ride there, because with all my talk about turning friends into family, there are certain things no friend of mine will ever know. Certain pictures of blood and disgrace of body and soul that only my family and I share.

No, I am not calm. I remind Sam several times which exit to take. It cannot come soon enough.

I tell the story. I do not worry about inflection or vocabulary, because I am home. I mention Alex as a lawyer, but that is only because it is a weapon. He could be a bricklayer, and then he'd hurl his bricks. But it doesn't work. Edythe hurries into the kitchen to make coffee and the expected burst of gunpowder—the tanks of outraged male protection moving inexorably through the calm and graceful besieged medieval town—just never happens.

Instead, Alex says these commitment things are an ugly business. I am confused. He touches on the legal anomalies of fathers committing sons on drugs. And then, inexplicably, he too is back on the army. Alex, who learned to touch-type in his six months in the reserve, insists on telling Sam the story of his buddy in the next cot who was taken away and locked up for twelve hours by M.P.'s who turned out to be practical-joking buddies of his law-school classmates.

I must have missed the transition clause. Sam tries to keep the subject on me but finally he too brings out memories of being assigned the wrong gear in Basic. Then Alex tells Sam the story of one of his clients, a World War Two prisoner in a North African prison camp. The British had set up an intricate system of barter, which the captured Americans destroyed upon arrival. The Americans wanted everything immediately, said Alex's client, traded everything for chocolate and chocolate for anything.

"That so?" says Sam.

I sit confused. I'd expected to be pulling with all my might to stop my men from straining at the bit to pulverize a dying boy. Instead they twist and curve, they attend enthusiastically to everything invoked except the issue at hand, and I myself am the chorus of bloody Trojan women yelling kill, kill.

"You make a strong impression," says Alex.

Edythe urges me into the kitchen and inexplicably begins to show me her wedding gifts. Although her children are eleven and fifteen. She is talking about exchanging my mother's shower gift—the shower so many years ago, my mother so long dead. Does she suspect something? Is she trying to impress me with the solidity of the hearth, the financial underpinnings of the marriage vow? The horror of straying?

Now Edythe is telling me stories about going to the ballet at the New York State Theater, the garage under Vivian Beaumont, or the late buses that are not so late. Does she want me to accompany her to the ballet for cultural distractions?

She tells me she took the serving pieces my mother gave her to Hoffritz, exchanged them for a credit, with which she bought the assorted gifts she shows me now—oyster knives, cutting, paring, boning, shucking. She urges one on me, narrow and curving—oyster knife? Sliding it out of its sheath, I slice a flap off my index finger's cushion. Sylvia Plathsville? No, says Edythe, Japanese molybdenum. Where is her sense of humor?

When we come back into the room, Alex advises that I go away for a while, till it passes over.

And that is such crazy disconnected non-sequiturial stupid advice that I am shocked into fury.

"I can't," I cry out.

"Why not?" he says indulgently in his everything-is-possible-if-we-sit-down-calmly-and-work-it-out-together-little-sister   tone— the very tone I made Sam drive through two traffic-jammed highways to hear.

And it's such stupid advice on so many levels, I don't know where to begin. Go away where? To some motel under an assumed name as in *Psycho*, afraid to take a shower? Till *what* passes over? The film? Harry's intention to kill me? My crazy suspicions? Harry's time on earth?

"Once you're away, he'll forget about you," he says. "Really sick people have a lot on their minds. Look, people just say things."

My look at him stops his big brother memory smile on his face.

Shocked by the first fury of my life toward Alex, I defuse, recede. "I can't leave now, I have professional commitments," I say.

"Well what's your arrangement with the magazine?" Alex asks. He offers to send a messenger to my agent's office tomorrow, have a copy of my contract on his desk before ten. No? Am I sure?

Once out of sight, he'll forget about me. He has a lot on his mind, you're not that important.

I just want to go home. We say goodbye.

And even if I were to go away—there's Sam.

I can take care of myself.

In the car we are silent.

Oh, what is it with these men? Len with his White-Paper court-martials, Alex with his M.P. tales? Do they slide into army memories because it was in the army they were last forced to act like men? No, more complicated and various: The circling themes were army, false witness, prison—prison? Is that it? Sam, who would not drive the ten miles to see my play performed in a Connecticut penitentiary last summer? Who sat beside me at *One Flew over the Cuckoo's Nest* while on the screen Jack Nicholson stood talking by an open window instead of making his escape, and told me later he had to strain with all his will to stay put in his seat instead of running up the aisle and out the door?

I go home and think about usable power.

Suddenly, all I want is Harry.

Harry seems my only friend. He doesn't want to do anything theoretically to someone. We're not a nasty business or a tricky business or a matter of fathers and junky sons or Hershey bar currency or children he loved before me and after me. It is to *me*. Because of *me*. And against me.

So I must fight back myself. I think of usable and unusable power.

There is some element in all this that I cannot understand, and making lists has always been my stab at straight thinking.

Unusable power:

1. Mothers with children. Mothers can't say to children, "You're too clumsy, you don't move the way I want a child of mine to move." (Although parents do hint at it, it shocks me.)

2. Children with parents. Children cannot say as weapon, "I don't love you, Daddy"—it would cause too much pain to parents. It's too big a weapon.

3. Wives with husbands. They cannot invoke physical limitations. Wives can't say to husbands, "He got the job instead of you because he's bigger, or because your hand gets clammy."

4. Teachers with pupils. They can't say to pupils, "You are a strangely unattractive child and I am reluctant to touch you."

5. Pupils with teachers. They can't say to teachers, "Do not try to be our friend, it embarrasses us."

And looking over this, it is a ridiculous list on its own terms because people do and have and are, as we speak, doing and saying these very things. So this is not about unusable power, it is about tact.

"There is no weapon," says La Rochefoucauld, "against a man with no tact."

And an excess of tact is the defect of the privileged child, the child so loved, approved of at home and abroad that she carries her privilege with her, assuming the elements of grown-up life will fit into its image. The myopia of luck.

What they lack, these children of privilege, is the edge that unfairness gives. The no-matter-what-I-do-Mama-loves-sister-Toby-better syndrome. The bitterness, the rawness, the openness to what experience really is, comes from nothing left to lose. As opposed to the vested interest in the established order that belongs to the privileged child who knows that the way things are, everything is referring to her, increasing, getting better and better.

The way I used to feel.

My personal sense of unusable power:

I am afraid of retaliation, of making enemies in dodge ball, political argument, Monopoly. Enemies who will really get me. You leave me alone and I'll leave you.

Len says he never shot his gun in Korea. Most soldiers never shoot their guns. William Buckley worked on a study of why most artillery fire was so crazily far afield in Korea. He'll never understand.

Off war. I've caught it.

Back to me. In games—Ping-Pong, badminton, Monopoly—I'm afraid of slamming, snaking one into a corner, taking any kind of advantage. I learned to play Monopoly at twenty-one. I won't make a deal unless the other person agrees it's a fair deal. So he won't do me in later.

I thought all of this was about the power I have over Harry. Now it seems it is about the power he can use over me. That he will use. It is his generation—one historical beat younger than mine. The Ethical Culture–educated revolutionist/anarchist who will decapitate the board of regents with dynamite but hesitate over a beetle, break the foot of the wardrobe man because he insulted me on the first day . . .

What?

Fairness is based on luck and privilege. I said this already. On not rocking a boat whose speed suits you and whose course is working with the currents to speed you to your most desired and desirable destination.

Boats against the current?

Okay, for me, fairness is fear of retaliation.

But this is not about *me!*

When life flares through your bones *un*fairly, then it's all systems off. I try to reach to imagine the wild instants of such anarchy. It's easy. Squeezing my eyes shut, I am instantly back at moments when I thought my body would be peeling forever from Marilyn, my mother, my baby girl . . . Harry. Peeling away forever and forever from what gave it life, and so it would never come alive again.

I'm talking about the death of my own body.

And there my straight thinking will end. But let's stay on the board a moment, against a player no longer feeling lucky, ceasing to care, no tact, death sweeping through him, using all weapons, nothing left to lose.

The whole notion of unusable power is having the nuclear bomb but using foot soldiers instead because of a fail-safe mechanism that will bang right back on you.

What's my play?

"Control, control, now be smooth," called the coxswain over and over when my Princeton boyfriend rowed back and forth past me for a whole winter and spring on Lake Carnegie.

Ride with the times.

Close your notebook, move slowly over Sam, tips of breasts grazing his cheeks, his chest, his diaphragm, his belly, hold his balls in your mouth gently, softly, the softest covering delicate smooth like transparent velvet, softly, gently, lull him to sleep, holding him in your cheeks . . . with a sudden bite, crunch, could tear, destroy him, unusable power, ridiculous, dumb, such thoughts do *not* go through my mind.

control control now be smooth

Ride with the times.

SECTION TWENTY-ONE

NIGHT SHOOTING: LOTS OF SCENES OUT OF SEQUENCE

JUNE 1, 2, 3

The times are springlike. Heavy spring has broken through and we are shooting all night every night.

Sylvie is rushing. She wants to finish her scenes first so that she can leave for Israel when her new lover leaves. He is wide and ugly, with amazing light eyes.

It is clear she wants to be gone. We shoot all night, and in the predawn she puts on white canvas pants and a black turtleneck sweater and leaves with her light-eyed lover. Everyone else stays for runny eggs and sausages on the city streets. The caterers set up trestle tables with scuffed silver chafing dishes on Seventy-eighth and Columbus or Twenty-fourth and Tenth—wherever we are stopped, when the dirty daylight begins.

Sitting on the Columbus Avenue curb with the crew, powdery tortillas wrapped around our eggs, all streets seem lonely and I cannot believe I made so much of which street we picked. The streetlights are still on from the night. The crew, burly, gray, weary, looks ready to cry. Perhaps it is the occasional sound of a brisk step, someone in the distance about to start their normal day. We are eating, trying not to be too alert, not to speak too loud, preparing for a day of sleeping with the blinds drawn. There is an awareness that for Sylvie in her black and white the electric time comes when shooting is over. If the crew on the curb speak at all, it is with self-reproach. "I should have used the lantern, the other filter, the green dress."

"I should have insisted on that last reverse," says Harry. He is angry.

The scenes are being shot wildly out of sequence so that Sylvie can finish up. Phil is rewriting furiously, Barney is grim and curt.

New, brightly covered scripts are all around. Everyone has to find the next project, and at mealtimes, even between setups, everyone from the sound man to Sylvie reads and makes notes in the margin. The cold-bloodedness of it startles me. Now? While we're still here?

Sylvie's vermilion-colored script is titled *Serendipity Smith* and she laughs out loud while reading it.

Marie says, "When they have all left, Jessie, we shall have to have lunch, to console each other over the withdrawal."

So she too fears their leaving. But the minute I relax into the safety of friendship, I remember she doesn't have the facts. I fear their leaving, I fear their staying, I fear and envy their future projects. I fear the future, or lack of it. I fear everything.

JUNE 2

We do a series of scenes—inside, outside, don't stay too long in one place. Like con men, we keep moving so that no one on any one street gets too annoyed with our all-night presence.

We always seem interesting, at first. We're out on Broadway shooting a scene in a paperback bookstore. Children, couples holding hands stop and watch.

The scene is simple: Sylvie browses for a book, forgets it, leaves it at the cash register. The young girl clerk runs out and gives it to her. Sylvie, on impulse, embraces her.

Barney whispers to Sylvie. No one can hear. Sylvie takes the book from the clerk, whispers to Barney, she does it again, then retreats to her trailer. We're all used to this sense of exclusion, but it makes the crowd restless and annoyed. Why stay?

Sometimes I want to scream at the watchers, "Why do you stay? Leave! You must have some better life waiting for you!"

Because if they leave—maybe I will too.

On the other hand, I keep thinking someone will say to me, Do *you* have to stay, Jessie, all night? Every night?

What will I answer?

Once I took a walk, went from the honey wagon on a walk around Second Avenue. Two blocks away one could still see our trailers, but people were sitting on stoops, laughing. Children argued over stick ball, a man in an undershirt stroked the forearm of a dark-skinned woman. When I came back, Harry emerged from the shadows just out of the light.

"Where were you?" he said.

"I took a walk," I said. "I wanted air." Air? When we're shooting outside?

Am I not allowed to leave?

"I just wondered," he said.

JUNE 3

When we shoot on a residential street, the neighbors hang out of their windows and invite their friends and relatives over to watch,

217

as with the Fourth of July fireworks. They serve potato salad and cold cuts, position chairs at the window. Then we set the shot up endlessly, there's a short spurt of energy when we shoot it, and then it's over. Like buying a great nightgown for bad sex.

By the second night, the hosts themselves are wild with boredom and go on to bed. When they wake up in the morning, lean out of their windows half-shaved, you can see their scorn. Still there?

TWENTY-THIRD STREET

We do one shot hanging out the door on Twenty-third Street. Sylvie and two other girls saying goodbye to someone driving off. They stand in the doorway. "Goodbye, goodbye," say the other girls.

"Jesus Christ," says Sylvie.

They do that half the night, with Georgeann standing at the doorway for the first two hours while they set the shot. Harry's placed arc lights on scaffolding in the trees, and he mounts and remounts them to cast the shadows he wants on the street.

Then Rich shouts, "First team!" and Sylvie's brought in from her trailer to say, "Jesus Christ."

Next, she's supposed to come onto the street and bang her head against a lamppost. It's a special rubber lamppost, and when Georgeann bangs her head against it, it wobbles. The crew breaks up, and after a moment so do the onlookers.

The set decorators come and steady it. Georgeann comes out on cue, and it happens again. Now the spectators see us as bumbling incompetents. Fourteen-year-old boys on skateboards cackle meanly. Georgeann bangs her head again and again on the wobbly rubber.

The onlookers call jeering remarks they think are funny. At last, the post holds in place.

Sylvie comes out, bangs her head and it wobbles. Now the spectators start mocking chants, laughing wildly at each other's dumb remarks. The anger at us is startling. Like slaves rising, throwing our pistachio nuts back in our faces, as the apartment dwellers would have liked to do. They stopped their lives to watch us whisper to each other, mill around. We let them down.

Barney consults the crew and changes the shot. Instead of thumping her head, Sylvie just stands near the lamppost, shakes her head despairingly as if trying to rid it of its thoughts. She tells Barney she thinks it's a false gesture, but she does it. The cameras roll and we wrap for the night.

Seconds later—no one saw it start—Georgeann and Sylvie are careening down the street on commandeered skateboards. Where did Sylvie learn that? They're shrieking like adolescents in a shopping mall, doing half turns, jumping up, clumping down. Georgeann is the skilled one, she leads the way. They twirl and spin. Sylvie loses her balance, about to fall off, but she shrieks, rights herself, and keeps going. Barney covers his eyes. The crew watches, unsmiling. If Sylvie breaks an ankle, no amount of insurance will help.

Georgeann and Sylvie screech around the corner out of sight, then back, hop off the boards. They look very pleased with themselves, and they giggle and whisper. A closed corporation, as we said in high school.

Barney goes over to lecture.

I have no balance, high center of gravity, even roller skating is a trial.

Their wild best-girlfriend laughter floats back.

* * *

We all go home and sleep in the day. The chambermaids in the crummy crew hotel know about our schedule—my world does not.

"Up early?" ask friendly jogging neighbors as I stagger in.

"We're weathered," I say one morning in the fog when we had to stop early.

What?

I come to the set in the beginning of dark. There is a dusky feeling under my skin that everybody is about to collide.

For the moment it is held off, waiting. Something went wrong. I told my tale and nothing came lurching along after my words. It is why I write plays, good or bad, in bodies/actions. Something happens as a result of my words. People/actors move and speak. A girl in a pink dress moves three feet to the right of center stage and sits on a table.

And I understand Harry so well that when our eyes meet there seems no space between us. It is his eyes looking into his eyes or mine into mine.

Between setups, Sylvie sits on her camper steps giving interviews about the love of her public. "So I used to think, if they're pulling my sleeve, who am I anyway, some famous doctor? And then I think if they love me . . . it's for my work, then it's really me, right?" She looks up at me.

We spend some time together, Sylvie and I. She's wearing awful clothes I couldn't get away with, crinkled cottons that button under her throat, and eating everything in sight with her fingers, covered with grease, long fingers, not wiping them, though not staining the clothes I would never have thought of wearing. Men come over to join us on one pretext or another and do not look at me. I seem to have accepted all these things and to have decided she is smart.

"People don't think I'm smart," she says to me often, and we smile.

Then she praises my eyes behind my glasses.

That's the trade—pretty for smart.

She likes to tell interviewers the story of camping on the doorstep of the casting director who thought she was wrong for the part that was her breakthrough. She remembers this as the great unfair event of modern times—up there with the massacre of Smyrna—when she wasn't a star, when no one gave her parts, treated her like a star.

Pale-faced, bony, smaller in person than expected, why does everybody recognize her on the street?

We are always in a milieu, never alone. Gus, cauliflower ears with the multi pots of brown-toned creams, Florian, back-combing with natural bristles, Lorraine, the petit point groupie making Sylvie a Confederate flag pillow, the short Glen Campbell's mother, the union hairdresser assigned to sit there who offers to do my hair and whom I refuse. It's Florian or no one, I think as the topic of conversation is Sylvie's going onstage again.

The waves of love/hate she felt from live audiences terrified her, and the subject's come up because the new small theater at Lincoln Center has offered us—me and Sylvie—a workshop to develop a play and launch their season.

One can see their reasoning. My small oeuvre, all six plays, is called "fierce and uncompromising," Sylvie flickers on a giant screen. "Clash and flash"—a midcult entrepreneurial winner to launch their subscription series. Should Sylvie be flattered? Should I?

The electronic-press crew arrives, electronic journalists whose mandate is to generate interviews and little on-the-set vignettes, footage for "later," which the studio can then put into an electronic kit to send to all the networks, hoping they'll air it for free promotion to push the film. A little hairless girl in a black turban and jeans who looks like Madonna and a young, very hairy man wander the set shoving the microphone in people's faces, hoping for a poignant clip. They ask people what they think of the movie, why are they doing it? They ask Sylvie.

And what her answers make clear to me is that *Daughters and Sisters* was only the barest excuse for what Sylvie's wanted. Because it's the heroine's ordinary life she longed to play, not her wild flashes of extravagant, fantastic historical memory.

But the fact is, it is a book about loneliness, funny, no glamour—you can't escape memory, about memory and desire . . .

And that's why Barney wants to do it, he says to the hairless Madonna, who is eating french fries while they talk—"So I'll have zits," she says, off mike. "Politics suck," says Barney. "Even in the womb, you're a prisoner of your past and the memories of the world."

The book connects the heroine to history, both political and erotic. Sylvie wants each encounter to be true love—full of motivation—when in fact, as Marie wrote them, they were little more than random. "I wouldn't do it if I didn't care about them," she explains earnestly to the electronic-press-kit mikes—which, added to her preference that the men be unreal except in their devotion to her, is turning it into a feminist-style primer on how to find your true man. I have a brief sympathetic flash for what it's like to be Barney in their huddled discussions.

Does Sylvie protest too much? *McCall's* and *Glamour* have articles about how she goes from one man to another—not the *Enquirer*, thank you, but *McCall's* and *Glamour*.

The *Serendipity Smith* script is Nancy Drew with kinetic powers who has adventures—a female Indiana Jones—lots of locations, hanging off rooftops in Peru, Chichén Itzá, Bali, and Singapore, lots of money.

As usual, our conversation is oblique and en famille.

"It's scary," she says. "I'll say it out loud. I'm scared."

"Not if you plan," says Georgeann. "I have a steel cord around me attaching me to the building, we do an insert of your reaction shot."

"It's immoral the amount of money they're offering me," she says.

"You're worth it, my darling," says Florian, who wants to go to Peru with his new wife and her tiny daughter, Gillian, whom he adores. Gus will bring gels and terra cotta creams good for tropical climates. He remembers from being stationed in Guam—look ruddy but stay moist is the trick.

The money they are offering her would pay for Petra in perpetuity, keep an as-yet-unconceived child in Brearley plaid for good, a trip to Paris anytime for me and Sam.

Note: Under any kind of stress, I have developed the habit of sticking out my lower jaw to separate my teeth. This came from my bad year, when I damaged a nerve in my gums by grinding my teeth in the night. Sylvie sticks out her jaw in the same way.

When I'm about to say something I'd rather not, I jam my fist in front of my lips to physically monitor the impulse, so that no words make it through that aren't a conscious decision.

She does this too. On camera. She does both of these things on camera.

Are we more alike than I thought? Then I see her using my cadences—long sentences, asides—and realize she's patterning a character on my mannerisms.

I mention the speech patterns to Sylvie in an offhand professional way—it doesn't fit the dialogue of the *Daughters and Sisters* script, I say. I explain how in my own plays, I change the diction consciously, so that I don't end up unconsciously making all my characters speak alike.

She catches on and stops using the diction, but what am I to do with the fist and the jaw? I try to consider it homage.

Once, in a stand-in shot, Georgeann puts her fist in front of her mouth, aping Sylvie who aped me.

Will Georgeann copy Sylvie copying me—a Xerox copy of a dim gesture of mine going on and on and on?

FRIDAY

Sylvie's agent appears. Sylvie's turned down *Serendipity,* and they called back with "meaningful gross participation" money. She shrugs—glitter and be gay—"They keep giving me more."

"So she'll really do your play, then?" asks my agent. I hang up. Will *I*? is the question.

Can I?

It would force me to finish the play in the drawer—have a real audience, not the dear, hopeful one on West Forty-second Street whom I don't want to let down, and who'll think I'm serious and promising till I rot.

I'm not at all sure I want to commit. I refuse to be committed.

Wrong. No one tries to pin me down.

Again our conversations are a juxtapositional chorus.

"If I do *Serendipity*, turn down a serious play, how could I face someone like Marie?" she says. Marie, the arbiter of serious things? I briefly sketch out the mass dimensions of Marie's ambitions.

"But a live audience?" says Sylvie.

Florian's wife says Florian only married her to be near tiny Gillian, with whom he fell in love. The truth.

Sylvie says, "I'll be so exposed."

Gus shows her where he's marked tropical moisturizers in catalogs.

Georgeann says, "That's what planning's all about. There's a steel cable attaching me to the building, and the worst that could happen is it loosens and I slap against the building, get a little black and blue."

Sylvie says, "Georgie, love, you can't do stunts forever or one day you'll buy the farm. Look what happened on that first day at Cinema I."

"It shouldn't have," says Georgeann, "it was all planned. You just concentrate and blot everything else out."

"Hear that, Jessie?" says Sylvie.

I know it's a jibe.

She means, Concentrate, finish your play, girl.

I try describing it to Sam at home—Georgeann with her concentration, Sylvie with her soul, Georgeann with her cords against the building, petit-pointing confederate groupie, cauliflower ears with the beige creams, Florian and his natural-bristle teasing combs and nymphet romance, me with my block and my integrity, Sylvie with her gross points, the groupie with her petit point . . . I build and enlarge for extravagant humor, but he doesn't laugh, just says, "You've always been interested in her."

FUNNY BREAKFAST SCENE, TAKE ONE

At 2 A.M. one morning, on a soundstage on West Fifty-ninth Street, almost at the river, they set up the funny breakfast scene.

There is one small elevator, manned by a young black man named F.J. The first night, he opens the wire cage and says, "My name is F.J. and there's only me. If you ring twice or three times, you're only gonna get me and I'm not gonna come any faster than I come."

It so daunts the crew that once they're upstairs, no one goes down for breaks.

The windows are lit from outside through fake waving translucent ferns, so early-morning light will seem to be shining through.

The only way to fit it in on the schedule. It was a risk on Harry's part—he swore he'd get the matching morning light, and though his crew's been working golden time for days, he did.

The scene takes place the morning after Sylvie has gotten out of a new man's bed. Marshall, to be exact—lusty, gray-bearded, cafeteria intellectual. She comes out of his bedroom for breakfast and there at his kitchen table are his sixty-five-year-old twin sisters, his ninety-year-old arthritic aunt, his deaf father in a wheelchair. It is a parody of Tom Jones eating-into-sex, in reverse. Sex into food with your new lover's ancient relatives, who ignore you, shout at each other, eat off his plate, and finally off yours. They intend to intercut with footage of the preceding night's sex—a kind of joining of the

226

sex scene in *Don't Look Now* and *Tom Jones*, everybody tells me. Nobody seems troubled by the fact the sex scene this presumably follows has not yet been shot.

The family comes, straight from wardrobe, and is seated around the table. It's hard to believe they've ever met before, much less eaten together.

Rich spends a lot of time arranging the food on the plates—who's eaten how much of the eggs. "Now eat the bread, you take the jam, the whitefish . . ." says Rich. He puts them through it, and the continuity girl takes notes—but it isolates them even further. Barney seems indifferent to changing the ambience.

When Sylvie comes, it's worse. Their awareness of her is ferocious and paralyzing. They don't talk as if she's not there, they shout over her with deference. They eat food off her plate, not with absolute indifference to her presence but with show-off bravado. And when she speaks, they can't stop themselves from missing a beat.

It isn't working.

Barney whispers to them, explains. Nothing improves. It's three-thirty, coming close to four, we'll be fighting the dawn—and then the lighting will have to change.

Harry is slumped against a wall. Two days and nights of no sleep, borrowing lights from another production in town, planning, matching . . . his crew is grim. They did it all for him.

The smoked fish is smelling too fishy, salty and gross. But finally they're a group of old actors in it together and gradually it changes. No, Sylvie changes it.

She whispers a suggestion: one of the ancient twins throws food to the other, skimming by Sylvie, and it starts to work. Sylvie is, I remember, first a comedienne. She flicks out her tongue, tastes the herring and sour cream on her chin in bewildered response. It gets wilder and reverse bawdier. It's very, very funny. What's wry in the book is slapstick dirty here.

They spin off ideas—"like we could use this when he's on top," says Sylvie gleefully, and the deaf father spills orange juice over her. "He's moving over me now," she says—his aged aunt with the moustache spears her whitefish and so on. Marshall, her past lover-to-be, gets into it. He's lewd and funny, and looks—ugly as he is—as if he'll be a real woman lover in bed. Fat men often are.

They are giggling and planning all kinds of routines, both for the breakfast and for the sex when Marshall and Sylvie shoot it. And when they wrap, Sylvie comes downstairs with us in F.J.'s packed elevator, stays in the dawn to eat breakfast tortillas on the curb.

I tell her the first time I saw her onstage—her first small appearance—I got a lump in my throat that didn't disappear till her small part was over and she was gone.

Sylvie's light-eyed lover appears on schedule. She urges him to join us, but he disappears, and she leaves soon after.

THE NIGHT AFTER THE FUNNY BREAKFAST.
SCENE: THE NEXT AFTERNOON AT THE SAME TABLE.

Sylvie comes in strained, having neither slept nor gone over her lines. She keeps blowing them.

She's supposed to be bursting in just before sundown to bring them the four hundred memorial candles the family lights every Yom Kippur for their friends and relatives who died in the camps. The local grocery has been bought by a supermarket chain that doesn't stock them. Sylvie, the heroine, has found a way to bring them, and she bursts in, explaining:

"There's a factory in Paramus, I got off the bus, hitched a ride to get back here before sundown." She's supposed to say it in a rush. The lighting is complicated. The electricians are making the sun go down as she speaks.

The lights start going down. Sylvie says, "There's a Paramus in factory, I got off the ride, hitched a bus . . ." She says, "There's a factory in Paramus, I got off the bus, hitched a ride to get back here before sunrise shit shit shit . . ."

The actors try to help her. They tell her stories of the times it happened to them. The crew starts the lights in progression again. She tries it again. Nothing helps.

The lighting crew begins to mutter under their breath. It is four in the morning and they've done five sunsets already.

Harry naps under the table, and coughs when someone wakes him.

Phil changes the lines. "Look, I came all the way back from Paramus, hitched a ride to get back before the sun went down."

Ruth, the serious actress from the other day, arrives. The dailies of her scene will be shown at the 4 A.M. lunch break.

Phil suggests an improv. He's been defensive about his lines and out of joint since everyone praised the Ruth improv in my apartment.

Sylvie brings the candles, begins to put them on the table out of the paper bag, and everyone improvises their reactions. "So what's that?" is the first line. It's supposed to move from surprise to relief. They try some improvised lines, and Sylvie runs out of the frame. She comes back in, apologizes, and they start from the beginning.

She brings the paper bag of candles, the improvisation starts and she simply stares at them. She shakes her head in apology and they run through it again.

The third time, she hurls the candles to the floor, says, "Fuck you, so don't light them," and bursts into tears.

Barney rubs his chin and exchanges glances with Willa, the set decorator, in a knitted tank top (soft but not angora), who gets more candles. She exchanges looks with Margaret, the continuity girl. The dolly operator looks over at the focus puller. The actors look down at their plates—humble pros.

But Sylvie was right. They hate her. Because she kept blowing her lines, they lost their close-ups. They were each supposed to get a two-shot, a shot of only two people in the frame. And a one-shot, only one character in the frame. (The frame and then the screen all to yourself, in other words.) Some of the scheduled two-shots were: the twin sisters saying to each other in Yiddish, "What did the little tramp do?"; the father and Marshall, the lover, having a man to man about what she did in bed. The arthritic aunt was going to force herself to thank her, a one-shot all to herself as she struggled to get the words out. Then all the others were going to get close-up one-shots reacting one at a time to the action—i.e., Sylvie running in, her speech, the candles on the table, etc. All gone.

Sylvie is right to run out. The improv showed up hatred. I saw the face of the father in the wheelchair. Anyhow, Barney explained to me, their close-ups would have been only an option for the editor, might not be used in any case. A question of priorities. If they weren't rushing . . . but they don't have all the time in the world. It's the 4 A.M. lunch break, and then they've got to move on.

They reassemble, and Sylvie gets the lines stiff but right. They do an insurance shot of the back of her head. They'll have the option of looping her lines.

The "family" changes their clothes and doesn't stay for 4 A.M. lunch.

I'm glad to see Ruth. She's a presence of such calm. Sylvie urges the electronic-press-kit duo to talk to Ruth, but all they want to know is what it's like to work with Sylvie and what Sylvie was like in class.

Ruth takes it with cheer and sanity. "An opportunity to work with Sylvie, a role that means something to me. I read the book."

The dailies are being shown at 4 A.M. because, on our schedule, they're backing up. We take sandwiches inside. Ruth sits by herself, and I leave her alone. First there are several versions (takes) of Ruth and Sylvie sitting on the makeshift couch in my dining room as Ruth does her monologue. A two-shot, as they say.

Then there is a series of takes of close-ups of Sylvie reacting to Ruth's monologue as Ruth says the lines off camera. Ruth's off-camera reading is full out, as moving as when she's on camera, giving Sylvie full chance to respond to the passion and timbre of her performance.

Actually, this is the first time I've ever heard an off-camera reading like that in dailies. Most of the dramatic speeches are Sylvie's, and when she's done her lines off camera—so the actor in close-up can react on cue—her readings have tended to be flat and automatic. And then, too, she more often than not leaves after her own close-ups, leaving the script girl to read her lines to the reacting actor in a nasal monotone. I never realized what ungenerous behavior this is till I see the reverse—Ruth doing her monologue off camera as fully as if she's on-screen, giving Sylvie the tools to respond with nuance and precision. Which she does.

And then we're on to the establishing shots of the brownstone exterior, and I must have been concentrating on my sandwich, missed the more exciting parts of Ruth's performance I remembered from that day.

I didn't realize at the time, or probably didn't understand, that they never shot a take of a close-up of Ruth talking, a one-shot of only her, talking. They also never shot her all alone just reacting. She's just in the two-shot with Sylvie, which they already showed at the beginning.

I join up with Ruth outside, tell her she was truly fine, then share my theory that the reason Sylvie blew her lines all night was that her controlling Israeli lover enjoyed consoling her when she was unhappy, didn't like it when she had too good a good time, so kept her up all day . . .

"Doesn't that make sense?" I ask, and she begins to rage. "I brought up so much stuff," she says, "so many years of stuff I didn't even know was there . . . I brought it up . . . and you can't even see it."

"You don't even see my tears," she says, beginning to weep. "The light is on Sylvie's shoulder, my eyes are dark, you can't see anything."

"It was probably stupid to shoot it in my dining room," I say.

"No, what's stupid is to have a D.P. who doesn't know what he's doing," Ruth says bitterly. "Sylvie specifically spoke to him, but that space cadet was probably off on crack somewhere. You know, once he shot Sylvie in the *dark*? Why didn't they spend a little more and hire a real pro?"

My words tumble urgently, hotly. "He's the best, the *best*. He shot her in the dark because she had a goddamn pimple, did she tell you that?" and my voice stays hot and angry and Harry hears.

I realize he's close to us, close enough to hear. He looks at me. Oh what a long look.

We used to kiss a lot, kiss and kiss until I felt my heart stop.

Ruth swerves off. She's through with me.

Harry touches my shoulder with his finger and he's gone. The rest of the day I am aware of my shoulder the way you are aware of your forearm when you've had a vaccination. Everyone pushes, pulls, touches it, my shoulder bag bruises it.

DAY LATER

They offer her perks, script approval, things she's never been able to get. They say only for her.

"Look, Jessie," she says, "I could do it the way you take a magazine assignment like this. You know, for fun."

Fun?

She calls at Harry by the camera. "You're passing up the chance of a lifetime, you know. Chichén Itzá, Bali, Singapore—we can go around the fucking world together!"

"Best cameraman I ever worked with," she says to me. "Only one who ever understood my face."

"He's doing his own film," I say sharply.

"So let him do it next year, then. His price will be higher."

"And then we'll do your play, Jessie?"

He looks over at me. Making plans, Jessie?

My phone rings late at night.

There are a lot of pick-up shots. Trance, the comedian, comes by and does a small dialogue scene with Sylvie in the exercise room of a neighborhood health club.

The whole crew is on the verge of collapse, and the manager has opened the steam room for Sylvie at four-thirty in the morning. She invites all the women inside. Stephanie bursts in, newly back from California, got what she needed to accomplish done in record time. Everyone greets her, hugs her naked.

"I missed you guys," she says, and I wonder if this means Harry, too. I feel as if a lifetime has passed, and am glad we're not alone.

The women come in wrapped in towels, which they drop, just to sit on. The puffs of steam drift around, one sees one woman's breast, another's thigh . . . most men I know would ache to be in here.

There is offhand talking about boyfriends, low-voiced conversations in twos and threes.

"I may have to go to bed with him this weekend, it's been three dinners," says one of the production secretaries. "But I really don't feel like it."

"Don't do it," the room of women suddenly choruses.

"No?" she says. And something in her tone gives me a brief flash of sympathy for the unknown young man whose weekend has just been destroyed. Because I think she wanted to.

The steam goes by and one sees a part of one woman, of another, but now we're a group, together.

Sylvie says, "You know, Jessie, this fog makes me think I could run through the fog after Trance—you know like Scarlett after Rhett in *Gone With the Wind*. You know, like he's the one guy she loves but she doesn't know it till it's too late." She is still lobbying not to have to do a sex scene with him. "So Trance could be the one man she *won't* sleep with, got it, because he's really the one."

She thinks it could be great, like Rhett in *Gone With the Wind*. Trance must truly make her skin crawl.

The conversation switches to *Fatal Attraction*—a man's movie about women. Most of the women hated it. Yes, they'd do a lot, but not that!

A puff of steam reveals a slippery hip. "I went through a guy's garbage once, when we broke up," says an unidentified voice.

Another girl said she hung around on street corners, waiting to bump into him by accident.

Stephanie said her last boyfriend's old girlfriend used to call him in the night and plead for him to take her back. "I'd hear her screaming through the phone, and I'd think, That's gonna be meee." Stephanie? Does she mean Harry? Harry's girl before her? I cannot ask.

Willa of the angora says, "My old boyfriend told me how when he broke up with his last girl she lay down on the floor in front of him and howled, and when he broke up with me I almost didn't hear him, I was just thinking, Don't lie down on the floor, don't lie down on the floor. Like I never would have thought of it otherwise, you know?"

"I taped something on my phone saying DON'T CALL KEVIN," offers one girl.

It's clearly a great hint—up there with colorless nail polish to stop runs in panty hose.

"On the receiver or over the dial tone?" asks someone.

Georgeann keeps her towel on—her chest is faintly blotched. A heated gel blew up in one of her stunts on a previous film—the signs are almost gone. She looks around from person to person.

And then it's my voice speaking, cool, intellectual. "Listen to us— a guy leaves and we're scared we'll hang on, make fools of ourselves, but not that we'll boil a pet rabbit or kill a wife. That's just out of movies about women written by men."

"I see it as the opposite," an older woman's voice says suddenly. "Remember Bertram Pugash—threw acid at his fiancée?" She's the auditor from the office. Her breasts are hanging low.

"Bonnie Garland?" says the Madonna electronic-press girl. She's around all the time now, like one of the crew, like me. "I was at Yale with her. She was a sweet girl. She just wanted to break up with him."

"It's always somebody's ex-fiancé . . . the car goes up on the lawn, they burn down her brother's house." Everyone has a story.

"There was a Phil Donahue show on it," says the Madonna girl. "This guy says he used to follow this girl from work, he now realized she never really encouraged him, but finally she had to *move*. So there's this whole show about guys like this and how they're feeling now, and they're all saying, 'It must have been hard to be obsessed like that'—and I'm home all alone, and I'm yelling at the TV—hey, but what about that girl who had to *move?*"

"No," says one of the wardrobe assistants. There's a voice like this in every steam room. "Every man I've ever been serious with still has the highest regard for me, I can't imagine it any other way."

She's ignored.

Georgeann, next to me, starts to shiver in her towel. The steam is starting to die down and it's getting chilly.

"Do you ever feel that any man you've slept with thinks it's out of the natural order for you to leave?" I ask quickly. "I mean, he can do as he pleases, but once you've been with him, that you have no real right to leave?"

"Only every guy I ever knew," says Sylvie.

The puffs of steam start settling toward the floor. We need to leave so they can prepare the room for the real members. We gather our towels.

The women are shivering. But I haven't finished yet.

"Do you ever think an ex-lover wants to get you? When you pick up the phone and no one's there, do you think just for a second, maybe it's *him*?"

The puffs of steam settle to the bottom valves leaving some valleys of light as the women leave.

"Yes," says the first to go. "Yes," says the second, "yeah, yeah," says another as they file out. Yes, yes . . . Their eyes are flat.

The steam's been turned off. The lights go on and I'm alone on a white bench that's slick with sweat.

As the days go on we are rushing rushing rushing. They're trying to arrange the board so that Sylvie doesn't have to do two sex scenes back to back—Marshall and Trance—but it may be the only time available.

Marshall, the fat cafeteria lover, is on call every night because if possible, they'll slip his scene in if we finish early. He's making his way through lots of the women. The rest of the crew, the big blond dolly operator and the ex-football focus puller, marvel. "He's the one shtupping all the girls," they say.

Sylvie and I talk about him and agree. He's like the fat boy in the washroom grown up. He'll make any woman in his bed feel generous and terrific. He tries with everyone. Fat and red-faced, but whose eyes light up with wonder. "Oh Jess," he says, "you wanna do it?" and kisses me on the lips.

Sylvie says she likes the transportation captain, bearded and wild-eyed, who used to live in France, who told us both he could stay hard for a very long time, it's why the French girls liked him. Hmmm.

Girl talk.

"He's married," says Georgeann, her face a prune of disapproval. She's just come back with fresh pasta for the caterer to make for Sylvie's lunch.

"We were just kidding," says Sylvie. "Yeah, I guess it's not a funny joke. You know, Georgie, I think it's getting time for you to scare the world again, hang off buildings, jump off cars. . . .

"You have a talent," says Sylvie, "you should use it."

Jugular village.

Don't *tell* me it's not me she's needling. A talent? Hanging off a building? Being slapped by people? It's a slap at me.

How long since you wrote your last play, Jessie?

She is smart.

I feel everybody is watching me, though Florian is back-combing and Lorraine is pulling thread with her teeth and Ed is screwing lids on eye pots . . .

"I thought you said I should stop," says Georgeann. "I thought you said it was too dangerous."

"What am I, your agent?" Sylvie snaps.

We all pause. We know this tone.

"I wish I had ten percent of me, for God's sake."

She's off on her agent, who wants her to do *Serendipity* so he can get a sauna set up on his Bel Air ranch. A star turn.

Then it's over, she remembers the pasta.

"The refrig, Georgie, the *refrig,*" she says, and Georgeann goes off to refrigerate the fresh pasta and I'm off the hook for now.

"I have more fights with her than with a lover," says Sylvie, and she imitates a famous actor who was her first lover. "He told me he needed me," she says, "and I was so impressed. Then I found out they all say that."

We start to laugh and laugh and laugh. She says, "Sometimes I can talk to people I hate their guts and they never know it." Charming.

* * *

239

We are shifting time now, starting earlier in the day, shooting day into night.

One last push. Almost over.

In the dusky light as, one by one, the people on the set do the last of each thing—the last action scene, the last interior—each person wrenches away from the last of his job in an agony of self-reproach.

"Shit, I should have relit that scene, used an African screen instead of the Japanese one, should have used the other solution on the processing, taken more stills when the bridge was up, used another dolly, run another cable, moved the Mack and John scene into the front room where the shadow was softer."

They will hang like a burr on anyone around, and out it all comes. And this from these same self-promoters, these carriers of plastic-covered Xerox copies of every word of praise ever received for any work whenever done.

All food restraints are by the boards. The Crafts Services food table is a jumble. The Oreos are the first to go. Even those who supped on yogurt cups now grab a fistful—Oreos smeared with cream cheese, peanut butter, people mainline Oreos in clumps of six.

TUESDAY

We see the sex dailies. Sylvie with two different men. They've been saved to screen at the same time. Not many people are allowed in. Sylvie sits between Harry and Jeb, the editor, Barney is behind leaning forward. I sit in the back so as not to be noticed. Sylvie gives them notes. Very matter-of-fact. Calls them back to the script girl behind her, "Make sure you use Take Three, I like my eyes better. Is there an edit point around the nipples?" The tinkly music plays. Someone has edited out the groans.

The young brat-pack star who's the bad kisser is there. When their scenes come on, someone makes room for him and he sits next to Sylvie. Their heads are huddled.

Sylvie is on top. "I like the sheet falling away here," says Sylvie. "Can you see my panties?" Yes, you can. It's a close shot of her rising thigh, and there, like a lacy mountain ridge at the bottom of her flesh, is the wisp of panties. She laughs. The young man who kissed badly says something in her ear.

I try to think what the phrase ex-lover really means. Does it mean someone who has loved and loves no more?

Sylvie whispers to the bad kisser, says something to Barney. She dictates something flung over her shoulder to the production secretary behind her, too low for me to hear, and they laugh and laugh. All of them laugh.

Do I care? Yes I care.

Harry disappears as soon as the lights go up. I walk out next to Makeup, Wardrobe, and Lighting, all of whom, as usual at dailies, are scowling.

Today I assume it is because they are as embarrassed as I by the soft-core aspects of this professional enterprise. We stop at a log jam near the door and I say to a man in the art department—just to put him at his ease—"I finally figured out dailies are about what everybody did wrong."

"You're talking about the pink stone behind her head," he says instantly. "Believe me, if I'd had any warning they were going to sit her there, I could have replaced it with a gray one."

LATER THAT DAY

It is hot and humid and some of the crew got dizzy from the heat and no sleep and insufficient salt in the food, so they're sending around Gatorade in plastic cups—like Jim Jones did in Guyana; it goes around and everyone gulps it down unthinkingly.

Harry gulps it down with his pills. There's no time to do anything privately.

"Damn, damn," he says, "I should've checked." It seems the wisp of panties was his domain.

"It's no big deal," I say. "You can't do everything."

"I should have *checked!*" he snaps.

The *Serendipity* folks have come back to Sylvie with money and terms, a new wing on her house to save taxes.

Hair, Makeup, and Wardrobe crowd me, take my chair, so I'm literally backed up against the wall in her trailer. And Sylvie has stopped saying, "Hey, get a chair for Jessie." So why am I here?

Georgeann sits folded under herself on the floor in triple-jointed ease, reading *Falling for Stars*, the stuntman's publication.

She's listing the *Serendipity* stunts in a spiral notebook.

"It's when a stunt looks easy, watch out," she says.

"The script's a piece of shit," says Sylvie, "but we can do interesting things with it."

I've switched to tinted glasses because my eyes are tired and we move constantly from glare to dusk, but I'm always shoving them on top of my head, the better to see the true colors.

When I pull the sunglasses down, more often than not, my hair catches in them and I yank and yank till the glasses come away with small tufts snarled inside the screws. I have hair to spare. It happens.

I see Wardrobe bring Sylvie sunglasses after sunglasses in the same style. She puts them on top of her head and pulls them down, but her hair, which is silky as mine is snarled, slides through. They loosen the screws and the lenses fall out. I watch it from afar. Sylvie seems determined not to give it up.

They try frame after frame, finally settle for a variation on the kind I wear, and open the screws slightly. Her hair sticks—not as wildly as mine, but little wisps do stick up.

After the scene is shot, I see the prop glasses lying on a table. They're almost identical to mine, but maybe the frames will be sturdier. I pick them up, try them on.

"Hey, Jessie, they look nice on you," someone says.

Sylvie looks over.

"Somebody wants to be an actress?" she says. "Eve Harrington?" I don't understand at first.

The mouse in *All About Eve*. My blood boils in black little bubbles.

Everyone is crazy.

Extras are assembling from all over for the finale, which is out of sequence, actors coming in to reprise in dreams scenes they haven't yet shot. Rich is screaming at people, yelling at elderly extras who want to go to the bathroom.

"Yeah, they go and they never come back," he says. Because of the reprise of the concentration camp fantasies, there are lots of old extras.

Ruth, Trance, the first young lover, Jean-Claude, whose erection I saw—they all come back for fittings. The logistics planning of meals is huge, and there are shouted commands and Wardrobe is going crazy. Ginny, the costume designer, is stung by a bee through the Bedouin black she wears to avoid such eventualities—she's allergic and flat on her back.

Harry is staying, leaving, going off, dropping his arm around electronic Madonna, watching me, waiting, everyone waiting on me.

She'll turn down this money, this new wing on her house, she'll count on me to write her play, suppose I'm dead?

We're all exhausted from not enough sleep.

She's been talking to her agent.

"Let's cut to the chase," she says.

Her agent's phrase.

"I can always come back and do it next year when and if you're ready."

When and if. It seems it's all arranged, discounted . . . I'll get over my block, do magazine articles while she makes a fortune in Peru with Florian, Gus, and Georgie . . .

Something for everyone.

I have a screaming fight with Sylvie.

"You'll never guess what I figured out, Jessie," she tells me. "Our Marie's not a survivor child after all. Her mother is still alive, living here in Kew Gardens. I saw her at the synagogue."

"That's what a survivor child is," I snap.

She looks startled. It was I who cued her to mock Marie.

"A survivor child is the child of someone who was in the camps."
I start out reasonably enough, then my voice rises again, louder, "It
wasn't enough her mother was in the camps, she has to die, too?"

"Besides," I say cruelly, "if you go ahead I can't wait for you for
a year for the play. It's about a woman in peak childbearing years."

ALMOST DONE

The Production Designer doesn't want turquoise on the extras,
though almost every extra seems to have either a turquoise pullover
or a scarf. Turquoise is not for memory, he says—so all vestiges of
turquoise are being yanked off, and precious expensive time is being
wasted. Ginny is as furious as Willa was the day we changed the
carts.

We're over on Tenth Avenue in a cavernous soundstage with an
outside compound. Sometimes the extras will be outside in gossamer
clothes, sometimes inside with no circulating air in their heavy
striped concentration camp uniforms. Often they're given their numbers and called from inside to outside just to block out the numbers
of bodies that will be needed for a shot.

"I'm cold," they whimper, for the 3 A.M. night air is cold.

"At least let them go to the bathroom," I mutter. No one does.

Next Thursday it will all be over. Anything can happen.

Sparks are zigzagging around in my skin.

Everyone is jammed together by exhaustion, the necessity of using
every second to try the filter, match the master, use every second

before it's too fucking late. The boom man, husky, phlegmatic, holds his towering pole with the mike on one end, runs behind a departing taxi, to get the sound of gravel crunching. He trips, gasps, recovers, comes back covered with sweat; the crackling of the sweat on the mike, his gasp will mix with the crunch of gravel. He begs for one more chance. "Please for God's sake just one more," and no eyes meet, afraid to trip, lose stride—all eyes are wild and fixed on different sparrows in a disappearing flock.

I feel Harry's presence everywhere, behind me, at my side, above my head, swinging on a movie crane, but in the darkness we don't exchange a word. I cannot tell, in the darkness, where his eyes are looking.

And then it happens. The event that makes us coincide, you and me and the public, that relieves me of the responsibility to select and reveal. Because you can, of course, read about it in the paper.

SECTION TWENTY-THREE

I am approaching the set. It is June 15, and as with the first day of keeping a diary, I will always remember everything I am wearing this day, a green-and-white-striped tank top, an off-white canvas wraparound skirt, Italian sandals. When I swing off the bus, I think there has been a street accident. My next thought is that they're shooting Buzzing Activity and for once Barney's caught it. Then I see the network camera crews, police cars, strangers.

As I try to get in, a big policeman—black leather belt as wide as a brick wall—says, "No," and blocks me, really blocks me. Then he steps back, not to let me through, but to let past us three policemen carrying a large heavy dark green plastic bag, tied at the top like a Baggie, sagging in the middle. And though memories now coincide, it was, in fact, several hours before I put together those particular facts—inside that dark green plastic oversize Baggie is the body of Sylvie.

She'd been found in the early hours of the morning in her trailer, hacked, slashed, her white pants crusting with blood, throat torn, deep wounds in her stomach and thighs, hair pulled out in clumps from her scalp, hacked, slashed till she was dead and then some.

She has been dead at least ten hours.

SECTION TWENTY-FOUR

All familiar faces are stricken, all stricken faces are familiar. The stricken faces of people on the set are a community, allied, and perceived as the "other" by all the strangers.

We need to talk, recoup, explain in private. We need to sit down with Margaret, the continuity girl, and be told exactly what we were wearing, what we were doing, what words we were using when everything paused as usual at the end of yesterday. We need to take up exactly where we were then, so we can be together like a family that has suffered a disaster. Oh, go away.

But everyone comes. The police, the cameras, the reporters, the microphones, the rolling media lights, and the phone calls to me.

Everyone believes me now. Alex calls me, Sam appears briefly, Len calls. Everything held in abeyance is ready to lurch forward and be the large-ended wedge of my life's action. But no, stay away. I want no wrong-man scenario. This wasn't Harry. This was not Harry. I am adamant until I am believed. Leave me alone.

Once our eyes flicker over each other, Harry's and mine. Then flicker away.

If war is mud and shit and noise, then celebrity murder is lights in your eyes, hoarse commands yelled out in media jargon, and people falling into step beside you as you head out for a grilled cheese sandwich, slipping onto the next stool, trying to slip casually into a conversation that is fraught with things you don't want to talk about. So you sit there shoving greasy cheese through your sealed lips, because in times of crisis, regular habits and protein help, chewing endlessly and blurting noncommittal words.

The world is clearly divided now between we who are part of this, who were here before and remain, and the others, who misunderstand, abrade, and want something from us we do not want to give: our reactions in public.

The television crews mow down the movie crews, their deadlines parting the world. They shove microphones in our faces as we whisper together. They isolate and freeze us, leaving us to inhabit our bodies like stick figures, afraid to move except in the most unobtrusive, nonemblematic of ways.

Sylvie's entourage is beyond protection. They sit huddled in classical postures of anguish and disbelief. Her wardrobe person, who found her, is being encouraged again and again to tell the story of how she found her and how it might have all been different if she hadn't left early because her husband was too sick to watch their retarded son. Sylvie's hanger-onners are weeping—Lorraine, Gus into his pots of cream, Florian fingering his hairbrushes, Georgeann among them in a triple-jointed fetal posture of grief.

Barney's bones are showing again. No comment.

My skin is prickling, burning, smarting on my throat, stomach, thighs, itching on all the spots. I soak in a milk bath when I get home and it does no good.

Microphones in our faces, strangers all around everyone driving us crazy—oh, go away.

SECTION TWENTY-FIVE

Everyone comes.

The journalists come.

Sylvie's ex-husband comes.

The police come (no, they've been here all along). Now it's detectives, too.

Barney's daughter and granddaughter come.

SATURDAY, SUNDAY

Nobody remembers what time the news is broadcast on weekends, which makes it all easier. Nothing is ordinary time, there are no regular weekday habits to depart from.

Although I have convinced my brother Alex and Sam, I have a harder time convincing Len that it has nothing to do with Harry. "If he struck once, he'll strike again," he says. I say he's wrong and cannot talk now.

Why does he call when everyone else comes? Afraid he'll be shot down on the set?

Alex appears, looking out of place, gets through the police cordon with authority. Once he's here, like visiting family and spouses in earlier days, people try to make him feel at home. "Oh, you're Jessie's brother—can we show you around?" The soundstage? The murder?

No one has found the right tone with this yet. We fill the time with speculation about whether they're going to close down the film or try to finish it without Sylvie. The studio guys have flown from Hollywood for closed-door meetings with international financiers from Germany. The crew has to know—they've got to hustle for their next jobs.

Alex hints I might leave now, I'm not part of this, but this is so wrong and stupid. When he tries to make it up by saying, of course, it's my chance for a terrific story, he sees he's said something even wronger. It is awkward. We have no joint experience of his being ineffective in family matters. Finally he hugs me and goes away.

MONDAY

The next wave on the set is relatives come for the funeral. There is large Victor, who shows up talking about Big Lew, Sylvie's father, and how, had she stayed home and married large Victor, he could have saved her. There are cousins, uncles, first sweethearts, a paunchy accountant-lawyer from her Jersey town eighteen years ago, accompanied by his bewildered wife, face powder creased around her lips. Each in his own way is sure things would have been different had they done, "Oh sweet baby Jesus, only *said* somethin' different, it was in my heart but I never spoke it . . ." This latest was from Anthony, her driver on her first TV special, shot in Arizona. He and all the others think they could have saved her.

The journalists start to arrive. Not hard-bitten reporters from the crime desk, but journalists. They huddle with me to make firm our mutual commitment to minds, pads, pencils (as if I care).

And careful of my material they all are, always telling me they recognize, nay, respect the fact that it is my material. Why? Because I've been on the scene before? Because I once wrote a play with a murder in it?

No one knows anything.

Most of the journalists have checked in. Many of them speak of Sylvie as victim, and do not mean her shredded flesh. They mean the media, the Hollywood system, or being a sex symbol for men. They are all deeply and earnestly into ambience. I spend some time and effort trying to protect the crew from their ironic highly educated marking pens.

Note: Am I trying to turn the journalists into the material they keep assuring me they'll respect, and which I do not have?

Gordon, Sylvie's psychiatrist ex-husband, comes to collect his little boy. I'm struck by how little I saw the child after the first few days.

Gordon wears Italian seersucker and suspenders with little elephant figures on them. He wants to tell me—anyone who will listen, in fact—that he tried to help his star/wife, who was a sweet baby, crazy baby, but finally, terrific fucker though he was, is, smartest man, only real man, in fact, she ever knew, or loved, he had to get out or she'd destroy him. (Deep breath) She didn't destroy him, mind you, nowhere near, he was still intact, you betcha, in his elephant print suspenders. And then he starts it all over from the beginning.

My fellow journalists drift over quickly. Respecting my material obviously doesn't include my sources. They all speedily connect, incorporate his trying to save her from the people destroying her, only she didn't want to be saved.

He's into "didn't want to be saved," they're into "people destroying her," but it's on the same melodic scale and they trill along.

And then the heavy comes by, this guy, this Hollywood agent turned studio exec. His shirt is open to the waist, his loafers have "bits" in them; nesting in the curling black-gray hair on the bronze chest, he wears a medallion. An amalgam of all the things that amuse women like me and make us condescending, but on him it is terrific. And he attracts me. It's power—crude and stupid, no, not stupid—but power. He's here for two days to look, make the judgment.

He moves near us. "We were just saying she was used by guys like you," says a young reporter, staring at him, her lips a little parted with anger, but breathing him in, her boobs shimmying under her embroidered work shirt. "You guys ran all over her."

He smiles faintly, inclines his head, moves to the buffet.

And I, in the name of tough pragmatic women, sidle over behind him in line. "That's the East Coast intellectual's idea of power in the real world," I murmur. "They don't even realize it was her company financing the movie—that she owns all these people walking all over her."

"Well," he says kindly, "they were her companies, but she never got paid for her last two movies, and she was in litigation against her ex-manager. Bad guy."

Wrong again. And in his presence I feel myself back in my early days being courted to write scripts on spec (which means for nothing) by crude young producers like him, who took young serious playwrights like me out of the daylight and sat me in dark bars positioned in sight of long lines for successful movies.

"See that line," they'd say, "everyone on that line would rather be fucking." And me, too, I'd feel it too, instead of talking about script outlines and treatments (on spec), punctuated with gesturing knuckles, dark hair springing from them, brief caresses while they talk about giving the public what it really wants, not what it thinks it wants.

But we're years later, and this studio executive—one of those eager hustlers grown up—is pouring ketchup on his lamb stew, telling me (not in so many words) he was a poor boy, doesn't give a crap what I think of his style, of his power. He likes it. And so, oh so do I. Can he see it? Oh, get control, Jessie. Am I bending toward him? "It's the foreign investors calling the shots here," he says. "No telling which way they'll jump."

I say, in a cool intellectual's voice (but it skips a little), "Well, what do you believe, industrial espionage, betrayed lover (skip a beat), who killed her?"

"Probably some crazy spade jumped over the fence," he says, smiles and walks away with his full plate. It takes me a minute and then I understand it was his way of saying, "No thanks, I'm not interested in what you think of me."

Later in the day I see him talking with the journalist in the embroidered work shirt. When he leaves she tells me, "He's a savvy guy." But he does leave, thank God, taking a plane to LA. I don't think I could take another betrayal. Another?

I go off for lunch with Gordon psychiatrist to a crappy Chinese restaurant, where he does most of the talking. Mainly it's a rehash of what we've said before. "I'm no Mr. Norman Maine," he says a few times.

(James Mason—A *Star Is Born*)

When the waiter removes the mu shu pancakes, he says, "But look at her, she has this life force that wipes everyone else out, it's this strange thing about her. Look at us, we're halfway through lunch and we're still talking about her." Because she got murdered, dummy!

I try unsuccessfully to tear my moist towelette into shreds.

And where is Harry in all this?

Len calls again—no, you've got it *wrong*.

Why do I know Len is wrong?

Because he's got a sort of alibi. They were all going over promotional dailies with Barney and the PR people sometime around that evening.

No, I'm trying to fob you off.

How do I know Len is wrong? Because I'm sleeping with Harry again.

Sleeping with Harry?

Sleeping with Harry. Oh what is it you/I would want to know? Mainly, it's a relief. We've tumbled into bed and it all makes sense.

HARRY AND ME

It started up again, really, when we were always looking over our shoulders to talk, and the only place we could really be alone was his room, and the only place to sit was his bed, and it was easier to lie down, and we laugh and tell tales and sort out what is happening.

Is it relief that there really was something there that was sweet? What is sharp and unhappy and terrifying on the set becomes sweet with Harry.

We start by counting the number of people who say Sylvie was treated like a "hunk of meat" or put on the "flesh market" or some other prime rib/brisket term. Then we advance to dichotomies. We tote up the times people refer to the body-of-a-woman-with-the-mind-of-a-child, the-body-of-a-whore-with-the-mind-of-an-angel, the-body-of-an-angel-with-the-soul-of-a-bitch. Double points if people said one thing one day and reversed themselves another; but only a point and a half if people used both in one sentence: i.e., most-people-think-she-had-the-body-of-a-whore-and-the-mind-of-an-angel, but in fact she had the mind-of-a-whore-and . . .

The set is crazy; this is order, innocent order. If you could understand the disorder of these days.

I have occasional sense memories when I am with Harry, relaxing, dying away, growing excited under him, lost in him, watching him.

They are swift and overpowering—senses, textures, smells, and then they are gone. I sniff after them like a detective trailing clues. Who knows?

One I have is of standing in the discount drugstore on the day George Wallace was shot. Of hearing the news item break through the soft-rock radio music while I rummaged in the racks. I am a very young girl and I am buying cheap young girl cosmetics. I smell the toothpaste, the Bonne Bell astringent lotions, Jergen's hand cream samples. Because Sylvie was killed? Because she wears lots of cosmetics though, granted, not Bonne Bell?

No, but it may point somewhere, and in the interest of being unsentimental and truthful with you as well as myself, I must announce I am not back in Harry's bed in response to forces beyond my rational control or in spite of myself. No, I am determined to continue, I am willing this along.

A long slow kiss standing up, only our mouths touching.

The police are all around, but no one asks if they know who killed Sylvie. The days are turning close and evil.

No one on the street asks me who killed Sylvie, but they say everything else. On Sunday, a young lawyer in our building, riding down with me in the elevator, says suddenly, "I never thought she was pretty." This is only the beginning. On Monday, Tuesday, and Wednesday, Sam's secretary, the laundry delivery boy, my cleaning woman, people in our neighborhood who identify me with Sylvie because of the scene shot in this building, say things to me about her. All the things are ugly.

"She looks like a girl I used to date, couldn't stand her, dropped her." "She's like a girlfriend I hated, really hated." "No good, I worked for a woman had a daughter like her once, I looked at her first time, saw her for what she was." "Bad news, that chick, know chicks like that, can always spot them first shot."

"Someone sure hated that lady," the unit publicist says to me lightly. Why did this never occur to me? When the only fact I *do* know is that the knife was an ordinary butcher cleaver available at hardware stores, and took considerable power in shoulder or wrist to do the damage it did?

Why do I recognize these waves of hate coming down the street? Because I've felt them myself, coming toward me as my features emerge, someone wincing as they see me coming. Who?

The journalists are driving me mad. They've all hit on the same tack for their pieces. That is, *the story of my life as inextricably woven with the presence of Sylvie,* e.g., "I went on my first movie date obsessing about whether when I bent over you could see my panty line through my lilac Capezio tights, and there she was on the screen . . ." or, "I used to sit for hours in the balcony of the Falls River Dreamland Theater watching her on the screen and beating the meat," or "The year we moved from Flushing to Lawrence, all the girls in Lawrence wore Laura Ashleys, and the day I saw her they were all laughing in the theaters, the movie where she fell off the bicycle, and I was feeling very weird, and when I got home I found out my first period had just come."

The point is, they're all into the same message. See how Sylvie wove in and out of my feelings about my earliest sexual feelings—lilac Capezios, beating the meat, and first Tampons. And it's so truly dumb because it's an actress's view of the world, it's like a conversation I had with Sylvie last week, when I said, "Sylvie, try to imagine a room without you in it."

"You mean a room before I come into it."

"No, without you in it at all."

"Oh, you mean just after I've left."

I never got further than that.

And to understand why this makes me so crazy, I think I should explain the way I work. The way my mind works. The way I can only plan our route to the Cape on our New England map if I imagine a miniature red car moving slowly along the black printed lines. And so, I can only write with a particular dolly in mind. Other actresses can play the role later, but for conception there is only one, and I need her before me.

So we come late to the fact that it was Sylvie the actress who interested me, who kept me fixed on her movements, on her trusting aging eyes filling, in spite of herself, with a knowledge of staying power and what it costs.

Because there was something that claimed me in the way her face was changing and was still hers—the way it disappeared into yowling open kitten cries and still she was there.

She'd been ignored too much and praised too much, she'd been loved temporarily by men she made permanently powerful. It was a face that had been told that life has many turns and everything that goes around comes around. But also a face equipped to spin everything around by the force of how she looked at you—the way you looked at her.

I found it disconcerting to walk down a street with her—or have a conversation with her with others watching. I lost control, drowned inside what they thought they were seeing.

I think I never saw her relax—repose was tense, watchful.

So if it's my work they want, it's really me, right?

I remember her turning the breakfast scene around—the actors springing off her eyes. That was the day I told her about the lump in my throat. And how the actors came to hate her—not only for losing their close-ups, but for making them better than they'd ever been before and then taking it away.

They didn't see her at all, the people we passed on the street. She willed what they saw, which used to be radiant and young and lucky but now was changing, changing. She was no longer automatically beautiful, I'm no longer automatically safe. Put another way, she lost her beauty when I lost my optimism. Life doesn't get automatically better—at best you have to insist on it, claim it—pray for it. And how do you survive? You need one pair of eyes to say it's you, it's you and only you—let everything else of value change, but you are you.

She tried a shrink because she wasn't educated. I tried Sam.

"I'm no Mr. Norman Maine nor was meant to be," said Mr. Cool Shrink over the General Tsing's historic chicken. Hip jerk.

Stop saying, "Over the General Tsing's chicken"! Over what food would it have been better?

She told her agent to turn down *Serendipity*, no more offers, the end, she'd wait for me, however long, to finish a play that will now never be written. A killer, we called her, but she's dead, and as Harry and I mourn and fear and play the odds she's already there, and yes, it's Sylvie I lost, so how can I mock at Gordon shrink when I, I grieve for having lost my most particular, aging, deepening dolly?

The decision's been made to finish the film. It came out of the closed-door meetings, the call of the foreign investors. A gamble either way.

Cast and crew are being notified, but it's a big mess. Lots of crew are peeling off to go on to other jobs—temporary crew is being hired. Wardrobe had already packed up and gone to Lima, where their next job is, leaving only the third assistant, who in the wake of the murder threw away all the clothing schedules and the body measurements of the extras. (There was so much paper around, she said. Someone had to do it.)

Scenes are being added, rewritten, and the big dream finale is being resurrected and expanded. Extras Casting is wild. Essential to the plan is rounding up and resurrecting the original crowds of extras. It's late June—many of them have gone off God knows where. It was going to be a slow summer for movies in New York, no reason to stick around.

The Extras Casting people set up long tables of phones as in a political campaign, leaving messages, following up, marking N.A. (no answer) on their photocopied lists. They man the phones till 2 A.M., in the hope that someone's back from a late night party.

Phil, huddled around the scheduling board all day with Rich and

Barney, has become a star, as they say, in his own right. The actors from previous scenes, being recalled to Wardrobe, bring him gifts of Chivas Regal and flattery—"Just to say thanks for your beautiful words—I've worked with the best, but *your words* . . ."

They come up with ideas for increasing their parts, only vaguely couched as jokes. "How about I tell her I've just killed someone? It'll remind her of the camp. She can have her back to me while I do this monologue and sort of have her shoulders shake with tears while I talk. *Phil?*"

The first priority, it seems, is the sex scenes. I thought Trance was done for, but au contraire, Pierre—he'll most definitely get his. Sylvie's most easily replaceable in a shadowy bed. "Once you know somebody's face . . ." They'll shoot sex scene followed by sex scene, first Trance, then Marshall—they're toying with adding another not in the original script.

Trance goes first, hits the bed with a body double for Sylvie, whose hair is not quite right, but is adjusted, and whose face we never quite see. The lights are low. Can I describe how mean this is? Sylvie so badly didn't want this. Trance is smiling. He is happy. He suggests caress after caress to Barney. He'll tell the story of the ants, but he's ready to give that up. Not necessary. He can have it all. The crew seems uncomfortable. The body double has a nasal voice—not high and light like Sylvie's. Trance describes the qualities of the groan he wants from the actress. We have a voice double who will loop the sighs, Barney says.

"I wouldn't do it," says Georgeann next to me. But did anyone ask her, trooper that she is? No amount of on-the-job concentration could turn her breasts and hips into anything resembling Sylvie's.

"I want a sigh like this . . . ahhh," says Trance. A real auteur. "Make sure it's like that . . . ahhh." He negotiates to be at the looping.

I thank God he never heard Sylvie's grunts. Barney is noncommittal.

The body double's breasts are wrong—high and thrusting, with swollen pointing tips. They'll never match Sylvie's. She's doing three nude scenes. Sylvie only did two, so if there's a matching problem in the editing room, there'll be two of her originals against three of the body double's—the body double will win. Sylvie'd asked to have her nipples not shown at all—but does she want the wrong nude body to be her definitive one in film history? Oh, how am I supposed to know?

I ask Barney to give the voice double the line, "I'm happy with you." Why? Because Sylvie wanted it so much. He looks at me straight. Lady, lady, his eyes are telling me. He just wants to survive.

The body double bends over Trance. Her breasts sway smoothly like soft frozen yogurt cones. "I'm happy with you," says Trance over and over. He chuckles. He rolls her over and moves on top of her. He casts a shadow on her face. He gets a close-up. He tells the story of the killer ants. He says, deep throaty chuckle, "I'm happy with you."

No wonder his mother, daughter, and grandmother don't want to touch him.

After the meal break, they do the sex scene with Marshall of the randy breakfast. He and the body double in her white terry cloth robe study the storyboards with Barney—all the motions to match the spearing of whitefish and the spilling of orange juice. I never see the double's face. They move to the bed on the soundstage and go through the maneuvers one after another.

"She was one complicated lady," Marshall says to me of Sylvie as he leaves. I give him credit. He hated it.

Lavender paisley is everywhere. All the actors in any kind of scene with Sylvie are being called back for the expanded dream finale—anyone who was ever seen on-screen with the real Sylvie. The dresses, duplicates of the one she wore in the finale, roll by on racks like a Macy's markdown. They'll have lots of Sylvies in long shot—they plan running Sylvies, fainting Sylvies, skating Sylvies—there'll be sweat under the arms, and no time to clean or replace.

I see Jean-Claude pass by, the beautiful young man from the first sex scene—"Don't show my crack." Are they going to give him a second go-round with the double? No, he's being fitted with clothes for the finale. He was supposed to be a lover from her past, but they're keeping all their options open—fitting him for modern dress, a camp inmate's uniform, or a Nazi guard.

He is French Canadian, with a strong accent. He didn't mind not speaking, that was the deal. He is working with a voice coach so someday he can play an American boy. He pokes around subjects tentatively with me, finally trusts me, because he needs someone to talk to. He checks with me cautiously—I was there, wasn't I? Yes, I say, moving the truth a little.

He says to me, ever so shyly, that Sylvie was very upset at the time. " 'Do you know what just happened?' she says to me, and I says, 'Oh yes—we are acting a part.' "

We are speaking, of course, of Sylvie's sounds.

"It was not because of me," he says to me. It is important to him that I understand this. "I was just, how you say it, there. I could not get, how you say, hard." But I saw his erection getting out of bed. I saw it. He says, "I try . . . I think of Nicole, my girlfriend in Montreal, I think of my first girl, but nothing worked—it was humiliating."

"No," I say reassuringly. I tell him obliquely I saw him. He looks at me as if I am a kind woman, but lying, as kind women are known to do. How can I convince him? Say I was on tiptoe peeking in the window from outside in the shrubbery? There are some secrets I do not owe an earnest young French-Canadian stranger, even to give him sexual confidence.

"No," he says, shaking his head. Then he says doubtfully, "Maybe when I get out of the bed, the air hitting it, it was like a balloon?"

Now we are recreating the finale already shot so as to match it, expand it, build on it.

Tapes of the existing finale footage are being run on large TV monitors, and Wardrobe, Makeup, and Lighting study them, as do the new extras. The unlocatable extras are being matched as carefully as they match Sylvie. I think of how the previous extras would enjoy it if they knew—having stand-ins for themselves, that is, which shows that unavailability in an actor is the great leveler.

Georgeann is busy, running, jumping, going in and out of doors. Harry is placing her here and here and here. He is moving her around, adjusting her arms and legs. She is gallant. She can be used for motion, for long shots. She stands and moves, from a distance looks the same height. They're adding to scenes shot wherever possible, so she's ducking into taxis, approaching doorways from the back, hurrying down streets toward us, away from us.

She's the only stand-in permitted to give interviews. They want a minimum of publicity on this.

"A wonderful person," she says, "never heard her say a mean word about anyone. I just can't imagine anyone not loving her."

Ruth comes back for finale fittings and suggests to Phil she could narrate the thing as Sylvie's friend. I don't know why I ever expect anything from actresses.

She's marked passages in the book that could be voice-over narration, tries to enlist Marie, who's not only powerless but urges her own wistful point of view—if they all threw different pies in the face of the body double—all the people from her past—in the dress and pies in the face they would think it's Sylvie/Sasha, and it would be very funny, doesn't Ruth think?

Ruth suggests *Sasha's Friend*, or *Mothers and Friends* as a title. She giggles a little, as if she's teasing. Phil smiles. Grateful for all ideas, he says.

I confirm my suspicion with Harry about the original scene in my apartment between the two of them. Sylvie specifically came over to instruct him about the lighting of Ruth—"It's not about *her* tears, remember."

Still no one knows who did it. I keep expecting an inspector to call us into a room. I expect to steadily assure an officer with a stainless-steel-covered notebook that the fired P.A. didn't really mind, that the wardrobe man had an innocent accident, and that yes, Sylvie did drive Barney crazy, but it was in the context of the stress of moviemaking.

I finally realize this is not going to happen. This is murder in an urban zone, Dame Agatha, scriptless, plotless. No one will turn out to be a half-brother from New Zealand, and evidence like an argument between Barney and Sylvie over who says "I'm happy with you" doesn't matter worth a damn.

Barney's splayfooted granddaughter upsets the soup kettle for the crew's lunch. Oh, what a mess.

Back in Harry's room, I swarm all over him. Wet, spermy, swarming. Kissing him, loving him, I feel the texture in my hands, the crinkle of the Kodak envelope between my fingers, cheap cosmetics, Jergen's cream, smooth glass bottles in my fingers when I heard that George Wallace was shot. The smell makes me think of my long-dead cousin Jeremy, and then terror that Sam will find out about my presence in this pungent bed—my daily four o'clock terror come at three. But it all has to do with this moment and nothing matters. Rather, our sticky substances seem to glue them all together, envelopes of Kodak prints, flashes of adultery on the six o'clock news, Jeremy's option.

LATER

"Will she?" I hear them saying.

"Ask *her*," says Harry's voice.

They want me to sit and pull my sunglasses over my head so the hair sticks up. Sylvie never got it right. The hairdresser would make my hair look like her hair. It would be from a distance, it would be a comic scene, back of a bench. They would dress me in lavender paisley.

So it comes to this, with the difference in our height, hips, similarity in breasts, sometimes congruence of ineffable expression, they want me with a wig on from the back to look like Sylvie.

NO, I say, no, no, no.

And when I refuse, they jam the wig on Georgeann's head, so it's the ontological absurdity of all—Georgeann from the back acting out a gesture borrowed from me by Sylvie, first offered back to me to do my own gesture in a Sylvie wig, to pretend to be her copying me.

"Did you know they were going to ask me?" I ask Harry.

"I thought we could have fun with it," he says.

Sam won't sleep with me. I make a move and he lies cool and even and calm. Okay.

He has an urgent call to go away for ten days, and we turn it over. A county in Maryland needs him to testify; he is the only one to whom all parties will listen. Yet if he goes, he will miss Petra's birthday. Sometimes Petra bakes a cake and they go out together. But sometimes they don't. We chase it around. We learn Petra has already made plans with Jerome. He decides to go. The Zoning Board of Appeals needs him, the Recreation Commission needs him, the Sewer Districts, Water Districts, and Mosquito-Control Districts all need him. He will be away at least ten days. We are both relieved. And decision unnecessary for this month.

While the finale is being shot, I begin to stay with Harry. Even though Stephanie is back, it's clear that is over. Too strongly put. Was never really on. Was just marking time between friends.

Preparations for the finale are like battle plans—strategic maps of crowds of people flying past, everyone in the film's past swirling in and out, an odd score, percussive, with Middle European folk music, part Smetana, part movie strings. The pink-jowled composer comes on board, urges people to admit they hate John Williams, John Barry, Andrew Lloyd Webber. "Oh, me too," he says, and clasps his hands, but in fact the score is not yet ready as it was promised, so we are doing it to a click track, i.e., like a metronome, a series of mechanical clicks set to the varying tempos the music will be following. So the emotional beats—faster, slower, sadder, more passionate, fearful, angry—are being choreographed against a series of mechanical thudding beats, faster, slower, all together, spaced apart, etc. . . . click click click click, then the occasional Smetana . . . click click click.

The finale is going along to its click track and Harry is negotiating with me, but it is to a different rhythm. And what do we think, you and I?

When the finale is over, one way or another he will leave me for dead?

The finale is a dream of memory—the new king, the steadicam operator. A steadicam is a camera strapped to a man's body, he swoops around. Man into bug, Gregor Samsa as camera . . . a camera fringed by scampering arms and legs. He swoops over and around and under like Peter Pan, perches on floating platforms that swing him even more freely and wildly, but with wire strings so strong to tie him down.

He and Harry confer. They have megaphones and earphones and special walkie-talkie microphones—boys with toys—and they call to each other. "Now over there, old couple laughing, stage left boys crying, stage left, cross over right . . . girl on the right Sylvie Sylvie, back to center left . . ."

Marie asks to be in the finale as a woman with a pet dog with a pooper-scooper, and the click tracks go on and on and on.

So it goes on—the Eastern European forward motion, toward/

away/nightmare/dream of love, erotical/pastoral/mystical . . . "Lit," says Harry, "like the dark side of the moon."

It suits his aesthetic. Mystery is important, beauty that you understand in a few minutes is boring . . . no one will question the dailies now. "Too dark, too dark," they often said of Harry, but now there is much to disguise, to hide. He plays with contrasts of light and sometimes they misfire . . . and one day they burn rubber tires to make smoke and he's sick, oh so sick.

The important thing, Harry says, is to do a difficult thing with ease, a big scene with movement that shows no sense of strain, use the richness of texture.

Barney is following along for appearance' sake, but he's abdicated completely. His nerve, muted as it already seemed, is gone since Sylvie died, and Harry is free to try whatever he wants.

He doesn't care about matching gestures. "If the camera is moving right to left, then left to right," he tells me, "with strong enough action, no one will notice."

I follow alongside with my notebook and write it all down, but I will never forget it, even the sentences like the last one, that I don't quite understand. I am next to him at every moment.

In Harry's room at night, when it is over, when we wake from exhausted sleep, it is to the sound of Rodgers and Hart on a portable tape cassette by our bed—"Have you met Miss Jones? someone said as we shook hands. . . ." We are a cool piano bar, Ella Fitzgerald supper club. We turn into each other's arms to an emotional tempo of our own choosing. We'll not have this movie be our track of hope, irony, memory of a time gone by.

We are not turning in and around each other for memory. We are doing this for now.

I watch him darting across the huge floor of the soundstage for hours and hours and hours. Rich is screaming, Barney is trying to keep up, golden time, platinum time—and sometimes Harry is so tired I bring him his pills and watch him as he sleeps.

I say, "Everyone is tired, everyone is exhausted," meaning even everyone healthy, until he says, "Don't do that." I learn his mother was a nurse, did not love him enough unless he was sick . . . his mother who now cannot do anything right—the kind of information I hate finding out now, this way.

The finale goes from lyrical/pastoral to erotic/helpless and through it all Georgeann in lavender paisley—in and out and around, one sees her everywhere. Four cameras, and the steadicam haunts my dreams, Harry placing her here and there . . . and then at night in my arms, in my bed, I want those hands only on me on me and they are, they are if we sleep at night, or during the day . . .

(I will say, if anyone asks, the company had an extra crew room booked at the hotel and it was easier to sack out there. Nobody will know where I am, no one will ask. I have an answering machine, can always check in for messages.)

"I have to be asleep in half an hour," he says, "and I want to spend it in your arms."

I touch him in public. No one knows or cares. The head makeup man puts his head in my lap during a scene. It was the softest place to hand. Everyone is exhausted.

I try to separate Harry.

Sitting with him, I love to anticipate what is to come. Sitting at his feet, staring at each other, kissing till we sway . . . sitting apart in the two hotel chairs, the tips of our shoes touching—so many layers, so much leather—across a space of chairs. I can arch my toe on the set and look toward him. And that is enough.

The making love itself is black, wild. It's almost an indifference to dying, although it's full of fear. The sharpest fear—for an instant— is living without it.

No one understands. I can't take another grief. No one knows what it's like to have bliss after bliss peeled away from you forever. To anticipate it happening. Harry does.

And once, so unearthly it is with him inside me. He looks at me, startled. His face floating above me. It startles me, too. We talk as if it isn't happening.

And then another night it happens again. I see his eyes leap. He touches my face. My lips freeze. Inside someplace where I have never felt him before—inside my soul, it must be—we stare at each other wild-eyed in the light. He puts the pillow over his face.

I imagine we have a life. I plan to cook for him. He drives me to my apartment, then sits downstairs in the car while I get my pots. We go back to the hotel, where there is a small burner. Dinner takes forever. Chicken with forty garlic cloves. I burn my fingers squeezing the pulp. I hoped the aroma would last forever.

Sometimes I wear his clothes—one piece at a time. The rest bare.

Sometimes I bring a shopping bag of my clothes to try on for him. I bring winter clothes—for the air-conditioning, I say. But it's not that. I want us to be living in all seasons.

Once he wears a tie and spills something on it. His eyes are briefly ashamed. I hate the mother who didn't love him enough.

Our only weekend, we watch television and sleep on the Sunday newspaper. We fall asleep reading. We wake up, light in our eyes, make love with our clothes on, pushing them aside. And then we make love all night till dawn, can't stop, we never stop, we lie weeping, tears in our eyes, and keep going.

Once he holds me, strong and harsh, I cannot move, my breathing stops. He is stronger than I am but I am spread open in so trusting a pose I cannot even begin to fight. When he lets me go, my breathing resumes, harsh and ragged in the air—it rasps as click track to my held-in terror. We listen to the ragged breaths thoughtfully till they grow fainter to normal.

If I were sure he means me harm—what could I really do? Call for help? Bring the world into our cries in the night?

Find the words? What words, what world?

And besides, I tried that, didn't I?

We are negotiating, both waiting to see the answer. We lie trapped—he in what he has to do, me in understanding it.

And then, so long ago—weeks only?—we wondered, watched, maneuvered through the darkened set, and while we watched, waited, negotiated, if you will, and played with fire, Sylvie died.

Which is why we are in the same bed. It would be stupid and arbitrary to be apart. The war is between him and me. No two are closer.

Of course we are in the same bed. Meet the enemy in a clash of swords—don't scrunch alone in your muddy foxhole, smoking pot. If every day may be your last, why spend it alone, huddled, wondering in the dark what your enemy is doing?

No, engage in the sunlight—heroic, shining swords, crash of trumpets where the stakes are everything, out in the sunlight—rather the moonlight, moonlight of desire and touching. As we touch and kiss, my body leaps like the sharp clash of cymbals that announces ceremony, parts the air, parts life. It announces we are fully alive and for this moment we've made our joy, it's up to us.

And what is all this cymbal imagery when we are here and she is dead? They called her a killer, but she is dead, and Harry fears death, but she is dead, and I fear killing, but she's gone before me . . .

A room without me in it?

Sometimes I lie on our damp bed while Harry sighs and groans in his dreams. I hold him in my arms and think what are we doing? What have we done?

The man checking into the hotel room below us puts a note under our door. He has Tourette's, hopes his medication will keep it under control—if not, please forgive him, do not call the authorities.

The next night, after we thrash around on the bed, he curses and curses us.

And in the finale everyone flits and flits, sweep of dancing, steadicam, scenes supposed to make you cry, laugh, the family with the four hundred Yahrzeit candles, loads of extras, Rich screaming at them incessantly . . . and late at night and again and again it's been blocked out and has to be changed—dream sequences, little scenes, lots of goodbyes, people at wakes, the funeral crew, lovers, lovers.

One night—in a moment of calm, in fact—Rich has an alcoholic seizure. It upsets the crew to have someone they so dislike literally fall before their eyes.

The extras are less sentimental. A shit is a shit is a shit. They're softly pleased.

And that's the night Harry shouts me out. He throws me out. I am saying nice things about him. I am saying, "You are a good person." He is furious.

"Please leave," he says. Says it calmly, at first, then again. I see he means it. I start to leave slowly, chattering all the way as if this was only because tomorrow will be a big day. "Leave," he says, and finally he shoves me. He cannot bear my presence at this moment, and I don't care why as long as it is not the end. I hurry. My feet clatter too much, like Madama Butterfly in her bound clogs, give me away, say this is taking place right now.

But the next night—day, actually, we were shooting all night—we act as if it has not happened.

I start to leave before he doesn't want me there. I will ease my way back in. I slip out of his arms, put my feet on the floor. I feel his arm across my knees. I cannot get away. He says, "Why are you leaving? Do you want to be here?" Yes, no, I say. Yes.

And a few nights later he sends me away again. I understand there is no appeal from this one, but I am not ready yet. I try not to panic. I believe I can get through one day if I can spend just this one night seeing him, watching him. He asks me not to. I look at the floor. Any second I may howl like the girl I heard of in the steam room. Instead, I hurl my earrings at him. Past him, actually. They hit the wall, glittery black dangling stones. It was with all my might and they dent the wall. He's thoughtful. Stares at the wall.

I am allowed to stay, but only tonight. I wake. He is wearing clothing to bed. I take him in my mouth. Stop it, he says in his sleep, he moves my hand, my mouth from place to place.

In the morning he bangs his head on the wall of the shower, bangs it and bangs it and bangs it. I keep on brushing my teeth.

He shaves with his shirt on—cuts himself, blood on his shirt.

I keep talking.

"Aren't you sad?" he says.

He is setting me free.

* * *

Looking at the call sheet, I realize there is a way to look at it as simple timing.

When the finale is over, he lets me go.

THE NEXT DAY

I turn my ankle on the street and fracture a small bone. It is the day before my brother Robbie is coming to town for the American Historians' Convention.

No one was near me, even the pavement is not responsible. My leg lifted up in the normal course of things and instead of going straight down it twisted around. Blame the air. I am in a gel cast; I am on crutches. I am told to be careful of the nerves under my arms; they can be permanently damaged if I use the crutches wrong.

If I were onstage, I would immediately be Girl on Crutches. I use temporary wooden crutches—not the tubular stainless-steel ones that imply permanent deformity—so strangers are galvanized to action to help the *temporarily* infirm.

Edythe has been calling, having tickets for this and for that, now finally understanding vaguely why I cannot comfortably attend the New York State Theater, offers to see me, cook for me. But she still doesn't register what it is to be on crutches.

And even Sam, still away, who does not see the crutches, is only in touch with Jessie who is slightly hurt but managing well. He offers to come home but it is in the middle of the hearings. We both know it is a bad idea, and I am slightly hurt but manage well.

My first day back on the set I see Harry laughing with the Madonna girl. I think a wire has cut my throat and I will die from the agony of its edge working its way steadily through my neck, till my head rolls off. But he is only helping her with footage for her electronic-press assemblage. She didn't have enough, and it amuses him to round it off.

I am with Harry, who has let me go but will let me hang around. He crawls over me delicately as I lie prone, my feet propped up. Only his penis touches me. For some odd reason, he uses dirty words now that I am on crutches. He seems interested in synonyms for genitalia.

Is he trying to excite me? It is strange to be naked except for a gel cast.

He says "thank you" for no reason once, when lying in my arms, and is different with me, gentle, so gentle. He kisses my ankle, my eyes, holds my hair all night while I sleep, I only know when I wake and pull away. I'm back inside, grateful, moving smoothly, carefully, except for my stupid cast.

WEDNESDAY

My brother Robbie and his wife, Abigail, come in for the Organization of American Historians at the New York Hilton. I go to meet them early, before the call—so I don't miss much on the set. I lurch through what seems like miles of dark Formica tables, bowls of peanuts, and men with badges. It is too dark to see my cast, and I wear long floppy white pants, so everyone there averts his eyes lest my hobbling progress be infectious. But then they are job hunting, and the field is bleak. I look forward to seeing Robbie. He comes in from Ann Arbor only rarely.

Abigail, the first girl my age I knew for sure wasn't a virgin (because Robbie told me), is wearing a black wool empire maternity dress. June—it's ridiculous. Except the bar is frigid with air-conditioning (dark, cool, odorless sex).

"How smart of you to dress for the air-conditioning," say I.

"It's the only dress I own," she snaps.

An old story. Abigail claims she loves Ann Arbor because you only have to have one black dress you can wear to all the functions. Abigail and I are truly not friends.

When they married, she said she was a sculptor; now she works, I think, in the university publications office.

Robbie, who has his tenure at the University of Michigan, is surprisingly having interviews at Wesleyan, Williams, Colgate, Bryn Mawr . . .

What's up? He doesn't want to be so far from his family, he says. But his family is just burgeoning, forming and growing inside Abigail. Anyway, we go up to his hotel room and while Abigail goes back and forth to the bathroom, we sit on one of the twin beds and I tell Robbie what Alex had already told him about what's happened, about my fears.

I stretch out—one pillow behind my head, the other under my foot. My foot on their pillow? "Sorry, Abigail," I say, "he insisted."

And Robbie, historian with tenure, gets it straight—bang on. The sequence, that is. That the crutches have nothing to do with anything. That Sylvie's murder came after my concern about the accidents. It makes me think very well of Robbie as historian. I wonder if it appears somewhere on his résumé. *He gets things in the right order.*

He wants me to come stay with them. I have learned from his colleagues—always a surprise—how he pushes my plays to be performed in Ann Arbor.

Anyway, I'm amazed by his grasp of events, and I think he'll put an order on everything. He'll know what comes next. What a fine surprise, having your family turn out so sane and competent. Robbie sums it up: The question is, of course, who killed Sylvie? What? I hadn't seen this as the question.

He puts me into the cab, sliding my crutches after me.

"Who could hate *you?*" he says, blowing his credibility.

Back on the set, messages are waiting for me from Edythe.

The crew is disbanding. The second unit is out in a camera car, but there are still a lot of transitions to finish up.

Harry is waiting for me, too, and we go right to his room. "Come fuck with me," he says very softly in the elevator, "Oh, do you want to fuck?" Oh yes, I do.

Swarming in bed, again I smell my cousin Jeremy. Because of my gel cast? Because he's dead? No. Because he hates me?

Why do I think of Jeremy?

More practically. Why track down my mind? Because it is my only chance of knowing what is happening in the world.

Everything I Can Remember About Jeremy: Or, what might you want to know about my cousin?

1. A young blood relation who died in the same city as me, who winced when he saw me coming.

I was afraid of the dislike, of his someday telling me all the things he disliked about me so persuasively that it would burn its facts on my face—and I would forever walk around with my face scarred into the lines of the person he saw me to be.

I was upset when I heard about people who thought he was brilliant. They became forever in my mind people who might despise and hurt me. A publishing house gave him an option on a comic novel he never completed, and walking by Simon & Schuster makes me shudder even now.

2. My cousin showed me what a man's ejaculation looked like when I was sixteen. He was a medical student. It was in Mount Sinai, in the interns' quarters. We lay on his bed and his pink penis protruded from his white intern's pants and trembled till it bubbled all over. It was a totally safe sexual encounter. We would never tell anyone in the family because the words would be inconceivable to find.

3. When I was a little girl, his presence made me so physically ill I could not finish my sandwich if he was in the room. I would see him—hair askew, button missing—and if it was anything fleshy like tuna fish that I would be constrained to gulp down in his presence, I could not eat it again for weeks. Even cucumber sandwiches. When I lingered with them in my mouth, the bread turned gummy and then that too seemed fleshy.

4. He was a brilliant mathematician. He left medical school in his sophomore year. In that time, in that place, it was an act of incomprehensible savagery toward one's parents.

5. He told me I sang badly. I was doing wispy Scottish ballads, full of wee-ohs, that did well for me with my boyfriends. He told me I sang very badly. He studied conducting for two summers at Tanglewood with someone who said he was the most talented pupil they had since Thomas Schippers.

6. He had a lot of big, laughing, foolish friends who called me up. For a while we swapped dates. (His girlfriends, and later his wives, looked nothing like me. Nothing there.)

7. "He was so proud of you," said my Uncle Merv after Jeremy died. But then, Merv was on long distance, wanting me to shuffle grave slots.

How could I say, "Look, Uncle Merv, I really would be interested to know, did Jeremy *say* he was proud of me? I'll shuffle the slots anyway."

8. Our families were enemies. He wanted my parents. Somehow it didn't connect with or away from my brothers. I think maybe he'd fantasized he was my parents' third child, and then it was me who came. About the time I was born, our fathers fought.

Why be evasive? He wanted his grave next to my mother's and he wasn't going to get it. The other side is my father, and then it's Alex, Robbie, or me—whoever gets there first.

9. When he grew terminally ill, he was in the same city as me. I did for him according to my bond.

I refused to let him drive after he got sick and had blackouts, told him if he renewed his license I would call the Motor Vehicles Bureau and his employer. I would not have random highway blood on my hands to wash off every night when he was buried and the grave dust washed away.

10. One day, during a remission period, he called my friend Marilyn, introduced himself falsely, using my name, and did an unspeakable thing.

When she told me about it, I told her what he himself did not yet know, that he was terminally ill. She properly didn't want to know. It was too big a secret for what he'd done. We differed over what was unspeakable and what I should have told her. He'd tried to seduce her, not telling her he was married, telling her I'd sent him. Only attempted rape. As long as you're not killed, said Marilyn. I'd settle for that, any time. And now they're both dead.

A nice straight girl, she was. She had a clown's face and a lush body, could have any man she wanted. She died in her apartment after a deliberate overdose of barbiturates, a few glittery stars still pasted on her arm, from who knows when. "They stick for weeks," she warned me, "even when you scrub." The newspapers said only that she died in the night, and several women who saw her obit—she was of some small, growing renown as a composer—knowing we were friends, called to ask me if she'd been on the pill.

She'd been there for me in the bad year as I railed at her. "A book for my mother? She can't see, don't you know what a tumor is? She can't read, she can't *see*, for God's sake!"

On the grim prognosis for my father's heart: "This is so hard on you, Jessie," "Oh," I snarled, "you don't understand anything, do you? It's hard for *him*, not me, for *him!*"

And another time I snarled the opposite. She was the one I counted on never to go away. She was six months younger than I.

After Jeremy and my father and my baby died, she asked me what she could do. "I'll probably need your time," I said. "I'll ask you for your time."

Busy as we both were, it was asking for heart's blood, which we'd always give.

"I'm not sure I can promise you that," she said.

I thought she hadn't heard me, so I said it again.

"I can't promise," she said.

I remember, from so stunning a statement, feeling only mild

puzzlement. Like Scarlett O'Hara, I decided to think about it to-morrow. When—in a manner of speaking—they found her dead.

11. Jeremy had two wives, both of whom still are crazy with love for him, though he is dead and gone, boys, and he divorced both of them after humiliating and nastily handled infidelities (on his part).

They each called me repeatedly, from Texas and from Nice, to argue with me about denying him his driver's license. They explained that he had always equated cars with being a man, somehow, that I could be killing him by my obstinacy.

12. In college, he worked with a scientist who later got the Nobel Prize. For years later—even now?—any mention of the Nobel Prize scared me, because someone in the Academy admired him and might have gotten the message about me.

13. He is dead.

Do I miss him? No, there was no comfort where he was. Yet there is a space where he was, which means he was somewhere in my life.

And he hated, hated my plays, said they were about wanting a penis like my brothers'. It was crazy crazy.

But I don't sing wee-oh lullabies anymore, and I was afraid to say he was crazy about that.

I don't know why I think of him in bed these days. I have tried not to organize the story because I never think of him in any consecutive way. He hated me, he made me preside over his death and so I had to deal with the death of someone I didn't love, along with those I did. Like one from Column B, I got to taste it all.

He said, when I left his hospital room, "Do you know, cousin Jessie, how lucky you are to be able to walk out of here?" Sylvie said she felt waves of hate coming toward her and I said I understood, had felt it, too. Did she mean the theater audience? The public on the skateboard night? I meant Jeremy.

I don't know why I think of him when I'm in bed with Harry at moments of pleasure in motion. I didn't want him, he repelled me, he put me off red meat, I can hear him howling in those last days in the phone to me. Why his two wives still adore him while his bones are rotting underground, I'll never know. They're both lovely girls, I went to one wedding, not the other.

"Don't look into your husband's heart," whispered my dying cousin Jeremy.

THURSDAY, JUNE 24

When I come onto the set in early afternoon feeling drugged and groggy—I slept all morning—Stephanie tells me Len has been calling and now wants to meet with her. I feel obliged to tell her that Len, husband of my husband's ex-wife, has this crazy idea that Harry might have killed Sylvie. I warn Stephanie so she won't talk to him. She is perplexed. She does not immediately understand that Len is crazy.

"Oh," she says, "you mean because of the thing he had with her in preproduction?"

What?

"The thing Harry had with Sylvie in preproduction."

Okay, you may well say. Big deal. But this is me, and I am sickened with physical jealousy and remembered hate. Him with her—a mass of images and sentences—her knees up in the air, his plunging down, her laughing, laughing . . . and at me . . . Did they tell me, hint? "The only one who understood my face" . . . ate together, laughed together, but the words evaporate like violet spider webs before my eyes, and the images flash sharp, knees up, legs high . . . bodies coupling, turning, recoupling, shouts of glee shouts of laughter . . . my own shouts of rage.

Waiting for the pay phone in the luncheonette near the shooting studio to be free, I think Lizzie Borden took an ax, gave her something forty whacks. I lost a job over that. It was eight TV half-hours— great money, would have paid our share of all Petra's bills. But it was a turn-of-the-century piece, and they wanted it to be about women learning to be actuaries, running typing schools for other women, and I wanted it all to be about Lizzie Borden. They said it wasn't their bag. Their funding was for a series on Everywoman.

Policemen are scurrying around and no one knows anything.

Sylvie was caked with blood, her canvas pants were caked with blood like Jackie Kennedy's pink bouclé suit in Dallas. She'd always wanted to have a life with dignity, like Jackie Kennedy. She'd used the phrase repeatedly. The words caked blood had struck me. My material? Why do they think women don't know about gore and blood when they see parts of their bodies dropping into glistening bloody clots twelve times a year from the time they grow breasts? No wonder we have a vegetarian frisson, we housewives handling slabs of raw bloody meat, Dione Lucas–Lizzie Borden cleavers in our hands, and me with my vegetarian frisson in the kitchen last Christmas alone with the half-eaten leg of lamb, lemon satin shirt, mohair hostess skirt, suddenly snatched it up, tore at it with my teeth, gnawing the bone, then put it down instantly, ran into the bathroom to wash. In the mirror, lemon satin shirt, mohair hostess skirt, shamed eyes, greasy face, like dog with feathers on his mouth. I am thinking of Sylvie, of course, Sylvie, hacked to pieces. Not to pieces, but to death.

I call Robbie, but his room doesn't answer. Probably in an interview. Will he take me away? I forgive him for all our old fights and I want to go to Ann Arbor. The inside of my head will not follow me there. I'll cook for Abigail and time her contractions and buy her Vitamin E oil for her stretch marks.

While waiting for Robbie to call me back and take me away, I must nevertheless confront what is here and now. I lurch and sway into Harry's temporary office/lab. It is pitch-dark. He is hunched over his Movieola, looking at some strips of film. I stand rigidly staring at his neck, thinking of him with Sylvie, black rage filming my eyes, draining the world of other color.

HE: What is it?

ME: Sylvie . . .

HE: What about her?

ME: You know what about her.

My breath is suffocating me.

HE: Who killed her, you mean?

He's trying to change the subject, get off the hook.

ME: I suppose you know?

HE: I might have an idea.

ME: Stephanie said you and Sylvie . . .

My jaw clenches in fury.

HE: (shrugs) She thought I'd light her right if she showed me what to see.

ME: And what do you see?

HE: I see a lot of things.

I don't like this riddling, playing in the dark.

I turn on the light.

He reaches for me, sees my face, his face shuts down.

That's right. I won't play. I won't play, I won't condone this kind of behavior.

ME: What things?

HE: I saw you trip Georgeann the first day you came on the set.

What?

Yes, I did. I'm sorry, I've realized it for some time, but till it was in words, even someone else's, I didn't have it to tell, do you understand? And also, it's not important.

And in my mouth, as I stand there, hovers the taste of Kodak prints, Listerine, afro combs, black salesgirls, old shufflers going senile, hippies and liberal '68 professors and boxes of Junior Tampax—the phenomenological paraphernalia, in other words, of being in Discount Drugs on Flatbush Avenue when the news came over the loudspeaker that George Wallace had been shot.

It's been dogging me all these days, because the terror I felt at that moment, at that time, in that place, thirteen-year-old child of my parents, knowing this is an evil man, of feeling suddenly that it means anyone might kill . . . no, it means we kill. And what does that mean? That means that someone kills not only the Kennedys and John Lennon, but someone almost kills George Wallace . . . as Georgeann was almost killed?

What?

That I tripped Georgeann—oh God, I tripped Georgeann—but it was a spasm, not an act. It was a tropism, having to do with Marilyn's suicide, death, bottles of playschool plasma. It was an impulse that, with the slightest movement, was put into action. I nudged out my toe in irritation and walls came tumbling. The fact is, I'm not mechanically alert enough to know what would have happened next. I think the coil was unsteady anyway. The crew will agree that it was an improperly conceived physical plan.

Bullshit. If asked, they will say, "Yeah, well it could've been stronger maybe, you know . . ." But Georgeann is fine, her body healed, building up her activity gradually as the doctor said—it was an irritated movement, less than the shrug of a shoulder, and it spiraled. God knows I'd snatch it back, undo the day, give up *my* spleen, but that's not the trade, no matter how I yearn and ponder, so what would you have me do? I'm sorry for it truly, but I cannot dwell. Thoughts fly up.

If it was an impulse—but I don't dignify it that much—it was a passing one. Over and out—gone. And then? I don't know. Barney knew, Harry knows, who else knows? Anybody?

Why didn't I tell you? Do you understand, can we understand I didn't have it to tell? I knew in some way but there were no words because, as now, putting it in words changes everything and makes me howl: "Yes, it's true, but not the way it seems in words."

I lurch out of Harry's trailer as fast as my crutches allow me. I half slide down the aluminum steps on my rump. But dignity has never been so beside the point or out of reach. I look around me.

Georgeann is all right. There she is, her lavender dress like the one Sylvie wore, doing connecting shots. She's walking in and out of doorways, running across streets, bending to pick up a child from far away. "A lovely person," she says of Sylvie when interviewed, "never heard her say a harsh word." She's bending down, adjusting the child in her stroller. She can walk and talk, her body could be combed inside and out with stainless-steel instruments and find no trace; it is all fixed. Is this absolutely true? Under the never quite disappearing flush of burns fully healed, does a spleen regenerate without a trace? She is turned toward me. I have been staring at her.

I start home in a dull, shocked haze. Of course, shocked. However much I explain, it doesn't count for much. Not when it's me and I'm still here having to move and shift and reason with this heart and mind and body that is me.

In the taxi I reenter the movement, and the back of my jaw tenses. I put out my foot and derailed the table. My toe jerks out, hits the gel cast. I gasp with pain. But the toe goes nowhere. I push it again and no response, no movement except an enclosed spasm, a rasp of pain that no one can see. Like being dead, but hurting hurting.

I tell the cabbie to take me to Forty-second Street for exercise weights. My doctor told me to buy weights to exercise my leg. Already the calf is growing flaccid. My breasts, however, are high and swollen from the exercise of the crutches. They sting. It is all in the pectorals? Do women on crutches have fantastic busts? Herman's does not have the weights. So that my taxi will not have been a loss, I hobble up, step by step, to the upstairs ski shop. They are having a late-spring sale on down parkas. I make my way through the deserted floor of mirrored posts and silent puffy rows of tufted down. A tall young salesman and a heavy black woman in a nylon smock stand staring at me. I continue circling the floor, but my hands are clenched and clammy on the rubber hand grips.

The downstairs salesman is unpleasant when I ask him to come out and flag me a cab—does he expect me to lurch down Forty-second Street hailing anything that will stop?—but he does. I tell the new cab to take me to Lord & Taylor. It is Thursday night, open late, and I need a new outfit. The only clothes I can wear these days are these loose, floppy white pants, which pull easily over my gel cast, and my long-sleeved blue T-shirt—all my other cotton tops are sleeveless, and I worry about the crutches under my armpits. But as we approach the store, I can't face going through counter after counter on crutches, and I can hardly send the driver in. My mother and Marilyn are gone, and there is no one intimate enough left to send on personal errands. Would any of this have happened, I wonder, if they'd stayed with me? So when we pull up before the lighted store windows, I lean forward and tell the driver to take me home.

I let myself in. Wearily, a little stagily, I put down my purse, take off my sunglasses. It's hard not to be a little stagy on crutches.

I turn back, and down the long dim corridor to the elevator I see the blur of a pale dress, and a contorted figure, arm upraised with a butcher knife, running toward me.

I drop my crutches and lunge against the door, slam it shut. The doorbell rings, someone knocks on the door. I lean against the door and beg, I plead to be excused for my rudeness.

"I'm so sorry," I whisper, "I'm on crutches, you know how you get." My heart pounds in my throat. Who is this "you" to whom I whisper? I dare not open the peephole, or the knife may slip through. I slip the chain lock into place as quietly as possible, whispering apologies all the time. There is no noise on the other side. "I'm on crutches, you know, they make you crazy," I plead. The aftercrash of my crutches rumbles in the silence like a shriek. I turn away from the door and step on my injured foot. A wave of sharp splintered pain rises from my ankle. The cast is cracked.

Did the crutch fall on it? I drag along, using one crutch as a cane, and make it to the back kitchen door to check that it is locked. It is. Back in the front hall, I feel that the presence on the other side of the door is gone.

A moment later the service elevator comes, and the porters get out, chattering in Spanish dialect and rolling the rubber cans to pick up the garbage. Clearly, they see no one there.

I drag down the hall to the bedroom, close the door, pile two chairs against it, and take the long view.

Why do I not call the police? Another night, two years ago, I called the police when I heard the burglar alarm begin to ring across the courtyard. Seconds later, through their window, I saw the fussed old women appear in bathrobes, shaking their faulty apparatus in irritation. I called the police back to say it was all right, they didn't have to bother. "No," said the nice lady on the other end reasonably, "we can't call the car back, you might be the perpetrator calling, you see?" And as we talked, three police cars screeched to a halt in front of our building and six men jumped out, guns drawn.

Do I fear ridicule? No, it is tactics. If I call them and they storm in, guns drawn, to investigate my call, they may leave my front door open, and whoever it is can slip in quietly and hide in a closet till they are gone.

And there's still tomorrow night. When whoever it is, who probably went away now, comes back and I can't call the police again because I will have cried wolf.

Huddling on my bed, I think of the long haul.

My ankle is numb inside its splintered cast.

I find I cannot think face front about what just happened or my body freezes and my arms and legs rise up in the air, rigid—a fetal shout?

I turn on the television and I try to read, and I turn on the radio too and all the lamps, even the tiny Tensors. I fall suddenly asleep and wake up terrified by all the light and noise.

There is a telephone book lying on the floor next to the bed and I take that as a piece of terrific luck, that it isn't out in the hall where it usually is. So what?

You might think of instant action, but I am all alone now and will stay so, must be ready for the long and steady haul.

My ankle now roars with pain, and when I reach down to hold it, I cut my finger on the jagged cast. The Band-Aids are a room away, so the sheets grow quickly streaked with bright finger blood.

I hear myself sobbing, but like a tree falling in the forest, the sound is quickly boring. I sing myself a little lullaby, and my voice out loud pleases me. When I fall asleep, I dream I am in blazing light and that brilliant tulips like crepe paper ones are spurting all over. They are like the ones you make in kindergarten. Are they crepe paper? Will they burn? No, they say. Flowers won't hurt. When I come forward to touch them, they are petal smooth, they spurt up straight and clean and shining and fragrant, fragrant crepe paper blazing with light. I wake up sheepish. I willed myself a pretty dream.

I turn off the lights and the television and dream that a huge man in a black turtleneck sweater has broken into the apartment, into the room, and is moving over me. I pretend I am not awake. I move compliantly. As long as I don't trust him. As I drift to sleep, I think foggily of Marilyn. She had a point. Rapists are less dangerous—the weapon shrivels and goes away. She knows about shriveled weapons. Her parents loomed so monstrous large in her imagination, I could never connect them with the aging wizened couple who sat huddled on her bright sofa. But parents are protection—even awful ones. I wish I had my parents. No one else has known me as long.

FRIDAY, JUNE 25

In the morning the ringing downstairs buzzer wakes me. Hobbling to the intercom, I think I dreamed of a rapist as wish fulfillment—safety. Oh, only this. Only the usual girlish fear. Not a woman with a butcher knife.

What did I see? The police will remind me I was not wearing my glasses—everything is a blur. How many ways can a blur form and reform in one's imagination?

The day doorman tells me my sister is coming up, and the doorbell rings and Edythe is at the door.

She is buxom and smooth in a mauve-colored leotard and flowered skirt. Her flesh seems creaseless, like a smooth taut curving sausage filled with the freshest prime ground pork and spices. She has been trying to reach me, she says.

I remind her I have hurt my foot.

She opens her tote bag—its stenciled letters say MY BAG. She has bought me a set of knives that, she tells me, are foundry stainless.

There is a boning knife, a cook's knife, a bread knife, and a particularly horrid frozen food knife with both a saw-tooth and a serrated edge. Edythe is enthusiastic. She points out the beautiful balance, the full tang handles, the razor edges for life, and tells me they cut through tendon and cartilage with a minimum of physical effort.

She matter-of-factly cuts away the rest of the splintered gel cast, tapes my foot, and helps me get dressed. She says she always wanted to be a surgeon. Once she took a splinter out of my foot with stunning skill. My nieces get a lot of splinters.

At her urging, I call the orthopedist.

Robbie calls, returning yesterday's messages. He says there's some trouble, Abigail is staining, but he insists on meeting me at the orthopedist's and takes down the address.

Edythe takes me there in a taxi. In the taxi she tells me that a mugger stopped her once near the Vivian Beaumont garage at Lincoln Center, and using the number five knife, the Japanese-made one with the curving blade made on a samurai principle, she slashed him in the gut. Clean, dead-on accurate. She looked, but it wasn't in the newspaper, still she was pretty sure she got him in the place right between the spleen and the liver.

We sit together in the doctor's office while around us people relive their injuries and advise each other not to sign a thing. I wonder if Edythe gave me the knives to make it a fair fight. Whether it was Edythe last night. I did not have my glasses on.

My doctor is an ass. "Did you take off your cast because you think you've healed yourself?" he says. "Do you think you can do what I and God cannot?"

He puts on another gel cast and tells me I can use a cane. Why didn't he say that in the first place?

Robbie calls me from his hotel. He will meet me at the cane

place. No, none of the orthopedic-supply stores the doctor has recommended. I'm to sit tight. He calls back in five minutes, having found a cane store in the yellow pages. He gives me the address. It is in the east seventies. Elegant.

The cane store is horrid as I could not have imagined. "It's better here," Robbie says. "You'll be depressed if you have an orthopedic cane." The cheapest cane here is one hundred and sixty-five dollars. It doesn't seem sturdy. Oh, and there is one that is eighty-five. It is black and spindly. Its pointed bottom skitters across the floor when I try it. The ever so slightly sneering salesman puts a big pale pink rubber tip on it. It is hideous; I shudder. Like a black shriveled leg with a pink orthopedic prosthesis.

"Don't be ashamed, there's nothing to be ashamed of having to use a cane," says the salesman, unpleasantly. Robbie is getting impatient. I hate this one.

Robbie is impatient and has to leave and the others are too expensive. But he doesn't say that. He says, "Can't you make up your mind? Whatever you want." He knows the choices as well as I, and he's not about to take me to another store or drop a hundred and sixty-five dollars on a cane. And Abigail, after all, may be bleeding his son away in clots. So we separate. I do not ask him if I may come to Ann Arbor.

I have hit the same nerve of exasperation in Robbie that usually comes out choosing caskets for funerals. "Oh take any one" (implicit—it's just like *you* to select). He's not good in emergencies.

But it's something else. I have always known he does not wish me well. What did I think, kneeling in the mud at our parents' graves, Robbie's rubbers positioned trimly near to my cheek? I thought, "Here I am crumpled at your feet, take some pleasure in this for

God's sake, there should be something in this for somebody." So much for brother and sisterly love.

I take a cab to the set.

Oh, do you understand? The awful isolation of having the inside of your head having *nothing* to do with the outside world? Only on the set will I find the milling of feverish activity, high-voltage light, and absolute absence of content that will correspond to my present state.

When I arrive, people are already drifting back from the lunch break, no more shooting. It will not be a late night tonight, and I begin to worry about darkness coming on.

They tell me Harry is in the editor's trailer. But I haven't asked. I think I cannot face seeing him. All I will think of is what he knows about me.

My throat is dry. I look at my arms—my terror is flaking them.

The last time I can remember the world most precisely acting out my head was that year—when I drove through a sunny Sunday of happy strollers to sublet my dead parents' apartment. As I pulled up to the door, the doorman sank to the pavement weeping. But those days are pastoral now—a maiden's simple sorrow. The inside of my head is no longer such a clear display. It is blank, buzzing, agitated, fearful.

I begin talking with Georgeann, who is waiting on the sidelines for some insert shots with the second unit, the other camera crew, showing her driving away in a car, wriggling in behind the wheel. I put my hand on her arm, ask her questions. I hold out my notebook as if it's time for real professionalism. I ask if she doesn't still think it's terrible what happened to Sylvie, who didn't deserve it. I say everyone's so grateful to her for doing such a good job, I know Sylvie would be grateful, too. The movie meant a lot to Sylvie.

I say I am very interested in her accounts of the different kinds of car crashes and hanging off ledges. I say I admire her skill and plan to rent the videocassette of the movie where a wire cord connects her to the building facade. The movie where she splattered on the pavement as the wicked spy. How did it feel to see yourself carried off dead?

"But I'm not dead," she says.

She looks at me in the same slightly puzzled way she did in the playground the day she came back, as if trying to place me. A star turn again?

No, it's that I asked her this same question before. Jesus.

"Yeah, well," she says. She takes her arm away from me, looks at it.

Harry comes out of the trailer and hurries me away. Is he afraid I am babbling an apology for her absent spleen? I do not want to look at him, I avert my eyes.

What does he want? He tells me to go home. He is tense, preoccupied, in a rush to get back to the Steenbeck, he has miles of footage to go. He tells me he will be at it all night; he tells me to go home, he will talk to me tomorrow. Once he looks at me oddly, and my cheeks grow hot. I turn to leave and he disappears back into the trailer, already focused on his little screen in the dark. Who cares about tomorrow? It's tonight I have to get through, and he's working tonight, no help, though I hadn't expected him to be, but why did I show up here if I wanted to avoid him? And in any case it will be dark tonight and I can't go back to my apartment, don't want to be, can't be alone.

I seem to know few men without women, and there seems to be no woman I trust. I do not, repeat do *not*, want to stay with Alex, my brother, Stephanie, Marie—do I remind Marie of some Dachau Kapo? Was it her? Stephanie? The old woman she told me she'd loved, found hacked to death, little Steffie found her—did little Steffie hack her? Stephanie, who turned Harry over to me without a second glance. I have no close girlfriend after Marilyn, no one to ask to be with me, no one to ask for time, to refuse or grant it. And men have more strength in their arms and wrists. As defenders? As murderers?

Though the police will remind me I didn't have my glasses on— what did I see of gender, anyway?

I think fleetingly of Sylvie's Israeli lover, a blue-eyed El Al purser, someone said—because an Israeli hero could protect me in wide-screen Technicolor, keep me safe forever—but he never did appear after she died. Oh, where does this trashy terror begin and end?

Gordon psychiatrist, Sylvie's ex-husband, comes along. Of course. He's clean. A doctor, after all. We go out to dinner and he talks about his son with Sylvie, a manipulative child, he says. He does not seem fond of him.

I am so afraid he will see through my reason for having dinner with him and think me manipulative and send me away that I begin to tell him my dreams, to amuse him. I often have funny, crazily plotted dreams.

He grows wary. I see he thinks I want free interpretation. I meant only to distract him from realizing I wanted to spend the night with him only to have a protected bed—a thought that surely never entered his mind.

In trying to redress the balance, to show that I have my own opinions, don't need his, I become a contradictor. I adjust every little word he says. It's one of the cheaper ways I have of linking dialogue on the stage.

His beard is spiky, like a porcupine. When he kissed me lightly getting into the cab, a spiky needle got in my mouth. By morning my skin will be a mass of welts.

But my linking dialogue isn't working either. "Well, it's not really that I'm concerned with character, it's more a question of . . ." He's turning off. Oh shit, he's afraid he won't get it up with a contradictor. I turn insistent, he is wary, then gone.

Now nothing can induce him to even get into the taxi with me to drop me off. I wonder, when he is gone, whether I would really have gone through with it.

I go back to the editing trailer. I can't think of anyplace else. Harry is back in his chair, staring blankly at the turned-off dead gray screen. He is preoccupied and full of energy at the same time, snapping his fingers, cracking his knuckles, things I've never seen him do. It's as if something is ticking inside him, a light clicking and burning, and it doesn't have to do with me. He looks at his watch. Might as well . . . and we go back to his room. Yes, I can spend the night. I feel I have been invited back to pass the hours till morning, but I am so relieved I do not care. I, too, have my own good reasons.

It is a hot night and the air conditioner in his room is broken. Gusts of hot air blow in through the white hotel curtain; the air is hazy, hallucinatory. In his arms I feel us each absorbed in secret, urgent issues, buried, separate from each other, while our bodies join, stroke, smile, moan . . . with every second passing I am hanging on to life, and life is Harry in my arms, moving, smiling, excited about something he will not say, and I am safe, escaped for now, for this moment, in an underground train or across the border . . .

It is love in a war zone—everything counts for everything and we are killer and victim, patient and nurse, medic and WAC, besieged lovers trapped in a war zone where loving is rare and for the moment. "I'm fucking your face," says Harry. "Your body doesn't exist, I feel I'm fucking your face."

But women are slashing, hacking with knives, if women are killing women it is a sad thing.

We make love again, and though I am terrified at what my dreams will bring, I fall heavily asleep. Harry wakes up just before dawn crying, crying. I wake up and say, "Oh, my love," and hold him, because I love him, and we go back to sleep.

SATURDAY, JUNE 26

Through the window, I see early dawn on Fifty-third and Sixth. No one will find me. In the street, only old bag women with shopping bags, checking the trash cans. My black cane with its pink rubber foot is propped against the aging vanilla hotel wall.

I tell Harry, in the sleepiness of morning, in my affectionate gratitude at not remembering my dreams, that someone in a pale dress came after me night before last with a knife. I am more concerned about my dreams than the reality. I want to say, "See what you did for me, you took away my dreams."

I am amazed by what happens. Harry leaps out of bed, wants to call my sister. He gags and grows ashen. I say I have no sister. Yes, he says, the one who dances. I know he means Edythe, my sister-in-law, but I stall. He says he will call my brother then. He cannot call my brother. That is absurd. It is crazy. How can I count the ways? They will know his name, put him in jail . . . how can I tell him any of this?

I insist we cannot call, there is no one to call, and Harry orders me to stay in his room. He makes me swear not to open the door till I hear his voice. I swear, and he throws on his corduroys—naked, so great is his rush he looks sick with hurry, throws on a polo shirt, and rushes out. He rushes back and makes me swear again.

Stay there, stay there, stay there, don't leave.

I am a grown-up, huddled in Harry's room.
Being in Harry's room
is being in Harry's skin
and he is dying, dying.

Junk. So I've ended with junky toilet articles, half-used tooth-paste—why, when the white covering is flecked off the Colgate tube, does what remains seem such a sweaty substance? Like my mother, I've always found other people's medicine cabinets repellent with the notion of substance half used by someone else, partly squeezed . . . half in or out of the world.

I see myself in the third person. There is something disgusting thudding inside her—her heart?—and there is this wormy room.

So she sits in this wormy room?

To end up sitting on an overripe, unmade bed in a seedy hotel room, ridden with rank, adulterous sex with a younger man—not an older man, a younger man, but dying, all possible combinations shoved in under the wire—flecking toothpaste and a room so sweet, so overripe it is next to rotten? So she's tried everything now, all possible combinations, will this be enough, anywhere *near* enough? and there is a rapping at the door. I yank my T-shirt over my head and sit motionless. I feel the sweat, the odor coming through the door. Someone tries the handle, and I sit. But which man has enough of sweetness to stop before it rots? Not I, not *I*, and mine is not a life yet fully lived, someone jiggles the door handle again and there is an urgent, low rapping.

I care more than I would have dreamed I did that I have not written a great play.

I test to make absolutely sure the knocking is not from inside my head. I say softly, "I am here, in here. Outside someone knocks." I say it gently, so the person outside the door won't be sure someone's here.

The door handle is rattling; someone is leaning on the door, thumping against it.

I am slick with substances I didn't know my body had—who knew the old girl had so much juice in her?—for the noise outside the door grows louder. Who will read my notebooks? I am afraid to make a sound or take my eyes off the door.

I squeeze my eyes shut for an instant, fling them open wide wide wide! I want them open!

My mind rackets wildly—what immoral act did I perform? Should I have delivered Meals on Wheels, baked cookies, rung doorbells, visited a migrant worker? What steps did I lose or lack to have ended here in this room at this moment in this way? and I am furious with Sam.

The thumping on the door grows more insistent, and suddenly I feel my body yearn toward it, as in a gym class dodge ball game I longed to fling myself before the ball, end the misery in one voluptuous failure—give it up, get it over with, here I am, here I am.

I dig my fingers into the bed sheets and reach wildly for a man's anger—Sam's anger? Attached to real cause, rises from calm, is sudden, murderous, a dying fall and then it is over, gone, off the end of the world. My anger is irritable, spasms attached to peevishness, lingering . . . dummy dummy dummy, someone's out to kill you!

I snatch the old black telephone—of course! No one is on the other end, only the dull static silence of an unattended switchboard, as usual.

The flood of hope that deafened my ears dies down, and through the door I hear a high-pitched keening, like grief. It is a wailing, keening, rocking—a wake—and then the thumping begins again. It is the steady rhythm of a body heaving itself against the door toward me.

It flies up, a body, and hits against the transom at the top, thumps on the ground, gathers its strength, jumps toward the transom again. I realize there is animal focus—no intelligence, but mindless muscular animal focus out to get me.

So nothing I can do, no charm, no sexuality, no thoughts or cares, can move it from its intentions. I am a grown woman huddled in a man's room covered with sweat, sour sperm, and sickness, hearing madness breaking in on the other side. I grab Harry's razor and shove it under the pillow. It may slice my eye—the person on the other side of the door may grab it from me, damn Buñuel, yes, no, chase the razor question around, yes, no, has the person on the other side of the door seen the Modern museum, yes, no, I have, but I am here, it is up to me, in the end it is always up to me, and the keening turns into howling, howling such as I have heard in my dreams. There is noise, inside my head there is a keening. The thumping outside stops. Is this so? I hear struggling, lots of people. The door opens with a key. I jump back against the wall, hit my shoulder. It is Harry, face tight with fear, his skull like a death mask, several policemen.

"It's okay," he says, "it's okay, it's over." They are blocking the doorway, the air, what has he told them? I try to run past them but they block me. I run at them knowing it is hopeless—a wall of male muscle and bone and stale blue cloth and buttons. I push at them and they put their arms around me. One of them strokes my hair.

"It's okay," says Harry.

I struggle against them to see, I must see what is being dragged away between two policemen, thumping wildly in protest. I try to see through their shoulders, can I see a reflection, is there a mirror at the end of the corridor? I hear a moaning, a harsh moaning moving away, dying down, a great heaving, and the two policemen stagger but right themselves and then they go on till I can hardly hear it over the moaning that has started once again inside my brain.

I cannot control my body. It slides to the floor, flops around as I try to rise. I cannot order the muscles, tendons, ligaments to stiffen and rise. But the form of a person is being led away down the hall, the sound dies away inside/outside as I lie—splat—half in, half out the hotel room door.

"It's okay, it's okay, it's over," they tell me.

But I know they're wrong.

It was Georgeann, the stunt girl, being led away. Blank eyes, agile limbs, triple-jointed, catatonic . . . even this catalog gives more consecutive attention to her than I ever did.

She says I made her do it. She says I was guilty, I made her kill Sylvie, so she had to avenge Sylvie by killing me. She says she and Sylvie were so happy, that Sylvie was possessed by evil, someone made her do it. She says if not for me. Or maybe I just made up that last part. If not for me.

Obsessed by Sylvie is the tabloid phrase.

Harry had some film of her going into Sylvie's camper late afternoon of the night she was killed. He'd been taking footage for the electronic-press kit, using a hand-held camera to amuse himself. The footage was buried in a sea of undeveloped celluloid.

He hadn't known where it was, or *what* it was, in fact, that he was chasing. But something had ticked in his mind, not sure what, the reason he'd been hunched over the Movieola every evening.

She went after me, the police theorize, because she thought I suspected her or because she was jealous of my friendship with Sylvie or because I alarmed her with innocent questions, but mainly, they imply wearily, because she was damn crazy.

But anyway they are incurious, and we will never unravel it all, because Georgeann is catatonic now, closed, locked, mad—probably mad forever.

She said I was guilty, she was avenging Sylvie, I made her do it, she said, though maybe I made up that last part. Nobody will discuss it and I can't ask many questions.

"She's one crazy person," they tell me.

It wraps it up neatly for everyone else. My family assumes she was after me all along—so much for the Harry story. First Sylvie, then me. Len came crowing. He'd had the order right, right? He forgets he had the wrong guy.

And now it is all completed. Everyone suggests I write it up. My material.

Georgeann will never refute it. She is locked up in California.

My Santo Domingan doorman tells me his wife went into a catatonic state at the age of twenty-six. At forty-six she snapped out of it as if it had never happened, stood bolt upright in her sanatorium corner and moved toward the icebox for the Jell-O she'd been on her way to get twenty years before. Maybe this will happen with Georgeann.

Cut to the chase, as Sylvie's agent would say.

Did I set it in motion by overturning her bed that first day on the set, trigger something that surfaced later?

Or, conversely, did I sense something destructive and dangerous about her from the first and act out of the purity of my soul to destroy evil?

Did Sylvie get in the innocent way of someone after me? Was Sylvie incidentally killed because of me?

A room without me in it?

Did Georgeann look up and see me when her table left its track?

Did she hear what Barney shouted? When she saw me as an extra, first she flushed and then she frowned. Was she trying just to place me—where I cannot but belong? In the center of the blame? For though the table overturned, "It shouldn't have," she said. It was planned for no surprises, safe, controlled, and set to roll . . .

"You just concentrate," she said, "and blot everything else out." Or chaos comes?

In her notebook, Georgeann made plans, alternate plans, contingency plans, for *Serendipity Smith.*

Which Sylvie said she wouldn't do because of me.

"I'll do it," she said about my play, which now will never be written.

"Georgie, love," said Sylvie, gentle, "you can't do stunts forever. Look what happened outside Cinema I."

Information from the grave—Sylvie never suspected about me. Or she wouldn't have said that.

She said of *Serendipity,* "Okay, who needs it, except for money, and I don't need that," and she put in a call to her agent, saying, "Turn it down, no more offers."

That, too, was because of me. Doing my play meant goodbye Georgeann. Cut her off at the knees, my fault. No more stunts as Sylvie, no more stand-in, no more pasta, no more smiles, those dazzling smiles. It must have been so casual a goodbye—Sylvie's dead to you the moment she's lost interest, chills your blood, no fights, no farewells, she's gone because of me and my ridiculous play, which will never be written.

Sylvie skateboarding round the corner with Georgeann, giggling, shrieking like the giddiest of girlfriends. Sylvie leaving.

Goodbye Georgeann, goodbye.

She thinks I made her kill Sylvie, so killing me would avenge Sylvie's death.

The chase. Cut to the chase.

She wanted to get me because I looked like Sylvie. She was the one who was supposed to, but I did, bad enough they didn't use her in the sex scenes, but then they came to me to pull my glasses off as Sylvie, and then they made her do it. Georgeann imitating Sylvie imitating me. No. That isn't the way her mind worked.

Cut to the chase.

She saw me trip her and wanted revenge. Unlikely.

I tripped her because I sensed evil. Unlikely.

I tripped her out of anger at death.

I tripped her out of anger at Marilyn, who killed herself and gave me no good reason, swaying bottles, suicide. I ran beside her down the hallways as the doctor, also running, raised his eyes across the table. A resident, also running, I could see it in his eyes—healthy female, thirty-one, who wants to die?—it's not the worst of what he sees.

She told me, though, I hear it now . . . but I was deaf with grief.

So do I take the blame again, that then she died? The way my mother did, my baby, my cousin Jeremy, whom I didn't love but died hooked up to machines, jars, bottles?

Events moved too fast for me. If in my fourth year my canary had died, in my tenth year, my dog, in my fourteenth, my kindly grandfather, slowly in his sleep, maybe now, at almost thirty-four, I would be a different person. It's that it was all my way and then it wasn't.

What did I think about Georgeann? Is this what Sylvie felt? Trapped in the trailer with Georgeann coming at her? With the raging and the keening, I wanted only to wrench her away from my door, make sure she was not inside my head. But I did not know *who* was there, I did not. I never did see flat-eyed Georgeann led away, so I made it up. I imagined all the details, the clothes, the face—you don't expect such an agile body on such a vacant face—the mind and spirit of a retard with an intelligent, oh so gifted body. No, not a retard, careful, slow, brooding preparation, unrelenting attention to detail, no understanding, closed mind attached to a quick body, mind convoluted, slow, exact, angry.

I see her skateboarding with Sylvie, laughing, talking, "You have a talent, Georgie, you should use it . . ." Sylvie cold, "In the refrig, Georgie, the *refrig*," "not when I'm *acting*, Jessie"—Sylvie's face suddenly with no soul behind it, no light. But punishable by death, for God's sake?

When Sylvie's live to you she's sweet, warm, when not, she's cold, mean, so clear the sweetness never meant for you at all.

Stop trying to understand Georgeann.

Restraining arms, the lobby, the squad car, the door shut on her, slammed, never to open again—I invented the images again and again until they were sufficiently precise and visualized in my mind so that I could summon them at will. I did with some constancy at first, less often now.

Phil says stunt girls are the cock tease of death, a writer's idea. Harry says when he moved her on the set, under his hands she was ugly, hard and ugly.

The stunts she wanted to do were falls, falls, her specialty—was slapped for Sylvie on her first job, didn't want to "buy the farm," was maimed, slapped, stabbed, slashed for Sylvie, for lots of stars, now only for Sylvie.

The inside of my head is detail and killing and death. No sunshine. I must start to stare at sky, off the ribbon of highway, stare up at sky.

I think hate is chemical—like madness—and implacable. Attaching it to motives is where I go wrong. Attaching it to me, people who know me, love me?

Am I saying it's random, hate like madness? Covert, overt, present like the sky? like a cloud? Trailing along over, away, a tendril, a blade, sharp, curving, waving soft blade of grass, blade of knife?

It's your material, the world tells me.

Oh, I'm tired, tired.

CODA

Long ago I told you I was to be trusted. We have both been given reason to doubt. Which is why I find it necessary to start with me. I would tell you to trust me again.

Why do I start here? Because this is not a Victorian coda, that is to say, the same stern and elegant pen that withheld knowledge it will now reveal, that measured hand that turns the copybook page and writes in firm strokes, "One year later."

I, owner of neither stern nor elegant pen, have just read the account of previous pages, modern felt-tip marker in hand. And if I brag—as brag I do—that I have resisted all temptation to obliterate errors in the past account of present perceived, how then, without explanation (or excuse), can I swing into a present account of a year gone by?

For if I say A is happy, B changed jobs, C swells with child, and D is dead—except perhaps for D, how can you trust my selection of events until you have reevaluated the selector? And however I may strike out for transparent prose, you are trapped inside my head and will have to come to terms about my head.

I. ME

I'm back to writing plays. It's what I do.

II. WHAT I DID

I was exhausted. I cried, and had to be carried to bed.

When I first got up, I couldn't move too quickly, or I remembered things that stirred inside.

I sought out films with no heart, books without love, days without hope. I flicked the channels ceaselessly, lest hope or happiness be hurled at me unaware.

I walked like someone on deck with a memory of seasickness, avoiding any hint of waves that could trigger an answering engulfing despair.

When I found I could walk just a little faster, I tried a guru, promiscuity, and a woman director.

The first was neither contemptible nor corrupt. In fact, I rather liked the fierce and angry way he played his tambourine. But I asked a question about death one day, and his answer—even allowing for Indian translation—was wrong.

Promiscuity. Feeling I had known what it was like to be inside someone else's body, I couldn't seem to move back inside my own. I thought sex might help me. I was so open, so stretched out of shape, I could scarcely eat. A mouthful of bread made me feel invaded and empty. I imagined it traveling my body like a wandering IUD that will never be found. The first two men slid around crazily inside me, and I stopped.

The woman director made me feel that I knew best.

III. "YOU AND YOUR STUPID DREAMS"

This is a quote. From *Shadow of a Doubt* (Joseph Cotten), a Hitchcock film.

Joseph Cotten looks at pure young niece, Teresa Wright, over wooden table in darkened town tavern. "You and your stupid dreams," he says. (They are dreams of Main Street, puppies, marriage.) This is the moment in the script when for the first time we know for sure that he *is* the psychopathic killer. His words are the irrevocable proof. When Uncle Harry calls Teresa's dreams "stupid," it is an act of public madness—although he has only whispered the words.

I had dreams again.

I dreamed I was lying with Sylvie on the seat of a station wagon. "Glad we had this time to talk," we say to each other. The car is a yellow Volvo. My friend Marilyn once told me of a dream she had where I was driving too fast. She begged me to slow down, and I threw back my head and laughed.

There are bloodstains on the gray seats. Large, clotted, rusty, sticky splotches with protruding rusty wires.

"Don't worry," says Sylvie, "it doesn't matter."

My dreams were drenched in rusty blood. They infected me and the sweet town where we rented our cottage for August.

On the pretext of needing steel-clamped file folders for early drafts, I took the bus to the nearest commercial crowded terminus, hoping the buzzing inside my head would commingle with the agitated urban air and so dissolve. It did. For a time.

I am telling you of my stupid dreams of blood and pain and crashes most probably so that you will not find me soulless when we move to HAPPY ENDING.

IV. HAPPY ENDING

But how, you say, how can you have a happy ending when Harry has died? Even in the Brechtian sense—but fuck Brecht, for the moment.

V. SODDEN WITH IMAGERY, SORROW LADEN

I sat, in late March, in the Museum of Modern Art café, next to the sculpture garden. The snow fell in the sculpture garden, sorrow laden. It lay, sodden with imagery, on the statues.

I sit in my modern orange plastic chair and miss sucking and touching and playing with Harry. I am swaying slightly, shifting, smiling, warming. Warm breath stirs in the room, warm flesh, moving, rising.

I miss him, his warm flesh, his slow smile, his responding warm, funny body, bending moving stretching kneeling . . . off in the California sunshine. The air around me turns cold and chill like cold sweat.

Sentimental eroticism on a chilly day in spine-cold new MOMA plastic chairs that are already dented, and it seems a soiled and brutal temporary world.

I think of Sam's face, smiling at me in the half light as we make love, and as if I have indeed shaken my fist at the heavens, my orange chair rocks slightly and I understand that the steel cord that connects us has been stretched too far, too far. If it should snap, it would leave me free and floating and ugly and dead to my own heart.

He is a father. He will always love two more people in this world than I do.

But it is with Sam I make my life, my love, my life.

And what of Harry?

Our fury was so great it turned into permanent loving.

Now he is dead and I still stare at the sky in the same blank yet focused way one stares at space, because I do not believe he is nowhere. His flesh presides over too much that happens in my real world for that to be.

But it is with Sam I make my love, my life.

If I am not careful I will bend his love out of shape.

VI. HAPPY ENDING

Brecht applies.

I first saw *Threepenny Opera* in the springtime of my high school senior year, with a boy I liked. The noose was round Macheath's neck. Happy Ending rang out, a mounted messenger arrived with a pardon, and the noose was stopped. "Oh good," I thought, shifting around in my embroidered organdy, "unexpected pleasure." Like Rhett coming back to Scarlett as she lay on the stairs? Oh good. Nice Mack the Knife will live.

Was ever anyone so young? Or was it the production?

I saw it again this year. The chill of horror that settled over me as the Happy Ending rang out made me wonder what kind of little girl I'd been then, anyway.

But I am older now, and I know of smiles freezing in midair, about thought and response going down separate tracks, about starting to feel one thing automatically and suddenly having your feelings stop, congeal.

HAPPY ENDING

Harry died slowly, on the phone with me. He was in California. His male nurse gave me all the details as they happened, from hair falling out to Keri oil on his rectum.

He is dead now.

Most of the calls spread over the spring, and I often stared over the river into the sun. I got off the phone with blinding headaches. I put up little signs around all the extensions saying DON'T STARE INTO THE SUN. Sam never commented on them.

The previous winter, Harry asked me to check on and keep watch on all his treatments, and I agreed.

He left to go west and shoot his film in late July, just after *Daughters and Sisters* was finished, just about the time we went to the island. He called the island just before he left. His voice filled the cabin—like rusty blood?

All fall and winter, while he was in production, I sat alone in my room writing mistaken plays. I was just emerging to arrange productions when he came back.

We met in a coffee shop on Hudson Street. The only intimacy between us was that we kept eating each other's cottage fries. He and his crew had shot a southwestern ritual for his film. "Fantastic," he said, both of the experience and what it did for them. A word he never used, so it meant something more wonderful than he had imagined on heaven or earth. I think he had a girl. That night, the whole crew was going dancing.

I went home to my silent house. He seemed briefly like my growing, blooming son. I wished him well with his girl—but dancing!

When his remission ended, I flew to Washington, D.C., and sat with his mother, the frightened nurse, in the Mayflower Coffee Shop and went over all the possibilities, what the doctors had told her and him and me, what the best to hope for and the worst were, and what options/gambles were available and for how long.

He stayed in California. For a while he was still working full days, doing the rough cut of his film, and we talked almost every day.

Shortly after the rough cut was finished, his voice began to howl over the telephone from an increasingly long tunnel. I had to do the talking. He insisted on specifics, detail. If I complained the water was dripping, he asked for the plumber's exact words: "Whole new drain, lady, or you'll piss away your Drano." And the only time words were forced out of him was if I wasn't specific enough. Script where? Producer when? The forced-out words were so agonizing that I spoke as precisely as I could. New Dramatists' Committee was not New Theater Workshop, and so on. Like my cousin Jeremy, who tested me to make sure I still took him seriously enough to hate, Harry insisted on every detail of a continuing life.

Sam walked by once, when I was talking sincerely into the receiver about a laptop computer, the tears rolling down my face, not affecting my voice, no tissues, and not bothering to get any.

"Do you have to?" he asked later.

"Yes," I said, "but I won't care that much. I'll do it but I won't mind."

I lied to Harry once about what I was wearing. Five minutes later I called back to tell him the truth: it was khaki jeans, not a flowered skirt.

I had thought if I could lie, then so might he—the brief rebellious relief of thinking it was all made up and that after our conversations he and his so-called male nurse chortled and went out on La Cienega to snort coke, to pick up girls.

"Look," I said, "I'm wearing jeans. I won't do this again."

The tunnel grew longer. Any calendar marked a date when he would not be around.

And now, the final balancing of temperature and drug and body response is over, and he is dead.

The cold chill of making you shift in your chair.

Harry is dead.

Happy ending.

VII. WHAT WORKS

1. Sam and I work.

Sam's best work is with systems. Coming in from the outside, head cocked to one side, feeling with his fingertips and instincts, moving within the system till he finds out where it goes right, wrong. He knows what makes a system work together or not. We are slowly rebuilding. For him I sometimes think it is interesting, a new moving part in a still viable system. For me it is painful. But he has taught me method.

For me to think of Sam with someone else is to be knocked down by a giant machine, obliterated.

Sam wrote to me: "I love my life as I never could have loved my life had I never met and loved you."

It is what we can do for each other.

2. My plays work. Occasionally.

The plays I wrote this year were mistakes.

3. Petra

Petra is out, well, avoiding pressure, and taking courses in engineering. Her teachers enjoy her a lot. She and Sam talk about suspension bridges.

4. Marie

I'm mad at her. I urged her to tell me what she really thought of my new play. She resisted. "One knows from one's own experience," she said, "one can't tolerate being told one isn't Shakespeare." But I urged and cajoled and swore my objective need for her opinion. "It was a mistaken idea," she said, "all wrong." She took me for my better. Now the thought of her makes me furious.

5. Sam's son

Daniel has turned hirsute and girl-loving. There is no mistaking it. Just last week, we sat with Len and Bun, watching him play Ping-Pong with a neighbor girl, watched him watching her breasts bounce with a shy zest that was unmistakable. It is somehow indecent for four adults to watch a fourteen-year-old boy involved with a young girl's budding breasts. But we did. Let's just say he was unhappy, now he's not.

Len, Bun, Sam and I went out to dinner that night. We've all had to put up with a lot from each other, and we're not doing badly.

6. Stephanie

She's a producer, riding the why-can't-there-be-good-roles-for-women wave. She gets top talent for less on ideological grounds. She is living in California but comes to visit us regularly on her frequent trips to New York. She is decent and matter-of-fact in a way that makes me bless her presence. Harry let her visit him in the last months, when he didn't want me.

7. Residue

Daughter and Sisters may not be released.

I cannot believe the anguish I feel at news of this. It is not, after all, like putting a dirty sheet over the Ste. Chapelle for life. But the truth is, it makes me furious and blots out the sun.

Is it that so much work of so many, doing this and nothing else for months, has gone for nothing? Surely I cannot feel for this the kind of rage I keep so rigidly for bodies not in the world, for deaths untimely?

But then not to have the film at all? Not to see Sylvie, the others, the lighting, the crowds, the supermarket, the playground, the cemetery, Sylvie laughing, throwing whitefish. I believe I am the only person on the planet who cares this much about it, except perhaps some German investor who stares morosely into the Baltic and mourns his money.

Barney is doing a television pilot, Phil is doing a workshop with Papp.

I didn't do my magazine piece. I returned the money grudgingly, months after it became apparent to me I could not write it. My presence, however, appeared in several of the journalists' pieces as playwright-on-crutches—one, at an event before I hurt my foot— and each piece got events in the wrong sequence in different ways.

Life imitating art imitating history?

Stephanie is bringing out Harry's film next winter in limited showcase release.

And Sylvie is dead—a death that will always differ from the others.

I think of her every day, but choose not to remember her as actress/ flower—a tender shoot of narcissism and harmless vanity. Rather, I take consolation in remembering the way she ate—voraciously, stuffing food inside her red mouth, gobbling so fast her fingers raced to stuff the next batch in.

"A killer," Harry called her, but that was about her lighting.

I cannot be sure she would be dead if not for me.

8. Alex's family

My niece was graduated from high school and on her way to Saratoga for the summer to the New York City Ballet company workshop, and then to college. I gave a graduation farewell party for her and her friends in our apartment. It was almost summer. The house was filling with her friends.

The phone rang. It was Harry's nurse. I had promised to check through some things and get back to him the following Tuesday. "He's asleep," he said, "and I thought I should call to find out if you've checked out those things"—it was about flying a body back East—"I was remembering, you know, how it used to be by train, someone had to be along with the coffin or you couldn't get a ticket."

"This is not a good time for me," I said. "Actually, I haven't checked it out yet, I'll call you back on Tuesday as I said I would, will that be okay?"

"Um, no," he said, "actually, I don't think it will be . . . hold on a minute will you, just stay there . . ." and he left. I held on to the black receiver, staring straight out the window, the sun wheeling around like fire inside my brain—and then he got back on. "He's gone," he said.

And such is the moment that Harry dies.

I went back to the party, showing no strain. I wished my niece well. I was dear to her friends, all of whom were also starting new lives. Late in the afternoon, I warmly sent them on their way.

I told Sam about the call only after all the guests had left.

"Did I do the right thing?" I asked. Life goes on.

"She'll have her day," said Sam somberly, "let her enjoy herself now." He, too, is fond of my pretty niece.

But hours later, from a phone booth on the highway, she called me. "Oh Aunt Jessie, what was wrong," she asked, "don't say nothing, I could see in your eyes, something was wrong, what did I do?"

"Oh, you didn't do anything, dear," I said, stung into giving information. "It's that a friend of mine, one who was very sick already, just died."

She burst into loud sobbing, and what she said next truly astonished me.

"Oh, you've had so much of that, I hate that for you, it's so terrible," she said, raw, sobbing, crazy with grief for me, "I can't stand that for you."

You? I didn't think I existed as a "you" in her mind with a history of my own, just the aunt with the Manhattan apartment, who gives toys, presents, and, this day, a party.

I gave her no name in this story, and I will not try to cover myself by inserting it now. I mentioned one wanted to be a tree surgeon. That was her also nameless sister.

Somehow she is tuned in to me and always has been. I knew and didn't know.

So there are jagged blazing wails of response to us that we simply will not see. The violence of her attachment to my fate is in contrast to the blandness of my years of undetailed pleasure in her and her sister. It reminds me once again that one is implicated in violence in the neighborhood of one's body.

My niece, in this way, is connected to Harry. Her wild, crazy, young, hiccoughing crying was a sound that eased me somehow. In a phone booth on the highway leading to her young grown-up life, it was the funeral dirge I would have chosen for Harry, for the funeral I did not arrange, would not attend.

I THINK HATE IS CHEMICAL, LIKE MADNESS

VIII. EDYTHE

And now we get to Edythe, my sister-in-law.

I thought about it a lot before deciding. Did she kill the man near Lincoln Center, who was, after all, a mugger? Is it up to me to speak up? Is this refusing a driver's license to cousin Jeremy time again? Where does my responsibility for chaos on the street begin and end?

For a long time, I said nothing.

One day we went to a Westchester street fair. A small thin girl, arms and legs like matchsticks, stood on Center Street, singing with a street band. She wore a granny dress, a stovepipe hat and high boots and sang, "All of me, why not take all of me?" with a smile so brilliant, it almost tore open her pale-skinned, delicate face. Edythe said to me later, "That little girl on the street, to be doing something she loves to do that much! I envy her so much I could hardly stand to look at her." Her tone was matter-of-fact.

When I found myself scanning the *Westchester Tattler* for news of the murder of a little girl in a stovepipe hat, I went to Alex. At first he didn't seem to hear me. Finally I told him the Lincoln Center story Edythe had told me.

"Oh, people say things," he said.

I was precise. I was unmistakable.

"Oh, people say things," he said.

He, just as precisely and unmistakably, was not going to listen to me.

His face in repose was humorless—a hanging judge perched above a trim, aggressive body. The face of my older brother, who will protect me only so far.

My reaction was simple. Good enough. I have made myself clear. If Edythe kills someone, I am no longer to blame. And my conversations now with Alex are as if none of this ever took place.

IX. BUT BACK TO HATE

But back to hate, chemical like madness. Oh to be sure, there is pure public impersonal madness—muggers in the pitch-dark and junkies with dilated pupils. But the rest of it I believe to be in the median area between impersonal and personal madness, when your image—however distorted—is lodged in the mind of your attacker. And then I believe murder is hate, hate is chemical, and accurate consumer labeling important only insofar as it makes clear to us that we live with the madness we arouse, need be alert to the madness we trigger.

And then what? Run, scream, carry mace spray, move to Bali? I give no advice.

"You like drama," says Sam, startling me. Actually, I have pared it down to a certain wariness at the personal services level.

That is, I ask the druggist to check the sample eye drops given me by the eye doctor who scowled at my chart on his fiftieth birthday, saying, "At least someday you'll be fifty, too."

I recheck the brakes at a second service station when the auto mechanic tells me that his wife, who he once said looked a little bit like me, has run off with his brother.

And when, in May, the exterminator reveals that the plan of a lifetime he shared with me last quarter, to be his own boss, has died forever with the prime interest rate, his bitter, "That's life, you better believe it," goes through my head as I run all my dishes and cutlery through the dishwasher twice lest some lethal poison has been sprayed on purpose. Silly precautions? Life's like that?

But my life is not a holding action. I walk down Forty-third Street at dusk, cross Broadway, ride freely in airplanes, and trust another person immoderately—all more reckless decisions, you might say, in terms of statistical safety.

I propose no theory of guilt or innocence, implicit, complicit, casual, any way at all. I hint at neither pinpointed menace nor universal love. I do not believe we are all mad, nor am I even certain we are all capable of triggering madness. But I did trigger madness, or so I think. And in any case, I do not suggest you follow my lead. Life's far too personal to ever get to the bottom of it.

But I do believe there is no limit to what I or anyone I know might do at any moment. I try to stay alert. And that is as far as I care to go.

I used to think that one day it was over. You accept your losses. You let them go. That was where I got it wrong, and my loved ones, my lost ones, hammered at my brain, saying, "You think you're through with us? You're not through with us," as Harry would now, except that he doesn't have to, because I don't even try. I know better.

———

You wanted to know what Harry did and didn't do to me. And I told you what I had in words, what I understood. I never lied to you. I had only so many words to give, only so much I understood.

I was claimed by Harry in the moment that he saw me. He recognized my face, my angry toe, my eyes, and reached out to claim me. He was as angry as I and as urgent.

And though he let me play at courting, he reached out, claimed me, got me back to life. And now I cannot think of life without thinking of him. Will not.

He courted me with hot bright eyes, a slow smile, firm hands kneading my shoulders—but they are the coin of low romance. He courted me in truth with the furious awareness of time, which neither of us wanted, but both of us shared.

The Coliseum? Sam's equipment? Escalators, cranes?

The day he told me Stephanie was dying, he saw me pull away. She was a trial balloon. The night he called me about lonely streets, he could hear I'd pulled away again.

Oh no, not for me, I said. He saw me slipping away, he had to bring me back, use whatever he had, all he had.

Don't count me out

When did he map it out? When I pulled away from Stephanie, when I said it happens to us all, when I saw lonely streets with a carefree heart . . . or chattered safely on the telephone while cradled in Sam's arms.

He used everything he had. The day he banged his head against the shower, he had nothing left to give. He was a beggar—he had given me my freedom, and begging is the nether side of love, the dark side of the moon. And when I came back, as how could I not, how would I not? we were what he'd wanted all along, what he had wanted to show me . . . the only way he knew to get it for himself—and to give it then to me.

Yes, he did go to the Coliseum, maybe just to watch Sam, and maybe not. Escalators, ovens, camera cranes? But don't you see, none of it matters? The obvious truth that you probably knew before me is that at any moment he could have destroyed Sam and me with words. Just told Sam. He did not.

XI. HARRY'S VOICE

Weeks after I thought Harry had lapsed into final coma, he rolled toward the phone while his nurse was talking to me and said my name. It is that last voice—weeks after I had understood it to be a sound I would never again hear on this earth—that I dream of now.

And Sylvie is dead and gone, and Georgeann languishes in catatonia.

XII. WHAT REMAINS

My limbs are intact. I walk fast the way I used to. I think of a baby without seeing tears splashing down on its newborn head. I need only to stamp my foot and my body flares to attention. I can hold pain and absence of pain in my head at the same time.

I itch to change this account, edit out the easy scorn and sloppy mistakes—Trojan women do not yell, "Kill, kill" but "Woe is me"—but once I start I will not stop.

XIII. ENDING

I wish I had said simply
Edythe made a casserole.
Stephanie is successful.
I bought an antique silk kimono.
Harry is dead.

I told you what I saw, and it was all I had. And what have we now?

I mourn and I celebrate all my loved ones, and you may well perceive me as a jolly joke, like the people with the four hundred Yahrzeit candles—a nylon backpack full of tombstones, a forgettable movie, and five golden rings.

From the moment Harry saw me he knew I would never let him go. I've never let any of them go, and now I never will.

I hold on to them so fiercely, forever, and it will never change. The child that grows within me, another love—or you, if you should come my way—I hold on to all those I have loved, or will, because they are my history, my life, my joy and my future.

And now I find it hard to let you go.

I linger in the doorway like some graduate student or analysand.

If we have been locked together, you and I, perhaps it has been my fingers, like a bony handcuff on your wrist. Now, repentant, I would lead you through surrounding streets as toward an urban sheep shearing, dancing to Elizabethan rock—crazy adolescent festival where everything is delirious and open, more possible than possible.

Or, perhaps, I long to involve you in some sudden and swampy ritual, where you are coerced to hug the hand of the person in the seat next to you, for, if I think any one thing, it is that the will to tenderness is all.

Then I would like to trail behind you as you leave the theater. Oh, not to hear what you say about me, but to watch you, see how you leave the lobby, hold your partner, maneuver around the Broadway skinheads in the street, look around when someone jostles you, talk of plans for Sunday, hail a taxi, or just watch the light.

And intrusive and presuming though it be for me to wish for you at all, what is it I wish for you, to mark that we have met? For you to live your life? to love your life? to tuck your life up smartly in your armpit and jump, cut, run for your life like O. J. Simpson—the hip *Our Town* my relatives would so dearly love to have me write? Or just to stay alive, hug your friend, spin around, stand your ground, shove back the crowd, smile, move—ah, do I wish for my name to be sweet honey in your mouth? The sky sinks down and spins you back and the velvet dark caresses, the sunset is electric on the hairs of your forearm and what I beg of you is kindness, for me, for you, for all around you, kindness in the face of all at every turn, for it is all the chance we have. And what I want for you in this brief moment just before you leave my sight is for you to feel alive. For the streets on which I let you go are dangerous ones—how can they be otherwise, when it's you and I who move on them?

ABOUT THE AUTHOR

ELEANOR BERGSTEIN is best known as author of the acclaimed political novel *Advancing Paul Newman* and as screenwriter and co-producer of the successful movie *Dirty Dancing*. Her short stories have appeared in many magazines, from *Transatlantic Review* to *Redbook*; her first screenplay was made into the Columbia picture *It's My Turn*. She is currently at work on a new novel and is planning a film set in the world of the homeless, which she will write and direct. She lives in New York City with her husband, poet and critic Michael Goldman.